THE LOST KEY

THE FBI THRILLERS

Power Play (2014)
Bombshell (2013)
Backfire (2012)
Split Second (2011)
Twice Dead:
Riptide and
Hemlock
Bay (2011)
Whiplash (2010)
KnockOut (2009)
TailSpin (2008)
Double Jeopardy
(2008): The Target
and The Edge
Double Take (2007)

The Beginning
(2005):
The Cove and
The Maze
Point Blank (2005)
Blowout (2004)
Blindside (2003)
Eleventh Hour
(2002)
Hemlock Bay (2001)
Riptide (2000)
The Edge (1999)
The Target (1998)
The Maze (1997)
The Cove (1996)

A BRIT IN THE FBI THRILLERS
(WITH J. T. ELLISON)

The Final Cut (2013)

THE LOST KEY

CATHERINE COULTER

AND J. T. ELLISON

G. P. PUTNAM'S SONS

New York

DOUBLEDAY LARGE PRINT HOME LIBRARY EDITION

This Large Print Edition, prepared especially for Doubleday Large Print Home Library, contains the complete, unabridged text of the original Publisher's Edition.

PUTNAM

G. P. PUTNAM'S SONS • *Publishers Since 1838*
Published by the Penguin Group • Penguin Group (USA) LLC
375 Hudson Street, New York, New York 10014

*Lg Print /
Coulter*

USA • Canada • UK • Ireland • Australia
New Zealand • India • South Africa • China

A Penguin Random House Company

Printed in the United States of America

ISBN 978-1-62953-143-4

Book design by Nicole LaRoche

This is a work of fiction. Names, characters, places, and incidents either are the product of the author's imagination or are used fictitiously, and any resemblance to actual persons, living or dead, businesses, companies, events, or locales is entirely coincidental.

**This Large Print Book carries the
Seal of Approval of N.A.V.H**

Here's to us, J.T., and to a partnership
I hope lasts for a very long time.
Catherine

For Catherine, and Karen,
and Anton, and Randy,
and all those on Eternal Patrol.
J.T.

ACKNOWLEDGMENTS

I would like to thank Clive Cussler for giving me splendid advice on how to find the perfect writer for Nicholas Drummond and Mike Caine. It's an amazing experience, Clive, and you know what? I really lucked out. May you live long and prosper.

I would like to thank my brother-in-law, Alex De Angelis, for his assistance with all things Chinese. Alex, not only do you amaze me with how much you know, you are an incredibly kind, generous person. But lest you forget, I can kick your butt at Scrabble.

My rock—Karen Evans—thank you for always being here for me, for helping me find the right word, for never treating me like the technological idiot you know me to be.

And finally, I would like to thank all of those valiant men and women who came before us who fought to keep us free.

—Catherine Coulter

ACKNOWLEDGMENTS

Life never ceases to amaze me. I always thought the ability to create characters, and story, was a lonely endeavor, something I'd spend hours locked away in my office developing, like a blind mole, hoping against hope that when I emerged, things would hold together.

And then Catherine came into my life, and I realized the combustible power of having two writers on a single project. Two approaches, two brainstorms, two brains!—it is a thing of glory. **The Lost Key** is a magnificent example of two brains being better than one.

I have to thank Catherine for the guidance and advice and too many laughs to count, and for loving the gulfstream-on-gulfstream violence. Working with you (and Mike and Nicholas) is a dream come true.

Darling Karen, for keeping us calm and focused;

Anton, for declaiming by the pool table;

Chris Pepe, for giving us brilliant notes

and constant wrangling;

Scott Miller, for getting me into this in the first place;

Everyone who loved **The Final Cut** and reached out to let us know;

Jeff Abbott, Laura Benedict, Paige Crutcher, and Ariel Lawhon, who listened and yoga'd and fed me when necessary;

And, as always, my darling husband, Randy, who realized this book could only be made better by mararitas and new kittens. Love you, bunny.

—J. T. Ellison

O Captain! my Captain! our fearful trip
is done;
The ship has weather'd every rack,
the prize we sought is won;
The port is near, the bells I hear,
the people all exulting,
　While follow eyes the steady keel,
　the vessel grim and daring:
　But O heart! heart! heart!
　O the bleeding drops of red,
　Where on the deck my Captain lies,
　Fallen cold and dead.

Walt Whitman, "O Captain! My Captain!"

Prologue

**Lower Slaughter, Cotswolds
England
September 1917**

Ansonia was dead. And all those brave men who'd risked everything to end the bloody war were dead with her, and they'd left wives and children to wonder what had happened to them, to mourn, endlessly. Had their deaths been quick? Crushing tons of icy water and then it was over, quickly, so quickly, they didn't know the end was on them? He prayed it was so. All he had left of her was the letter she'd stuffed in Leo's coat pocket to give to him, his first name written in her hand on the envelope. **Josef.** All that was inside were her hastily scribbled words explaining what she'd done and why, and how much she loved him and Leo, and how, with God's help, she would see them soon. Stay safe, stay safe, and all would be well. Signed simply, **Ansonia.**

Josef closed his eyes against the pain

of it, a pain so deep he didn't think he could bear it. But he had to, he had no choice, for there was Leo, their son, depending on him since his mother was gone. He saw her now, his brave, foolhardy Ansonia, saw them together that last night, and thought now her smile had been sad, accepting, as if she'd known she would die. He shut it off.

Josef Rothschild would mourn her forever, but not yet, not just yet. He stared through the front window down the long, dark drive, then over at the thick night dark woods. Pearce would be here soon with five other Order members. William Pearce, Viscount Chambers, the head of the Highest Order, his friend and ally for such a short time. He knew it would last until they both breathed their last breaths, this odd friendship of theirs, a German and an Englishman, forged that long-ago night at the battleground of Verdun. He wondered if William would one day be the Prime Minister. Josef wouldn't doubt it. Even though William was young, he already had power, wealth, but most important, he had an excellent brain, a clear head, and honor.

Josef stared into the darkness. Where were they?

Six men of the Highest Order were coming to hear him announce that their plan had succeeded. **The Highest Order** —Josef had always thought the formal title of their society sounded so lofty as to be ordained by God—but now all members simply called it the Order. Yes, six members of the Order were coming to hear not only that they now had the kaiser's gold, but that they also possessed Marie's key and her book of secrets. Yes, they'd won, they would deal the kaiser a death blow, and they would raise a toast to Marie, magnificent Marie, architect of a weapon so powerful the one who owned it would rule the world.

But there wasn't to be wild triumph, because the scores of gold bars worth millions of deutsche marks, the kaiser's private treasury, the book, and the key were lost to both Germany and England in waters so deep he couldn't imagine the U-boat ever being found. In England's hands, having the gold would cripple the kaiser's war, but having Marie's horrifying weapon would deal a death blow. Now no one would have either the gold or the weapon, ever. Still, he wondered if someone in the distant future would find the U-boat and the kaiser's gold and Marie's key. Would they marvel at the lunacy of men long dead? Marvel at their greed, their eagerness to crush one another, their butchering of the innocent? Would they look at Marie's weapon and be unable to fathom how any man, any country, could sanction its use?

Josef pulled the thin curtain back from the window and stared out into full darkness. There was no moon and the few stars shimmered off the ground fog covering the field beyond the cottage. The men would leave their cars hidden and come into the cottage one by one. The Order was always careful, rabidly so in wartime. Soon, soon now.

Josef looked over at the trundle bed in the corner, at his son, Leo, exhausted from his ordeal, still in shock. At last he was sleeping soundly, legs pulled up against his chest, one thin arm dangling over the edge of the cot, the small white hand open. Josef felt such fear, such love, that for a moment he couldn't breathe. If his son had died, it would have been his fault. But he was alive, he'd survived the hellish trip from Berlin to Scotland, the specter of death constantly riding on his small shoulders. Josef prayed Leo had understood all he'd told him on their trip from Scotland to William Pearce's cottage, understood that what his father and the other men had tried to do had been for him, for all the children of this useless, bloody war. Every time he'd said Ansonia's name, he'd tasted his own tears. And when he was through talking, the tears shiny on his cheeks, Leo had slipped his small hand into his father's and whispered, "Before we left her, Mama told me you were a hero. Now I understand why. What will happen now, Papa?"

Josef was humbled. He had no answer.

He looked out the window again. He saw a shadow running across the field, and another, wraiths in the night, the darkness bleeding around them. They would stagger their arrivals, each coming from a different direction, a few minutes between them. Six men, dressed in black, weapons at their sides. Three carried Webley .455 Marks, standard issue, and two had Mauser C96s tucked in their holsters. They were prepared for anything even though they should be safe enough, here in a small cottage deep in the Cotswolds, expecting to hear news of their triumph.

The first man stopped, whistled loudly through his teeth in a poor imitation of a whip-poor-will. Josef whistled in return, and the man started forward again. A series of calls and answers began behind him.

The first knock sounded. Four taps, then two pounds. The signal.

Josef took one last look at Leo, then pinched out the lone candle. He opened the door, welcomed each of them. Their only goal was to stop Kaiser Wilhelm's war.

Only five men arrived. Where was William Pearce? He was never late. Josef gave all of them coffee, then, unable to wait, said, "The U-boat went down. The kaiser has lost both his gold and Marie's book and the key. And we did, too."

Dead silence, then, with succinct finality, Wallace Benton-Hurt, head of the Bank of England, said, "So it's a stalemate."

"Yes," said Josef.

"I hear something, it must be William," said Grayson Lankford, and went to the door.

Josef said, "Wait until he knocks."

"No one knows we're here, Josef. You're being paranoid."

"Yes, I am," Josef said, "and that is the only reason I am still alive. Wait for the knock."

Everyone waited, watching the door. Footsteps, then a knock. Two raps, sharp, like the end of a stick, or a rifle butt.

Not the right signal.

Josef knew they'd been found out. **Leo.**

He grabbed Leo into his arms and carried him to the closet. Leo's eyes opened, unseeing at first, then he focused on his father's face. "Listen to me, you have to stay here until I come for you. Do not make a sound. Do you understand me?"

Leo knew fear, and he saw it on his father's face. "Are we in danger, Papa?"

"Yes, the enemy found us. You must keep quiet, Leo. Remember what I told you. If something happens to me, you tell no one what I told you. Trust no one. Remember, no matter what you hear, you keep quiet." He kissed his boy, wrapped the blanket around him, and closed the closet door just as bullets shattered the glass windows and the front door burst open.

DAY ONE

1

**FBI New York Field Office
26 Federal Plaza
7:25 a.m.**

What in bloody hell have I done?

Nicholas Drummond reported for duty at the FBI's New York Headquarters smartly at 7:00 a.m., as instructed. After twenty minutes with human resources, he felt a bit like a schoolboy: stand here, walk there, smile for your photograph, here's your pass, don't lose it. It was worse than the FBI Academy with their strict rules, the uniforms, the endless drills, and more like his training at Hendon Police College with Hamish Penderley and his team.

The administrative realities of moving from New Scotland Yard to the FBI in New York were decidedly less romantic than the initial prospect had been. Months earlier, Dillon Savich, head of the Criminal Apprehension Unit at FBI Headquarters in Washington, D.C., had encouraged Nicholas to make a new home in the FBI, and he'd accepted. It was now the end of May, graduation from Quantico and the FBI Academy two weeks in the past, and he was officially an FBI special agent, and technically at the bottom of the food chain.

Again.

Twice he'd done this. The first time he'd left the Foreign Office to work for the Metropolitan Police in London. He'd survived those first days and he'd survive these, too.

And even better, you don't have Hamish Penderley to ride you now, making you do tactical drills at 5:00 a.m. Zachery's a very different sort. So buck up.

Nicholas knew he should have started out in a small Bureau office in the Midwest, gotten his feet wet, but Dillon Savich had gotten him assigned to the New York Field Office, as promised, working directly for Supervisory Special Agent Milo Zachery, a man Nicholas knew and trusted, with Special Agent Michaela Caine as his partner.

When at last they issued him his service

weapon, he felt complete, the heavy weight of the Glock on his hip comforting, familiar.

Freshly laminated and now armed, he'd been walked to the twenty-third floor, led through the maze of the cube farm, and ushered into a small space, blue-walled with some sort of fuzzy fabric, the kind Velcro would adhere to, with a brown slab of wood-grained Formica as a desktop. There was a computer, several hard drives, two file trays labeled in and out, and a chair.

The cubicle was so small he could easily touch each side with his arms outstretched, and that made the tiniest bit of claustrophobia sneak in. He needed more monitors and more shelving and maybe he'd soon feel at home. Once in the zone on his computers, the close quarters wouldn't be a problem.

He dropped his briefcase on the floor next to the chair, stashed a small black go bag in his bottom drawer, and took a seat. He spun the chair around in a circle, legs drawn up to avoid crashing. Small, yes, but it would do. He didn't plan to spend much time sitting here, anyway. Part of the deal he'd made with Savich meant Nicholas would be working ad hoc with him at times, running forensic point on cases in Washington. From what he'd already experienced working with Savich and Sherlock and Mike Caine, he was in for a ride.

A low, throaty voice said near his ear, "Needs a bit of sprucing up, don't you think? How about a nice photo of the queen, front and center?"

Speak of the devil.

"The queen is hanging happily over my bed in my new digs." He bent his head back to see Agent Mike Caine looking down at him, smiling widely. She was wearing her signature black jeans, motorcycle boots, her blond hair pulled back in a ponytail. Her badge hung on a lanyard around her neck, and her black-rimmed reading glasses were tucked into her blouse pocket.

"I wonder why I didn't smell you first." And he leaned up, sniffed. "Ah, there it is, that lovely jasmine, like my mum. Hi, Mike, long time no see."

"Yeah, yeah, all of two weeks since your graduation. So you're all settled in to these new digs of yours? By the way, where are your new digs?"

He didn't want to tell her, didn't want to tell anyone, it was too embarrassing. Fact was, he'd lost a big argument with his grandfather about where he'd lay his head in New York. He shrugged, looked over her shoulder at several agents walking by. "All settled in. A fairly nice bed in an okay place over there—" And he waved his hand vaguely toward the east.

She cocked her head at him, and he said quickly, "You look pretty good after being on your own for four months. When can we get out of here?"

"Champing at the bit for a case already, Special Agent Drummond? You've only been here fifteen minutes. We haven't even had time to go over the coffee schedule and introduce you around. Are we calling you Nick or Nicholas these days?"

"You know what they say about rolling

stones and moss. Nicholas will do fine."

She looked at her watch. "You're in luck. We've caught a murder."

He felt the punch of adrenaline. "A murder? Is it terrorism related?"

"I don't think so. I heard about it two minutes ago. Time to get briefed."

Milo Zachery joined them in the hall. In his tailored gray suit, white shirt, and purple-and-black striped tie, Nicholas thought he looked a lot snazzier than Penderley ever had. Slick clothes, fresh haircut. He looked like a big-dog federal agent all the way to his highly polished wing tips. Nicholas knew Zachery was focused, smart, and willing to let his agents use their brains with only subtle hands on the reins.

Nicholas shook his new boss's hand.

"Good to see you, Drummond. I'll handle your briefing myself. Walk with me."

Mike gave him a manic grin, her adrenaline on a level with his, and he was reminded of that night in Paris several months earlier, Mike barely upright, leaning against the overturned couch, bleeding from a gunshot to the arm, her face beat up, and smiling. He thanked the good Lord she was here and whole and ready to kick butt.

Nicholas smiled back and gestured for her to go first.

"Such lovely manners from the first Brit in the FBI. I could get used to this."

"Still cheeky, are we? It's good to see that some things haven't changed."

"Come on, you two." Zachery walked them past his office, down the blue-carpeted senior management hallway, straight out the door and to the elevators. As he punched the down button, he said, "You're headed to Twenty-six Wall Street. Stabbing. The NYPD called us since it's on federal land, so it's our case. I thought it would be a good idea to get Drummond here liaising with the locals as soon as possible. And aren't you two lucky, someone managed to get themselves dead on your first morning. Go on down there and figure out what happened."

The elevator doors opened and Zachery waved them in. "Drummond, I know you're going to be our big cyber-crime computer-terrorism guy, but we also need to teach you to drive on the right side of the road, get your boots dirty on the ground first." He smiled and clapped Nicholas on the shoulder. "Glad you're with us, Drummond. Welcome to the FBI. Good hunting." He turned, and said over his shoulder, "Oh, yes. Mike, keep him in line."

2

Mike's black Crown Vic waited for them in the garage. She jangled the car keys at Nicholas, then drew them back. "Maybe I should drive, even though you need the practice. Wall Street's pretty crazy."

"Contrary to popular belief, I do know how to manage the streets of New York. I have American blood, too, you know."

She laughed and got behind the wheel. Once they were out of the garage, she said, "Next time out, you'll drive. It's a requirement that you know all the streets. But not today. So tell me, did you really live up to Savich's lofty standards at the Academy? And Sherlock's?"

"I tried my pitiful best, Agent Caine." He watched her come within an inch of a lane-cutting taxi without blinking an eye.

"What have you been doing here in New York for the last two weeks?"

He never looked away from the pedestrian zigzagging in front of the Crown Vic. "Oh, a bit of this and that, getting set up, that's about it." **Not to mention I**

shopped for furniture until I nearly cut my own wrists, fought with Nigel on where all the bloody furniture should go, and was forced to have dinner with my ex at a French in-place big on presentation and light on food. In short, I haven't used my brain for two bloody weeks—but he didn't tell her any of that.

She sped through a yellow light. "I've missed having you around. Come on, now, tell me about your new place."

Not in this lifetime. "Nothing much to tell, really. It's a place to live, that's all." Nicholas's grandfather, in a magnanimous show of support for his grandson's decision to move to America, had pur-chased Nicholas a brownstone. No matter how hard Nicholas had protested, the baron, and his parents, he suspected, refused to allow Nicholas his wish, an anonymous apartment somewhere in Chelsea.

He was now saddled with a behemoth town house on East 69th Street, much to his butler Nigel's delight. Five bedrooms, five floors. Oh, yes, this sort of opulence was just the ticket for fitting in with the rest of the agents in the New York Field Office.

Mike slowly turned onto a street packed with pedestrians. "I can't wait to see it. Invite me over for a beer later, all right?"

And again he thought, **Not in this lifetime.** He said, "Where is our crime scene?"

"Just off Wall Street. Right there."

Mike threaded through dozens of people across to Pine Street, not far from Federal Hall. He saw the yellow sawhorse barrier with nypd on it, three blue-and-whites, lights revolving, reflecting off the stone buildings.

They badged the NYPD cop at the barrier, signed in to the scene, and were led to the small side street. It was going to be a beautiful day, he saw, already warming nicely. Considering the number of crime scenes he'd handled in the pouring rain in London, this certainly was preferable.

"What do we have here?" he asked the young NYPD officer standing inside the tape. His badge read f. wilson, and he looked barely old enough to vote, much less be a cop. Even though Nicholas knew he couldn't be more than five years older than the cop, he felt ancient, until Wilson spoke like the seasoned professional he was. "Stabbing," Wilson said, "and aren't you in luck, it's right there on your land. Another five feet and it would be ours, but no, this guy decides to get himself dead and make it all yours. I hear it's your first day on the job. Welcome to New York."

"Thank you."

Wilson grinned. "We've been canvassing, got a small group of people held aside who were nearby when it happened. Most say the suspect was a Caucasian male, brown hair, medium height, wearing jeans and a white hoodie."

Nicholas looked over at the small knot of people standing on the street corner, gaping at the scene, some recording everything with their phones, others standing quietly, obviously shell-shocked. He said, "Rather a detailed description, that."

"I know, right? Amazing, really, since

most witnesses can rarely agree on the sex of the suspect. Talk about lucking out—from the statements so far, there were two men arguing, then a struggle, then one guy turned away and the other man stabbed him from behind and took off running."

Mike said, "Hold everyone here, Officer Wilson. We'll want to speak to them as well. We need to get a look at the body, and we'll be right back."

Wilson saluted her and moved away from the tape to let them in.

Nicholas took his time walking toward the dead man, noticed Mike was taking in everything as well. Special Agent Louisa Barry, one of their crime scene techs, was snapping on nitrile gloves, ready to get to work. Nicholas smiled at her, then went down on his haunches beside a man who was seriously dead. He was in his late forties to early fifties, his brown eyes staring sightlessly into the sky, salt-and-pepper hair combed slightly to the side to cover the beginnings of a receding hairline, his suit rumpled and creased.

From the angle of his body on the pavement, and the way his arms were flung out from his body, Nicholas thought he'd fallen to his knees, then onto his back and died. The blood pooled beneath him, dark and thick, but it was disturbed, like a child's finger painting, swirls and whorls whipping across the sidewalk. **What were you arguing about? Why'd he stab you in the back?**

"See anything interesting?" Mike asked, studying the blood pool.

"It's what I'm not seeing that's interesting," Nicholas said. "No murder weapon. The guy stabbed him, then pulled out the knife and took off. I wonder if any of the witnesses saw the killer do that."

Mike said, "He still had his wallet, isn't that right, Louisa?" She looked up at Louisa, holding the man's belongings.

"Right here."

Nicholas asked, "What's his name?" He hated calling a once living, breathing man a corpse. He deserved more than that.

"Jonathan Charles Pearce. Lived on the Upper East Side. Money and cards left in the wallet. His cell's a BlackBerry Touch, and here's a nice old watch and a set of keys. Cell is password protected, I can't access it without my tools."

Nicholas said, "Do you carry a UFED in the field, perchance?"

"Is that British for Universal Forensic Extraction Device?" And she grinned. "Yeah, so happens I have a Touch Ultimate on the truck. Hang on a minute."

"Good," he said. "Are there any cameras around?"

Louisa said, "Nothing that points directly to this spot, but there's a traffic cam at the intersection of Pine and William, and the building itself has a camera on the corner. Might have something from one of those."

"Excellent, Louisa, thank you."

"By the way, Nicholas? It's good to have you on board. Welcome to New York."

"It's good to be here."

In the next instant, Louisa was headed to the mobile command unit.

Mike said, "Glad she brought it. With the UFED we'll get the pass code broken and access the data in no time. So, Nicholas, it doesn't appear Mr. Pearce was the victim of a robbery."

"No, it would seem not. A fight between two men. About what?"

"Whatever it was, the killer lost it and stabbed Mr. Pearce in the back with a dozen people looking on."

3

Nicholas looked up at a sharp whistle to see a tall, beefy older man heading their way, people getting out of his way. He looked like a guided missile, ready to clear the scene and move on to his next case.

"Here's the ME, and good news for us, he's the best," Mike said. "You'll like him."

The man reached them and stuck out his hand. Nicholas thought he meant to shake, but he was handing them both nitrile gloves.

"You're not allowed anywhere near my body without proper protection. See to it, now."

Mike snapped the gloves over the ones she was already wearing. She never argued with Janovich. "Good morning, Dr. Janovich. Now we're double protected. I'd like you to meet my new partner, Special Agent Nicholas Drummond. We worked together on the Koh-i-Noor diamond case. Today's his first day."

They shook hands. Janovich immediately pulled off his gloves and put on a fresh pair. "If I remember correctly, you knew the woman who died during that case. I'm sorry, that was tough."

Nicholas felt a familiar stab of pain. "Thank you, it was. I was Inspector Elaine York's superior at New Scotland Yard. But now I'm here in America, working for the FBI."

"Welcome, welcome. I don't know why we have a foreigner working for us, but in the long scheme of things, it doesn't matter, does it? We shook hands, change your gloves."

Mike said, "This particular foreigner was born in L.A. Do you remember the sitcom **A Fish out of Water,** with Mitzie Manders? She's Bo Horsley's sister, and Nicholas's mom."

Janovich blinked, his mouth widened in a huge smile. "You're kidding. I loved that show. She is a beautiful lady, and she had wonderful comic timing. Tell your mother she has a fan in the New York OCME, will you?" He gave Nicholas a closer look and smiled. "Since you're a foreigner, that stands for Office of the Chief Medical Examiner."

"I'll tell her, and thank you," Nicholas

said, amused, but Janovich had already begun examining Mr. Pearce's body, talking as he worked. Nicholas crouched down so he could listen in.

"Stab wound to the right kidney. Took him down fast and hard from behind. Created quite a mess. I'd say this poor man bled out within three or four minutes. The blade would need to be at least five inches long to make a gash that deep. Not much of a cut in the shirt, I'm betting a stiletto of some sort."

"Who's our killer, then?" Nicholas asked.

Dr. Janovich glanced up at Nicholas and started, as if surprised to see him there at face level. He flashed a rare smile. "I guess I'll have to let you figure that out."

Nicholas stood, groaning a little as his knees popped. Louisa hurried over to them. She handed Nicholas Pearce's cell phone. "I got in, no problem. You'll see Mr. Pearce received several texts recently. He was supposed to meet someone with the initials **EP** here this morning."

Nicholas said, "There was a short conversation between Pearce and EP.

Listen to this: **'I have news. Meet me at the Pine Street entrance of Fed Hall.'**

"And Pearce wrote back: **'Can't get downtown this a.m. Meet me at store instead?'**

"EP: **'Nine-one-one.'**

"Pearce: **'I hope this is the good kind of nine-one-one. On my way.' "**

There was a fifteen-minute gap in time, then another outgoing message from 8:15 a.m. Only thirty minutes earlier.

'I'm here, where are you?'

Both Mike and Nicholas could imagine Pearce walking quickly, distracted, worrying about what this EP and his 911 alert were all about, wondering what was so important it couldn't wait.

The good kind of 911? What did that mean? And who was EP?

"Evidently," Mike said, "EP didn't show up. Do you think it was a ploy to draw Pearce here to kill him?"

"Or maybe EP did show up and it wasn't a good kind of nine-one-one. They argued first, then EP killed him. Whatever, Mr. Pearce knew his killer. Maybe."

Janovich began his prep to take the body back to the OCME. Nicholas went down on his knees next to Mr. Jonathan Pearce. He said quietly, "We'll find who did this, sir. Mark my words."

Mike said, "You know, we've had a lot of trouble with gangs recently. Committing a murder in broad daylight is a surefire way through initiation."

"Anything is possible. But it seems rather unlikely that a New York gang would congregate on Wall Street and send text messages to their victims."

"No, generally not. Unless it was a gang of stockbrokers."

He grinned at her. "I know what you mean. They're a deadly bunch in London."

"Here, too."

"Well, then," Nicholas said, "let's get out of Dr. Janovich's way and see what the witnesses have to tell us."

They made their way to the group of witnesses huddled on the corner. There was another crowd gathered across the street, gaping and pointing, shooting more video with their phones, probably calling all their friends. He didn't think there was a single crime scene in the world today that wasn't recorded down to the blood on the sidewalk.

Most of the witnesses were clearly upset, but a few were annoyed at having to stick around to talk to the police and be late to work. But most were eager to tell what they'd seen.

Mike took the lead. "I'm Special Agent Caine, and this is Special Agent Drummond, FBI. We'd appreciate your telling us exactly what you saw." A furious babble erupted, and Mike put up her hands. "One at a time, please. Sir?"

He was the eldest of the group, a businessman in a gray wool suit. "I was walking across the street and heard the two men arguing. I looked over to see the older man fall." He swallowed. "The dead man."

Nicholas asked, "How much older was he than the man who stabbed him?"

"Twenty years, maybe. The guy, the killer, he looked about twenty-five, thirty. No more."

Mike was taking notes in her small

spiral-bound reporter's notebook. "Could you hear what they were arguing about?"

"Not really, but they were fighting over something, I don't know what."

"It was the phone," said an older woman dressed in head-to-toe white cashmere, holding a small Chihuahua. "The guy wanted his phone. After he stabbed the older man, he grabbed the phone and used it. I had the most absurd thought—that he was calling nine-one-one. But who would stab someone, then call nine-one-one? But then people started yelling at the man and he dropped the phone and took off running."

She'd clearly been crying, her eyes were red and bloodshot. "I'll never forget the way he looked right at me, before he ran away—" She shuddered and broke off. Mike watched her frown, then she yelled, pointing, "That's him! He's come back. Right over there—he's standing in that crowd of people across the street!" People around them were shuffling to get a better look, and the Chihuahua was barking his head off.

Nicholas jerked around to see the man looking straight at him. The man didn't hesitate. He shoved his way through the crowd, pushing people down, then he was free, running full out. He disappeared around the corner.

The crowd was shouting, an NYPD officer who was nearby hesitated a moment, then took off after him. Nicholas shouted to Mike, "Come on, come on, after him."

The streets were packed with people at the start of the workday. Nicholas passed the cop, his long runner's legs eating up the sidewalk. He saw the suspect half a block away, darting in and out of the crowds. He was in good shape, strong, fast as an Olympic sprinter, the bastard, pouring on the speed.

A woman fell in front of Nicholas, and he yanked her to her feet as he passed, shouting to the man, "Stop, FBI. Stop running now!"

Of course the man ignored him, continued

running south. Where did he think he could go? Battery Park at the end of Manhattan? If he tried to jump on the Staten Island Ferry, Nicholas had him, no way he'd be able to speed through the throngs of people. But if he caught the tube—**no, the subway—** then he'd be gone.

Mike, where was Mike? He glanced over his shoulder, she was two yards behind him, her stride smooth and fast. His mobile rang, but he ignored it. The man turned a corner, and Mike shouted, "Turn right, turn right now, there's a street across to Broadway, Exchange Place, cut him off. I'm going straight, we'll box him in."

Nicholas was nearly hit by a wildly honking cab, heard the driver cursing him, but he never slowed. He burst out onto Broadway, nearly behind Mr. Olympic. Ten yards, five—Nicholas could smell his sweat—yes, now he had him. Nicholas reached out an arm to snag the man's shoulder when he turned, something in his hand, and he pointed it at Nicholas—

And Nicholas was on the ground, doubled over, pain shooting through his body. His muscles jerked and jittered, his teeth clenched, his entire body cramped in on itself until he was sure it was all over for him. He couldn't breathe—then the pain stopped.

His breath came in short gasps. He shook his head to clear his brain. Slowly, he rolled onto his hands and knees.

Mr. Olympic was long gone. Nicholas saw a small rectangular black box on the ground five feet away. It was a Taser. Frigging Mr. Olympic had Tasered him.

Then Mike was on the ground with him, hands running over his body. "Where are you hit, where are you hit?"

"I'm all right, really, I'm all right."

"Then what happened? Where's our guy?"

Nicholas pointed at the Taser.

Mike couldn't believe it. She stared at the small black Taser, her heart still kettledrumming, pumping blood and fear through her. "I saw you go down. I thought he'd shot you, the way you were jerking around on the ground, but I didn't hear a shot. Thank heaven it was only a Taser."

"Yes, **only** a Taser," he said as he ripped the Taser barbs out of his side. At least it was getting easier to think and put words together.

"Can you walk, or do I need to carry you?"

He wanted to laugh at that visual but couldn't get any spit in his mouth. He slowly got to his feet.

Agent Ben Houston's voice crackled from the walkie-talkie Mike carried in her jacket pocket.

"We're here to back you up. We've spotted the suspect. He's on foot heading north on Trinity Place. Mike, Nicholas, he's parallel to your position. We're moving to intercept. Cut across Rector and stop him."

Nicholas was rolling his shoulders. "What? Did Mr. Olympic hang around to see what would happen next?"

"Come on, come on," Mike shouted, pulled on Nicholas's arm and took off again. "Can you do it?"

"I can. Bloody hell." Nicholas shook off the last of the Taser effects, felt his adrenaline kick in, and triangulated the area in his head, grateful his brain was back in working order. If they cut up to Rector they could intercept, especially if Ben could drive the man toward the box. Then a phalanx of agents could converge on the target from four sides.

He rushed after Mike, slower than before, but found the more he moved, the better his body parts worked. One block gone, now two. Shouts from the walkie as they closed in on three sides.

They turned the corner onto Trinity and there he was. Nicholas wanted him badly and pushed to his limit, shoving people out of the way, ignoring shouts, cries, curses. Mr. Olympic ran into the street to get away from the hordes of people and took off, one fast disbelieving look at Nicholas. Nicholas followed, heard Mike shouting, "Push him south, push him south." He glanced back, saw her coming fast, knew how determined she could be. He signaled for her to duck to the left and he'd turn Mr. Olympic right into her waiting arms. He hoped she'd deck him.

This time it went right. Mike flanked him,

ignoring the shouts and screams, the honking cars and taxis, and Nicholas pushed on the last of his speed, launched himself and tackled the man hard.

They were locked together, pummeling each other, as they rolled into the street right in front of an oncoming NYPD patrol car. Nicholas saw the bumper coming and shoved Mr. Olympic to the curb. He rolled as the patrol car slammed on its brakes and came to a stop an inch from Nicholas's leg.

Nicholas lay there for a heartbeat, not believing the car hadn't hit him. He sat up slowly, sent a prayer of thanks heavenward. But there was no time to rejoice that he hadn't been smeared across the street. He grabbed Mr. Olympic's leg and landed on top of him. No way was he getting away again.

The idiot tried to twist around to hit him, but Nicholas clipped Mr. Olympic in the jaw with his elbow, stunning him. **Perfect.** Nicholas jumped to his feet and pulled the man up with him. He thought of the Taser and how he'd been sure he was dying and slammed Mr. Olympic hard against a parked Audi, face-first.

Mike grabbed his arms behind him while Nicholas frisked him. He found an H&K MK23 pistol, a mobile phone, and two long-bladed stilettos, one of them still stained with Mr. Pearce's blood.

Nicholas jerked the man's head back. "Listen to me, we're federal agents. What in bloody hell are you up to, mate? Why did you kill Mr. Pearce?"

A sneer, nothing more.

Mike got in his face. "You assaulted a federal agent with your Taser, you idiot, and that means no one's going to play with you anymore. Tell me your name, now. Tell us why you murdered Mr. Pearce. What were you arguing about with him?"

Mr. Olympic bared his teeth, meant to be a grin, but wasn't.

Mike said, "No wallet, no ID, but you'll be in the system. We'll know who you are within the hour, so you might as well tell us now."

"Come on, mate, don't be daft. Who are you?"

The man opened his mouth, but no words came out. They saw a look of horror in his eyes, then panic, sharp, cold panic— Mr. Olympic's eyes rolled back in his head. He seized, a bubbling white froth spewed out of his mouth, then he slumped against Nicholas.

Mike screamed into the walkie, "We need a medic, right now." Nicholas let him slide down to the sidewalk. Mike felt for his pulse, started a CPR checklist, but Nicholas pulled her back.

"Let me go, we need him alive."

"It's too late," he said. They looked at the man's face, gone blue now, dark eyes staring blankly up at them. A few more muscle twitches and he stopped moving.

Bystanders were in a circle around them, excited and horrified, knowing death when they saw it. The NYPD officer who'd nearly hit Nicholas rushed to help. He saw the man lying on the sidewalk. "What happened? I didn't think I hit you. What happened to him?"

"No, you didn't hit me, it's something else," Nicholas said, and turned to Mike. "Stay with him." He stood, raised his creds high, told the crowd he was FBI and they needed to move back, this was now a crime scene and there was nothing to see, it was all over. He heard Mike say to the officer, "I don't know what happened. We were chasing him—he killed a man on Wall Street, but he went down; why, I don't know. We were trying to help."

Special Agent Ben Houston pulled up in

a Crown Vic beside him, hopped out of the car. He took one look at the dead man and said, "What happened to him? What'd you do to him?"

Nicholas said to Ben, aware the crowd was pressing in again, "I didn't do anything to him. I'd finally managed to bring him down. He started seizing and foaming at the mouth. Whatever happened, Mr. Olympic did it to himself."

"Mr. Olympic? You mean, like he had cyanide in his tooth?"

"Maybe, not necessarily cyanide, but a bloody fast poison of sorts in his mouth." He frowned at the blue face. "But why would he kill himself? What the devil is going on here?"

No answer to that. Mike said to Ben, "We need an ID on this guy, pronto. Nicholas is right, something's not kosher here, and it's possible the Devil does have something to do with it."

Nicholas said, "I wonder why he stayed around." He looked down at Mr. Olympic. "Why?"

6

Berlin, Germany
4:00 p.m.

The mission was shot to hell. März watched, tense, unable to do anything. He knew every single individual in this huge room was even more frightened of failure than he was and that was because, simply, they were scared to death of him. They were right to be; he was lethal and soulless and took pleasure in his work. No one dared to look at him standing quietly in the back of the large windowless room, watching, always watching. The nerve center, the workers called it, all of them focused on the single massive monitoring screen on the wall, covered in twenty blue and green quadrants. Fifteen analysts worked multiple computer angles. They were responsible for monitoring each agent's heart rate, his breathing, his visuals, his audio. They saw everything the agent saw, heard what he said, heard what those around him said. It never ceased to amaze März, this invasion of another's mind, but all the analysts were used to being inside a live human being and participating from afar.

Senior Analyst Bernstein was in charge of Mr. X, with him every step he took, inside him, watching and listening from the moment Mr. X had deplaned and the mission had gone live.

And gone to hell. März thought of his boss and tasted fear.

First Mr. X had killed the Order's Messenger. Then, because he stayed at the scene so they could see what was unfolding, he'd been spotted by that ridiculous woman and her little yapping dog. All of them had followed the chase, watched the big dark-haired FBI agent finally take down Mr. X, saw him hauled to his feet and cuffed. The room was dead silent, watching, listening. Then alarms began going off and the room exploded into action.

Bernstein yelled, "What happened, what happened? Mr. X has collapsed, his visuals are down, his eyes are gone."

"I've lost heart function!"

"Ears are down. Ears are down."

"He activated his gel pack! He must have thought he was going to be taken."

Panic rippled through the room, moving silently from man to man as they now focused on Mr. X. After a moment, the heart monitor beeped long and low, then went flatline. Mr. X's quadrant suddenly went black with a snap, as if a switch had been flipped off.

Horrified silence. März spoke quietly, no need to raise his voice. "Mr. Bernstein, since we've lost Mr. X, please give me the satellite."

Bernstein's voice shook and he hated it, but his belly crawled with the taste of failure, and fear. "Yes, sir. Coming, sir. Online in three, two, one."

All twenty-four quadrants flashed to a new scene, a bird's-eye view of New York rapidly winnowing down as the satellite's cameras telescoped toward the chaotic New York street. A quick screen refresh and the scene was in perfect focus.

"There are people hovering over the

body, I can't get a clear shot of Mr. X."

März said, "Alter the angle."

"I'm trying, sir. We'll have to wait thirty seconds while the bird is repositioned."

"Do it faster."

The analysts were perfectly still, breath held, while Bernstein madly tapped on his keyboard, moving the low earth-orbiting satellite a hundred miles above the scene a fraction to capture the proper image.

He managed the realignment in record time. Fifteen seconds flat. He wiped his sweating hands on his lab coat, then ran the camera sight down as fast as he could, and there it was, the shot slightly moved, the main screen taken up by the faces of the two FBI agents standing over Mr. X's body. The male FBI agent stood and moved away, forcing the growing crowd backward. The camera detail was so fine they could see the bruises starting on his jaw, hear a deep sigh from the blond agent as she stood and watched the medics work on Mr. X, who was clearly very dead.

"Why did he activate his gel pack?" März asked.

Bernstein said, "Sir, I don't know that he did. It seems that the agent who took him down may have hit him in the jaw at precisely the perfect spot to activate the gel."

"Show me."

The film was rewound and played again at half speed. With a red laser pointer, Bernstein showed the agent's elbow connecting with the back of Mr. X's jaw.

"One-in-a-million shot, sir. We couldn't have known an exterior punch would be enough to release the poison. Or maybe Mr. X was fiddling with it, debating whether it was necessary. He didn't want to be taken. He sacrificed himself to protect us."

Not likely, März thought. "Show me the FBI agent who hit him. Who is he?"

"The agents at the scene were calling him Nicholas Drummond, sir."

März said in his same calm, terrifying voice, "Well, you idiots, what are you waiting for? Give me data, right now, screen one. Who are we dealing with? I want everything you can find on Special

Agent Drummond. Who he is, where he comes from, what he ate for breakfast. All of you, go."

Five minutes passed in tense silence. The only background noise was the clatter of the keyboards. Finally, Bernstein stood, ran a hand through his thinning hair, and forced himself to walk to März. "Sir?"

"Yes?"

"About the target, sir. His last words."

"'The key is the lock.' Yes."

"Not exactly, sir. We've replayed it several times, and we believe what he actually said is the key is **in** the lock."

"**In** the lock. Not the lock itself?"

"That's right, sir. I've prepared an audio file and sent it to your screen. I'm sure you'll want to listen for yourself."

"Yes, I will. Get back to your station, Bernstein. Tick-tock, people. What do we have on Drummond?"

The analyst who'd replayed the video said, "Sir, Nicholas Drummond, grandson of the eighth Baron de Vesci, currently an FBI special agent, moved to New York last month after terminating his employment with the Metropolitan Police of London. He is former Foreign Office, and his father, Harold Mycroft Drummond, is currently listed as a consultant to the British Home Office."

"Pull his file."

"Yes, sir, I'm accessing the Home Office files now."

Another analyst said, "Sir, Drummond had one marriage, ended in divorce. He's highly trained and lethal with a variety of weapons, and he's a serious hacker." The man swallowed. "He was a field agent for a while, mainly in Afghanistan, but like I said, he's a serious hacker, sir, excellent, in fact, and that's why the Foreign Office wanted him. He was responsible for the underlying code of Mackay, similar to Stuxnet, the virus used to shut down the Iranian nuclear arsenal in 2010."

März didn't miss the note of awe in the analyst's tone. He said, "I thought that job was done by Mossad."

"Apparently they used Drummond as a decoy, sir. He was the one who wrote the original program, fed it to the Israelis. They took his Mackay variables and created Stuxnet. But he left soon after, there's no reason listed. Moved to New Scotland Yard as a homicide investigator. Drummond's personnel file from the Metropolitan Police lists a multitude of successes; he had an excellent close rate, and several write-ups for insubordination."

Another analyst called out, "Sir, he's the one who recovered the Koh-i-Noor diamond a few months ago. He went rogue with the female special agent, Michaela Caine. You'll remember they recovered the stone."

März smiled and the young man shuddered. "Went rogue, did he? Keep digging. In the meantime, I will inform Mr. Havelock of the situation we find ourselves in. He will not be well pleased by the news that both Pearce and Mr. X are dead. Bernstein, find a way to destroy any evidence of his internal surveillance capabilities before the Americans find them."

Both März and Bernstein knew this was impossible that Mr. X's implant would most likely be discovered in autopsy. Their only hope now was that the autopsy wouldn't be done today, that it wouldn't be thorough, but the chances were slim on both counts. And then the FBI would have the nanotechnology implant. And Havelock would have all their heads.

März stepped from the room, seeing the images of Mr. X running like a madman, then caught and brought down. Losing Mr. X so close to the end meant there would be repercussions, bad ones. At least they still had Mr. Z in play.

Since this was März's operation, he must take responsibility. No choice. Slowly, he raised his hand and knocked on the door to Mr. Havelock's office, and entered without waiting for a reply.

7

Dr. Manfred Havelock stared out the huge plate-glass window, looking at the Berlin spring afternoon. People crowded the sidewalks, bicycles parked in rows outside the red-umbrellaed sidewalk cafés of the Kreuzberg, so much traffic, so many people, yet there were scores of horse chestnut trees and ivy climbed up the buildings, beautiful and green, right in the heart of the city.

He lived here in the X-Berg, enjoying his anonymous life among the socially conscious Germans and the unwanted immigrants, the hip-hop culture and the gays, because no one would expect it. He was forty-seven and easily one of the richest men in Germany, if not in all of Europe. He was a success in all ways imaginable. He smiled, thinking of his global multinational nano-biotechnology firm, and the respect given him by his peers. Truth be told, though, he most enjoyed the fear of his enemies. He watched a boy and girl leaning across a café table below to kiss, like in Paris, he thought, a place he could easily live. Would he move with the rich and powerful? Honestly, he found them a boring lot, toadies, sycophants, but still, to have his boots licked was pleasant on occasion.

But only on occasion. He loved the X-Berg, it was where he belonged. Its darkened corners allowed him to indulge in whatever behavior he wanted, no matter how reckless, how profligate. On the streets he was known only as the man who preferred the most esoteric acts available, and paid well for them. Ah, but there was more, so much more. No one knew who he really was, no one knew who lived among them, and what he was capable of. What he could do to them, if he wished. If they knew, they would not go so easily through their days and nights.

Havelock turned to see Elise step forward from the shadows. Her black hair, loose, as he liked it, cascaded to her waist. He himself had selected the skintight black catsuit she wore, a fit so tight it drove him mad with lust, even more than if he had seen her naked. Ah, and those five-inch stiletto heels on her long, narrow feet, perfect, as was the diamond-and-jet choker he'd fastened around her beautiful throat three years before when he'd selected her for himself and brought her into his world.

He waved toward the window. "Is it not ironic, my dear? The way they move without knowing how precarious their lives are? How in a blink"—he snapped his fingers—"I can take it all away from them? Make them cry and scream if I wished? Make them dead and nothing at all?"

Her voice was low, deep, as he'd taught her to speak. Her soft rose scent filled his nostrils. "It is, Manfred, very ironic."

She came to stand by him, smiled directly into his eyes as she took his hand, caressed his palm, and began to press hard and harder still until his eyes went wild and he cried out.

She released him, still smiling. Once the pain fell away, he said, "Thank you, Elise. Well done, just as I taught you. But now we must think of other things. My plan is under way. Let us have a drink, to celebrate."

She walked to the opulent walnut bar in the corner of the room and fixed him two fingers of Lagavulin, dropped onto two perfectly square ice cubes. He studied her as she walked back to him, her stilettos the only sound, and felt intense pleasure at seeing her shake her head in a practiced move that made her hair spill around her shoulders, soft, beautiful thick hair. He felt greed and hunger, hunger so intense it was naked in its force.

He took the glass from her, feeling the brush of her fingers. It took all his willpower not to throw the drink on the floor and run his hands over her body, feel the tightness, know there was softness and strength beneath the catsuit.

Elise saw the mad lust in his eyes and shifted her hips, offering, should he choose to have her again so soon, but he shook his head and looked out onto the pulsing streets of Berlin, sipping the scotch. Still, he tightened all over thinking about the bruises she'd given him only an hour ago.

But there was a time for indulgence, and a time for focus, and so he shook his head, pointed toward the discreet door, and Elise melted away into the darkness with no hesitation, saying nothing at all, a faint smile on her mouth.

He truly wanted her, but not yet. Knowing she waited for her summons to come to him again helped. He took another sip of the scotch to steady himself.

His time had come at last. All the years of waiting, sitting by while his father was in charge, were finished. It was his time now.

He frowned. There were so many operations, too many opportunities for failure, and he had to admit it, he'd been careless lately, indulging too much, losing himself for hours at a time in Elise's capable hands. He must keep focused, there was too much at stake. **With focus and quiet comes clarity.** Odd that his father had taught him that valuable lesson; indeed, he could hear his father's voice—suddenly, he froze. He knew, knew something was wrong, terribly wrong.

He turned in the next moment when März entered quietly, shutting the door behind him. His face, as always, was blank, no clue to his thoughts, and, as always, Havelock felt revulsion at that long scar bisecting the shiny, stretched flesh, more a death mask than a man's face. März was deadly, uncompromising, and brutal, and he was Havelock's. He owned him. He'd come to believe März was his perfect complement.

But Havelock had learned over the years that when März's icy blue eyes were narrowed, something was terribly wrong, and fury was bubbling, ready to kill, to destroy. März said only, "Mr. X is down, sir."

"Tell me," Havelock said, his voice perfectly controlled.

"His gel pack was activated. As far as we can tell, it was an accident."

"An accident," Havelock repeated, and März, hating himself for it, knew deep grinding fear. "Before the gel pack was accidentally activated, did Mr. X manage to retrieve the package from Pearce?"

"No, sir. He was being taken into custody when the incident occurred."

Havelock shut his eyes and turned to face the windows again. "And the prototype?"

März kept his voice clear and calm. "It is possible the American FBI are in possession of the prototype, sir. We are endeavoring to intercept and remove it from their hands before they are able to study it, but there is little chance." Actually, there was no chance at all and both of them knew it.

"I see. Were you able to tap into the Messenger's systems before Mr. X's untimely demise?"

März hated his fear, wondered briefly if Havelock would quickly slide his favored Spanish stiletto into his neck. "Yes, but we were not able to upload Mr. Pearce's data before Mr. X was killed."

Havelock felt such rage he wanted to kill all of them. Without Mr. X finishing his part of the mission, hooking into Jonathan

Pearce's computer for Havelock's remote access, they couldn't retrieve the coordinates for the lost sub, and time was running out.

Havelock's voice went deadly quiet. "First Mr. X kills Pearce, against my orders, then he gets himself dead? Better for him, perhaps, but not for you. You're lucky Mr. Z is still functioning as he should.

"You will fix this, März. We can't afford to have the plan derailed. Nor can the Order realize we are behind it or there will be problems, huge problems, that could destroy everything. Find a way to retrieve the information from Pearce's computer before the FBI find it."

"Yes, sir. There is another route to the files, sir, though it involves a human asset."

Havelock waved a hand. "I don't care what you have to do."

"Understood. Also, it turns out we were incorrect earlier about what Pearce said as he died. What he actually said was **'The key is** in **the lock,'** not simply **'The key is the lock.'** Does that make any sense to you?"

Havelock took a sip of scotch. "I will think about it. Pearce was fond of riddles. I'm sure this is yet another of his trying games."

"We may have another problem, sir."

Havelock met his lieutenant's eyes, and März flinched, knowing the deadly sarcasm was coming. "**More** problems, März? Am I not paying you enough? Providing you with the proper tools? Are you incapable of running the most simple of missions without cocking it up?"

"No, sir. Not at all. This is about the FBI agent who responded to Pearce's murder, and was responsible for Mr. X falling in battle. His name is Nicholas Drummond."

Havelock slowly set his scotch glass on his desk. "I don't suppose you know who that is?"

"Yes, sir. He is former Foreign Office, then he went to—"

"You idiot, I don't care about his résumé. Drummond's the one who tracked the Fox across Europe and retrieved the Koh-i-Noor in three days. He brought down Saleem Lanighan. Lanighan was a tough son of a bitch, too, and now he's in a nuthouse in Paris, they say he'll never have his brain back. And Drummond's father has the ears of all the British government. Do you understand, März, Drummond is very high in the government?" He banged his fist on the desk, making the scotch splash up over the edge of the crystal glass. "These are not men to be trifled with, März. They will eat us whole if given the chance. The Drummonds must not be allowed to interfere in our plans."

"If you want me to have Drummond eliminated, I will arrange it. It would not be difficult."

Havelock calmed, narrowed his eyes at März. "You're wrong. It would take more than Mr. X or Mr. Z to take down Nicholas Drummond. He is dangerous, and unpredictable. I would take great pleasure doing it myself, and I'm the only one who could, truly, but I can't be under any sort of suspicion, not if the Order are going to accept me into their fold. No, leave Drummond alone for the time being. But watch him, März. Watch every move he makes, keep him off the scent. If he gets close, then you deploy. Do you understand me?"

"Deploy, sir? You mean deploy the micro–nuclear weapon? But the MNW has not left the testing grounds. We do not know if it is traceable. Nor do we know what the fallout will be. It could be worse than we anticipate. We do not know—"

All Havelock had to do was shake his head, only a small movement, but März was instantly quiet. "I do not recall asking your opinion, März. Besides, we are past that point. Now that Pearce's son has found the submarine, we must move quickly before others find out. The moment you access the coordinates from Pearce's computer, we will leave and retrieve the key.

"Understand me, März. If we have to use an MNW on Drummond, we will. Once we have the key and the weapon and adapt it to my MNWs, it won't matter, we will then be invincible. The Order won't be able to do a thing to stop us. Do you know, my father told me about the kaiser's private treasury of gold that was also supposed to be aboard the submarine along with the key? If true, which I doubt, the gold would be a nice bonus. Now, gather all the micro–nuclear weapons for possible deployment."

März nodded slowly. If he felt doubts, they didn't show on his face. "It will be done, sir. Will there be anything else?"

"Why, yes, there is. Send Elise back in."

"Sir, I believe she has retired to her quarters."

"Your point, März?"

März said, "I'll send her right away," then turned and left the room. Havelock waited for the door to close, then carefully wiped up the spilled scotch, fixed himself another, and sat back in the chair.

Drummond. **And** his father.

But no, he couldn't use an MNW on Drummond, even though the image of him being vaporized on the spot by a small nuclear bomb radiated pleasure and anticipation in the deepest part of him. No, he couldn't authorize it, not yet. It could allow them to trace the technology back to him. They were too powerful and their questions would resonate and multiply and lead to inquiries at the highest levels, and the delicate spiderweb he'd woven would unravel before he was able to find the key. And the kaiser's gold?

8

Near Wall Street
10:00 a.m.

Mike knew Nicholas was tense, angry, just as she was. She touched his arm as they watched the techs load Mr. Olympic's body into the medical examiner's van. "It's always tough, the waste, the not knowing why," she said. The van doors closed with a clang. "And now he's dead and can't tell us. But we will take care of Mr. Pearce, we'll get him justice. You know that, Nicholas. Are you okay?"

He let out a deep breath. "Yes, I know that. I'll be fine."

Mike shielded her eyes from the sudden glare of the sun off the glass windows of Trinity Church, to their right. She saw a crowd was gathered a little farther down the street, in Zuccotti Park, watching them.

"Good." She popped him in the arm, grinned at him. "You know, I really didn't expect you to be Superman on your first day, but there you were, flying right out of the gate."

"Talk about fast, Mr. Olympic would have gotten away from us if you hadn't known that shortcut. This is strange, Mike, all of it. I mean, Mr. Olympic hung around, then he was so afraid when we got him, he popped cyanide in his tooth?"

"Or whatever it was. You're right. Leave your cape on, okay?"

"I wonder, did Superman ever get a pilot's license, or did he wing it?"

"He winged it, absolutely." She glanced again at the growing crowd. "Let's go back. Maybe there's an update on the video, and we can see for ourselves what happened."

"Yes, let's. I'd like to see how Pearce was taken down." He paused, gave her a long look. "You know, you could be Ms. Olympic."

She said coolly, not looking at him, "I tried, but I wasn't good enough."

He pictured a younger Mike, all long, strong legs, blond hair in a ponytail, focused, determined— "Long distance or sprint?"

"Long distance."

He believed it. He paused for a moment, frowned. "It's strange. I feel like someone's been watching us, but how could anyone do that? Forget it, come on, let's get back."

It took them only a few minutes to walk back to Federal Hall. Officer Wilson stood by the crime scene tape, keeping people out.

"We heard there was an incident with the suspect and he's dead," Wilson said. "What happened?"

Nicholas said, "Well, he led us on a merry chase, Tasered me, then managed to get himself dead when I caught up to him the second time."

"Did you have to kill him?"

"No, it was something else entirely, something he ate, maybe. Next time, Wilson, you can chase him."

"Nah, I'm not as young as I once was." He gave Nicholas a manic grin. "You look worse for wear yourself, Agent Drummond. Anything we can do for you? You need a medic?"

"I'm fine," Nicholas said. "What we need are the video feeds of the murder, if you have them."

"Happens we do. The agent over there, Louisa? She has them downloaded."

Louisa was sitting on the edge of the truck's gate with a laptop balanced on her knees, her bobbed blond hair blowing a bit in the light spring breeze. She looked up. "Hey, you're back. Good." Then she really looked. "Whoa. You guys look like you've been in a war. What in the world happened to you two?"

"Not all that much, really, and the suspect is dead," Mike said. "We really need that video feed now, Louisa."

"Or yesterday, whichever is fastest," Nicholas said.

"You got it. You're in luck with the video. I'm almost done enhancing it. Like the witnesses said, the men actually argued for a while before he killed Pearce."

She turned the laptop around and hit play.

The feed was grainy, angled down, so Mike knew immediately it had come from a traffic cam, but it was clear enough that they could see Mr. Olympic loitering on the corner when Pearce rushed into the frame. Pearce had been jogging. They watched him bend down to catch his breath, rub his knees, check his watch, and look around. When he didn't see who he was expecting to see, he sent a quick text message on his cell.

Such mundane acts, Mike thought. He had no clue he was about to die. She'd seen death videos too often, and it always made her sad and angry to watch a person's life end violently.

Mr. Olympic walked over to Pearce and said something. Pearce jerked in response. They spoke, then it became more heated. Mr. Olympic slipped a knife from inside his Windbreaker. He was careful with it, practiced. No one on the street level would have been able to see it; the angle from the traffic cam showed it gleaming between the two of them. When Pearce turned away, obviously angry, the knife sank into his back. They watched Pearce's face change from bewilderment to disbelief. And then he was down, Mr. Olympic with him.

Louisa said, "I know, it's horrible. Now, listen, I was able to catch up the audio to the video before he knifed him."

The voices were faint; they had to strain to hear.

Pearce said, **"He won't come. He's too smart, he'll know, he'll see you."**

"He'll come, see me with you, and he'll think everything is fine. We're going to wait for him to show, and then we're going to have a little chat."

"So you're the one who sent me the text?"

Mr. Olympic held up a cell phone, waggled it in his hand. **"The power of technology. While we wait, you can tell me what he told you last night. The call between the two of you lasted for thirty minutes, then you made some very interesting calls yourself. Exciting news travels fast, yes? He found it, didn't he?"**

"I won't allow it, I won't let you have him." Pearce jerked around, but Mr.

Olympic was fast. He said something they couldn't make out, then suddenly the knife was out, five inches of tempered steel, and seconds later it slammed deep into Pearce's back.

Pearce went down on his knees, the suspect cradling him.

He said, **"Tell me. Tell me everything, or I swear to God, I'll kill your whole family and everyone they love."**

Pearce had little breath left. He was facing the cameras, his eyes blank with shock.

"Tell me or they're both dead!"

"The key—"

"The key what?"

"The key is—in the lock." Pearce's head lolled against the man's chest.

"What? What the hell does that mean?" He shook him, but Pearce was gone. He pushed Pearce onto the pavement, and Mr. Olympic, clearly furious, pulled out Pearce's cell and punched in numbers, but then looked wildly around at the shouts, saw two large men closing on him, and jumped to his feet. He tripped on Pearce, dropped the cell phone, and ran.

The screen showed people running to the body, several people calling 911, then Louisa turned the computer back around. "That's all I have for now. I'll keep working on this, see if I can further enhance it. You say our suspect is already dead; at least Pearce got payback, right?"

Nicholas said, "Mr. Pearce's dying words: **The key is in the lock.** What does that mean? Louisa, play it again, please."

She did. He listened and watched, and when it was finished, nodded to himself. "We need an ID on this man, Louisa, as quickly as possible. Upload this video into the facial-recognition database. There's a good still shot to be taken as he turns to run away. Put in a parameter to have it search the European databases through Interpol as well, and all the incoming flights from Germany to New York."

Mike asked, "German?"

"I caught it the second time through. A moment before he stabs Pearce, he says, **'Deinefruedemögevergehen und** übelmögedichereilen.' "

So he spoke German, did he? She said, "So that's what he said exactly, is it? Excellent. Thanks for clearing that right up for me."

"A bit of sarcasm? Sorry, yeah, I speak a little German, enough to catch what he said. It's a curse of sorts. It roughly translates to **'May your joy vanish and evil be with you.'** "

"Lovely sentiment."

"It doesn't sound all that dramatic in translation, but it's powerful in German. I suppose in this context, it's more of a way to ward off evil spirits following him, which turned out to be us."

"Too bad the curse didn't work," Mike said. "But, Nicholas, Mr. Olympic sounded American. He was fluent, colloquial."

He nodded. "I'm willing to bet, though, that German is his first language. I've often found it true that a person curses in his native tongue automatically."

"Good catch," Mike said. "Louisa, I'd also like you to upload all the video onto the servers so it will be ready for us to look at again when we get back to the office. And please be sure you add in all the footage from the crime scene, throughout the morning. There might be more there, small details we're missing right now. The two men were waiting for someone, someone Pearce was willing to die to protect."

"And still he told him when Mr. Olympic threatened his family, **'The key is in the lock.'** Was he lying? Or was it true? And another question: Why did Mr. Olympic hang around? Did he think this EP would still show up?"

"Maybe he did show up," Mike said. "This EP is obviously someone close to Mr. Pearce, that's all we know. Keep an eye out for someone you don't think really fits, Louisa."

"Like anyone not wearing a suit, and hanging around," Nicholas said. "Find out about Mr. Pearce's family as fast as you can. That threat Mr. Olympic made, we're taking that seriously. Call me as soon as you know."

"Got it." Louisa smiled and disappeared

into the mobile command unit. Nicholas watched the ME, half a block away, move Mr. Pearce's body into a black bag for transport.

He said slowly, "I don't think murdering Mr. Pearce was part of the plan. At least he wasn't meant to be killed before Mr. Olympic got what he came for. Whoever he was, he wanted information about what EP had found, and Mr. Pearce wasn't about to tell him."

Mike shook her head. "We'll back-trace the cell phone number. Speaking of which, dropping Mr. Pearce's cell phone sure wasn't part of the plan. Thank heavens he got rattled when people started coming at him and dropped it."

"Good luck for us. Clearly this was a trap, but we need more information. Mr. Pearce wasn't wearing a wedding ring, but we know he has a family. Let's go to his home."

Mike nodded. "I hate this, but we have to do it. Hopefully, someone knows what this was all about. What Mr. Pearce said—**The key is in the lock**—don't you wish just one time things would be straightforward?"

"That wouldn't be much fun, now, would it?"

9

Jonathan Pearce's Apartment
117 East 57th Street
10:30 a.m.

The doorman was too upset by Mr. Pearce's murder to give more than a token protest about letting them in without a warrant. He took them in the lovely 1920s elevator to the twenty-third floor and unlocked Mr. Pearce's apartment.

Mike and Nicholas first saw the walls of windows on three sides overlooking Manhattan, the clear blue skies, the warm sun spilling through the glass.

Mike whistled. "This is breathtaking."

Nicholas joined her, pointed. "You can see the George Washington Bridge."

She nodded, then turned to study the long, narrow living room. "It doesn't seem to be disturbed—nothing seems out of place. I want to get it fingerprinted before we go poking around too much. But we can have a look." She tossed him a pair of gloves.

He snapped them on and cocked an eyebrow at her, hands raised like a freshly scrubbed surgeon. "Where's my patient?"

"Idiot."

The apartment was large, well furnished in a mix of modern and traditional, with neutral colors and exquisite paintings and sculptures. "This is the sanctuary of a Renaissance man," Nicholas said.

"And a very neat man who slept alone," Mike said. "There are no female signs anywhere. Only a single toothbrush, shaving kit, and brush were in the bathroom. The five bedrooms have been redone so there was one large master with a huge walk-in closet with built-in cabinets, plus a private library, an office, and a massive theater room."

Nicholas stepped into the library. It was darker than the rest of the apartment because the windows were tinted, all the shelves behind locked glass. He saw books ranging from antiquity to what he bet was a first-edition Hemingway. His fingers itched to open the cabinet and touch the beautiful leather. The books were not only special, they were very valuable.

He called to Mike, "What does Mr. Pearce do?"

She stuck her head into the library, looked around for a second. "It looks like he's in the rare-book business. Would you look at this, he has letterhead on his desk."

Made sense, for a Renaissance man. "What's the name of the company?"

"The letterhead says Ariston's, Second Avenue, between Fifty-fifth and Fifty-sixth. I wonder where he got that name, Ariston's?"

Nicholas said, "From whom sprang all rational thought. Ariston was Plato's father, a fitting name, considering. The business must be successful. See all the books in here? They're very old, very rare. And very valuable."

Mike looked around. "Maybe this explains the locks in the master bedroom closet, which is, I might add, bigger than my whole apartment."

"It seems like overkill. Let's take a look. Was there a key in his desk?"

"Better." Mike reached into her pocket and pulled out the key chain Louisa had given her at the crime scene. "Let's go see what he keeps under lock and key in his bedroom closet." She looked first at the lock, then studied the keys, picked a small silver key on the ring. Sure enough, it went in, and the lock clicked free.

"More books," Nicholas said. "Old, very valuable. Let's see what's in this second locked cabinet."

She studied the lock for a moment, then found an even smaller key, this one gold, and it slid in perfectly.

There were three shelves of books. Nicholas gently touched the spine of a small vellum book that looked like it might crumble away into dust. "These must be the ones that can't get exposed to light. Let's lock them back up. The crime scene techs will have to inventory everything for us—they can take their time and do this properly. I don't want to be the one responsible for devaluing a masterpiece."

Mike tried to shut the cabinet, but the hinge hung. She fiddled with it for a minute, then said, "This one doesn't want to close and I don't want to force it."

"Let me see." Nicholas ran his hand along the edge of the door. He pulled it toward him, but the hinge stayed stuck open. "That's strange. Maybe these haven't been opened in a while. Let me try once more." Instead of pulling again, he pushed, and the hinge suddenly popped free, the door coming away with it. They saw a small compartment, one that would have been impossible to see if Mike hadn't overextended the hinge when she'd opened the door.

"There's something back here, Mike."

"What is it?"

"I have no earthly idea. Best take a picture, then I'll fish it out." Mike snapped a shot with her cell, then he stuck his finger into the dark slot and pulled out a small clear plastic bag. He turned it over in his gloved hand. "Looks like a common everyday SD card, nothing at all special, like one you'd have in your digital camera to stick in your computer to upload your photos. It's 256 gigabytes—this holds a lot of data. As much as some laptops."

"All on that tiny card. Amazing."

"Mike, let's head to the computer in Mr. Pearce's office. I saw an iMac on his desk."

"Trust you to stumble into something."

He waved the SD card at her. "It was all you. Let's go see what Mr. Pearce was hiding away."

Of course it wasn't that simple. Like Pearce's phone, the iMac was password protected. Nicholas sat at the desk in the expensive high-end Aeron chair—Mr. Pearce's business was clearly quite lucrative—and inserted a small thumb drive into the slot. The machine booted up with a system prompt. Nicholas launched a program he'd designed to crack pass codes, and a few minutes later the solution came up on the screen. He wrote it down on a sticky note, then ejected the thumb drive. There would be no trace of his program in the system. Elegant, and useful.

Mike watched him carefully. "I certainly like you being able to do this kind of forensic accounting work legally, Special

Agent Drummond. Keeps my blood pressure under control."

He smiled, inputted the newly acquired pass code into the machine. It whirred to life, bringing up the clean desktop with a face-on photo of a young dark-haired woman about Mike's age. She was smiling, eyes shining at the camera. "Mike, come look. I think I found a photo of Mr. Pearce's daughter."

Mike leaned over his shoulder. "She has something of the look of her father. I really hate this, Nicholas. Louisa should be calling us with a name and her information any minute and we'll be able to contact her. I saw a photo in his bedroom of a boy maybe about eight years old, and the girl, she looked about fourteen or fifteen, their mother between them, hugging them close." She sighed. "I pulled the photo out of the frame, but nothing was written on the back. But I do know that no woman lives here, so either they were divorced or Mr. Pearce was a widower."

"So his family now consists of a son and a daughter." Yes, she did have the look of her father, he thought, and hated it as much as Mike. They'd be the ones to change her life. He kept working. "Okay, we're in. Now let's see what sort of skeletons Mr. Pearce was hiding in his closet, literally."

Nicholas inserted the SD card into the slot and opened it. Again, an encrypted password screen came up. He ran the program again, and like putting a key in a lock, the computer screen suddenly filled with a stream of extensive images and files.

Mike leaned close to the computer screen. "Good grief, what **is** all that?"

"I don't know, but there's a lot of it."

10

**11 Downing Street
Office of the Chancellor
of the Exchequer
London
4:00 p.m.**

The phone rang, a discreet buzzing, but Alfie Stanford ignored it, remained focused on the screen in front of him, which moments before had blinked to life unbidden and alighted with data. Horror filled him as he watched the pages streaming across his desktop: images, letters, some hundreds of years old, e-mails. Someone had accessed the Messenger's private files. The Messenger had been compromised, and thus the Order itself. Decade upon decade of information, research, and secrets had been seen by the wrong eyes. By an outsider.

Who could have found the SD card and accessed Jonathan's files? All the Order members believed his death was a New

York street mugging. But no longer. Stanford knew to his gut the murderer had also accessed his files. He couldn't imagine what would happen now. His heart thudded hard. This was a nightmare of epic proportions.

He had to warn the others. There was a protocol for this very situation, one he was supposed to have memorized. But he wasn't a young man anymore, and he wanted to be sure the protocols were done correctly, all the proper steps followed in the correct order, the alerts given as quickly as possible.

Stanford rushed across his office to the small Cézanne on the opposite wall, a favorite from his boyhood. It swung away to reveal an embedded safe he'd had built when he took office. A place for secure documents, far from the prying eyes of the rest of the British government. The only other person who knew of the safe's existence was the man who'd built it, and he was one of them, so they needn't be concerned with leaks.

Stanford's fingers fumbled on the dial

and he cursed softly. His nerves were shot. He felt fear building up, as caustic and dark as a violent fever.

Finally, the lock clicked, and the safe opened. He reached inside, felt for the package taped to the top of the safe. A small file with coded instructions, codes no one could crack unless given the codex, something only the members of the Order knew.

He released the package from its hiding place and turned, slamming the safe shut with his right hand.

He didn't feel the pinch of the needle right away. It took a moment for the sensation to catch up to him, and then it was agony. His chest felt like it was on fire, and he dropped to his knees. He couldn't catch his breath. The package fell to the carpet, and he saw a hand reach down to snatch it up. He wanted to scream, but he couldn't. He heard footsteps, running away, fading, and he knew the file was gone, but then he couldn't seem to think properly. Had he been mugged? In his own office? No, that couldn't be right.

He remembered now the hand reaching into his back pocket, taking his wallet. Hadn't he?

He went into a seizure on the thick Aubusson carpet as the poison spread through his veins, and it was like his blood itself was on fire.

With sudden clarity, he realized what had happened. He was the leader, Pearce was the Messenger. The Order was under attack. But who could get inside 11 Downing Street without being seen?

The protocols. Dear God in heaven, the protocols.

Stanford tried to roll, to heave himself up off the floor, to reach the phone, to warn them of what had happened. But his hands splayed feebly against the soft, thick carpet, unable to lift his weight.

He began to fade, his heartbeat slower and louder in his head, like the bong of a massive internal clock, counting down.

Five.

A man's voice, shouting, then he was touched, pulled hard, and he flopped onto his back. The pain was so intense, like a lightning bolt repeatedly striking him. He'd heard it said that death did not hurt; they lied. His chest was seared, he was choking, he couldn't breathe. The room began to spin.

Four.

His assistant, Wetherby, a good sort, was on his knees, hands pressed hard against Stanford's chest, his face white with shock.

"Sir. Oh my God, sir. You're having a heart attack. I'll get help."

Stanford knew in that moment who'd ordered him killed, the same man who'd ordered the rape of the Messenger's computer. The man who wanted to be Stanford, who wanted all he had, wanted to know the secrets of the Order, wanted the Order itself. He tried to give his assistant the name of his enemy, the two syllables hard against his tongue—Have, lock—but the words came out more like "Ngam."

Three.

Wetherby was back, shouting out, "Where's the medic? The chancellor is having a heart attack!"

Two.

They need me. The Order needs me. I cannot die, not now, not when we're so close. He tried to force the words out, praying that he could be understood.

One.

But the words wouldn't come. He had failed them, failed them all.

Oddly, he saw his mother's face. Was she telling him he'd done his best? Yes.

Peace flooded through him. And then all was dark.

11

Berlin
5:00 p.m.

Havelock watched Alfie Stanford die. He wanted to stay dispassionate, but the writhing and flopping about was so clearly painful, and the old fool was so helpless, he couldn't help but become aroused. He was tempted by the thought of trying the smallest bit out on himself, not enough to kill, but no. That wasn't a good idea. The dosage needed to bring on cardiac arrest was so nominal, he could miscalculate and end up killing himself all in the name of pleasure. He replayed the footage to watch again.

He wondered, had it been this way for his own father, dropping to the floor in the middle of his gym, everyone gathering around to watch him die? The old man had been in the ground for less than a month now, and Havelock had done his part, looking all grave and somber, in black, finding an errant tear, and he'd thought, finally, **I've cleared the path for my journey to begin.** Had he really wanted his father to die? He didn't want to think about that, only that his death had been a necessary evil.

His mother, on the other hand—the wondrous terror in her eyes before he flung her into the sea was something treasured and precious, brought out to be examined at his leisure like his favorite painting, Goya's **The Colossus.** He wallowed in the dark brute power of it. He was the colossus with his raised fist, the giant that men feared and worshipped.

He fingered one of the scars on his arm through the heavy fabric of his bespoke blue oxford. His mother's voice rang in his ears, the waking nightmare he returned to every time failure was possible. Her stark, never-changing litany bit deeper than the belt, even after her cherished death.

You are not good enough. You are not smart enough. You will never lead men. You are a sniveling child. And now you will be punished.

He tossed back the scotch and poured

another, raised the glass toward the sky. "A child, Mother? I was strong enough to take your life from you. I do hope you are rotting in hell."

You are worthless.

Did he hear her words again? Was her ghost mocking him still? Havelock hurled the glass across the room, watched it shatter against the marble floor. He felt better now, more in control.

He smoothed down his black hair, gone gray at the temples in a most distinguished manner, shot his cuffs, straightened his collar. At least Mr. Z had succeeded in eliminating Stanford, and now confusion and mayhem were under way in London. At least one part of his day had gone according to plan.

But Mr. X had failed, and how could that have happened? Havelock had designed the perfect plan, and it had been, until the fool had died with Havelock's implant in his head. All of them knew the chip would be found in autopsy, knew the Americans would figure out what it was, and then they would come. It forced his hand. He would have to move faster than he'd planned.

He needed the Messenger's son, he needed Adam Pearce, and he needed him now.

Havelock sat back in his chair and uploaded all the video from Mr. X's brief New York sojourn. He tapped a few keys on the flat dynamic keyboard embedded in the wood, then placed a small metal neuro-cap on his head, snapping the edges down tight so it would have perfect contact with his skin. He waited for the neural pathways to link.

Ten seconds later, he was viewing video footage from Mr. X's last twenty-four hours. He saw the world through Mr. X's eyes, heard the voices Mr. X heard, all of it uploaded to Havelock's servers.

Havelock was working on a way to merge two sets of brain waves, so he could actually link into his assets' thoughts and tell them what to do from afar, almost like calling on a mobile phone, but with his mind. He hadn't perfected the technology yet, nor did he know how to solve the one huge obstacle: those test subjects who heard a second voice inside their heads—his voice—had gone irrevocably insane.

So he looked and he listened, wanting more, but content to know that soon he would be able to enhance his micro-nuclear weapons, his MNWs, and set them in place, ready to deploy at whatever target he selected. Or whatever enemy. They'd never know what hit them. All he needed were the coordinates of the lost sub and the key, and for that he needed Adam Pearce.

He fast-forwarded through the footage: arriving at JFK, the ride to the ferry terminal, to the moment Mr. X slipped unseen into the Messenger's apartment. Mr. X had done a thorough search, carefully opened all the cabinets, the closets, the wall safe behind the Modigliani painting in the office so no one would know he'd even been there. Many locks. But no SD card.

He watched Mr. X insert a thumb drive into the iMac on Pearce's desk, quickly break through the encryption, do a hard download of all the files. A pity he wouldn't be able to get the thumb drive, since it was now in the hands of the FBI. But it didn't matter. He doubted there was anything more than correspondence and records of sales of rare books to clients. No great loss. He continued to let Mr. X's images wash over him, all the way until the end, when that bastard Drummond had taken him down. He saw Drummond's elbow hit Mr. X's jaw, bursting the gel pack, killing him. A fluke, but it was good to know that could happen. He'd have to find a better solution, a better placement. He couldn't have his assets dying at the hands of the enemy by accident. Inside a tooth would be better, the molars would protect the gel, less chance of splitting the gel pack open. But the tongue—

Havelock unhooked himself from the neuro-cap and lifted it off his head.

Mr. X had proved to be a disappointment. He hadn't found the SD card, hadn't gotten his hands on Pearce's son, Adam, had all but handed the American FBI his magnificent implanted chip on a platter.

He pressed a key and the screen

disappeared. He stood and walked to the window, where the light was rapidly dying. He loved the night, the possibilities the cover of darkness brought. He loved to watch the lesser beasts wander through their lives, unknowing, unseeing. He had faith, and sometimes that was all he needed. Soon he would have his perfect weapon, and they would all know his name.

What would the world see when they bowed down before him? The powerful genius, the unparalleled inventor, the man who, very soon, would control the lives of millions with a single drop of fluid? **I am a leader of men, Mother, I am good enough, smart enough. And you, dear Mother, are dead.**

12

United Nations Plaza
11:00 a.m.

Sophie Pearce accepted Ambassador Xi-Tien's thanks for her work this morning, and nodded in agreement about their dinner date later this evening. She didn't cup her hands and bow deeply in the formal Chinese farewell, since the ambassador was a modern man. She shook his hand, saying, **"Zai jian,"** and waited, not moving, until he turned and walked away with the delegation, then she relaxed with a deep breath. Her services as a translator wouldn't be needed for the rest of the afternoon. She'd have lunch, then run over to her dad's place to pick up the rare first-edition Mark Twain she'd promised the ambassador. Her father had pulled the book from his private collection for her. He was amazing, he could always find exactly what people wanted, like a magician pulling rabbits out of a hat. And at $8,000 for this single gem, her father could afford a lot of hats.

She knew it wasn't a first/first—that would have set the ambassador back at least thirty grand. She liked that he was happy with the second printing; it made her respect him. Xi-Tien wasn't flashy like many of the others she'd worked with in her five years at the UN. He was kind and subtle and, even better, had already wired the funds to Ariston's private bank account.

Sophie hurried down the stairs past security, pulling her badge over her head and stuffing it in her pocket. Her heels clacked on the marble steps, then she was on the street, headed up to Lexington, then over to Fifty-seventh. It was a gorgeous day and everything and everyone seemed cheerful. The oppressive heat of the past few summers hadn't begun to swallow New York whole yet.

Sophie caught a glimpse of herself in the plate-glass window of a leather boutique, her dark hair pulled up into a ballerina bun at the top of her head, long legs, strong, moving fast. She was in the best shape of her life after all the yoga and running and kickboxing she'd done over the winter. She wasn't terribly vain, but she looked good, no matter all the long hours of sitting in her small glass booth at the UN, listening, speaking, and repeating endlessly. She'd firmed up, lost weight, and jettisoned a husband along the way, too, the jerk.

She was happier now, helping her dad out on weekends when she could. Life was good. She'd find the right guy, someday.

She wasn't even out of breath when she arrived at her dad's building. She'd grown up here, in the Galleria, with the stunning views of Manhattan and white-glove treatment. She'd insisted on getting her own place when she graduated, knowing if she didn't move out, she'd suffocate under a stack of musty old books. Her dad wasn't thrilled, but he didn't stop her. Her trust fund was healthy and she could afford to move out, unlike many of her friends.

She wasn't too far from home, though, less than a dozen blocks, down in Turtle

Bay. She made sure she saw her dad at least once a week. She usually caught him at the store, since he seemed to live there these days. She felt a brief stab of guilt. Since her mom died, and her brother moved out west for school, it had been only the two of them, and she'd been so busy lately, she'd missed some of their normal dates.

No more, she promised herself. Once a week wasn't enough, not anymore. Divorcing the jerk had taught her a hard lesson about betrayal and loss, the importance of keeping those who really loved you close.

Gillis opened the doors for her, merely bowing, saying nothing—unusual, because he was normally chatty. She didn't realize something was wrong until Umberto rushed over to her, tears sheening his dark eyes.

"Miss Sophia, I am so sorry, so very sorry about your father, we—"

Sophie went still. "What happened? Was there an accident? Did he fall? Umberto, is he okay?"

Umberto was shaking his head. "I'm so very sorry, your father, he's dead, Miss Sophia. The FBI is upstairs. They didn't call you? Forgive me, but I do not have the details."

She ran to the elevator, ignoring everything else in a mindless chant of **No, no, please, no.**

The elevator doors slid open, and she slammed down on the button once, twice. She knew it took exactly twenty-two seconds without stops to reach the twenty-third floor—a sign, her father always said, that this was truly their home. Twenty-three was the family's lucky number. For twenty-two long seconds, she didn't breathe, stood deathly still, counting.

She raced down the long hallway to the front door. It was unlocked. She burst in, saw a man and a woman, both with guns clipped to their waists, speaking in front of the picture windows. She watched their hands go to their guns as they whirled around to face her.

"What happened to my father?" She

knew she screamed the words. She was getting hysterical and took a deep breath and tried again, more calmly this time: "Please, tell me what happened to my father."

The man spoke first. He was British, not an American. "I'm Special Agent Nicholas Drummond, with the FBI. This is Special Agent Michaela Caine. You're Mr. Pearce's daughter, aren't you?"

She was shaking, couldn't help it, and grabbed the back of a chair. "Yes, I'm— I'm Sophia Pearce. Where is my father? What's happened?" The internal **No, no, no, no, no** beat through her body in time with her heart, but she knew, deep down, she knew.

"I'm very sorry to tell you, but your father was killed on Wall Street this morning." He'd spoken slowly, quietly. "We've been trying to track down his next of kin. I'm sorry. Please, come and sit down."

She waved her hands, trying to ward off his words. "No, no, there's got to be a mistake. It doesn't make sense. My father had no reason to go to Wall Street. He'd have been at the store. How could anything kill him? What happened? Please." She heard the hysteria rising in her voice again but couldn't help it.

"Come." Nicholas took her arm and sat her down on a large burgundy leather couch. He kneeled in front of her. Sophie realized vaguely that he was a big man, young, and she saw pity in his intense, dark eyes and knew this moment would be seared indelibly on her brain forever.

His voice remained low and calm. "We believe he was lured to Wall Street with a fake text message from someone named EP. But EP wasn't there. Another man was waiting for him. They argued, then he stabbed your father. I'm so sorry."

She couldn't think, couldn't move. Hearing the words made it real, horribly real.

"Can you tell us who EP is?"

Something flashed in her eyes, but she didn't say anything. The room began to spin, the man on his knees in front of her, holding her hand, blurred, and then she didn't see anything.

13

Nicholas kept his hand on Sophie Pearce's pulse, still fast, but steady. It was a shock, he knew, it was always a horrible shock to have the death of a loved one come swiftly, violently. She'd closed down.

Mike appeared at his elbow with a glass of water. "When she comes out of it, we'll give her some water. I doubt it will help, but it's something."

He set the glass of water on a side table and rose. "I think she knows who EP is. Try to get her to tell you when she gets herself back together. I need to get the ETA of the crime scene techs. I'll be right back."

"Nicholas, be sure to tell them someone else accessed the hard drive before you did. I'm betting Mr. Olympic was here and he did it."

"I agree, but he didn't find the SD card and I'll bet it was the key to access the good stuff on Mr. Pearce's computer. I'll try to find the origins of all those files, see what they have to tell us." He looked again at Sophia Pearce, moaning now, her eyes fluttering open.

He said abruptly, "I need time to sort everything. I've never seen anything like this."

"Listen up, Nicholas. You don't have to do everything alone. We're all in this together, you and me and Zachery and Louisa and Ben, plus I've asked Gray Wharton to be attached to the investigation, you know how good he is. You're now a part of a big team. No more carrying the world's weight on your shoulders."

Sophie Pearce opened her eyes. "I heard you talking about my father's computer. What was on it?"

Mike handed her the water and watched her drink, then set the glass back on the table.

"Please, talk to me. Tell me what you've found. None of it makes sense to me."

Mike said, "I know this is a shock, Miss Pearce. We'll go slow, one step at a time. Now, when you say the store, you're talking about his bookstore, Ariston's?"

"That's right." She was getting a little

color back, though she was still too pale. Mike helped her sit up, and introduced herself and Nicholas again, waving toward Nicholas, who was speaking on his cell in the entryway. "My father is an antiquarian, one of the best in the field. Ariston's is renowned for rare books. He has a worldwide network."

"So he's very successful."

"Oh, yes, he has a gift for this, always has. Agent Caine, I don't understand, who would kill him? He didn't have any enemies. Everyone loved him."

Nicholas stepped back into the living room. "We don't think it was premeditated, Ms. Pearce. You know as well as I do that enemies can be seen and unseen. As your father was a preeminent businessman in an esoteric field, he surely had rivals, people he upset when he bested them. My grandfather's a bit of a collector; I know how cutthroat the auctions can get."

Sophie nodded. "So you understand, then. It's such a small field. He had rivals, certainly. But enemies? No. Not my dad. No way." She sat straighter. "Now tell me again how he was killed. You said a man stabbed him?"

Rather than answer her, Nicholas asked her again, "Tell us who EP is."

He was looking closely this time and he saw it again, a flash of knowledge in her pale eyes, then it was gone. She didn't look at them, didn't say anything, simply shook her head.

Mike said, "Your father was stabbed on the street after an argument with another man. As he died, your father said to the man who stabbed him, 'The key is in the lock.' Does that mean anything to you?"

"The what?"

"The key is in the lock."

"No, I don't know." Nicholas saw nothing in her eyes, no clue to give away that she knew what this meant.

"Could it have been a robbery?"

Nicholas said, "No, Miss Pearce—"

"Sophie, please."

"Sophie. No, he wasn't mugged. He had his phone and his wallet on him when he was found, and nothing appears to be missing."

Quick as a whip, she faced them again. "You said you found something on my father's computer. What was it?"

14

This was interesting. Nicholas gestured toward the office. "I'll show you, and you can tell me what you think your father may have been involved in."

He walked down the hall to the library, Sophie behind him. She hesitated for a moment at the door. He could have sworn she scanned the doorjamb. Why was that?

"Everything all right?" he asked.

She gave a short jerk of her head.

"What do you do, Sophie?"

"I'm a translator at the UN. I specialize in Asian policy and economics," she said, as she stepped into her father's office. He watched her look around, swallow, then cross her arms over her chest, steeling herself. "Show me."

Nicholas thought, **Be careful now, no reason to give it all to her, since for whatever reason she's not being straightforward with us.** He leaned down and hit a couple keys and brought up the schematic of a satellite.

"Do you know what this is?"

"It looks like a satellite."

"Correct. The problem is, this isn't just any satellite. This is a high-tech LEO-synchronous spy satellite, one the military will be using. Not to mention it bolsters the NSA's ability to listen in to pretty much any conversation it wants in the Northern Hemisphere."

"Um, English, please, Agent Drummond?"

"LEO, short for low-earth orbit. It's where most spy satellites are placed." He clicked a few times. The image was of another satellite, similar to the first, but with a few changes.

"This particular satellite hasn't been launched yet; it's still under development. Classified development, on a classified military project, on a classified server owned by a very big aerospace firm, who will be quite displeased when they find out the plans for their super-secret spy satellite are residing in the computer of an antiquarian in Manhattan."

He stood straighter, to intimidate, and said very quietly, the threat clear in his voice, "Would you like to tell me what your father is doing with classified material on this SD card?"

Sophie Pearce smiled for the first time, not much of one, but still a smile. "It's not what you think, Agent Drummond. My father's not a criminal, he's an expert in military history. He has friends who perhaps share things they shouldn't, because he's known for his discretion. He could write a book with all the stuff people send him."

"You're telling me his **friends** send him classified material that could be used against the United States if it were to be discovered by the wrong people?"

Narrowed eyes replaced the smile. "Yes. What are you implying?"

"I'm saying a civilian having access to these plans violates hundreds of laws. And the **friend** you speak of, the one who e-mailed these plans? He masked the e-mail address, bouncing it through about forty servers all over the world, so it's virtually untraceable."

He stopped, reached down and clicked

the mouse, closing the image on the screen. That was enough for now—the satellite image didn't even scratch the surface of what Nicholas had seen, but she didn't need to know that.

"My father would never do anything to hurt this country."

Mike paused in the doorway, listening. She saw Nicholas was towering over Sophie, but Sophie hadn't moved. She looked mad, ready to square off with him. Mike had the distinct impression Sophie Pearce was more than the sum of her parts. Like the Fox, she thought, who'd very nearly brought them down, Sophie had that same feel to her—softness covering steel. She knew more than she was saying, a lot more. How to make her level with them?

Mike stepped into the office. "Excuse me. Nicholas, can I speak with you a moment?"

He shot her a look, nodded. Mike said to Sophie, "Do you have other family here in town? Someone who can come be with you?"

Sophie shook her head. "It's only us." Her voice cracked, and they knew the fact of her father's death was sinking in now.

"Who is 'us'?" Nicholas asked.

"My . . . my brother."

"What is his name?"

"Adam." Her voice shook. "Please, where is my dad? I mean, where is his—body?"

Mike said, "At the morgue. There will be an autopsy. We need to be one hundred percent sure about how he died."

Sophie swallowed hard. "Someone shoving a knife in his back isn't clear enough?"

Mike touched her shoulder. "I'm sorry. I truly am. Are you sure there's no one we can call for you? Your brother, Adam?"

Sophie said, "No, Adam's not here. I forgot—I have a meeting this afternoon and I need to call and cancel. Tell them what's happened."

Mike said, "All right. Go ahead, we'll be out in a moment," and watched Sophie pull her cell from her pocket as she stepped into the hallway, closing the door behind her.

"You think it's safe to leave her alone?"

Mike said, "Worry not, crime scene's here. They'll watch her, see if she does anything hinky. We're in here, so she can't hop on this computer and delete anything."

"Wouldn't matter," Nicholas said. "I've already copied his hard drive and downloaded the files from the SD card." He held up a small thumb drive. "I also encrypted the drive with my own program so no one can tamper with the files now."

Mike grinned at him. "I knew I asked to partner with you for a reason. I listened to some of your conversation with Sophie. Do you think she's clean in all this?"

"Mike, she works for the UN. She's a translator."

She nodded. "Yes, and that means international connections. We'll keep a close watch on her."

"She also knows who EP is. I don't think she knows what her father meant when he said 'The key is in the lock.' What else does she know that she's not telling us? The big question is why isn't she telling us everything she can think of? Her father was murdered. I can't tell you if Pearce was up to no good, but what I saw on the SD card—I think this is big, Mike, we're talking government secrets, big-money secrets. We need to pull apart Pearce's financials, and Sophie's, too."

"And we need to protect her and her brother, Adam, given what Mr. Olympic threatened. Zachery called to report someone's been hanging around Ariston's this morning, as if he's waiting for the store to open. We need to get up there and check it out."

"I bet Pearce has another computer at the store. I'd like a chance to see what's on it. We should take Sophie with us, if nothing else, to keep her safe. Maybe, too, she'll break down and tell us what else she knows about all this."

15

**Ariston's Antiquities and Rare
Books Second Avenue and
East 57th Street
Noon**

They walked to Ariston's, only minutes from Mr. Pearce's apartment, the perfect commute for a Manhattan businessman. Mike assumed the vast majority of Pearce's life was carried out in the few square blocks between his store and his apartment.

Nestled between a boutique clothing store and a high-end jewelry shop, Ariston's was in an older, handsome building, tall and narrow, the brick paled over the decades. The windows were dark, a hand-lettered closed sign draped inside.

East 57th was busy, people hurrying to lunch, to work, to their lives. Mike had her hand on Sophie's arm, holding her back. They watched carefully for signs of anyone paying special attention to the store. They saw no one out of place.

Mike was on her cell with the Facial Recognition guys who'd spotted the man lingering around the store. "Anything?"

Nicholas glanced over. She shook her head and clicked off. "It's a guy, young, that's all they could tell us, that and he seems to have left for now. They'll call the minute they see him again. We're clear to go in."

Sophie unlocked the front door, opened it slowly, and disarmed the alarm. So this was Ariston's. It was a comforting smell, Nicholas thought, familiar—it immediately shot him back to his family's home in England, Old Farrow Hall, and his grandfather's extensive library of rare books, the smell of old vellum, the warmth from the fireplace.

Ariston's was a bibliophile's dream: floor-to-ceiling bookshelves, some behind glass and many under lock and key. There was row upon row of shelves, all clearly labeled according to genre, sub-labeled according to century.

There was a small register area up front,

and a larger seated space midway back, with two well-worn oversized brown leather chairs edged in nail heads. A gooseneck reading lamp hovered over each chair, and every other inch of space was filled with books.

Nicholas realized Sophie had stopped just inside the door. He heard her swallowing. He knew this was difficult for her. He couldn't imagine hearing that his own father was dead, hearing that someone had killed him. He prayed she'd keep it together, maybe even tell them what she knew.

He watched her square her shoulders and turn on the lights. He heard the pain in her voice when she said, "Dad spent most of his time here in the store. It was his whole world. The entire time I was growing up, he had me in here every spare minute, dusting, curating, answering the phones. When I got old enough, I started handling the orders. We have a worldwide clientele, especially for military titles."

Mike ran her fingers along the spines of the shelf nearest her. "How exactly does all this work? Do people come in off the street to buy rare books?"

"More than you'd expect, actually. But the bulk of the sales are online. The Internet was the best, and worst, thing that happened to our industry. It used to be all the work was done by letter, then by phone, but both had a distinctly human touch. Once people could buy the books without any direct interaction with Dad, well, it wasn't nearly as fun for him. He loved meeting new people. He lived for the auctions."

"Auctions?" Mike asked. "Like Sotheby's and Christie's do with furniture and artwork?"

"Similar, yes. He could pay the rent for a year on this place with a single rare-book sale."

Nicholas thought back to the books he'd seen under glass at Pearce's apartment. "Did your father keep the rarest books at his place?"

"Some, yes, but for the most part, those are the ones he really loves—loved."

Her face went blank, then she gestured

for them to follow her, and went to the back of the store. She unlocked a door, and they saw a small office with a desk and ledger books, and a brand-new twenty-seven-inch iMac computer on the desk. Sophie didn't hesitate, walked to the back of the room, pressed a series of buttons on a rectangular steel lock, and the door swung open with a pneumatic hiss. Behind it was a circular stairway.

"This leads to the basement where he keeps—kept—the really valuable books." Her voice hitched. They watched her gain control. She flipped a switch inside the door and the basement was lit with the soft red glow from a single light, like a small fire on the wall. They walked down the narrow stairs into a space that didn't run the full length of the store but took up at least four hundred square feet, all bookshelves behind tempered glass.

Mike whispered, "I feel like I'm in the Vatican vaults."

Nicholas felt his chest tighten. "Low-oxygen environment?"

Sophie shot him a surprised look.

"Exactly. Plus humidity and temperature regulation. Sixty-four degrees, with an ambient humidity of forty-five percent. It's the only way to keep the books from crumbling into dust. We had to reroute all the water pipes, too, and the fire retardant is a special chemical mix that's safe for books and papers."

She stepped to a case and pointed at a book with thick-edged gilt lettering. "This was his favorite. He's had so many offers over the years, but I never could convince him to sell."

It didn't look remarkable, but when Nicholas read the spine, a chill washed through him. "William Blake's **The Book of Urizen**? That must be worth millions."

Sophie smiled. "Only eight copies in existence. One went at auction for two and a half million in 1999."

Nicholas said, "I wouldn't give it up, either. I love Blake."

Nicholas looked like he might begin to quote Blake's poetry, so Mike quickly said, "We're looking at some incredibly valuable books here. Is there anything in this store, a book, some papers, some secret archives he's been getting offers on and refused to sell, like this Blake?"

Not an instant's hesitation. "Not that I know of."

"Is there anything someone might want badly enough to kill your father?"

She shook her head. "I'm telling you, the antiquities world has its fair share of cutthroats, but none that would be capable of killing my father. He was a great man, and had the respect of a lot of people."

That wasn't the point. Money was always a great motivator for murder, but it wasn't right. Mike said, "Think of the man who sent him the specs on a classified satellite system. Who was he?"

They watched a tear streak down her face. She made no sound, simply wiped it away with her fingers. "I told you before, I don't know what you're talking about. My dad was into books, that's it. That satellite specs on his computer? Perhaps someone who admired my father thought he'd enjoy seeing it."

Nicholas showed her a photograph of

Mr. Olympic that he had saved on his mobile. "Have you ever met this man before?"

She looked at it closely. It was obvious the man was dead. His eyes were slitted open, his face a dusky blue. "He's dead, isn't he?"

"Yes," Drummond said. "Do you know him?"

She slowly shook her head, swallowed bile. "No. I've never seen him before." She watched him change the photo and quickly stepped back, her hands up. "Please don't tell me you have a photo of my father on your phone. I don't want to see it. I don't want to see him like that." Her voice ended in a yell, and Nicholas put a hand on her arm to steady her.

She gathered herself, took a deep breath. "That dead man, he killed my father?"

"Yes."

"And now he's dead, too. Good. Thank you."

Mike lightly touched Sophie's arm, her voice low and calm. "Sophie, let me ask you again. Can you tell us why your father, as he was dying, said to his murderer, 'The key is the lock'? What does it mean, Sophie?"

She was back in control. She shook her head. "I have no idea."

Mike said, "Sophie, don't you think it's time for you to level with us? You know your father's murder wasn't a random mugging. You need to tell us everything you know."

"I have told you all I know. I don't feel well. Can we continue this conversation later? I want to go home."

There was a bump above, and they all froze.

16

Nicholas put a finger across his lips. "Sophie, did you lock the door when we came in?"

Sophie nodded. She was staring upward, her eyes fixed.

Heavy steps now, clumping on the hardwood, moving toward the back of the store.

Both Nicholas and Mike moved in front of Sophie, their Glocks at the ready. Mike whispered, "They were supposed to call me if they saw anything. Something's wrong."

Sophie now looked frightened, even paler in the odd reddish light. "There's no cell service down here."

Nicholas jerked his head at Mike, then started slowly up the stairs.

Mike whispered to Sophie, "Stay here," she followed Nicholas.

When they reached the top, Nicholas used the reflection of his mobile's screen to see if anyone had come into the back office. It was empty, the door still closed.

They eased their way out of the staircase.

Nicholas held his Glock against his leg. There would be no more surprises, like this morning's debacle.

When they reached the door, he mouthed a **one, two, three** to Mike, and they went into the bookstore, Nicholas high, Mike low, perfectly coordinated, as if they'd been doing this together for years.

No one was there.

They went silent, walked slowly through the stacks toward the front of the store, guns up, clearing each stack as they went. Nicholas saw the front door. It was closed, but the hand-lettered open/closed sign was twisted halfway between the two.

Three stacks to go now, two, one, and Nicholas stepped around the last bookshelf to see a young man, a kid, maybe, no more than early twenties, blond and brown, sitting at the front reception desk, his hand literally in the till.

Nicholas said, "FBI. Stop what you're doing and show me your hands."

The kid saw the guns aimed at him and froze. He raised his hands slowly, his face a blank mask, his eyes on Nicholas, a twenty-dollar bill still clutched in his right fist.

"Don't you move an inch. Who are you?"

The kid merely shook his head. When Mike moved to get behind him, he exploded from the chair, leapt over the counter, and headed toward the door.

A bad move, that. Nicholas was ready for him. He slammed into him, then landed a solid punch to the kid's stomach, stopping him in his tracks. The kid's eyes went wide and terrified because he couldn't breathe. Mike pulled him to the ground, her knees against the middle of his back, her hand in his back pocket for his wallet, but it wasn't there.

The kid took a deep breath. He was clearly panicked, terrified, his legs churning to get away. Mike cuffed him and hauled him to his feet.

She shook him. "Who are you? Tell me or I'll sic Superman on you, and believe me, you don't want that to happen."

Sophie pushed her way past Mike. "What are **you** doing here?"

Nicholas was looking at the young man. There was something familiar about him, but he couldn't nail it. "Tell us who this is, Sophie."

Sophie said, "Yes, of course. This is— um—Kevin Brown. He's a family friend. He used to work here at the store. But he left a few months ago."

Mike eased back a bit. "Well, your family friend was trying to rob you."

Kevin Brown shook his head. "No, no, I wasn't. I was leaving Mr. Pearce a note. He called me last week, told me I could come back to work part-time, weekends only."

Sophie stared at him. "Really? I thought you were in school."

He nodded. "Yeah. Well, it didn't work out. I contacted your dad and he told me to come back. Look, can I go now? Like I said, I stopped to leave Mr. Pearce that note. I gotta go have lunch with a friend. Really, I need to be getting on."

"I don't think so," Mike said, and pushed him into the chair behind the register. "First things first, Mr. Brown. Where is your wallet?"

"I left it in my backpack, in a locker at Grand Central."

"Yeah, that makes a lot of sense. How did you get in? The door was locked."

"I still have a key."

"Then why did you have the register open?" Mike asked him. "And why did you try to run?"

His chin came up. He gave her a cocky grin, despite the uncomfortable cuffs around his wrists. "Hey, I was making change for a twenty. I knew Mr. Pearce wouldn't mind. Suddenly you two Feds are sticking your guns in my face. What was I supposed to do?"

Sophie rolled her eyes. "Maybe, Kevin, you could have simply done what they asked you to do."

Kevin shrugged. "I don't bow to the man, Sophie."

"You're an idiot. Get out of my store."

"Hey, I only wanted to let Mr. Pearce know I could come back to work. I, well, things aren't going the way I thought in school, so I came back, and I could use the coin."

Nicholas watched Sophie draw a deep breath. "Listen, Kevin, my father is dead. He was murdered this morning."

Kevin Brown's face seemed to leach of color. He leaned toward Sophie, almost as if he was going to hug her, but she stepped back a foot and Nicholas could have sworn she shook her head slightly. Brown stopped and eyed her, as if she were a bomb that might explode at any moment.

"You're not kidding, are you? What happened?"

"I would never kid about something so horrible. They don't know what happened yet. Why do you think they're here?" Sophie pointed to Nicholas and Mike, then said to Mike, "Can you uncuff him, please? He wasn't doing anything wrong. He's right, my father wouldn't mind."

Mike's cell phone beeped. She ignored the request to uncuff Brown, and instead answered her phone. Nicholas listened with one ear to the conversation until he saw Mike tense. She said, "Channel two?

Okay," and hung up, pulled out the walkie-talkie she carried in her pocket. She adjusted the walkie to the right channel, handed it to Nicholas. "The man they saw casing the store earlier is coming. He's a block away."

Sophie said, "Who's coming?"

Mike quickly uncuffed Brown and gave him a little shove toward Sophie. "You two go to the back office. Now. And lock the door."

17

Ariston's
12:20 p.m.

Sophie knew they had to hurry. She slammed the door to the office, threw the deadbolt, and ran to the circular stairs. When they were safely belowground, she faced him.

He'd grown some more, at least a couple inches. Now she had to look up at him. But right now she was so mad at seeing him, so afraid for him, that she didn't know whether to hug him or hit him.

"You're supposed to be in California. Caltech wasn't to your liking? Did the brains there catch on to who you really are? Tell me the truth now, why are you here?"

"You know why I'm here, Sophie. We have a major problem. Someone in the Order has betrayed us."

She slammed her fist into his shoulder. "The grand search again? Adam, when will you and Dad give that up?" Her voice caught. She looked stricken. "Oh, no, no, Dad's dead."

Adam Pearce ran a hand through his too-long hair. "I know, I'm sorry, Sophie. But this is so important, the most important thing in Dad's life. And now that they killed him, I've got to keep on with it.

"Sophie, listen to me, I found it, I found the sub. I called Dad last night and told him, and he was going to share the news with a few members of the Order. And today he's dead. Either the Order has a traitor or there's something even worse going on."

"Really? You actually found the sub, after all this time? Nearly a hundred years? You actually found the **Victoria**?"

Adam nodded. "I'm ninety-nine percent sure this is it. But now, Dad . . ." His voice trailed off and he simply stood there, looking at her helplessly, tears trickling down his cheeks.

Sophie pulled her brother against her and held him, crying with him, and let the pain come.

Their lifelong search for the lost World

War I U-boat was really over? She said, "Was it worth Dad's life?"

He shook his head against hers. "No, no."

She said against his neck, "The FBI agents asked me if I knew who EP was. I didn't tell them anything." She slowly pulled back, took her brother's young face between her palms. "You did it, Adam, if anyone could find it, you could. I'm so proud of you. Dad was, too, wasn't he?"

"Oh, yes. But you know Dad, he said something like, 'Well, it's about time.'" Their father had known his son would find the sub when Adam's genius had burst forth at the age of eight, and he'd hacked into their bank's checking-accounts system. He'd been caught that one time and everyone had marveled and laughed and given the little genius a pat on the shoulder. It was the last time he got caught. Soon he'd been able to dig deep into computer networks, circumvent firewalls and other security measures. At fifteen, their father had given him the mission: find the **Victoria.**

She tried to smile, seeing her father speaking, but she couldn't. "The FBI agent said Dad had some satellite specs on his computer that were classified. I take it you know how he got those?"

He swiped away the drying tears on his face, waved his hand. "That's irrelevant."

"Adam, it is not irrelevant. The FBI are pissed, and looking in to who sent the info to Dad. I think they knew I was holding back. Those two, they're not going to go away. I know they'll keep after me. And they want Adam Pearce very badly. And they saw a photo of us as kids, you know, the one in Dad's bedroom."

"I look different. Don't worry, I'm Kevin Brown—quick thinking, sis. I've put hundreds of layers in to protect us both." He grabbed her shoulders, made her look him in the eye. "I narrowed down the location of the sub last week. Last night I took command of a private satellite that was passing over Scotland to take a look. Dad and I always thought the **Victoria** was lodged deep somewhere, under an outcrop of rock or land. It's only been in the last year that the satellite technology is to the point where it can see past underwater shelves. I mean, it can see right through the land under the water. And that's where I found it, nestled up under a huge rock ledge in northern Scotland. Like I said, I told Dad last night, and we were supposed to meet today so I could show him. I couldn't tell him where it was over the phone, it was too dangerous."

"Why didn't you show him last night?"

"Because I was still in California. I took the red-eye from L.A. I got here as quickly as I could. And then this morning, when I got the text, I headed straight from JFK to meet him here."

Sophie sat down on the floor, taking it all in, trying to make sense of the story. "You're telling me Dad was killed **because** you found the sub? Why? Isn't that what the Order wanted? I thought they'd be thrilled at the news, not homicidal. They're supposed to be united on this matter."

Adam's lean face was etched in misery. "They are. That's why I need Dad's phone, so I can see who he called last night. At least we can narrow it down. But there's more, Sophie. I told you Dad texted me this morning and told me to meet him down at Wall Street. I did, even though I thought it was weird. But when I got there, he was already dead. So—I knew before you told me upstairs." His throat clogged with tears. "I knew."

"Why Wall Street?" she asked. "Why there? It makes no sense."

"Because it's away from Dad's territory. I think the man who killed Dad sent a text to me from Dad's phone, and one to Dad from mine. To draw us together."

"So the murderer was after both of you."

Adam nodded, chewing on his lip. "Yeah. Maybe. The minute I saw what was happening, I got out of there, headed up here. I was careful, took a couple of cabs, the train, to make sure I wasn't followed."

"You weren't followed. At least not by the man who killed Dad. The FBI got him, he's dead."

Adam's voice was hard. "Good. That's good. I'm glad the bastard's dead."

Sophie asked, "How would he text you and Dad? Did your phone get stolen?"

"No, not mine, but it's possible to spoof a phone number, you know that. Kid's play. If someone broke into Dad's and got their hands on his cell, they could do it easily."

He reached out a hand, squeezed hers. "Your hands are like ice."

"It's all right, it's nothing."

"Don't shut me out, Sophie. Please. Not again."

"I'm not." She began to pace, winding around the vitrine case in the middle of the room. "I'm trying to figure all this out. The two FBI agents are acting really strange, like there's something they know but aren't telling me. And they don't trust me, not that I blame them. I'm not a very good liar. But you know I couldn't tell them the truth, it's far too dangerous, and since every cop in the known universe is after you—" She paused, then added, "They showed me a picture of the man who killed Dad."

"Did you recognize him?"

"No."

"Well, you know as well as I do there's lots they aren't telling you. If they found Dad's hidden SD card, then it won't take them long to figure everything out. They haven't had time yet. I have to get out of here before they come back, see if it's too late to access Dad's files remotely and delete them. I already got into his e-mail account. I didn't see anything unusual, no outgoing messages."

"Could he have sent an e-mail, then deleted it?"

"Yes, but I'll have to break into his e-mail client's server to see what they have, and we're running out of time. Soph, get me Dad's phone. Whoever he called, whoever he wrote, that's who had him killed." His voice cracked, and suddenly he was a little boy, and she his big sister, there to protect him. "I can't believe he's dead."

Again, she held him close for a moment. Could he, nineteen years old, barely a man, could he fix things? She didn't know. "Adam, if the Order killed Dad and want you dead as well, then you're in danger. I don't want you hurt."

"You know we can't stand by and wait to see what they'll do, Sophie."

"I know, I know, we have to find out who did this. I'll see if the FBI will give me Dad's phone, or at least tell me who he called last. You need to disappear."

His face was pale in the red-tinged light. "Now that I think about it, I don't understand why they'd want to kill me, since I'm the only one who knows where the sub is located and could tell them. And they want that sub. Yeah, if they got that info, then I'd no longer be necessary to them, and whack."

They would kill him, but she didn't say it aloud, no need. She couldn't, wouldn't, lose Adam, too.

"Tell me where the sub is. Exactly."

"No, no way, not until we figure out what's happening. You didn't know yesterday, and you don't know today. It's safer that way."

She saw he wouldn't budge. He was more stubborn than she was. "Fine. We have to get you out of here. Use the back door, out into the alley. I'll contact you if I find anything out, and you do the same. But don't come back here, and don't go to the house. You hear me? And watch your back."

He thought for a moment, then nodded. "I'll be in the Village for a while with Allie. You know how to reach me." He turned to go, but she grabbed his arm.

"Wait, wait. There is something else. Dad said something before he died, they have it on video. It's nonsense, really, but maybe it will make sense to you. 'The key is in the lock.' Do you know what that means?"

"Well, sure I do, but—"

She heard the voices of the FBI agents and cut him off. "Damn, they're coming back, you have to go. Now."

She opened the fire door and waved him away, but he stopped, looked back, and gave her a rakish grin. "'The key is in the lock'—it's not what you think, sis."

"Adam, where's your wallet? Really?"

"In my shoe."

Then he was out into the alley, up the stairs, and out into the bustling New York streets.

18

Nicholas and Mike waited for Sophie and
Kevin Brown to disappear into the office,
safe, out of harm's way, then Mike grabbed
the walkie from Nicholas and moved to
the right, to the nearest stack, so she'd be
hidden from sight. Nicholas melted into
the first stack on the left, and together they
waited to see if the man came through the
door. Mike clicked the button on the walkie
so they could hear everything being said
outside, but turned the volume down so
the intruder couldn't hear anything at the
store's door.

Nicholas listened to the surveillance
team intently until they suddenly went
silent. He nodded to Mike, who whispered,
"What's he doing, what's he doing?" into
the walkie.

Nicholas recognized Special Agent Ben
Houston's voice. "He stopped two doors
down. We've got a loose box around him
so he won't get away. He's watching the
street, probably looking for us. Hang in
there, let's see what he does. Okay, he's

moving now, coming toward the door. Bald, about six feet, wearing jeans and a Windbreaker. Young, rangy guy, looks buff, real strong."

Nicholas said to Mike, "I'm half tempted to let him come in, see who he is and what he's after."

She duckwalked to his position. "Too chancy. He could come in guns a-blazing."

Ben's voice came through the walkie. "He means business, people, he's being deliberate now, not looking around or watching for a tail. Okay, here he is, at the door. You should be able to see him now. He has something in his left hand, I see metal, might be a weapon—"

Nicholas grabbed the walkie from Mike's hand, said, "Take him. Take him now."

Nicholas and Mike stepped out into plain view, weapons raised, and watched the surveillance team converge on the suspect. They saw his head was shaved and he wore a black goatee. He took one look in the glass door, met Nicholas's eyes, saw the weapons pointed at him, and threw his arms up in the air.

"Don't shoot, don't shoot!"

Ben appeared behind him, shouting, "FBI, FBI. Put your hands on your head, get down on your knees. Do it, do it now!"

The man went down on his knees, no hesitation. Ben wrenched his arms back behind him and cuffed him as Mike opened the shop door.

She stood over him, hands on her hips. "FBI. Who are you?"

The man looked confused. "Whoa, whoa! FBI? What's going on here? What in the world is happening?"

Mike slipped her Glock back into its clip at her waist. Nicholas very nearly smiled. She looked as tough without the Glock in her hand.

Nicholas stepped forward. "Tell us your name."

"I'm Alex Grossman. I have a lunch meeting with Jonathan. He's got a book I ordered; he called me last night. My phone's in my pocket, you can check."

"What else? Maybe some needles, a weapon?"

"No, man. Only my keys, my wallet, and

my phone. What do I look like, a terrorist?"

Mike said, "That isn't funny, sir. Not at all."

"I'm sorry, I'm sorry, I'm a little freaked out here, okay? Can I put my hands down?"

Nicholas frisked him quickly and retrieved Grossman's wallet, phone, and keys.

He said, "Where were you this morning, Mr. Grossman?"

"Asleep. I own the Bullet Pub. It's also a restaurant. We had a private event last night, the group stayed way later than planned. I didn't get home until after three a.m. I caught some sleep, then headed over here to meet Jonathan. Please, tell me what's going on."

Nicholas nodded at Mike, flashed the small cell phone. "Pearce called him last night at eight-thirty p.m."

Mike nodded. "Tell me what Mr. Pearce said, exactly, Mr. Grossman."

"That the book had come in. That's all. He always called when an order arrived. We chatted a bit, caught up. It's his personal touch, why everyone likes doing business with him. What's happening?"

"Mr. Pearce was murdered this morning," Mike said, then nodded at Ben to unlock the cuffs.

"Jonathan's dead?" Grossman sounded blank-voiced with shock. "But how? Why? I mean, it doesn't make any sense." Then he became very still, going inward, Mike thought, accepting his friend's death as fact. He whispered low, "God rest his soul. Jonathan's a great guy. Please, tell me you know who did it."

Mike ignored his questions, leaned against the counter, crossed her arms. "How well did you know Mr. Pearce, Mr. Grossman?"

"Well enough. This can't be happening. I don't feel well, can I sit down for a minute?"

Nicholas heard the back door open. Sophie stuck her face out, pale, scared. He waved for her to come to the front.

Nicholas said, "This man says he's here to pick up a book. Do you know him?"

Sophie let out a big breath. "Oh, yes, I

know him. He's a very good customer. Alex, Mr. Grossman, how are you?"

Grossman looked at her pale face and pulled her against him. "I am so sorry, honey, I'm so sorry. What can I do?"

She gulped down tears. "Nothing, at the moment. Did you have an order in?"

"Yes. Your father called me last night." He glanced over at the register. "That's it right there—the Tiffany blue cover. Auden's **Poems.** Inscribed by Dick Grossman on the half-title."

Mike saw Sophie was frowning at Grossman, upset that he'd spoken to her father. But she said, "Agent Drummond, may I? It's already been paid for."

"I'm sorry, he'll have to come back another time."

Sophie glanced at Grossman, then back at Nicholas. She stood straight, in good control of herself. "Agents, please. I'm going to have to close the store for the time being, until I can get caught up on everything. There's no reason to hijack Mr. Grossman's book. It's already paid for. Please, my father wouldn't want his store or his customers to suffer because of him." Her voice stayed strong and steady, and Nicholas gave in.

"Fine, but we need to get moving, so be quick about it."

Sophie packaged up the small book, wrapping it in several layers of brown paper and twine, as if it were glass and easily breakable. Nicholas had to resist telling her to hurry up, but again he had the feeling she knew more, and now she was using the time to get herself calmed and in control. He could be wrong, but he thought something about Grossman, about the phone call, had upset her. If so, why? They'd take a closer look at Alex Grossman. As Sophie wrapped the book, Grossman gave his information to Mike. If he owned a nearby business, he wouldn't be hard to track down.

Finally, Sophie handed the wrapped book to Grossman. He rested a hand on her shoulder. "I'm really sorry, Sophie. If you need anything, please don't hesitate to call. I'm sure you won't be interested in cooking for a while; stop by the pub, I'll feed you. It's the least I can do."

"Thank you, Mr. Grossman. I—thank you."

She turned away from him. Grossman watched her for a moment, then nodded to the agents and went out the door, the bell tinkling behind him.

Mike asked, "Out of curiosity, how much was that book worth?"

Sophie glanced at the small sales slip her father had tucked into the register the night before. "Forty-eight hundred dollars."

Nicholas walked to the back of the store, opened the door to the office, and shouted down the stairs, "Mr. Brown? You can come up now."

Nothing. Sophie was busying herself with the register. Nicholas called out, "Sophie, where is Mr. Brown?"

Sophie cocked her head to one side. "Oh, he had to go, he had a lunch meeting, like he said. I let him out the back."

Nicholas stalked back up the aisle toward her, clearly pissed. "You shouldn't have done that. We weren't finished talking to him."

Sophie's chin rose. "Kevin's not a threat, nor did he have anything to do with my father's death. He's a kid, nice enough, but not old enough to get it together, you know?"

Mike said, "We don't know he didn't have something to do with your father's death, Sophie. It was odd, Brown suddenly in the store the same day your father's been killed. Give us all his information. We'll have to find him, check him out."

"I don't have it. It's probably on my dad's computer, but all his files are password protected." She glanced at her watch. "I want to see my father. Where is he?"

Mike said, "I'll make arrangements so you can see him. Tomorrow, maybe."

"I've got to go. Dad's funeral arrangements—all his friends, I don't know, there's so much—when will I be able to bury him?"

"Probably a few more days. I'm sorry, Sophie, but I can't give you an exact day yet."

She was crying again, and Mike drew a

deep breath and let her go.

Nicholas narrowed his eyes after her. "She was lying through her teeth. Oh, her grief for her father was real enough, but Kevin Brown? She simply let him go? And the identity of EP?"

Mike was shaking her head. "I don't understand her. Why wouldn't she tell us everything she could to help us find out why her father was killed?"

Nicholas said, "And why was she upset over Alex Grossman speaking to her father last night?"

"You saw that, too, did you?"

19

Lexington and East 53rd Street

Alex Grossman wanted to run full out, but he couldn't, the FBI might be watching him, so he forced himself to walk the four blocks to his apartment at a steady pace, the only secure place he could make the call. And he needed to make the call, right now. More was at stake than Jonathan's death. He had to keep the charade in place, no matter what.

He took a deep breath. Jonathan Pearce, the Messenger—dead. He couldn't get his brain around it. It was a disaster. The Order—every link in the chain was meant to be unbreakable, and yet the most important link—the Messenger—was dead. Not only dead, he'd been murdered. Sophie was barely holding it together, and Adam, dear God in heaven, what would Adam say when he found out? No one even knew where he was.

What would they do now?

Thank the Almighty he'd managed to

get the book with the SD card hidden inside, as they'd arranged. And Sophie, quick on her feet, had managed to get the book to him right under the noses of the FBI. If they'd lost Pearce **and** the files—

No, don't think of it. You have the SD card. Call in. Weston will know what's to be done.

Grossman's apartment, despite the Midtown location, was a fifth-floor walk-up two blocks down from his pub. He didn't mind the stairs, they kept him in shape. When he burst into his flat, he locked the door and went straight to the safe in the kitchen, nicely disguised in one of the cabinets, right behind three cans of kidney beans.

He started to put the book inside, but something made him stop. He held the book for a moment, staring down at it. Slowly, he untied the twine, unwrapped all the layers of paper.

He opened the book. There was a space cut inside the pages, the perfect size for a small micro–SD card.

But the space was empty.

Panic slammed him. He tamped it down. He had to think. There were only two possibilities—either Jonathan Pearce hadn't put the SD card in the book after all or someone had gotten to the store before Alex had and stolen it.

There were only two copies of this SD card in existence—standard operating procedure for the Order. Redundancies. One card was supposed to be in the book. The other was in Alfie Stanford's safe at 11 Downing Street.

He reached into the safe and pulled out an encrypted satellite phone. He noticed his hands were shaking. Adrenaline. **Calm down, lad, there's much to be done.**

He dialed the number from memory. It was answered on the first ring.

He blurted out the words, his American accent gone to reveal his natural crisp British. "Pearce is dead."

Edward Weston said calmly, "Yes, I know. Did you retrieve the book?"

"Yes, but the SD card wasn't inside. FBI agents were in Jonathan's store."

"Yes, I know. Do you have any idea

where Pearce's SD card could be?"

"I'm not certain at this time, sir. Sophie was there in the store as well. She was a mess."

"Yes, yes, I'm sure she was. We all are. What about Adam Pearce, was he there?"

"I didn't see him. I don't know how to contact him directly."

Grossman could hear Weston tapping his fingers on his desk, a longtime nervous habit. "I see."

"What are your orders, sir?"

"I need you on a plane to London straightaway."

Grossman was surprised. "I shouldn't stay in place? My cover will be blown. Try to get ahold of the SD card? The FBI agent, Drummond, he was at the store this morning. He and another agent are investigating Jonathan's murder, so I'll bet he found it at Jonathan's apartment. I could try to waylay him, maybe—"

"Absolutely not. It doesn't matter, not now. Prepare yourself, Alex, there's more." He heard Weston take a deep breath. "Alfie Stanford died in his office at Eleven

Downing Street two hours ago, and the contents of his private safe were stolen."

"No," Alex said, stunned, disbelieving. Stanford was their leader. He'd run the Order for more than thirty years. To lose both him and Pearce in the same day was unthinkable. "It's murder, surely, sir, it must be. We're under attack."

"I believe you're right, Alex, but we won't know anything until the inquest. Scotland Yard is conducting an investigation, as well as the Security Service. We're coming at this from all angles. Now you understand why I need you to come to London right away. Forget the SD card. There's no way you can get it. Right away, Alex, tonight."

Pearce dead, Stanford dead. And—"Sir, Wolfgang Havelock died not above a month ago as well. I know he had a stroke, but with three members of the Order dead in such a short period of time—"

"Exactly, Alex, exactly. You're absolutely correct, it seems the Order **is** under attack. The information stolen from Stanford's safe can cripple us all. We are convening an emergency meeting of the

Order, and I want you here."

"Yes, sir, of course. My cover will be blown, but it hardly seems to matter now."

"Good. I'll share some news with you, Alex, because I know I can trust you, and you're going to know it soon enough, anyway. I know that Pearce was in direct contact with Alfie Stanford last night. As for the message you passed to me last night from Jonathan, it was indeed good news—the very best news, actually—Adam located the submarine at last. We don't have the exact coordinates as yet, but we will soon. Once we get to the sub, we'll retrieve Marie's key and her book and be able to find the weapon, and the kaiser's gold, if that isn't a myth."

"Do you think it's possible English spies really did manage to steal the kaiser's private treasure?"

"Probably no, but we'll see. I don't intend to let anyone get in the way. Now, I'm not sure who to trust right now, Alex, so you must be careful."

"The pub—"

"That is why you have a partner. Call

him, tell him your mother is ill and you must return to—where does your current legend say you're from?"

"Chicago. Lincoln Park, a few blocks from the zoo." He said the words automatically, the information so ingrained in his being he could recite it in his sleep, with a knife pointed at his throat.

"Right. Tell him you must return to Chicago immediately. We'll take care of the rest and send a plane for you. It will be waiting for you at Teterboro. And Alex? About Drummond having the other SD card. I believe you're right. Drummond used to be with the Foreign Office, and he was Met Police for a stretch, before moving to America to join the FBI. We detected a breach on Pearce's computer this morning. I think this Drummond character may have made a mirror of the files. If he has, certainly it's very likely he found the SD card during a search of Jonathan's apartment.

"If that is the case, we must simply forget about getting it back. Drummond has already turned the SD card in. I'm sorry the American FBI have it, but there's nothing to be done about it now. So what I want you to do is bring Sophie Pearce with you. She's in danger, and until we understand what's going on here, who else is also after the sub and the key, she must be protected."

Alex looked out the window, watched the pigeons alight on the sill, cooing and preening. Oh, bugger it all, how was he going to get Sophie to come willingly with him? She wouldn't, no way, it wouldn't matter what he said. "What about Adam?"

"Do not worry about him. I have others looking for him."

"Very well, sir. May I ask who is taking over the Order now that Mr. Stanford is dead?"

There was a slight pause, then a hitch in Edward Weston's throat, which he quickly cleared away.

"I am."

20

26 Federal Plaza
1:00 p.m.

Zachery was waiting for them when Nicholas and Mike returned. He'd been alerted they were on their way up, and stood right outside the elevator doors, his hands on his hips. He did not look happy.

"Two dead bodies before lunch, Drummond? You're having one hell of a first day."

Then, of course, Zachery saw clearly that the two bodies were the last thing on Nicholas's mind, but he snapped to quickly. "Ah, yes, sir, I know."

Nicholas was accustomed to being on the radar of his superiors for all the wrong reasons, but two dead bodies, that was surely pushing it. No one could have anticipated how his first day would turn into a bloodbath, without his assistance, not really. He stood straight and tall and waited for the hammer to fall, Mike beside him.

Before Zachery could say anything else, Mike asked, "Sir, any word on identification of Mr. Olympic? That's what Nicholas named our man because he could run as fast as Bolt."

Which meant Nicholas had run faster, Zachery thought, looking at her. "Not yet. Fingerprint, DNA, and facial-recognition software are running as we speak on—Mr. Olympic—but so far, nothing. The autopsy has been scheduled for two-thirty this afternoon. You need to know what killed this man."

I love autopsies, my very favorite way to spend an afternoon. But the fact was, though, they did need to know if Mr. Olympic had indeed chomped down on some sort of poison pill in his mouth.

"Yes, sir, not a problem."

Mike said, "Sir, what about Pearce's hard drive and the SD card we had messengered back? Any word there?"

"It's all still running. Gray Wharton has the video feeds uploaded as well." Zachery glanced at him, one eyebrow hiked. "Once you're done at the OCME, Drummond, perhaps you can lend a hand there."

Nicholas smiled. "With pleasure, sir."

"Good. Before you go uptown, I want a full rundown of everything that happened this morning. I'm beginning to gather we're dealing with something very complicated, very sticky."

"Yes, sir," Nicholas said. "On both counts."

Mike shot a glance at Nicholas. She knew him well, a surprise since they'd really known each other only a handful of days. Something was cooking, but exactly what, she didn't know yet.

Zachery had made it clear to her when he'd agreed to pair her with Nicholas that one of her main responsibilities was to manage the Brit, and that meant to make sure Nicholas followed the hallowed rules to the letter. Creativity was welcome; hotdogging was not, although any FBI special agent knew that the New York Field Office was known for its cowboys, particularly under Bo Horsley.

Control Nicholas? She wanted to tell Zachery that would be like trying to control a plume of smoke on a windy day, but she didn't. One of the reasons she liked working for Zachery was that he was steady, even-keeled. But now he looked strained. Was something else going on, something big? Well, Zachery would tell them in his own good time.

He led them to his office, shut the door, and Mike gave him a moment-by-moment rundown on their morning. He did not interrupt her because she was good, clear, no unnecessary information, always on point. When she'd finished, Zachery said, "Your suspect—this Mr. Olympic— when he unexpectedly died, are you certain, Drummond, that you didn't hit him in a way that could be misinterpreted?"

"Not at all. I saved his life, pushing him out of the way of the patrol car. He was very much alive when we started to cuff him. He went down, with no warning. It was clear to me he'd activated some sort of poison, and it did its job. We'll know after he's autopsied exactly what killed him."

"There won't be any video surveillance footage showing your hands anywhere near this man's face? No witnesses to claim you brutalized him, in fact, caused his death?"

"There won't be. I did nothing wrong here."

Zachery held up a finger. "Don't get riled up. I have to ask. You had your hands on a man as he died in broad daylight on a busy New York street. You know an inquiry is mandated since you are still in your probationary period, and there is no fooling around in these proceedings.

"Agent Caine agrees that you did nothing wrong. If, however, there is anything either of you wish to tell me, now's the time."

They both shook their heads.

"All right, then. Before you leave, you have some time to look deeper into Jonathan Pearce. He was clearly not a simple antiquarian bookseller. You said he'd been lured with fake text messages to Wall Street; the computer in Mr. Pearce's home office had been compromised before you were able to access the files, and there was all the classified material you found with the SD card, and e-mailed to him. Tell me exactly what the classified material was."

Nicholas said, "He had specs for a military satellite still in the developmental stages, which will be launched in a few months to bolster the Milstar II military communications satellites already in orbit."

"Not what you'd expect from a book-seller's files."

"Especially when sent through an anon-ymous repeater, so there's no way to tell who provided the information. That satel-lite is so top secret no one outside the program and the launch schedule know anything about it. It certainly isn't some-thing laymen have access to. The SD card Gray is processing was full of files and letters and photographs. I didn't have time to sort through them all before his daughter, Sophie Pearce, showed up. I need some time to make sense of all of this, but the information was clearly of a secret nature."

Zachery nodded. "We'll get to the bottom of it. We always do." He drew a deep breath. "Now I have some bad news, Drummond. We received word an hour ago that Alfie Stanford has passed away."

21

Nicholas took the news like a fist to the gut. "You don't mean Alfie Stanford, the chancellor of the Exchequer?"

Zachery nodded. "From the look on your face, I see he was a friend of your family? I imagined as much. I'm sorry, Drummond."

Nicholas finally found his voice. "Yes, he is. I went to school with his three grandsons. I've known him my whole life."

"I'm very sorry, Nicholas," Mike said. She touched his forearm lightly. "Sir, what happened?"

"He collapsed in his office at Eleven Downing Street. It seems to be natural causes, though they don't know for sure yet. He was eighty-two, so I suppose it makes sense. The media is going to be all over the story, of course, Stanford being who he was. Drummond, if I hear anything more, I'll let you know. Both of you, keep me posted."

The audience was over. He gestured toward the door, then reached for his phone. "And Drummond? Do try not to get anyone else dead today, will you?"

"I'll do my best, sir."

Nicholas looked shell-shocked. He didn't wait, pulled out his mobile and dialed. Mike said nothing, merely stood close, giving him silent support.

It was only half past six in the evening in England; at least he wasn't going to wake anyone up.

The Drummond family butler since the beginning of time answered, "Old Farrow Hall. May I help you?"

"Horne?"

"Master Nicholas? How wonderful to hear from you. All is well in New York?" Nicholas heard the unspoken question— and is Nigel well?—though Horne was too ingrained in the proper etiquette to permit him to ask after his son.

"We're fine, Horne. Nigel has me so set up I can't find my knickers by myself. I'll tell him you asked after him." He swallowed. "I need to speak to my father, Horne. Is he home?"

"He is. He's in the midst of a very serious

situation with Mr. Stanford dying so unexpectedly today. Oh, my apologies, Master Nicholas, you do know about Mr. Stanford?"

"I do, Horne. That's why I'm calling."

Horne let out a sigh. "Of course, nowadays everyone knows everything at nearly the same instant. I'll go fetch Master Harry for you. And Master Nicholas, permit me to say—we do so miss you here."

Nicholas was hit with a wave of homesickness. It mixed with his shocked grief at Alfie Stanford's death and for a moment he couldn't speak. He missed them all, his grandfather, his parents, all the denizens at Old Farrow Hall. He even missed Cooke Crumbe's very bland porridge.

"Thank you, Horne."

Then his father was on the line, and he knew exactly why Nicholas was calling.

"Horne told me you'd already heard about Alfie," Harry said. "I can't believe it, Nicholas. It's so sudden, there was no warning, no life-threatening illness that I knew about. I know he was getting on in years, but still, he was a tough old bird. He had a touch of rheumatism, the occasional attack of gout, but no heart trouble that I ever heard. Your mother has gone to Wembley Hall to be with Sylvie, and their grandchildren are coming home from their various overseas posts. We had to pull Anson off a submarine in the Balkans."

"If he wasn't ill, then what do you think caused his death?"

There was a pause, then his father said, "Are you on a secure line?"

"Yes, I am. What's happened?"

"We believe it was murder."

"Inside Eleven Downing? That's madness. Surely not."

"The medic from the Diplomatic Services spotted a mark on his neck, near the carotid artery, said it was made by a needle. Alfie's body has been sent to the Coroner's Court. The autopsy has been fast-tracked. They'll test his blood, so we should know more by night's end."

It was all unbelievable. Nicholas said, "But who could have done it? And why?"

His father sighed, clearly exhausted, and Nicholas heard the weight of the world in that sigh. "We don't know. The video feeds are being run, but so far no one who doesn't belong there has been spotted."

"You know that means someone inside Eleven Downing Street."

"Yes, and the very idea makes my blood boil. You can trust we'll get to the bottom of it, soon enough."

"What can I do to help?"

"I wish there was something, but there's nothing you can do from New York. I will let you know what happens, but for now, please, do keep this quiet."

"But sir, I've got to—"

His father interrupted him. "Nicholas, I've always admired how your first instinct is to right the wrong, and I'm proud of that. But for now, I'm going to insist you keep this to yourself. No one's said a word about murder. It is at present a very fluid and delicate situation. Very delicate."

Delicate? What was his father not telling him?

"Tell me, sir."

Harry sighed. "I'm afraid I can't. But if Alfie Stanford **was** murdered, trust me, Nicholas, this is bigger than anyone could imagine."

22

Berlin
7:00 p.m.

It had been a glorious evening.

First a wondrous interlude with Elise—his back was still stinging from her superb whipmanship—then the good news from London. After the morning's screwup, despite the knowledge the FBI might already have their hands on his implant, his day was rapidly improving. One very big thing had gone just right. Mr. Z had managed perfectly. Alfie Stanford was dead, and good riddance to the old buzzard. And what a glorious distraction it was, a wonderful, brilliant distraction.

He'd been glued to the **BBC World News** for the past half-hour, gleaning and parsing every word out of the announcers' mouths about Alfie Stanford's untimely demise. It was all too perfect, too delicious. Stanford had always been an overbearing ass, and now he was in the grave, and no one would ever be able to figure out what happened to him. Mr. Z was that good.

He sobered for a moment. Drummond was on the case and Havelock knew to his gut the damned Brit would come for him soon, fast and hard, which meant he only had days, maybe even hours, to get the coordinates of the sub and collect the key, and who knew? Maybe there'd even be a sack of the kaiser's gold lying about. Soon all the governments in the world would bow down before him, and to hell with the FBI and Nicholas Drummond.

Havelock prided himself on being a measured man; he realized neither panic nor celebration was in order. While the news from America hadn't been perfect, it had not disrupted the plan entirely. Even knowing who he was up against, and how things would go down if he didn't find the sub in time, he remained calm and focused.

But he did pump his fist in the air when he saw the body of Alfie Stanford exiting 11 Downing Street feet-first, encased in a black body bag.

Guess who will hold the power now? And that made him smile.

A knock sounded at the door. He called, "Come," and hit mute on the television.

März entered, holding a tablet computer, looking pissed, which was unusual, since that pale face of his was usually without expression. Something major had happened.

"What's wrong? Out with it, März. You look like someone's died. Which, of course, they have." The maniacal grin was back, he couldn't help himself. "Have you ever seen anything so wonderful? The FBI are looking left, while we feint right, Scotland Yard believes Stanford passed to the hereafter from a heart attack, and before the week is out, we will have everything we've always wanted. Now, tell me, has the Order called?"

"No, sir."

"Oh, no matter, no matter. We shall call them. Now tell me, März, what terrible event has upset you?"

März knew he was being mocked, knew Havelock was the only man on the planet who could get away with it. Because, simply, Havelock was the only man März feared in the world.

His kept his voice calm, icy calm. "I have learned that one of the top medical examiners is shortly to perform Mr. X's autopsy. He will not fail to find the implant. It won't be long before they trace it to you."

Havelock shook his head. "They won't trace it to me in time, März. This is why we created the shell company, and I had it shut down five minutes after Mr. X drew his last breath. It will stall the FBI long enough for us to find the sub and retrieve the key. Now, get Mr. Weston on the phone. It's time I gave him instructions."

März nodded, turned to go.

"Oh, März? Do tell me, where is Adam Pearce?"

März turned back slowly, not reacting. "As you instructed, we are looking for him, sir. All of his accounts have been silent. We are still working on the files uploaded from Pearce's computer—so far, nothing in them gives the exact location of the sub. But we know Adam Pearce had narrowed it down to northern Scotland."

Havelock jumped to his feet. "Why didn't

you say so? Move the **Gravitania** into position now! We'll be within a few hours' sail when we locate the final position. I always thought they'd gone to ground near the Hebrides."

"I've already had the ship notified. They are under way to the closest coordinates we've found. Also, I have sent the assets we discussed earlier to Adam Pearce's last known address in New York."

"An address? After all this time? How did you find it?"

März gave an eerie smile. "When Mr. X spoofed Pearce's phone, we were able to download all the data and back-trace the text messages. There were a variety of phone numbers from which the texts were sent, but we were able to identify more than one instance of a single GPS coordinate where the texts were sent from. Mr. W and Mr. Y were sent there to reconnoiter the position. Adam Pearce has a girlfriend living there; he bought her an apartment last year. With all that has happened today in his world, he will go back to her, for safety, perhaps. And when he does, we will take him."

"Make it happen faster. I very much dislike waiting. Now get me Weston."

März left, then a few moments later, the phone on Havelock's desk buzzed.

"Yes?" Weston sounded harried and annoyed at the interruption. Well, the poor man was quite busy now, after all, what with Stanford's sudden death.

"Hello, Edward. It's me."

"Manfred, now is not the time."

Weston was already trying to act like the leader of the Order. It was charming. "On the contrary, my dear Edward, I think now is the perfect time."

"I have guests arriving in half an hour."

"This is very good news. The Order is moving quickly, as it should. You are to be congratulated. Do tell them I'm so very anxious to step in and help. What with my father's untimely passing, and the sudden horrors this lovely day has brought, it would be my **honor** to continue his legacy. I can be there at a moment's notice, to serve at their pleasure."

Weston was quiet for a minute. "It will

happen, I'll see to it. There has been no luck finding Adam Pearce?"

"Not yet, not yet, but all the pieces are coming together. Soon we will have the exact location of the sub."

Weston said, "In that case, I think you should come as soon as possible. I've ordered Alex Grossman to bring Sophie Pearce to London tonight. If we can't find Adam Pearce, she's the lever we need to make him come to us."

"I'm impressed, Edward. Well done."

A moment of uncertain silence, then Weston said, "It's added insurance, in case your plans fail—and they already have today, Manfred, don't think I'm not entirely aware of how badly your boys screwed up this morning. Damn it all, that idiot killed Pearce! Of all the people, he's the one we needed the most."

Havelock said, "Pearce refused to cooperate; his death was an accident. But it's no matter, Edward. Adam is the key, not his father. He has all the data we need, locked up tight in his brilliant little brain. Yes, yes, I see having Sophie Pearce under our control could be very helpful. Yes, that is very good thinking."

"I also told Alex not to worry about Pearce's SD card, since we have the other one, from Alfie's safe. But I do worry. The FBI have it and they are not stupid."

Havelock only smiled into the phone. "Do not worry about Drummond. He is nothing."

"Well, are you coming, then?"

"I will be there by morning. When is the meeting?"

"Noon tomorrow."

"Excellent, capital, well done. By then, if we don't have Adam Pearce and the location of the sub, we'll at least have Sophia Pearce in our hands. Until then, dear Edward."

Havelock placed the phone in its cradle, a smile still playing on his lips.

He hit his intercom button. "Elise? Begin packing. We are going to London."

23

**26 Federal Plaza
1:45 p.m.**

While Nicholas was on the phone to his family, Mike took a quick look at some of the information Agent Gray Wharton had taken from Pearce's computers. She glanced at Pearce's client list, stopped cold—she saw names she recognized— an international who's who of power and wealth. Sophie had said her father's business was global; she certainly hadn't been kidding.

Mike scanned the list, seeing name after familiar name, and knew from experience that there was something more here. She glanced at her watch; it was nearly two and they had to get to the OCME for Mr. Olympic's autopsy. She started to close the file when she saw a name that really stood out. She read it over a few times, then closed the file and ejected the thumb drive. Nicholas needed to see this. She didn't know what it meant, but he might.

She grabbed two bottles of water and two apples from the small fridge she kept under her desk. She was hungry; they hadn't had time for lunch. The apples would have to do for now. They could stop and eat on their way back downtown. A full stomach before an autopsy wasn't a smart move, in any case.

She looked up to see Nicholas standing in the door to her cube. "Are you ready to go?"

"I am." She handed him a bottle of water and an apple. "I know we have to hurry, but you need to see this before we go."

She inserted the thumb drive back into the secure, red partitioned side of her FBI computer and opened the mirrored hard drive. She clicked on the file labeled clients. Hundreds of blue folders came up on the screen, neat and orderly.

"Thank goodness Pearce was an organized bloke. His files are almost too easy to find."

Mike punched the third blue file, got up and gestured to her chair. "Sit down and take a look. Tell me what you see."

Nicholas sat with Mike perched on the chair's arm. Her blond ponytail had grown in the past few months and it was right next to his face. He breathed in the jasmine scent, shifted himself away.

She leaned, pointed, her ponytail touching his face. "Look at that, Nicholas."

He leaned away again, looked at the screen, whistled. "Good catch, Agent Caine. Alfie Stanford bought several books on military history from Mr. Pearce over the years. Mostly World War One titles, though there are a few from the Franco-Prussian War and some on the Russian oligarchs."

"Weighty stuff."

"Certainly. Stanford was a very bright man, very dedicated to study and scholarship. You don't get to his position otherwise." He clicked a few other folders. "I wonder who else we may recognize in Mr. Pearce's clientele."

She tapped her watch. "No time. We need to go, Nicholas. We can talk about it on the way up to the OCME."

Ben Houston jogged around the corner.

"Oh, good, you're still here. I was about to call you. Before you go, you need to see this." Ben's red hair was mussed, his suit rumpled. Nicholas thought he looked like he'd had a rough morning of it, then thought to look down at his own bespoke trousers. There was a line of mud along the crease and a thin ash of dirt covering his knees, right above a small rip in the fine wool. He brushed at it, shaking his head. Nigel would have his head tonight when he realized he'd ruined his trousers. Six hours into his first day and he was already falling apart.

Ben handed Mike a brown file. She opened the brown folder and both of them stared at Kevin Brown's photo.

Ben said, "Looks like Sophie Pearce wasn't exactly telling you the whole truth."

Nicholas laughed. "I thought he looked familiar. Remember that photo of the Pearce family? With the boy and the girl? There he is, all grown up."

"Yep," Ben said. "Adam Pearce, the nineteen-year-old son of the late Jonathan Pearce, alive and well and running around in his father's store this morning, well protected by his sister, Sophie. You're going to love his file. The kid is serious trouble. Here's his arrest record. Look at the list of places Pearce has broken into. I bet you want to get your hands on him, right, Sir Nicholas? He's as big a hacker as you are."

Nicholas didn't look up from Adam Pearce's photo, simply said, "Careful, Red. I have not been knighted."

Ben patted him on the shoulder. "I'm sure it's only a matter of time. I mean, you do have the right accent for it, after all."

Mike ignored them and read the list. When Ben had said "broken into," she'd expected stores and businesses. Instead, she was seeing major multinational corporations, military targets, the Pentagon. It hit her. "Whoa. I know about him. Talk about a hacker, he's right at the top."

"Yep, he's become rather notorious around here, actually. We've tied him to Anonymous, WikiLeaks, several remote break-ins on some very high-level military sites, the whole shebang."

"What's his **nom de guerre**?" Nicholas asked, and Mike heard the excitement in his voice.

Ben said, "Eternal Patrol. He has friends in almost all the dissident and domestic protest groups. But he's good, I mean really good. We've never been able to pin him down. And he's been off the grid for a while, hasn't been seen in the city for the past two years."

Nicholas laughed, shook his head. "So now everything makes sense."

24

Ben said, "EP is famous in the underground computer world, but what's cool is that he isn't a black-hat hacker—you know, the ones who take down governments and sell credit card information and the like. But he's not purely a white hat, either, trying to improve the Internet. He's walking a fine line, could go either way as he gets older."

Nicholas said, "Eternal Patrol—EP, Adam Pearce—he's a real talent. If you can catch them young, and turn them—well, I wouldn't mind getting my hands on him. He'd be brilliant at risk assessment."

"Takes one to know one," Mike said. "I'm glad you're now working with us, legally." Shortcuts were okay, she thought, as she glanced through more of Adam Pearce's file. She saw echoes of Nicholas, no way around it.

She said, "Adam Pearce is a genius, no question, into computers from the time he could walk. He hacked into the Pentagon's secure internal e-mail system at the tender age of twelve."

"Oh, he was an old hand at it by then," Nicholas said.

"So it appears. Here's a list of transgressions, long and varied. So, does he do this only for social acceptance among his peers or just for fun?"

Nicholas shrugged. "Fun, credibility, secret stealing. Who knows the motivation?"

Ben said, "I'd say Eternal Patrol is more of a merry prankster than a truly malicious hacker."

Nicholas said, "You know, hackers make the best employees."

"Why's that?" Mike asked.

"They're always willing to think outside the box. I used to use some of the brighter international ones for my work in the Foreign Office. They are barely controllable unless you have something on them. Or they want something from you. Sometimes you even have a bit of luck and they'll turn against their compatriots. They'll bargain the information away. You must be the most careful with those, they're unpredictable at best, moles at worst."

"So how can you be sure they're being honest and legitimate with your information?" Mike asked.

Nicholas said simply, "You need to have someone who's just as talented to keep an eye on them. If you hire one to build you a back door, you need to be sure the code he's using is clean. A clever hacker can build a trapdoor in his back door, and then you're up a creek, as my uncle Bo likes to say. Would you look at this—he's managed to stay off the radar for what— two years? He's very good, considering he's wanted all over the world. NSA, CIA, Interpol. Kid has a lot of powerful people very peeved at him."

Mike said, "You were right, Ben, about Sophie Pearce. She flat-out lied to us, and, of course, so did Adam. Now, why is she hiding her relationship with him? And why did he show up out of the blue hours after his father was killed?"

Ben said, "Maybe he wanted to see his family, maybe he thought we'd be off his scent. I'll admit, though, the timing is certainly coincidental."

Mike said, "Is there a special meaning for Eternal Patrol?"

Nicholas said, "It's an old naval term, actually. For a lost ship. There are hundreds of ships and submarines that have been lost in the various wars. Traditionally, when they go down and no one knows where, they call it being on eternal patrol."

"Well, that makes sense, at least. His dad was a naval history buff. Ben, put out a BOLO for Adam Pearce, and we need to go talk to Sophie again. Find out if this was all she was keeping from us."

Ben said, "Already did. We also need to look at what Adam Pearce has been into lately as EP. If he crossed the wrong people, perhaps his father was killed in retaliation, or to draw him out. If that's the case, Sophie isn't safe, either."

"She's safe enough," Mike said. "We've got eyes on her. No one's going to get close to her. Have them pick her up, Ben, we'll see if she knows where her brother's hiding. Nicholas, we're outta here."

When Mike had cleared the garage

doors and turned the Crown Vic onto Worth Street, Nicholas said, "I have something to tell you."

She knew that tone, he'd decided to tell her something that he'd thought to hold back. Good, it meant he trusted her, at least every once in a while.

She looked over at him. "Your dad told you something super-secret, and you're not supposed to say anything?"

Nicholas had to laugh. "You're too smart for your own good. Yes, he told me something very disturbing. The Home Office believes Alfie Stanford was murdered."

"You've got to be kidding me. I thought he was old enough to die on his own?"

"Yes, he was, but he wasn't ill. One of the medics found a needle mark on his neck."

"That's not good. Do they have a suspect?"

"If they do, he didn't tell me. I don't believe in coincidences, Mike, and here we are, hit in the face with a huge one. Alfie Stanford and Jonathan Pearce have clear ties, and they're both murdered on the same day?"

She didn't believe in coincidence, either. "And Adam Pearce is an über-hacker, and his sister lied to us. But how is it all related?"

"I don't know yet."

"Ah, here we are, your inaugural FBI autopsy. Let's hope Dr. Janovich found the poison pill."

25

Office of the Chief Medical Examiner (OCME)
2:20 p.m.

Dr. Janovich was waiting for them in his office, dressed in stained scrubs, his eyes shining brightly with excitement. He tapped his watch face when he saw them, but without rancor.

"Finally, you're here. I didn't want to wait, so I started without you. Come on. I have something to show you."

They stood over Mr. Olympic's naked and partially autopsied body. Janovich spoke quickly, pointing to a nasty scrape on the man's shoulder. "Did quite a job on him, didn't you, Drummond?"

"I believe the tarmac was responsible for that particular mark."

"Ah. Well, this isn't the interesting part." He pointed at the wall, where X-rays hung on a light box. "Look closely. Do you see the foreign object in his skull? I went digging in his brain, and I found this."

He used a small set of calipers and showed them a tiny bit of metal, no larger than a thumbnail, thin as paper.

Mike said, "It looks like shrapnel."

Nicholas's heart rate jumped, adrenaline poured into his bloodstream. "No, not shrapnel, Mike. Dr. Janovich, can I see it under the microscope?"

Janovich beamed at Nicholas. "Good, good." He set the rectangle of metal on a clear glass slide. "Try it at one-hundred-times power. It's quite illuminating."

The metal object came into clear focus. Nicholas's breath caught. He hadn't wanted to be right, but—"It's an implant. There must be two hundred filament leads off this." He stepped away so Mike could take a look. "Dr. Janovich, where did you find this, exactly?"

"Embedded behind the optic nerve. The incision was well healed, which means it's been in his brain for a good while. I also found a very small feed into the auditory nerve as well, so small I nearly missed it. All in all, it's amazing."

"Sight and sound? Is that even

possible?"

Janovich said, "Evidently, it is. I've never seen anything like it. This is incredibly advanced technology. And this implant? It isn't a metal alloy I've ever seen. It's biologic in nature, meaning it can merge with the brain tissue it's implanted in and not be rejected. If it does what I think it does, well—" He shrugged. "It's huge, terrifying, really."

"Could it be running now?" Nicholas asked.

Janovich shook his head. "I don't think so, not without its processing power. It shouldn't be able to stand on its own."

Mike held up a hand. "I know about implants used for people who've lost limbs, to help them control new arms and legs. Through thought-controlled action."

"Yes," Dr. Janovich said. "Yes, implants are very big in robotics and nanotechnology. There are even implants for the blind, those with progressive diseases like macular degeneration, to restore their sight."

Mike said, "Let me look again; talk me

through this." As she studied the implant, Nicholas said, "Do you see the filaments coming off the edges? They're thinner than a piece of hair."

"It looks like a metal millipede. So this is a brain implant. It's tiny, wafer-thin. It was implanted behind Mr. Olympic's optic nerve?"

"Yes," Dr. Janovich said.

"And not because Mr. Olympic was going blind."

Nicholas said, "Oh, no, quite the opposite. Dr. Janovich, correct me if I'm wrong, but I assume it was mono-vision— meaning the people who were getting the feed from the implant could only see out of Mr. Olympic's left eye?"

"You're right, Drummond."

Mike's head was cocked to one side. "You're saying that someone could see through Mr. Olympic's eye? See what he was seeing?"

Nicholas said, "Implanted into the optic nerve, it's possible this works something like a video camera, uploading images as the user sees them. And since Dr.

Janovich also found the thin thread that fed into the ear, I'm guessing the person behind this could hear what Mr. Olympic heard as well."

"A visual recorder, then," Mike said, "and the audio part as well. Sight and sound."

Dr. Janovich said, "Since I pulled this implant out of his brain, your wild speculations aren't so wild after all. If someone was watching, and hearing, remotely—"

"Holy crap," Mike said. "It makes sense and it sounds insane."

Nicholas was so excited he was nearly vibrating. "It's possible, though. Look how tiny the implant is. Think of the uses. You could send someone into the field and all they'd have to do is stand around looking at the target, and the chip would do the rest, relaying the information to a remote server. And if it can be done live, it would change the face of intelligence gathering forever."

Dr. Janovich said, "It's entirely possible."

Nicholas said, "Dr. Janovich, you're certain the device only works with active brain waves?"

"I believe so. It definitely runs biologically. There is no battery, nor any way to take it out and recharge without surgical intervention. It used the suspect's brain to charge and run. Without its electrical plug, so to speak, it can't work. Once his heart stopped, transmission stopped as well."

Mike said, "Who has the capabilities to make such a thing? And the ability to make it work?"

Nicholas said, "I reckon any of the private firms who do this sort of research. It's one thing to develop a prototype. It's a whole different level to put them into action. We're talking billions of dollars. The list of firms capable of doing this can't be very long."

"You could look at universities, too," Janovich said. "No, forget it, not enough money."

Mike said, "No chance there's a serial number, like we see on other implants?"

Janovich said, "Good thinking, but I wasn't able to find one. If I can get the device open, I might see something, but I really don't want to try it. I think we need someone well versed in nano-biotechnology to autopsy the chip. I have a friend at MIT who's quite accomplished in the nanotech field. I'd recommend bringing him in to have a look inside, see if we can identify a manufacturer."

"Do it," Mike said. "Right away, if you please, Doc." Mike drew in a deep breath. "Imagine, someone was watching remotely as Mr. Olympic murdered Jonathan Pearce. Hurry, sir, we don't have time to waste."

Dr. Janovich said, "There's a lot of money in nano-biotech, a lot of private investors. It might be harder than you think to find out who developed and placed this particular device. Especially if he doesn't want to be discovered."

Nicholas said, "Oh, we'll find him. I have an idea of where to look."

Mike squared her shoulders. "And knowing who Mr. Olympic is will go a long way toward helping us ID the maker of the implant. There still haven't been any matches on his fingerprints?"

"Not yet," Janovich said. "I don't think he's a local. If he's in CODIS, we'll have a match soon."

Nicholas said, "We heard him curse the victim in German."

Dr. Janovich nodded. "Sounds right. He was wearing a pair of socks with a small Metro label, and that's a European store, in Germany as well."

Mike asked, "In all this excitement I nearly forgot. Have you isolated what killed him, whether it was a poison of some sort? Or how it worked so quickly?"

Janovich stepped back to the body. "I need toxicology to be specific, but it was some sort of deadly neurotoxin. It caused an almost immediate heart arrhythmia, followed quickly by cardiac arrest. Take a look." He used his calipers to spread the man's upper lip back from the teeth, showing a small gap in the gingiva. "It came from right here, I think. There's a pocket of sorts, almost like a small abscess, but it's definitely man-made. There's a scar, in the tissue, from a laser cut. There was also some sort of residue, in a gel form. Thicker than saliva, clear and tacky. I swabbed it and sent it to tox, but like I said, it's going to take some time to identify what exactly it is. Currently, I have to list it as undetermined. But whatever was in here, I'm certain it's the culprit."

"Did I kill him?" Nicholas asked.

Janovich put a hand on Nicholas's shoulder and said, not unkindly, "You fought with him, true, but based on his facial bruising, I believe the gel pack was hit externally, and that broke open the abscess and activated the poison. But, Agent Drummond, it was an accident, you are not to blame."

26

26 Federal Plaza
3:00 p.m.

Mike called Ben the moment they got in the car. "We're on our way back. We have big news. Do you have Sophie Pearce?"

"We do," Ben answered.

"Good. Ask Gray to scan photos of all the German nationals who entered the United States in the past week, see if he can find Mr. Olympic on a flight manifest."

"Will do. See you in ten."

She hung up her cell and looked over at Nicholas. He was staring at his tapping fingers on the dash.

She said, "I know you're frustrated, Nicholas, but stop it, okay? Dr. Janovich was right, it wasn't your fault."

"Of course it was. I was the one who popped him in the jaw with my elbow, I think. And that means we'd know what all this was about if I hadn't killed him."

"Your activating the poison was a fluke. Look at it this way. If Mr. Olympic hadn't died, and Janovich hadn't found the implant in his brain, we could never have known that someone was watching everything through his eyes, listening to everything we said. And now we know it's someone who's connected to one of the big nano-biology firms. It's all good."

Nicholas stopped tapping his fingers. "Yes, of course you're right."

Still, she understood. Any death, even accidental, unleashed demons that visited in the night. She said simply, "We all live with it, Nicholas. You know even better than I do that it's something we have to deal with. Now snap to, Superman, I need you." And that made him smile.

"Good. Now, we've got to figure out what we're missing. Jonathan Pearce was lured to Wall Street by Mr. Olympic and killed. Sophie Pearce lied through her teeth to us and her brother, Adam, is probably wanted by the intergalactic police. What are they hiding? What are they up to?"

He was focused again. "I'm going to go out on a short limb here and say Mr.

Olympic, our dead German, was sent to access Pearce's files. He's definitely the one who broke into the system before we arrived at Mr. Pearce's apartment."

"You don't think it could have been Adam Pearce?"

"No, no reason for him to access his father's computer since he'd have every-thing duplicated on his own computer. If you were looking for something specific, and you had a man you could send in who could visually upload everything he saw, and heard? I'd say Mr. Olympic."

Mike said, "We really need an ID on Mr. Olympic, like now."

"We also need to look at another possibility here, Mike. The information on the spy satellite is certainly worth spending some time tracking, if that's what they were after. Again, for a layman to have those plans on his personal computer is more than worrisome."

"What are you saying? Do you think Jonathan Pearce was involved in some sort of espionage?"

He said, "You saw the list of people he

dealt with, they're all over the world, and all very powerful. Was he simply mailing classified information to the highest bidder inside the books they bought? If so, it's rather elegant, actually, and very old-school. Al Qaeda, for example, uses handwritten notes for their biggest operational plans since computer communications between terrorist franchises aren't secure."

She nodded. "Okay, yes, it's the only safe way of moving information in this new digital age, especially since it's virtually impossible to erase information."

He said, "You're right. I can resurrect nearly any hard drive. Everything leaves a footprint, no matter how ghostly. And to think, Pearce's son is a well-known hacker. I'm going to say father and son were in cahoots."

"**Cahoots**? From a Brit?"

He glanced at her, saw she was smiling. "I'm flexible. And yes, cahoots. Now I hope Sophie Pearce is going to give us some real answers."

When they stepped off the elevator,

Nicholas said, "I recall something in Pearce's files about a company out of Germany doing groundbreaking nano-biotech work. There wasn't a name, but I'm sure it would be easy to find. Do you remember Pierre Menard, from FedPol?"

"Of course. How could I forget him? He was smart, fast on his feet, and the biggie, he really liked me. Maybe you, too, but not as much." Menard had been a vital part of their search for the Fox and the Koh-i-Noor diamond.

"I'm going to call him. Maybe he'll know of a German nano-biotech firm that would fit the bill."

Ben ushered them into the room next to the interview room where they could observe Sophie pacing, back and forth, muttering all the while.

"She's mad," Nicholas said. "It's fun when a witness is mad, they tend to lose control more easily. I really don't understand, though, why she's so upset."

"Pretty obvious, don't you think?" Mike said. "Her dad was murdered this morning and now she's trying to protect her brother.

We're the cops, her brother's biggest enemy."

"Here's something else," Ben said, handing Nicholas a transcript. "There was so much, we got Agent Jack McDermitt on loan from the Investigation Unit. He and Gray took apart the forensic data from Pearce's phone and computer, looking for ties to his son, and to any foreign entities who might benefit from the plans of the spy satellite. Here's the extended transcript of the texts from Pearce's phone back and forth to EP—Adam Pearce. Father and son were searching for something, what we don't know since it's all coded. But Gray and Jack both think it's something major."

Ben was right, the conversations were indecipherable, full of abbreviations and numbers. Nicholas wanted to study them himself, but they didn't have the time now. He folded the papers, stuck them in his jacket pocket.

"See anything?" Mike asked.

"Like Ben said, it's all coded. We need some time and the key, a codex of some sort. We'll ask Sophie, odds are she knows what it all means. Ben, will you watch, see if anything stands out for you?"

"Of course."

He said to Mike, "Do you want to be the good cop or the bad cop?"

She punched his arm. "Can't you tell I'm the spitting image of Glinda the Good Witch?"

"Let's do it, then," and he crossed the hall into the interrogation room.

27

Nicholas stomped into the room, impatience and annoyance rolling off him, heavy as a noxious cloud. He took a seat across from Sophie Pearce and stared at her, his look dark, violent, scary, because he didn't say a word. Mike followed him more slowly, stood against the wall, her arms crossed, silent.

Nicholas said without preamble, his voice hard and low, "We know you've been lying to us, Ms. Pearce. We know the young man you called **Kevin Brown** this morning wasn't an old employee. We know he was your brother, Adam. We have a warrant out for his arrest, and every law enforcement official in the tri-state area has been informed of his acts of treason against this country. They won't go easy on him when they find him. Trust me on this, you want us to be the ones who take him into custody. Now, tell us how to find him or we'll arrest you as an accessory to murder."

Nicholas had taken her off guard. Mike

watched Sophie Pearce press back against the chair, maybe a bit afraid now, but then she got hold of herself. She even sat forward, ready to face him down. She said very deliberately, "I don't know what you're talking about."

He leaned forward as well, their foreheads nearly touching. He looked ready to strangle her, but still, she didn't move, didn't pull back. "Of course you do. We don't have time for any more evasions, any more lies. You will tell me where your brother is." He sat back suddenly, tapped his fingers on the tabletop, loud in the silent room. "Don't you understand? After your father's murder this morning, we learned we aren't the only ones looking for your brother. It's clear his life is in danger."

Mike was right, this was the way to get to her. He saw a flash of fear in her eyes.

Mike said from behind him, "I know you love Adam, Sophie, and that's why you're protecting him. Believe me, I respect that. You've lost so much today. You shouldn't have to go through this, too. And—"

Nicholas cut her off, his voice steel-edged. "If you don't tell me everything, you're going to lose not only your father, but your brother, too. So where is he, Ms. Pearce? Where is Adam?"

She'd wavered, he'd seen it, but now she looked him straight in the eye and said flatly, "I don't know."

Nicholas slammed his fist on the table, making her jump. "You're lying. I can see the pulse in your neck race faster with every single lie."

Mike said quietly, "Sophie, you know what this is about. You know the men who killed your father are trying to get to your brother. You don't want his blood on your hands. Help us, Sophie. You know we're the good guys. We don't want anything bad to happen to Adam. I have a brother, too. I'd do most anything to protect him. Maybe even go so far as to try to hide his identity to keep the cops from arresting him. But if he was in danger, I would stop pretending I didn't know where he is."

That did it. Sophie cracked wide open. She jumped to her feet, splayed her palms on the battered table. "What was I supposed to do, give you his real name? He's a hacker, he has a record. You know he's wanted. You'll put him in jail. Adam isn't the reason my father was killed, he isn't."

Nicholas said, "You think not? Where is he?"

She shook her head. "You don't understand. Adam wouldn't, couldn't, be the reason my father was killed."

Nicholas shoved the transcript Ben had given him toward her, knowing it looked official. "It's all here. Your father was lured down to Wall Street this morning with a text message from someone calling himself EP. EP, Sophie. **Eternal Patrol,** your brother's underground call sign, which you know very well. Your brother asked your father to meet him. Your father was killed doing so. It doesn't take a genius to see what's happening here."

"But you said the men who killed my father are searching for Adam." She looked at Nicholas, right through him, and her face suddenly turned hard.

"I see now, you're lying to me. You're playing me. You already know who killed my father. You never thought his own son could have done it, you're not that stupid. No, you want the boy hacker who's made your lives a misery because he's so talented, so smart, much more than any of you."

She jumped to her feet. "I won't help you put my brother into prison! I'm through speaking now. I'd like to call my attorney."

She stood there, her arms crossed over her chest.

"You're not under arrest, Sophie," Mike said, pushing away from the wall. "You're free to leave, but please understand, your brother is in imminent danger. Help us find him before it's too late for him, for both of you."

"Your father's dead, Sophie. Don't let Adam be next."

Sophie closed her eyes and swallowed. Finally, she said, "You don't need me. I know how you work, you can track Adam off his phone."

"We can't because your brother doesn't

use the same kind of phone as most people," Nicholas said. "You know he unlocks them, puts his own operating system on them, adds programming to make them untraceable, and the phones themselves are disposable. Think, Sophie. We can't protect him if we can't find him, and that's what's most important right now."

She gave it up. "He stays in the Village when he comes to town. If I need him, I leave word at the Starbucks on the Lower East Side, on Delancey between Allen and Orchard. His girlfriend, Allie, works there, she knows how to find him. He thought it was safer if I didn't have the address." She stood up. "I'm leaving now."

Nicholas rose. "Thank you for your help. And Sophie, I'm sure we don't need to remind you to be very careful out there."

A hint of panic, but only for an instant. She straightened her shoulders. "I always am."

28

East Village
4:00 p.m.

Nicholas and Mike left immediately for the Starbucks on Delancey. They didn't wait for agents to back them up, no time, and both of them knew it. Adam Pearce would be there or he wouldn't. If they needed help, they'd call in.

Agent Lia Scott was the eyes and ears on Sophie Pearce and was monitoring all calls, e-mails, and communications from Adam Pearce when they found him. She called Mike as they parked a block from Starbucks.

"Lia, what's up?"

"Hi, Mike, a quick update. We have the trap set up and live on Sophie Pearce's phone lines, so we're listening and watching. Our girl is calling all over town, looking for her brother. So far, she hasn't managed to locate him, but with this many people beating the bushes, he's going to know you're coming, and probably run."

"Did she alert this Allie we're about to see at the Starbucks?"

"Not that I can tell, but we had a ten-minute lag time while the paper cleared on the phone tap. It's possible."

"Where is Sophie now?"

"The phone shows her back at her apartment in the Alexander. As long as she keeps her cell phone on her person, I can trace her steps around town pretty easily. She's parked right now, and so am I."

"She doesn't know we're listening, so she should keep her phone on. Thanks, Lia. Let me know if she goes on the move."

"Will do."

All eyes behind the Starbucks counter were on them the moment they walked in. It was, Mike thought, like they were wearing a sign. She marched up and flipped out her badge. "I'm looking for Allie."

A handsome young black man with a Mohawk immediately stepped forward. "Allie McGee? She's not in today. She called in sick."

"Who's your manager?"

"I am. Stephen Torres. What's the problem, ma'am?"

"We need her home address, right now."

He didn't move. "Is she in trouble?"

Mike leaned on the counter with both arms. "She's going to be, if you don't tell me how to find her."

One of the baristas said, "I'm Shelley. I'm her best friend. She's over on Avenue A. One-oh-seven Avenue A, apartment five. She's probably not there, though, she has school today. She had a huge midterm today, and our work schedule was set last week. I traded shifts with her so she could take her test." The girl shot her manager a guilty look. "We're not supposed to trade shifts without getting permission first."

Mike said, "Nice of you. What school does she go to?"

"NYU. She's a computer science major."

"She have a boyfriend?"

The look on Shelley's face told them the answer to that.

"Does he live with her?" Nicholas asked.

"No, not really. In fact, I haven't seen

Adam in a long time. Allie said he was in California. She doesn't talk much about him, I don't know why."

Mike said, "What's her phone number? Right now."

Shelley gave Mike the number.

Torres said, "Hey, Allie's a good kid. What did she do?"

Mike gave her best scary Fed smile. "Don't worry about it. Thank you, Shelley, for the info. Now, can I have two grande skinny vanilla lattes and two cinnamon scones? To go."

"Surely, ma'am. On the house, for New York's Finest."

She left a twenty-dollar bill on the counter, aware of the phalanx of eyes on their backs as they walked out. They got in the car and Mike devoured the scone in three bites, Nicholas in two. He wiped his mouth. "That was well played, Special Agent Caine."

"Thanks. You so owe me a real meal, Nicholas. An apple, a scone, and a latte ain't gonna cut it." She brushed the crumbs off her lap, took a deep gulp of the latte, burning her tongue in the process.

"Let's go to her apartment," Mike said. "If I were on the run, I'd hide out at my girlfriend's place. It doesn't appear that Allie even told her best friend that Adam is a big bad wanted hacker."

Allie McGee's apartment was only a few blocks away. Mike checked in with Ben, told him where they were going, told him to be ready for a call if they saw something hinky. "And Ben, find out who owns the lease on this apartment."

Even though all they wanted to find was a nineteen-year-old boy, she and Nicholas had come prepared, vests, comms on the off chance they ran into trouble. She and Nicholas geared up while Ben ran the property record.

He said, "It's in the name of Allison McGee. Bought last year, for eight hundred thousand dollars."

"Pricey place for a kid in school, working at Starbucks on the side. Did her parents fund it?"

She heard tapping. "It was paid for in cash. Full purchase price."

"Interesting. Have the financials come back on Jonathan Pearce yet?"

Ben said, "As it happens, yes. Pearce is a very wealthy man. Both the son and daughter have healthy trust funds. And lookee here, there was a withdrawal for one million dollars from Adam Pearce's trust right before the apartment was purchased."

"Gotcha, thanks, Ben."

"Call if you need backup. Wait up, here's Gray."

Gray Wharton's voice came loud and clear. "One more thing, Mike, Sir Nicholas—Jonathan Pearce is a viscount. The Tenth Viscount Chambers, to be exact."

That got Nicholas's attention. "Chambers? Who is Pearce's father?"

"Looks like his dad's name was Robert, son of Leo, son of—no, wait—it looks like Leo was adopted by William Pearce way back in 1917, before the end of the war. As to who Leo's real father was, I'm going to have to dig to find that out. Do you think that could be important?"

Nicholas said, "No clue, Gray. I doubt it,

but if you happen to see it, let me know. Thank you. Quit calling me 'sir.'"

It was a secure building, requiring either a code or a buzz in from an apartment to open the doors.

Mike cupped her hands against the glass to get a better view of the lobby setup. "I don't see a doorman. We're going to have to buzz Allie's apartment."

Nicholas pressed the button for 2A. Nothing. 2B answered, though, and Mike adopted her best young girl voice. "Hey, it's five, I left my keys upstairs."

"Not again," came a harassed voice, but the door buzzed, and clicked open.

Mike gave Nicholas a grin. "Works every time."

Nicholas shook his head. "You'd think New Yorkers would be more careful."

"No kidding." They'd looked at the apartment floor plan, saw Allie's place was rear-facing, with a sectioned fire escape that let down into an alley.

They took the elevator to the fifth floor. Apartment five was the last door down a narrow, elegantly modern hallway with stained teak floors and small wheatgrass installations along the wall, the embedded lights reflected by beveled mirrors, giving a lovely glow to the space.

"Nice to have a rich boyfriend these days," Mike said.

They were at the door now. Nicholas leaned in, listened. It was quiet, too quiet. He whispered, "Something doesn't feel right." Didn't smell right, either. He smelled the sharp pungent odor of copper and that meant blood, a lot of it.

Not good, not good. Mike pulled her Glock from its clip at her waist, called Ben. "Ben, come down, something's not right here."

She knew they should wait, but she knew to her gut something was very wrong. She stood to the side of the door, and banged her fist three times, yelled, "FBI. Open up."

Nothing. There were no sounds.

Nicholas reached for the doorknob. Unlocked. He met her eyes, nodded. Mike called out again, then he opened the door and went in, quick and fast, Mike behind him, her Glock high, his low.

And everything around them seemed to explode into movement.

29

107 Avenue A, Unit 5
4:30 p.m.

The light was blinding, the force from the blast knocked him sideways against the entryway wall. Nicholas shook his head, trying to get his vision and his hearing back. Mike was beside him, shaking him, shouting something at him, but he couldn't hear her. He felt a trickle of wet from his ear; his hand came away red. He numbly realized someone had thrown a flash bang.

You're getting slow, Drummond. Maybe it was the aftereffect of being Tasered this morning, but he couldn't seem to get anything moving right.

It wasn't only the flash bang, he'd also taken a shot to the chest, center mass, and thank the good Lord above he was wearing a Kevlar vest, at Mike's insistence, or his first day with the FBI would have been his last.

Mike was yelling at him. "Can you get

up? Are you okay? Come on, Nicholas, talk to me. There's no one here, I checked, well, except—can you get up?"

With a huge wheeze, air filled his lungs and he was able to move again, his hearing and sight returning. Mike's hand was gripping his arm, helping him up. "That'll teach you for going in first," she said, and punched him.

"Better me than you." He managed to get up. "Okay, I'm fine now. Knocked the wind out of me, is all."

She closed her eyes for a moment. "Stop doing that to me, Nicholas. What happened?"

"A guy started shooting when I opened the door, then he tossed a flash bang at me as he went out the window."

"Was it Adam Pearce?"

"I don't know, the flash was too quick. We gotta go after him, now, before he gets away."

She drew a deep steadying breath. "There's something else, Nicholas," and she pointed. He looked into the living room, only fifteen feet away, directly to his right, and saw a dead girl, long brown hair spread about her head, lying on her side, near a pale blue sofa, her eyes blank.

"It's Allie McGee, has to be," Mike said as she ran to the side window that gave onto the alley.

She spotted the man climbing down the fire escape, not fast because he had to unlatch and lower each section as he went. Nicholas said, "I'll go down the fire escape, you take the stairs. There may be more of them."

As he went through the window, she speed-dialed Ben. "Allie McGee's been murdered, Nicholas is chasing a guy down the fire escape. Hurry, Ben."

It had all happened in only a few seconds, she thought blankly, only two snaps of the fingers. It had seemed a lifetime.

She looked back at Allie McGee, felt anger fill her gut and headed for the stairs. They should have brought backup, should have—Ben would be here fast. Besides, Nicholas wouldn't let the man get away.

He's going to get away. Nicholas saw the man had nearly reached the second floor. He'd lost precious time. Nicholas shook the rest of the cobwebs clear and went after him. He didn't have to unhook the fire escape sections as he went, so he could run flat out down the rusted metal steps. He saw a flash of dark hair, saw the man look back up at him. No way was Nicholas going to let him get away. He grabbed the edge of the second-floor ladder and slid down eighteen feet, landed hard, rolled, and jumped to his feet only seconds after the man had hit the ground and begun to run. He was limping, but he could still move fast. Good thing he was no Mr. Olympic. Nicholas caught up with him quickly.

He heard Mike shouting, running around the building toward him. Before she could get there, the man turned and lashed out with his leg, trying to catch Nicholas in the stomach. Not Adam Pearce, and not as young as Nicholas first thought. This guy looked like a hired thug, vicious, hard, a bright red scar slashing down his face. He looked no-holds-barred, a veteran of many a fight before, some he'd lost, given the ferocious scar on his cheek.

He saw the kick coming, turned so Scarface's foot hit his hip bone, a numbing shot that would have put him down if it had caught him full-on. Scarface was fast, and agile, whipping around for another kick, but instead he sent the edge of his hand to Nicholas's throat. Nicholas jerked back and the meaty fist glanced off his cheekbone, followed by Scarface's right fist smashing into Nicholas's shoulder. His damned limp didn't seem to be bothering him at all now.

Nicholas was bigger than Scarface, as well trained, and as dirty. He whirled around, leg out, tripped him, but the moment his back hit the ground he sprang back up like a jack-in-the-box and came at him again, forcing Nicholas back, ever back.

Nicholas countered every move grimly, and they danced together, arms and legs clashing hard, blood running freely from Scarface's nose. Nicholas gave up finesse and went for brute force, slamming both fists on his shoulders, pushing him hard.

As he stumbled backward, Nicholas found his opening. He got a good glimpse at the surprise on his scarred face as his fist crashed into the wide, whiskered jaw. Scarface went down, out cold, falling hard, his head bouncing on the asphalt. He was down, finally, no longer a threat.

Nicholas stood over him, breathing hard, hands still fists, until he realized Scarface was definitely not getting up. **Don't let him be dead, Zachery will skin me alive.**

Nicholas flipped him over on his stomach. As he snapped cuffs on him, he heard Mike scream his name.

He thought she'd been close, he'd heard her running footsteps before the fight with Scarface.

He whipped around to see his worst nightmare.

Another man, big, older, built like a boxer, had an arm around Mike's neck, and a pistol pressed to her temple. His mouth was stretched wide, a rictus of a smile, and Nicholas saw blood smeared over his mouth. Mike had smashed him in the face before he'd managed to grab her.

He licked away the blood, the terrifying smile still on his mouth. He said nothing at all. His finger began to move on the trigger.

Nicholas didn't think, his gun was in his hand, coming up smoothly, and he squeezed the trigger and blood blossomed out of the man's forehead a heartbeat later.

Mike went down, under him. Oh, God, he'd hit her, he'd hit her. But no, she was yelling his name and he saw her pushing and shoving, fighting to push the man off her. Nicholas realized he was frozen in position, chest heaving, arm still locked straight in front of him, his finger still in the Glock's trigger guard. He dropped his arm and holstered his gun and ran to Mike. He pushed the man's body the rest of the way off her, yanked her to her feet, ran his hands over her arms, her chest, touching her face. "Are you okay, are you okay?"

He was shouting and she flinched. The gunshot had come so close to her, and it had hurt her eardrums, but she nodded, forcing herself to breathe deeply, in and out, to calm herself.

Nicholas pulled her tight to his chest, eyes shut, the breath gone from him again. It was too damn close, he'd nearly lost her.

And the sirens began to wail behind them.

30

Nicholas held a chemical ice pack against his cheek, tapping away one-handed on a laptop they'd found thrown behind the sofa in Allie McGee's living room, and wondered, yet again, what in the bloody hell they'd gotten themselves into. In the course of a single day, three dead, one in cuffs, Mike nearly shot, him Tasered, beaten, shot, and flash-bombed. It wasn't even dark yet. And no Adam Pearce. But Allie McGee was dead. He hated it. He felt stiff, sore from the blows he'd taken and the jarring jump from the fire escape, his chest burned from the bullet in his vest, his clothes were ripped, actually quite ruined, and Nigel would not be happy, but, on the other hand, he was alive, he could see and hear again and he was trying to do something useful with the computer.

His life was becoming some sort of exceptionally violent country-and-western song, the kind his uncle Bo liked to listen to. **Tase me, shoot me, knock me down . . .**

He laughed to himself. **You're punchy, Nicholas, it's all the adrenaline, and yes, the deep and abiding fear you felt at the very idea of losing Mike.**

The image of the second thug with the gun to her temple, blood running down his face, that madman's smile, like it had been painted on and Mike's mouth moving silently. Now he realized she hadn't been silent at all, she'd been screaming **"Shoot him, shoot him."** He'd never even heard her.

NYPD was on the scene along with Ben and three more FBI agents, dealing with the aftermath of the battle in the alley. He'd answered about a thousand questions from the NYPD, and Ben told both of them they had to leave the crime scene now, and that meant this one and Allie McGee's apartment. He'd relented only when Nicholas agreed to go back upstairs. "Stay out of the way, both of you know the drill. Don't get us all in trouble."

He and Mike had trudged back to Allie McGee's apartment, waiting on the identification of the men who'd broken in and killed her.

The place was a wreck. The flash bang had thankfully not caught anything on fire, but Nicholas and Mike's mad scramble across the room to the window had resulted in an overturned table and chair, tampering with the initial crime scene.

But Allie McGee was the worst part of all.

Mike watched Louisa Barry carefully process Allie McGee's body for evidence. It hurt too much to keep looking, so she turned to watch Nicholas typing. She was still shaking, only inside now, and it was understandable, she supposed, given that if Nicholas had shot just two inches to the left, her head would have splattered all over the wall of Allie McGee's building. He'd seen the man was going to shoot her brains out and he'd acted, hadn't hesitated. She'd seen determination, wild fear, and something else before he'd fired. It was certainty, that was it. She was very glad he was on her side.

Nicholas never looked up from the computer. Mike finally made herself go to

Louisa, who met her eyes, read the unasked question. "Yes, before they shot her, they did a number on her."

"They were trying to get information."

"Looks that way. I don't know if she helped or not. We'll need the ME to give us a certain time of death, but she's not in rigor yet. You interrupted them, Mike, you and Nicholas."

"We may have gotten her killed, you mean."

Louisa shook her head. "No, she was dead before you arrived. They'd already torn this place apart. Now it's going to take the rest of the day for me to put this all together. Your shirt, Mike, you're a mess. There's a lot of blood."

"Thankfully not mine. Keep me posted." She turned to go, and Louisa said in a hard, flat voice, "She didn't have a chance, Mike, you know that. She was only a kid, against very well-trained professionals. I'm very glad Nicholas killed one of them. As for the other, I hope he rots forever in Attica."

"He will."

"This has gotten to you, Mike, I can see that. You've got to try to keep some distance, some altitude. It will all come together. It always does."

And with that, Louisa kneeled back down next to the body of a young girl who should have been at school when those men came looking for Adam, looking for something to show them where he was.

Don't blame yourself. But she did, because she'd failed to get the information about this apartment and Allie McGee from Sophie Pearce in time. She felt a raw burst of anger toward Sophie Pearce, but remembered Lia telling her about all her phone calls, trying to locate him. So she didn't know where her brother rested his head when he was in the city. Still, if she'd only told them sooner, they'd have been able to get here faster, and Allie McGee wouldn't be dead.

There were pictures of Allie all around the apartment, some of her alone, some with her family—she had a younger sister and an older brother and two blond smiling parents whose lives were about to be ruined—but the majority were photographs of her with Adam Pearce.

She crossed the room to sit on the arm of Nicholas's chair.

"How's it coming?"

A few more clicks. "This computer is shot to hell," Nicholas said. "The hard drive's been wiped, and I can't get it back. Maybe Gray can harvest something off the chip, but from everything I can see, there's bugger all there."

"Adam Pearce is a hacker, so he has backups, right?"

"Yes, but we need to get our hands on him first. Bloody hell, Mike."

"My thought exactly. At least we know Adam is still alive."

"We **think** he's alive. We hope he's alive. And all he's left behind is his dead girlfriend and a broken computer."

"And he didn't kill her. I find that comforting."

"Nor did he crash his hard drive. You're right, he had nothing to do with this."

Nicholas closed the lid on the ruined computer. "There is something, we've got one extra power cord here, to a Sony Vaio. That means there's a laptop missing."

She felt a spurt of energy, or hope. "It had to be Adam's. He was here, but then he left."

Nicholas's cop eyes got cold and hard. "Whatever he knows, whatever happened, he's now out in the cold, no friends, no father, no girlfriend. Only his sister, and we're watching her, and he's got to know that, and so she's off-limits. Which means there's no one to help him, and no way to predict exactly what he might do next."

Nicholas's mobile rang, and the screen showed Zachery's number. And he knew what it was about. He'd left another dead body. On his first day.

It was Maryann, Zachery's assistant, who was a longtime fixture in the New York Criminal Investigative Division. She'd seen it all, heard it all. And her voice said it all.

"Agent Drummond, the SAC would like to see you in his office."

"Would you please tell him I'll be back downtown as soon as we're through here?

I am not involved, I am only observing."

"I'm sorry, Agent Drummond, but he's requested you return to Federal Plaza immediately. With Agent Caine. We'll see you in fifteen minutes."

That was official. He was in trouble.

31

What's wrong now?" Mike asked.

"Zachery wants us back now."

She sighed. "I was afraid of that. He finds out everything so quickly. You know we're breaking protocol as it is by even being here. Don't worry, though, maybe he only wants to hear what happened firsthand."

"Three dead bodies, Mike." He glanced over at Allie McGee. "Make that four."

"Not your fault. It will be all right, you'll see. You did nothing wrong. Let me tell Louisa we're leaving. The traffic will be a nightmare, we'll put the siren on. Drive real fast. That should make you feel better."

He didn't think speed would help anything. He nodded. "I'll see you in the lobby."

He took the elevator down, replaying the fight, the shooting. He didn't see he'd had any other choice in the matter; another moment and the second thug would have shot Mike through the temple. He made a quick decision, pulled out his mobile, and punched in a number he knew by heart.

"Nick, good to hear from you. I was hoping you'd call and check in. How's the first day treating you? I wish I could have been there to see you walk through the doors."

"I wish you had too, Uncle Bo. Because you might have been happier to see me this afternoon than Milo Zachery is about to be."

Instant flatline. "Tell me what happened."

Nicholas gave him a quick rundown of the day. Bo whistled, long and low. "You do manage to step in it, don't you, Nick?"

"I wonder where I may have learned that. Do you have any advice?"

"Tell Milo the absolute truth. You already knew there was going to be a lot of interest in you, and with the deaths, and the shooting, there will have to be a formal inquiry. But you've done nothing wrong. Every action has been according to policy. So go in with your head high, my boy, and don't worry."

Nicholas saw Mike come out of the elevator. Her hair was falling out of the ponytail, her sleeve was torn, and there was all that damned blood on her shirt. He swallowed. "Thank you, Uncle Bo. I'll let you know what they say."

"You do that. And come for dinner this weekend. Bring Mike. We'd love to catch up."

"I will, and I'll extend the invitation, thank you." He hung up, and stuck his mobile in his pocket.

"Ready?" Mike asked.

"To face the executioner, you mean? As I'll ever be."

26 Federal Plaza
6:30 p.m.

Zachery was standing by the window, looking out onto the New Jersey skyline.

"Sit," he said brusquely when they came in. He didn't turn around.

They sat. Finally, he turned to face them, hands in the pockets of his suit pants. "We've identified the man who killed Jonathan Pearce this morning, as well as the two men you brought down on Avenue A an hour ago. All three are German nationals, all three have lengthy criminal records."

He nodded to the file folders on the coffee table, waited for them to open the files, then said, "You'll see the first man, Mr. Olympic you called him, is Jochen Foer. As you know, he had the brain implant—his sheet is long and varied, but almost all his warrants are for murder. The man you shot in the head in the alley is Siegmund Brasch, and Heiner Veblen is the one you managed not to kill but arrest. Both are wanted by Interpol for trafficking and murder."

"Hired assassins, then?"

"Seem to be. And Heiner Veblen, the gentleman you beat to a pulp, is currently in a coma at Bellevue Hospital. Ben is there, in case he comes to and decides he wants to have a come-to-Jesus talk. Though the doctors don't think that's likely, since he suffered a brain bleed."

Zachery met Nicholas's eye. "Did you have to put the man in a coma, Drummond?"

"One look at me and you'll see he was a vicious fighter, and tried to kill me. Fortunately, I'm a good fighter as well. I didn't hit his head, sir, everywhere else, but not his head. He fell down hard on that last kick, and his head smacked hard against the asphalt."

Zachery studied Nicholas's battered face, the swelling, the blood splatter on his shirt. He looked at Mike, imagined her with a gun to her head, and saw the aftermath, the man's blood speckled on her white shirt. He'd chew their butts tomorrow about having a team with them at all times, even if they were visiting an old man in a nursing home. They'd believed they were going to pick up a boy, nothing more. Well, so much for that fine analysis. It had been too close. Would a team have made a difference? He didn't know. He said, "Drummond, you do realize this is an all-time record for a junior agent?"

Nicholas went stiff. Mike didn't know if it was Zachery's tone or him calling Nicholas a junior agent. Or both. She said, without hesitation, "Sir, Nicholas did everything right, everything by the book. You would have done the same thing if you'd been there. You know these guys were pros, not some lowlife drug dealers. The German, Siegmund Brasch, he would have killed me if Nicholas hadn't acted. I'd be good and dead, my head blown off." She swallowed, seeing it. "He saved my life, sir. And Mr. Olympic, that was a fluke, Dr. Janovich surely told you it was. Nicholas did nothing wrong. Because of him, I'm alive."

Zachery gave her a long look. "And I expect you to say exactly that tomorrow morning, Agent Caine, when the Shooting Incident Review Team from Headquarters arrives for the inquiry. I believe both of you acted exactly right, but I have to make the call because I have no choice. Drummond, you are suspended, pending the results of the SIRT hearing. I need your gun, and your creds."

Zachery said nothing more, held out his hand. "Per regulation, another weapon will be assigned to you. You need to collect it, then head on home for the night. We'll sort all this out in the morning."

Without a word, Nicholas put his weapon and his freshly laminated credentials on the coffee table. He wondered what his former boss, Hamish Penderley of New Scotland Yard, would have said in Zachery's position. He probably would have grabbed one of his prized antique foils and run him through.

Zachery nodded briefly. "The SIRT hearing will be at eight-thirty tomorrow morning. Neither of you be late."

Nicholas saw Mike was about to blow. He caught her arm, shook his head.

"We'll be there, sir. Thank you. Is that all?"

"I'm glad you're not fighting me on this."

Nicholas shrugged. "Rules are rules, especially when it comes to the FBI. I knew that when I signed up. As a brand-new **junior** agent, I'm on probation for ninety days, and there are no special favors to be given because exceptions were made for me to join the FBI. I understand, and I will be back in the morning to explain my side of things."

"Good. Now go home, clean yourselves up, eat something, go to bed. As I said, we'll get it all sorted out in the morning."

Nicholas nodded, turned to leave.

Mike said, "But, sir, we can't afford to lose the time. Adam Pearce is on the run. He's in danger, and we have to find him. We think he's the key to what's happening."

Zachery narrowed his eyes at her. "There's a team in place working on this, Agent Caine. You're to see Agent Drummond home, do you understand me? And get a good night's sleep yourself."

Her back was ramrod straight. "Am I

being disciplined as well, sir?"

He shut his eyes, shook his head and gave an exasperated sigh. "Mike, you're being protected by getting your ass out of this building for the night. Read me?"

"Loud and clear, sir."

"Good. You two, out of here, now."

32

Mike called Ben while Nicholas went to get his replacement weapon.

"Please tell me the German is out of the coma and talking."

"Nope, the lights are still out. There's swelling, they put in a stent, so hopefully it will help things. He's pretty messed up, Mike. Nicholas did a real number on him."

"Thank goodness, otherwise it might have been Nicholas in the damned coma." She'd been there. She'd seen the fight, hands and fists flying, kicks and punches, the guy finally down, then in a flash, Nicholas facing her, firing point-blank, fast and unquestioning, and she wondered for the hundredth time exactly what kind of spy work he'd done for Britain's Foreign Office.

She refocused, shook it off. "Any chance they found an implant in the dead guy's noggin?"

"No. Clean as a whistle. Janovich did an X-ray first thing, no implant."

"All three are German, but probably only the one has an implant? That's interesting. Listen, Ben, call me if anything changes there at the hospital." She wasn't going to tell him about the inquiry tomorrow, but of course he'd find out soon enough.

Ben said, "I'm going to pull Lia off Sophie Pearce, and turn hospital duty over to her, come back and help Gray and Jack go through Pearce's files and that SD card. I'll be able to monitor Sophie as well."

"Where is Sophie?"

"She's at the UN, wrapping up. Gonna take her a while, too, from what it sounds like. She called her boss, told her she was coming in to clear her desk so she could take a leave for the next month while she handles her father's affairs. She's gonna burn the midnight oil."

"All right. You know, I can't help but feel like everyone is looking for something, and we have no idea what that something is."

"Maybe the something is a someone— Adam Pearce."

"Him, sure, but there's something more.

Hey, here comes Nicholas, I've got to go. Call me if you find anything."

"Mike, you and Nicholas look like crap warmed over. Get yourselves fixed up, okay? Oh, yeah, another thing, next time, even if you guys think you're just going to scoop up some kid, I'll have a team surrounding you. This shouldn't have happened, Mike, you know that."

What could she say? He was right. She punched off.

"News?" Nicholas asked, reaching her.

"Ben said nothing new. Why don't we get some dinner? There's a great new Chinese place down the street I've been wanting to try."

He ran a hand through his hair. He looked tired, and depressed and flat-out beaten up. "If it's all the same to you, Mike, I'd like to grab a taxi and head home. It's been a long day."

"A cab? What, you didn't drive your ejector-seat Bondmobile to work this morning?"

She didn't even draw a smile. "No. I don't have a car in the city. Taxis work fine."

"I'm right here, with keys in hand. I'll drive you home."

Nicholas thought of his magnificent town house, all five beautiful floors of it, thought of Nigel, doubtless dressed to the butler hilt. "No, no, there's no need. I'd like the time alone, to clear my head."

Mike grinned. "If you think I'm falling for that, you must really think I'm stupid."

"Never," he said. "Honestly, I'll be fine."

She hooked her arm through his and dragged him to the elevator, punched the down button. "I know you, the minute you're home, you're going to investigate Pearce and the Germans and Adam by yourself." She shook her head. "Why do you think Zachery wants us together? He knows things are moving fast and he figures we'll keep investigating, even though we shouldn't. He's pretty smart."

He waited for the doors to close, then faced her. She'd put her hair back up in its ponytail, but the blood had dried on her white blouse and turned black. "You really think so?"

"Yes. Remember how much he told us before he got to the inquiry part? He's not going to outwardly sanction us working off-book, but I'm sure that's the reason he sent me home with you. So don't fight it."

He smiled then, and Mike saw a hint of his uncle, Bo Horsley, her former SAC. "So you're not simply supposed to be my babysitter? Keep me out of trouble? I get the sense you wouldn't be a very good one in any case. Are you?"

"Nope, I never was. I used to have to babysit to earn spending money, and I hated every minute of it."

Up went a black eyebrow. "Don't like kids, Mike?"

"I like kids fine. It was all the parental rules I disliked. Dinner at seven, bath and bed by eight, no jumping on the sofa or pillow fights. Where's the fun in all that?"

33

7:30 p.m.

"Want to tell me where we're headed?"

Nicholas commended his soul to God and said, "Upper East Side. Three fifty-eight East Sixty-ninth, between First and Second."

She shot him a look as she turned onto the FDR. "So you're not far from Ariston's."

"No, not far at all." The sky was purple with the threat of impending rain, a fog drifting between the high-rises, creeping toward the Brooklyn Bridge. New York looked more like Gotham City tonight than he'd ever seen.

Mike said, "Don't worry about your job, Nicholas. The SIRT board will find you did everything according to the book, like Zachery said."

"It's not that," he said, turning to face her. "The high-tech specs on Pearce's computer, the three German assassins, the implant, Pearce's murder, Alfie Stanford's murder. It's all connected, and

I think I know—"

His mobile rang. "Good, here's news," and he put the call on speaker. "**Bonsoir,** Monsieur Menard. It's one-thirty in the morning your time. Don't you sleep?"

"**Bonsoir,** Nicholas. Not when I have such interesting research to pursue."

"You're on with Mike Caine, too."

"Hello, Pierre."

"It is good to hear your voice again. This is quite an interesting case you have. Nano-biotech is all the rage in the European underground. There are many uses for the developing technologies, and in the hands of the wrong people, it could go very badly."

Nicholas said, "We're looking for a specific company, Pierre, very advanced, very cutting-edge. A supposedly legitimate leader in the field with the possibility of a few off-the-book projects going on, too. We're looking for someone with money, who could provide serious funding. The equipment we found this afternoon is heads and tails above anything I've ever heard or read about."

Menard said, "This equipment, the implant, it was made of a biological polymer?"

"It seems so. My bet is, whoever developed it might also have worked on organ transplant research. You know the rejection rate on organs is always a problem. If there's a biologically based metal that won't be disruptive, there may have been a breakthrough on the other side as well."

Menard said, "There are only a few companies I have heard of who fit the criteria you're speaking of, but none of them are known to have criminal dealings."

"They wouldn't, I don't suppose. Whoever is behind this would have to be, on the surface at least, on the up-and-up."

"I will look into this for you, my friend," Menard said. "I assume the inquiry is of an urgent manner?"

"When is it not, Pierre? Oh, yes, we believe the chances are good the company is based in Germany."

"Ah," Pierre said and disconnected.

Nicholas said to Mike, "This is good. He'll have something for us shortly. Here we are."

Nicholas pointed, and Mike pulled into an empty spot directly in front of a stunning five-story limestone-washed town house. Why was she surprised, given who his grandfather was, who his parents were? Nicholas was fidgeting, he looked embarrassed. She said, "Well, it's not too bad, considering. Nice of the slumlord to throw in a parking place since this place is such a hovel." She put the Crown Vic in Park, unsnapped her seat belt. "Did it come with rented furniture?"

He shook his head at her. "Very funny. Thanks to my grandfather, this place is all mine, four floors of it at least. Nigel has the third floor, that's where the kitchen is and his rooms. He's in heaven."

"Close enough I'll bet he doesn't need an elevator," she said, still staring up at the house.

"Don't give me any guff over this, Mike. Like I said, my grandfather was behind it. I wanted something simple, and he would hear nothing of it."

She started to laugh. "Um, Nicholas, I did visit Old Farrow Hall. I wouldn't expect you to be living in a studio walk-up in Hell's Kitchen. It's a beautiful house. Let's go inside, I want to see how Nigel's set you up, and see if we can scrounge something up from your—no, his—kitchen. I'm famished."

He paused after he unlocked the front door. "Promise me you won't tell anyone."

"Nicholas, the entire FBI knows your grandfather is a baron. Not to mention all the women agents know he owns Delphi Cosmetics and are trying to get the nerve to ask you to get them free samples. No one will be upset about this. They might tease you a bit—I mean come on, you have a real live butler—but they won't hold it against you. We're all better than that." And she ruined it with a giggle.

"Sure you are." He opened the door onto a magnificent entryway, done in dark woods and white marble, very modern, and it fit him perfectly. "Welcome to my humble abode."

"Should I take off my shoes? No? Where is Nigel?"

Nigel suddenly appeared above them on the stairs. His face went white and he hurried into the foyer, looking Nicholas up and down. "Oh, my, whatever happened to you? And you, Agent Caine? There's a bit of blood, I see."

"We're okay, Nigel, nothing some Advil and ice won't fix. And a change of clothes, maybe one of my shirts for Agent Caine. We're both starving, we didn't have time to eat much today. Any chance of some dinner?"

"Yes, I have a lovely roast in the kitchen, with vegetables and mash. Shall I open a bottle of wine? I set aside a Château Margaux—the '67. It can decant whilst you change your clothes for dinner and fetch a shirt for Agent Caine."

"Yes, I'll find something. Nigel, this is a working dinner, so we'll have some Pellegrino with lime. Thanks."

"Of course, sir. Perhaps I'll arrange a nightcap later, some brandy perhaps, or some port. Yes, that's what's needed, the port to go with the pear tart I've made. They'll go together nicely."

Nigel was smiling, the bloody sod. He was loving playing the formal English butler, watching Nicholas turn red and tongue-tied. He saw Mike was grinning, quite enjoying herself.

"Oh, bugger off, both of you." He stomped up the stairs, the sound of Mike's and Nigel's laughter following him.

34

2 United Nations Plaza
8:30 p.m.

Sophie closed down her computer. Done at last. She'd filed her request for an official leave of absence, effective immediately, and sent a few personal e-mails to the members of the Chinese delegation, so they would understand why she was leaving them so suddenly.

The rest of her work had been distributed among the other translators. She picked up a photo of her father and Adam on her desk. She wanted to grieve for her father, but knew she simply didn't have the time. And there was Adam, gone who knows where, and her father's files, and at the end of the rainbow, the key. If Adam had indeed found the submarine, it was only a matter of time before the Order could retrieve the key, and the book, and then what would happen? Manfred Havelock was what would happen. He'd do anything to get ahold of the key and the book, at least that's what her father believed. Anything. Had Havelock ordered her father murdered? She didn't know.

She gently put the photograph in her large leather bag and straightened and remembered Drummond in that stingy FBI interview room. The bastard, the pushy, cruel bastard with his arrogant clipped British accent, and she'd ended up caving. Maybe Drummond and Caine had been right, maybe telling where they could find Adam was the right thing to do. But she still hadn't heard from her brother. Where was he? Had they found him? And were they keeping quiet about it? She didn't know.

She needed to find Adam, needed to arrange her father's funeral as well. She'd called their lawyer, who was shocked by the news, and promised to start the paperwork immediately.

Most of all, she needed to access her father's computer files. But how? She realized he'd given her all his bank codes when he'd left for a short trip to Leningrad two weeks before. He'd also given her his passwords. Had he changed them when he'd gotten home? Would the FBI know if she accessed his computer? She didn't know, but it was worth a try. What would they do?

The key is in the lock.

She had to know what those dying words meant, since Adam had refused to tell her. If Adam had really found the sub, then everything would change. Was Havelock the one behind this?

She turned on her laptop again and logged in to her dad's private e-mail account. He hadn't changed the passwords. She didn't see anything unusual—orders from abroad, a few newsletters from his favorite nautical history magazine.

She searched through it all, but there was nothing that screamed **Havelock's behind everything, Sophie, he killed me. Start reading, it's all here.**

She went to his correspondence. Maybe he'd written someone, even in code, to tell them about Adam's finding the sub, maybe he'd mentioned Havelock.

She found hundreds of letters, all neatly filed and organized by person, month and year. He kept up a rich correspondence with a number of people all over the world, about philosophy, naval history, particularly World War I, even about the loss of his wife, Sophie's mother, to cancer ten years earlier. But nothing about the submarine.

She scrolled through bits and pieces of her father, recalled happy as well as sad memories, but nothing about the submarine, nothing helpful.

She glanced at the clock, surprised at how late it was. She wasn't getting anywhere. She needed to find Adam, he was the only one who could tell her what was happening.

As she left her office, her cell rang.

She didn't recognize the number, but went ahead and answered.

"Sophie?"

"Adam. Where are you?"

His voice was garbled, she knew he'd have her on a cell repeater, sending the signal through multiple cell towers, trying to mask his true location.

". . . killed Allie. They killed her, Sophie."

She felt the words like a fist. Adam was crying. She'd never heard him cry before.

"Soph, they shot her, she didn't do anything, she was innocent."

"Who killed her? Do you know?"

He tried to pull himself together, she could hear deep, ragged breaths. "I hacked the FBI facial-recognition database. There were two guys, they were German. You know what that means. Havelock was behind it, Sophie, he must have been. He's behind Dad's death as well, and Mr. Stanford's. And now they're going to put him in the Order in place of his father—the meeting is tomorrow."

Her voice sounded off, even to her. "Who is getting Dad's spot?"

"I don't know." His voice was getting clearer, stronger. "I have to get to Scotland. I have to get the key before Havelock."

"Adam, how will you do that? The sub's been missing for nearly a hundred years. You'll need special equipment, not to mention the Order is going to be right behind you."

"I'll figure it out. Like I said, Soph, Havelock killed Dad, killed Mr. Stanford, killed Allie. The Order's been corrupted. And Havelock will be voted in. At least I'm still the only one who knows exactly where the sub is. I have to get there first. It's the only choice."

"Adam, no, don't go yet. Meet me at the apartment."

"No, Soph, I'm getting on a plane, right now, and you should, too. Take every precaution. Get away from here. Get yourself safe."

"Let me come with you."

"No! Staying apart is the only way to keep the sub's location secret. If one of us dies, the other will know the truth."

"But Adam, I don't know the coordinates, I don't know anything."

"You're right, both of us should know. Look in Dad's e-mail. It's hard to find, but there's a message in his outbox, you'll see it's marked unsent. It has the coordinates of the sub. Please, listen to me. Get out of New York. Go somewhere, anywhere else.

I'll call again tomorrow, at this same time. If you don't hear from me—" His voice choked off, and they both knew what he meant.

Suddenly, she was calm. If Havelock was behind the murders, then the Order was no longer as it was, and of course they were both in danger. "All right, Adam, I'm going now. I have my passport with me, I always do. Call me tomorrow. And be careful, for both our sakes, be careful."

35

Sophie unlocked her bottom drawer and pulled a plain manila envelope out of a small black backpack. She slid the contents onto the desk. The money was in two separate packets, five thousand in American dollars, five thousand in British pounds. Both easily exchanged for euros if necessary.

The passport was there as well, in the name of Sophia Devereaux, a resident of Lyons, France, with a work visa in the United States valid for the next six months. God bless Adam and his constant paranoia—**You never know,** he always said. He'd sent her this one two months ago.

In the photo, she had short brown hair and wore glasses. She pulled out the brown wig cut in a sharp-angled bob and the black-rimmed glasses, plus a pair of worn cargo pants, black Dr. Martens, and a zip-neck black sweater. She looked like a hip artist, or a writer. Certainly not a UN translator, or a woman whose world was crashing down. As disguises went, it was decent. Not perfect, but on short notice, decent. She spoke perfect French, and as long as she wasn't put under undue stress, no one would know she was American.

She stashed it all back in the bag, not smart to risk changing here. She'd need to go out through security like she always did, as herself, then go down into the garage. She'd change in the stairwell, go out the garage entrance, hail a cab to take her directly to JFK and get onto the next flight to Europe, regardless of the destination.

She hurried to the grand staircase at the end of the hall, stepped down slowly, and nodded to the security guys as she walked out. They knew about her dad, and looked grim. No one knew what to say. That was fine, she didn't, either. And now she was on the run.

The security guys were watching her, she could feel their eyes on her back. She stopped and dug in her purse as though she was looking for her keys. A stroke of luck, someone else came down the stairs, and their attention turned. She hurried to the basement access door and slipped through before they could turn back.

She went down a flight, stopped on the landing, stripped off her dress and heels. Forty seconds later, Sophia Devereaux walked down one more flight of stairs.

She opened the door, glanced around the basement. She'd timed it perfectly, no one was around.

The door opened out onto Mitchell Place. She stepped out and started toward the corner of First Avenue, certain she'd be able to catch a cab quickly.

"Is that you, Sophie? You going to a masquerade? What's with the disguise?"

She turned, startled, and saw Alex Grossman. He'd been waiting for her and she hadn't seen him. Some disguise, he'd still recognized her.

"Mr. Grossman? You scared me. What are you doing here? This is a tenant-only lot. Oh, it's just a party." And she patted her wig. Wasn't that a brilliant thing to say?

Grossman's eyes were dark in the dim

light. He hadn't moved, only stood there, staring at her.

"Sophie, please forgive me." He lunged forward and grabbed her arm, but she punched him fast and hard in the stomach and jerked away, only to stumble and crash against a car. She saw a needle in his hand and screamed, "What are you doing!" and lashed out with her bag, a good fifteen pounds. It slammed against his shoulder and he fell back, for only a moment. She turned to run, but he grabbed her arm, shoved up her sleeve. She felt the sting of the needle, felt her legs weaken, felt herself falling. As she faded away, she thought she heard the words whispered into her hair—**I'm sorry.**

Then everything went black.

36

358 East 69th Street
9:00 p.m.

The roast was delicious, as were the carrots and peas and mashed potatoes. A very British meal, Mike knew, and clearly a favorite of Nicholas's. They'd both cleaned their plates twice, to Nigel's nodding approval.

Mike found the relationship between the two men fascinating. Nigel was clearly deferential, but proud of who and what he was. Nigel was smart, strong in mind and body, and he kept Nicholas smiling. The two men were close, that was easy to see. She learned they'd grown up together. Nigel's father, the unflappable Horne, was an amazing, compassionate man, a man who knew exactly what to do and when to do it. She remembered how he'd taken her under his wing when she'd stayed at Old Farrow Hall for Elaine York's funeral. It appeared Nigel was cut from the same mold, only there was more. She'd bet they'd been together in Afghanistan, and if they had then Nigel knew all the secrets buried in Nicholas's past.

Nicholas had overruled Nigel's plan to serve them in the massive dining room with the crystal and china his grandfather had sent over. They'd eaten in the kitchen and Nicholas had insisted Nigel join them. She heard stories about young master Nicholas and his run-ins with the castle ghost, Captain Flounder. She was about to suggest Nigel break out the photo albums and embarrass his master further when Nicholas stood. "That was an excellent meal, Nigel, as always. Thank you. I think we'll skip the pear tart and the port, if you don't mind."

"Of course," Nigel said. "You will be working now?"

Nicholas nodded, stretched, and rubbed his bruised jaw, the only reminder of the afternoon. He was wearing black slacks and a white shirt, the sleeves rolled up to his elbows. She was clean, too, hair combed, and now wearing one of Nicholas's white shirts tucked into her jeans. Not exactly her size, but who cared?

"You ready to get to it?" he asked.

"Onward." They walked up a flight of stairs into a large living room with a vaulted ceiling and black-and-white leather furniture, very modern, and it screamed Nicholas. She pictured Old Farrow Hall, all its ancient antiques. She followed Nicholas through another door, into an intensely masculine library. No modern furnishings in here. It was beautiful, dark wood paneling throughout, a thick Aubusson carpet, similar to the one in Jonathan Pearce's apartment. There were floor-to-ceiling shelves, only most were still empty. She saw three large wooden crates stacked in the corner, waiting to be unpacked. The modern and the traditional, both suited him.

She leaned against a large leather wing chair that looked like he'd brought it from Old Farrow Hall, and possibly he had. "Tell me when you downloaded the SD files and Pearce's hard drive, you kept a copy for yourself. And you're ready to do your less-than-legal voodoo magic on the files."

"Think you're pretty smart, don't you?"

"Me and Zachery both, and he knows, of course he knows. Now, where do we start?"

He held up a small blue thumb drive in the shape of a British police box, waggled it back and forth. "I mirrored his whole hard drive, and the SD card. It's as if his computer is right here. And the Tardis never lies."

"As in the call box from **Dr. Who**?"

"The very same."

Nigel appeared in the doorway, carrying a silver tray with two big mugs of coffee. "Thank you, Nigel, that's perfect." Nicholas took a mug and drank deep, closed his eyes for a moment, and sighed.

She took her coffee, slipped out of her boots, and tucked her feet up under her.

Nicholas sat in the old leather chair across from her, as if he were settling in for a visit with an old friend. "I was telling you I thought there was a connection between Alfie Stanford and Jonathan Pearce. I don't know if you noticed, but my father's name was on Pearce's client list."

She shook her head. "Once I saw Stanford's name, I shut it all down and came to find you."

He drew a deep breath. "I think Stanford's murder is the key. He's an incredibly powerful man, on a number of levels."

"Outside the British government, I presume?"

He grinned at her, sipped on his coffee. "You're fast. As a powerful man, he naturally has enemies. However, for one of them to get inside 11 Downing Street is difficult to imagine. It would be like a stranger walking in off the street to your White House."

"An inside job."

He nodded. "I'm sure as can be that Alfie Stanford's murder ties into our case as well." He drew a breath. "The only way we can get anywhere near Stanford's case is if we can prove whoever killed Pearce also killed Stanford. My father is in a position to help since he's still part of the British government."

Mike put down her coffee mug and rose. "Then let's put them together. If the murders are connected, there'll be something in Mr. Pearce's files proving it. Let's see what we can find."

Pearce's files were clean, organized, and easy to follow. He and Mike examined the satellite specs on the computer, and a troubling amount of financial data from various governments around the world. He cross-checked and, yes, Germany was on the list.

Mike pointed. "They keep coming up again and again. I can't imagine that the German government had Pearce and Stanford killed, so there must be something more tangible to show us the connection. We're just missing it."

He clicked open a few more files, felt his heart begin to race. He heard her sharp intake of breath. So Mike saw it, too. "Nicholas, look."

"Yes, it's a pattern." He pointed to the screen, typing one-handed without looking at the keyboard. "Look at this letter from Mr. Pearce—see? Words and lines that don't make sense."

"It's a code," Mike said. "Can you crack it?"

"I can, but it's going to take some time. Well, well, would you look at this?"

"Yes, yes, only some of the people he corresponded with have this strange code in their letters."

He tapped on the keyboard a few more times, moved the mouse around. The files separated themselves and flew about, rearranging on the screen. When they finished moving, she could see fifteen small blue folders, each with a name. But the names themselves weren't logical, they were jumbles of letters and numbers.

She was nearly plastered against him, as excited as he was. "Will it take you long to sort out who these folders belong to?"

"Too long, far too long. I have a better idea, but I'll need some help."

"What can I do?"

"Hand me the phone. Time to go to a higher power. I want to call Savich."

"Savich? He's not your boss directly, but he's certainly part of our chain of command. He might feel like he's undermining Zachery."

He stared up at that blond ponytail, her scrubbed face. She looked like she'd be carded for sure for a beer. "Nah, he won't."

She picked up his cell and handed it to him, only to have "Born in the U.S.A." trill from its small speaker.

Nicholas looked at the readout, raised a brow. "And isn't this something. What is this guy, psychic or something?" When she didn't smile, he said, "What?"

"As a matter of fact, he is, at least that's what I've heard."

"Sure thing. Right. Savich? How are you and Sherlock keeping this fine evening?"

37

10:30 p.m.

Savich said, "Sherlock and I are tossing more popcorn to Astro than we're getting in our own mouths. Now, listen, Nick, you want to tell me why I've been asked to sit on a SIRT board about you tomorrow morning?"

"Ah, so you've heard." He looked at Mike, who had an eyebrow raised. "Savich, Mike's here with me. Let me put you on speaker."

"Hello, Mike. Now, Nick, I've got to say you've set a new first-day-as-an-agent record. Are you okay? I heard you'd been shot, glad you at least followed **one** protocol today and wore your body armor. I trust you're fine physically?"

"Yes, yes, I'm fine, no problem. But I can tell you this for a fact, a real bullet to the chest hurts more than the rubber ones we used in training at Quantico. The vest stopped the bullet in its tracks, a right relief, but it still knocked the wind out of me. Since there was also a flash bang in the mix, I went down. I thought for a minute it was all over."

"And Mike?"

"I'm good," Mike said to Sherlock.

Sherlock said, "We heard about Nicholas killing the man who had a gun against your head, Mike. Thank goodness you're both okay. Dillon's right, a very hairy day."

"An afternoon neither of us want to repeat," Nicholas said, but Sherlock heard the layer of excitement in his voice. "Mike didn't flinch, a gun to her head and she didn't move an inch. The woman's brave, maybe a bit of crazy, too, remains to be seen."

"Yeah, right," Mike said, and smacked him on the shoulder.

"Savich, don't worry about tomorrow, it was a clean shoot. Everything will come out in my favor."

"I believe it will. Now, I had a feeling you needed something, so what can I do for you, Nicholas?"

"Well, if you have a moment, I'd like to talk to you about the case."

You're on suspension, Agent Drummond. There is no case, but Savich didn't say that, rather, "Tell me what you need."

"I need MAX."

"As it happens, one of your agents, Gray Wharton, called me an hour ago and asked for MAX as well. Talk to me."

"What did Gray ask for?"

"He saw code in some of your victim Jonathan Pearce's correspondence. He said everything was moving too fast, and it would take him too much time to crack it, and asked for help."

Another reminder you aren't the only hotshot computer knife in the drawer here in New York. Nicholas said, "Gray's exactly right. In some of Mr. Pearce's correspondence, there are short sections in code, although at first glance, if you're reading quickly or just skimming, you won't catch it. Not only is there a sophisticated code, but there's also a pattern in the correspondence. I've identified fifteen people whose letters have the same code. The rest of the correspondence seems to be normal conversations. The problem is, the fifteen names are also in some sort of code. Do you think MAX can crack it?"

Savich gave a little laugh. "Gray pointed out the same things. I got the bit between MAX's teeth two hours ago, so it's already done. That was one of the reasons I called."

"I'm glad to know Gray called first, since I'd seriously wonder if you could read minds from afar."

Savich went quiet for a moment. "Not quite," he said finally. "You were on my mind, with the SIRT and all. Then after Gray's inquiry, and that got me thinking. When MAX broke the code, I cross-referenced the names. I came up with a very interesting list of people. I'm e-mailing you the list now. They're from all over the world, Nick, mostly Britain, and we're talking high-level, important men. There's a zip file with the codex, too."

"Anyone from Germany, by chance?" Mike asked. "The men we've been chasing today are all German nationals."

They heard tapping, then Savich said, "There is one in the file from Germany, Wolfgang Havelock. He passed away last month, had a massive stroke at his London office. Now here's where it gets interesting. His son owns a multinational nano-biotech company—Manheim Technologies. His name is Dr. Manfred Havelock. Forty-seven, brilliant, rich as Croesus, and from what MAX has to say, he's doing some groundbreaking work in the nano-biotech field. The guy holds over seven hundred and fifty patents in neural pathway nanotech."

Nicholas said, "Brain implants. Savich, this is our best lead yet. Is there anything in the files on him doing less-than-legal work?"

"Right now, it looks like he's legit, but I'll set MAX to do some more digging, see if there's anything off-book we need to know about."

Nicholas's heart was beating a rapid tattoo, adrenaline pumping in his veins. "Brilliant. Perfect. Thanks for your help, Savich. You remember Pierre Menard?

FedPol? He's looking into the technology companies for us as well, see what he has to say about Havelock."

Savich said, "Good. And Nicholas? You see that Mike does the legwork on this. We don't want you getting yourself in any more trouble since you are, officially, suspended. Am I clear?"

"Clear as glass, Savich. Thanks for the list of names. Sherlock, give your husband a cookie, he deserves it, although I've got to say the popcorn really sounds good."

After Nicholas punched off, Mike said, "Let's call Menard."

But Nicholas had stopped moving, was staring intently at the screen. "Hold on. What's this?"

"What?"

"There's another file, buried in the system. I didn't see it earlier, and I guess Gray didn't, either. It's encrypted and password protected. Pearce has it set up in a subfolder, and it's hidden deep in the system files."

Mike said, "I'll bet Adam set it up for him. Can you get in?"

He hit some buttons on his keyboard, accessed the file. "Ah, yes, and now that we have the codex, we'll be able to break the code easily and see what it actually says."

Nicholas started to whistle, a song Mike recognized from his cell ringtone. The Sex Pistols—"God Save the Queen." The keys clicked in a steady staccato rhythm, and after a few moments, he said, "We're in."

What he saw made his eyes go wide.

"What is it?"

Nicholas flipped the computer around so she could see the screen.

"Ever heard of polonium-two-ten?"

Mike nodded. "Sure. It's what the Russians allegedly use to assassinate people. Are you saying Pearce has something to do with polonium?"

"There's a letter here, from Alfie Stanford to another man, Edward Weston. Dated last week. It's very brief, I'll read it to you. **'Weston, Havelock's making a move in black-market Russian polonium. I trust you'll see it goes nowhere. He is not to be trusted, and with Adam Pearce**

getting so close, we must not allow Havelock anywhere near the key. I fear his father may have told him about the U-boat and Marie's key and book. If so, it isn't good. Stop him, Edward.' It's signed **AS.**"

"**AS**—Alfie Stanford. So it is now, officially, tied together. A U-boat? What key, what book? Who's Marie? What is Mr. Stanford talking about?"

"I don't know."

Mike said, "Well, if this Manfred Havelock is trying to buy polonium on the black market, then we know there's something rotten going on here. Two murders and counting, very bad indeed."

Nicholas nodded. "Weapons-grade polonium has a very short half-life, which means Havelock would have to use it fast or lose it. Mike, you're right, this is very bad. We have a very serious problem on our hands."

38

Mike said, "We need to call Zachery, right now, get a whole team on his trail."

"I agree. But first I want to hear what Menard has to say so we can give Zachery all the information he needs."

Mike said, "If a German national who was a technology leader in nano-biotech is making a play for polonium, this scares me to my boots. This U-boat, if he finds it—"

Menard answered on the first ring. "I was about to call you, Nicholas. I have a name for you, someone I think will be of interest."

"Is it Manfred Havelock?"

"I see I wasted my time since you found this person on your own?"

"No, Pierre, you've verified it for us. It's a long story, but we cracked an encrypted laptop full of files, and there was a warning about Havelock trying to buy up Russian polonium stores."

"**What?** Polonium? This I do not know about. **Mon dieu.** This is frightening news.

Havelock, **il est très fou**—crazy in the head, you know what I mean? He is quite intelligent, but there are whispers, and more, about his personal choices. He is known to be unpredictable. He is a scientist, and owns a company that makes brain implants for amputees and such. I believe he would be the most logical choice behind the implant you saw today. But this—polonium?"

Mike asked, "Pierre, what rules did Havelock break to get on Interpol's radar?"

"He has been moving small water-fission equipment around Europe. He bought a load of equipment from CERN—the European Organization for Nuclear Research—in Geneva last year. Little pieces, here and there. We always watch what sort of machinery moves through Europe when they come out of the nuclear fission laboratories. On the surface, it was not of concern—Havelock is a scientist, as I said, a visionary, with many irons in the fire. It wasn't unusual for him to be gathering this type of material. But if you combine this machinery with black-market purchase of polonium-two-ten—" He drew a deep breath. "This is frightening indeed."

Nicholas said, "Is he trying to build his own nuke, only in a nanotech environment? A mini-nuke of some sort?"

"I hope not, but I am afraid that is very possible. There have been advances made in nanotechnology weapons, certainly. North Korea, Iran, Russia—even Cuba has opened a nanotechnology university, and is studying the possibilities. The Americans have perfected their pinpoint laser technology, and I am sure they are quietly trying to develop miniaturized nuclear weapons. But I was not aware this technology had advanced past the theoretical. Even the smallest crop of suitcase dirty bombs are still fifty pounds. Imagine a miniaturized nuclear weapon the size of what? A wallet? Smaller, even?"

"So we could be dealing not with a mini-nuke, but a micro-nuke, one that's virtually undetectable to our current safeguards."

"**Exactement.** I must go, Nicholas. I will initiate an urgent investigation into

Havelock immediately. The most recent information we have on him shows he lives in Berlin. I will start there."

"What do you plan to do, Pierre?"

"Park a satellite above his home and listen in to his conversations. If he is importing polonium, we must find out what he plans to use it for. I will keep you informed of what we find. Thank you for alerting me."

Mike said, "Pierre, this is a really sensitive situation. There's a lot more going on here than the polonium. Be careful, don't let Havelock know you're onto him. Be very careful."

The Frenchman laughed, a hard, empty laugh. "**Naturellement.** You as well. **À bientôt.**"

When the phone clicked off, Mike said, "Zachery. Now."

"Yes, we need to warn him."

Zachery sounded half asleep when he answered.

"Yes? Mike, what is it? You two didn't get shot up again, did you?" They could practically hear him snap to.

"No, sir. I have news about the Pearce murder." Mike told him about Menard, and Havelock, and the files, the polonium-210, and the frightening possibility of a miniaturized nuclear weapon. He was quiet for a minute, then, "I'll take it from here, Mike. I need to talk to the director. Good work."

"Sir, it's Drummond here."

"Talk to me."

"There appear to be a group of fifteen men in Pearce's files who are conversing regularly, much of it in code. They are all high-level government people, or financiers, from all over the world. I think Pearce was a member of a secret organization. There's something big going on, and if one of their members has stolen spy satellite specs on his computer, and another's son is trying to buy up polonium, we could be looking at a massive international problem. I respectfully request to come back on board, officially."

"Nicholas, I can't do that, not officially, at least. After the inquiry tomorrow, you'll be reinstated." There was a pause. "Do I want to know how you've come across this information?"

"No, sir."

"Probably from the same place Gray Wharton got what he gave me. I'll need a full report in an hour."

"Yes, sir."

When Nicholas punched off, Mike said, "No matter he didn't officially lift your suspension, we're still a go. I'll call Gray, you keep searching these files."

Mike watched him out of the corner of her eye as she dialed Gray's number. He was completely focused, eyes calm, inwardly directed.

She spoke to Gray, who sounded punchy, his eyes were nearly bleeding, he told her, but they were nearly at the same point. She rang off. "Where's the loo?" For a British accent, she didn't think it was bad.

That got a grin out of him, but he didn't look up, merely waved a hand. "Down the hall, to the right, the third door, I think. I'm still learning the place."

She grabbed her purse and stepped out into the hall. He was right, the bathroom was behind the third door. She took care of business, brushed out her hair and put it back up in a ponytail. She was confident Nicholas would find out exactly what was going on. She'd call Ben, see what he was thinking.

She snapped off the light and stepped out into the hallway, right into the barrel of a suppressed nine-millimeter Beretta.

39

Mike's heart nearly flatlined, but she didn't make a sound, didn't move. There was a man on the other side of the weapon stuck into her chest, a man she recognized. She had a fraction of a second to think **Grossman—what in the world is he doing here?** before he was on her.

He moved fast, but she was quick, too. She punched him hard in the chest, sent him stumbling back. She started to lash out a leg, knowing she had to take him down or she'd be in real trouble. Grossman anticipated the move, grabbed her ankle, and gave it a vicious twist. She was forced to spin with the twist or risk having her hip dislocated. But as she did, she brought her left elbow around and slammed Grossman in the temple. He went down with her, both of them crashing to the floor. She kicked him hard in the stomach, scrambled up and started to run, to call to Nicholas, to warn him, but Grossman got a hand on her shoulder and hauled her back down, flipping her on her stomach and getting an arm around her throat. She kept struggling, but his arm tightened, cut off her air, his forearm mashed up against her mouth, and she started to see spots. She clawed at his arm, but he didn't move, didn't let go, and her struggles became more feeble.

Nicholas, she tried to cry out, **Nicholas, be careful!** But no words came out. She couldn't breathe, and fear was metallic and hard in her mouth.

She was about to black out when Grossman eased up on the pressure, enough for her to gulp in a huge breath.

His breath was hot on her neck, his voice cold, hard, so unlike the harmless bibliophile he'd appeared this afternoon.

"Don't you dare scream, Agent Caine, or I'll shoot you and leave you bleeding out in this hallway, and don't think for a second I won't."

She nodded, still unable to swallow or breathe properly.

She realized she'd heard a bit of British in his voice, the cadence clipped, consonants long, and wasn't that strange, because he was American, from Chicago, hadn't he said that?

Grossman said against her ear, "We're going to walk down the hall to the library, and your friend is going to give me Pearce's files. Then I'll walk out of here, and no one needs to get hurt. Do you understand?"

She managed another nod. She had to warn Nicholas, but she was starved for air and her muscles were still sluggish. She'd been gone for only a few minutes, he wouldn't come looking for her yet, no reason even to wonder.

She pretended to lose her balance and hit her head hard against the wall. She hoped it was loud enough, hoped he believed her. He didn't. Grossman grabbed her, jerked her forward and yanked her ponytail. "Nice try. Stay on your feet, Agent, there's a good girl."

No more Brit accent, but she was sure his American was fake. **There's a good girl. Oh, yes, the Brits were up to their eyeballs in this—this what exactly?** But Grossman couldn't have killed Stanford. Who did, then, a partner or another member of this organization in Britain?

He yanked her ponytail again. She ignored the pain, stumbled to her feet, being as clumsy as possible, shuffling her feet along the wood floor, hoping Nicholas or Nigel would hear. It wasn't much since she'd taken off her boots, maybe she could kick back and—

"You don't want to cooperate, do you?" In one fast move, Grossman pressed her face against the wall. He kicked her legs apart and leaned hard against her. She felt a shot of panic.

He said in her ear, "Don't pull that crap again. I don't want to kill you, but I will if I have to." He pulled her away from the wall and shoved her forward, his hand over her mouth. "Now, walk."

The gun dug deep against her ribs when he forced her into the library. She knew she'd be of no use to Nicholas if he shot her.

Nicholas didn't look up. "Ben gave me the transcripts of e-mails between EP and Pearce. It took me a while, some real digging, then I found something—I think it's coordinates, latitude and longitude. The files here say they're looking for an old U-boat, World War One era. Pearce sent Stanford a message last night saying he'd found it. These coordinates are probably the sub's location. Adam was using the satellite to look for the sub."

"Thank you, Agent Drummond."

He whipped around to see Alex Grossman, his hand over Mike's mouth, a gun stuck in her ribs. And then Mike was in motion. She bit hard on his hand and he dropped her with a curse. "Nicholas—"

Grossman slammed his fist into her jaw and she went down.

Grossman pointed the weapon at Nicholas. "No, no, don't move or you're a dead man. You're very clever, Agent Drummond. You're quite good at this."

Nicholas was already out of his chair, hand reaching for his Glock.

Grossman leaned down and pointed the gun at the back of Mike's neck.

Nicholas slowly straightened. "What are you playing at, Grossman?"

Grossman's tone was pleasant,

conversational, even. "Stop moving, or I'll put a bullet into the back of her head. You have something that belongs to me. I need it back. A simple transaction, and no one gets hurt."

"Except Agent Caine." Nicholas saw she was pale, not moving. He couldn't get to her yet, he had to take care of Grossman first. He saw blood on Grossman's hand. Good, she'd taken quite a bite of him.

Grossman said, "You have a copy of some files you took from Jonathan Pearce's apartment. I'd like them, if you please."

He held out his left hand, blood still dripping, palm up.

"And if I don't comply?"

Grossman didn't move, but he smiled and nodded toward his finger, which was tightening on the trigger. "I'm not playing. The files or you'll have to find a new partner. Now."

Nicholas tapped a couple of keys, ejected the Tardis thumb drive, and tossed it to Grossman. He caught the drive and smiled, eyes never leaving Nicholas. "I'll need the laptop as well, if you please. And don't even think of tossing it at me, there's a good lad. Put it on the floor, kick it over to me."

Nicholas hit two keys on the laptop as he closed the lid, then used his foot to slide it toward Grossman.

"Thank you. I hope we don't meet again, Agent Drummond."

Grossman reached down, grabbed the laptop, and backed out of the room, gun pointed at Mike the whole time. Weston hadn't expected him to retrieve the files, but he had, he'd gotten everything, and now he would join Sophie on the plane and they'd be on their way to London. What was incredible was that he'd be able to present the Order with the coordinates of the sub.

40

Nicholas hit the intercom. "Nigel, lock down the house!"

He pulled Mike into his lap, and offered up a prayer of thanks when her eyelids started to flutter.

"Nicholas?"

"It's me, Mike."

She touched her hand to her jaw, jerked it back. "That jerk hit me with his fist."

"Believe me, I saw. Let me check." She yipped when he touched her jaw. "Not broken, but you're going to have a lovely bruise. Hey, can't you even take a bathroom break without getting into trouble?"

"Har, har. Did you get Grossman? Nicholas, the files—"

"No, no, stay put, would you? Don't worry about the files. Before I gave Grossman my laptop I blew both the thumb drive and the hard drive. He's out of luck. The files are destroyed. But that also means we don't have the files anymore." He gently eased her onto the sofa and jumped up to fetch a pen. She saw him write something quickly.

"What?"

"I'm writing down the coordinates to the sub. Don't want to forget them."

"And Gray still has the files. I've got to tell him." She got to her feet only to have Nicholas pull her close, for a moment. He closed his eyes and swallowed hard. That was twice today she'd had a gun pointed at her head. He pushed it away.

"Look at that bruise starting to grow on your jaw, I'm thinking maybe the shape of India. Who's the lamebrain now?" He lightly tapped her shoulder. "I mean, why on earth did you have to go to the loo?"

"Again, I say har, har."

"You stay put, I'll get Nigel. He's a bang-up medic. Royal Army Medical Corps, he can make doubly sure your jaw's okay. When I went into the Foreign Service, he joined me as a medic in the field, believed it would be smart to know how to patch me up, should I ever get myself into trouble." He walked quickly to the intercom, pressed the button, and called Nigel's name, then once more. But he knew, of course. "Grossman got to Nigel before he took you down."

"Go find him. I'll be okay."

He ran out of the library, down the stairs. There was a window open on the landing. Grossman's escape. It was a long drop down to the street. Nicholas looked out, didn't see anything, save for the large oak tree in the front yard. So he'd stuck the laptop inside his jacket, grabbed a branch, and swung himself to the ground.

Bastard.

Nicholas found Nigel crumpled on the floor by the kitchen door, out cold. His neck pulse was strong and steady, but Nicholas's fingers came away with a small smear of blood. An injection site, a small lump of fluid under the skin.

Drugged.

He shook Nigel's shoulder, but no good. He lifted the phone off the wall and called 911.

Nigel had fought him. There were dishes cracked on the floor, remains from their dinner, and a knife on the tiles about three feet from Nigel's outstretched hand. So, when Nigel saw Grossman, he'd reached for the knife, but Grossman was faster, had the element of surprise, and had managed to stick the needle in Nigel's neck.

Nicholas felt rage roil in his belly. Grossman had invaded his home, his sanctum, and hurt the two people Nicholas cared most about in this city. His anger mixed with the surge of adrenaline into a wicked cocktail. He straightened Nigel's bent arm and rose.

Grossman, Havelock, all of them, they'd made it personal. And now there would be hell to pay. Nicholas picked up the kitchen phone and called Zachery.

Hell to pay.

41

Over the Atlantic
British Airways Flight 176
Midnight

The wheels lifted off the tarmac. Adam allowed himself a nice deep breath. It seemed like the first time he'd breathed in hours.

Adam settled back in his big first-class seat. He couldn't believe he managed to get out of New York with the FBI searching for him. But he was better at hiding than they were at looking. After the disaster at his apartment, with Allie—**No, don't think of her, you'll fall apart again**—he'd fled blindly, caught the first cab he'd seen, and had it take him across the bridge into Brooklyn.

There he stopped at an Internet café, went to the British Airways database, and booked himself a ticket to Heathrow under the name Thomas Wren, a completely clean legend he'd built for himself. Wren was one of four new identities he'd created in the past month. Adam was paranoid to a fault, and constantly developed new safeguards to cover his back.

He was surprised at how much the first-class ticket cost, not that it mattered, since the credit card was false, anyway. Besides, he needed the privacy of the seat on the overnight flight.

Once he had the ticket booked, he dug into his backpack—glasses, a baseball cap, and a blond wig, plus a set of cheek inserts altered the basic structure of his face. He was ready to go through security at JFK despite the FBI's facial-recognition technology at the airports. He was completely safe since Thomas Wren didn't exist, and wouldn't be in their system.

Adam rarely flew, opting instead to drive, but there was no other way to get to Scotland, to the submarine, and the key. To stop this whole mess before it got out of hand entirely.

At ten thousand feet, he brought out his laptop. Normally, he never hooked into a plane's wireless system—their networks were of the least secure he'd ever seen—but he had no choice. There was work to be done, work he hoped would keep Sophie safe, and allow him to stop whoever in the Order was working with Havelock. Havelock's father, Wolfgang, had been a decent man, Adam's father had always told him, smart and loyal to the Order, loyal to a fault. But his son had been raised by his mother, insane, Adam had heard, confined to an asylum for twenty years before she'd died. Though a brilliant scientist, Dr. Manfred Havelock was nothing like his father. He was very likely as mad as his mother, a fetishist, obsessed with the Order, even though he wasn't a member.

Adam needed to see how far things had progressed in the past twenty-four hours, since he located the sub, a German U-boat **Victoria,** and told his father, so proud and happy, he'd done a little dance.

If Havelock was behind his father's murder, and Adam was sure he was, well, he couldn't, wouldn't, let him get away with it. Would he kill him? The thought settled deep inside him, it felt right. It would be justice, it had to be right.

But before he planned how to kill Havelock, he had another plan to implement, a plan to make Havelock want to kill himself.

He hummed as he broke through Manheim Technologies' sophisticated firewalls, not a problem, since he'd designed most of the codes that had gone into building the firewall systems in the first place. These legitimate jobs paid the rent and allowed him quite a bit of freedom. The companies he worked for had no idea he was the notorious hacker Eternal Patrol. Nor did any of them know he'd built separate back doors on all of his jobs, which allowed him unfettered access at any time. He didn't abuse this privilege, it was more insurance than anything else. But it was time to see what was really happening.

He accepted a cup of coffee from the flight attendant, slipped on his headphones, and went to work. He'd see how Havelock liked having his world dismantled, file by file, before he killed the bastard.

What Adam learned from Havelock's private files chilled him to the bone. Havelock's technological advances in nano-biotech were astounding, far beyond anything Adam had even heard of in a theoretical way.

One of the things Havelock had managed to develop was a brain implant that allowed for real-time observation and audio. It would change the face of stealth intelligence, and if it ever made it out into the private sector, there'd be no such thing as privacy left.

But by far the more serious and frightening files hinted at a miniaturized nuclear weapon, a mini-nuke, so small as to be undetectable, which could be put in place by a remote human-controlled camera, and go anywhere, anytime, into any country, any stadium, any park, any government building. They could assassinate heads of state in the blink of an eye.

Incredible. Havelock was developing personally targeted nuclear weapons.

There was even research into theoretical

DNA-driven bomb plans—ones that would only explode when in the hands of the target, utilizing an instant DNA check to ensure the recipient's identity.

He'd never seen anything so scary in his life. Especially when he took into account the key to Marie's weapon the Order wanted to find and destroy. To keep the world safe.

From all he'd seen, Havelock wasn't only going after the weapon the Order had been trying to locate for the past hundred years, he was planning to overthrow the entire Order, planting his own people to coerce the other members to do what he ordered, until he could get rid of them. He'd killed his own father, why not Alfie Stanford? Yes, of course he had. His assault had begun and now all he needed were Adam's coordinates to the lost U-boat.

The Order. No, the Highest Order, the group's original formal name. Adam's father had steeped him in its long, tortuous history, beginning with its inception at the end of Queen Anne's reign. Powerful men in England did not want to see the Catholic Jacobites bring back bloody revolution to England. They formed the Highest Order to help quash the Jacobites, and succeeded. And once their initial goal of keeping the Catholics off England's throne was accomplished, they moved on; their goal, to keep England safe. His father talked about one of their biggest failures in the nineteenth century, the needless bloody war in the Crimea—and one of their successes—their discovery that Jack the Ripper was one of Queen Victoria's family—and they'd ensured he was confined since he couldn't be arrested, all the proof still in the old files, kept under lock and key.

After World War I, the Order became a multinational group of fifteen high-powered men whose primary goal was to maintain the safety and security of the world by helping countries avoid wars and other destabilizing events. Adam knew if Havelock managed to take over the Order, he would pervert all the Order's goals. He would also be in a position to take down all world powers—whether they were on his side or against him.

His father was gone. It was up to Adam to make sure Havelock's plan didn't happen. He must protect the Order, protect its legacy—his legacy. And now he, a nineteen-year-old hacker, was charged with being their hero. Him, Superman. He thought about himself in tights and laughed.

Adam didn't leave cyberspace until the six-hour flight was nearly over. He'd drunk five cups of coffee, his fingers were jittery and sore, his body hopped up on caffeine and adrenaline and fury. He'd done some of the most beautiful work of his life, and Havelock's world would never be the same. He'd actually amazed himself. He'd captured all the data from Havelock's computers and encoded it, sending it back into the system with line after line of bugged code. Adam now owned everything Manheim Technologies had on their databases. Havelock would have to back off or Adam would sell it off to the highest bidder.

He sat back in the luxurious seat and shut his eyes for a moment, resting them from the glare of the screen. He was good, he knew that, better than good, but still, he needed a fail-safe. Something to insulate the data he'd assembled and destroyed. This was bigger than his concerns of going to jail, of never seeing the light of day again.

He opened his e-mail, and wrote a single line of code. He then created a false e-mail account, and filled out his father's e-mail address. He knew the FBI were in control of his father's accounts, and that Drummond character had close ties to the Order, no matter he didn't realize it. Drummond would see this e-mail, if he was looking hard enough.

It was all Adam could think to do under the circumstances. He could not, would not, allow the Order to be compromised, nor, he realized, could he let the Order's existence come to light, every media outlet in the world would tear them apart, blame them for everything that had gone wrong, not even realizing the Order had always endeavored to keep things in check. Without the members of today's Order, scattered across the globe, the world would be in far worse shape than anyone could imagine.

But Drummond—he was the safest bet. Had he seen the coordinates to the sub Adam had sent his dad? If he had, well, there was nothing he could do about it now. At least if he had the coordinates, Adam wasn't alone. He didn't hesitate; he memorized the coordinates to the sub, and erased them from his hard drive.

Adam realized he'd taken on his father's role, the protector, the guardian of the Order's secrets. Adam knew them all, and now it was his job to protect the Order.

He reread the e-mail, the line of code. If Drummond was as much of a hotshot programmer as people said, he'd figure it out. This was the only thing to do. As much as he hated to even think it, Adam couldn't trust anyone in the Order, not now that Mr. Stanford was dead.

He hit send.

The e-mail scrambled through Adam's

system, then shot off with a whoosh, bounced off fifty servers around the world, and was gone.

He started to close the lid of the laptop, but something caught his eye. The screen began to flash. As he watched, horrified, the corners of the screen shattered, like a piece of glass, and began to fold in on themselves, getting smaller and smaller and smaller, until all he could see was a tiny brown three-dimensional box superimposed on the black background, spinning and flashing, his name underneath.

Adam couldn't believe this, didn't have a clue how it could have happened—he himself had been hacked. Who could have done this? The FBI? No, there was no way. They were good, but not good enough to get into his system, not that quickly. And they wouldn't play games, either. They'd just shut the whole thing down and track him to his nearest location.

Reality hit him. He was too late. Dear God in heaven, he was too late. The Order was already compromised. Havelock was already in control. Had he really destroyed Havelock's assets? He didn't know.

With shaking hands, he clicked on the box.

The screen went black, then a message began scrolling across the empty screen and Adam felt all the blood leave his head.

We Have Your Sister. Come to London. Now.

42

Nicholas's House
Midnight

The ambulance had been prompt, the EMTs thorough, and as Nicholas watched Nigel sitting up, an ice pack on his neck, arguing with the EMTs, he counted his blessings.

They wanted to cart Nigel off to Lenox Hill Hospital for overnight observation, but Nigel was having none of it. Nicholas wasn't sure he agreed. Even though Nigel had regained consciousness quickly, he seemed a bit loopy.

But he refused to go and that was that.

The EMTs reluctantly agreed not to haul him in. The injection contained some sort of mild sedative, and it clearly wasn't long-lasting. As a precaution, they gave him a shot of Narcan, an overdose medication that would knock whatever drug he'd been injected with out of his system, and he'd be good as new in the morning.

Nigel insisted Nicholas continue working

on the case, that all he needed was a lovely night's rest.

One of the EMTs said, "He'll be okay. Make sure he gets plenty of fluids. If he decompensates unexpectedly—he's not gonna, don't you worry, but just in case— you call us right back."

The ambulance pulled away, the neighbors shuffled inside, and the night became quiet again. The spring evening had grown chilly, and combined with the sudden silence, the air seemed oddly clear and easily breakable. Like glass.

Oh, yes, this was definitely how he wanted to introduce himself to the neighborhood, as the victim of a home invasion in his first month on the street. At least his FBI badge had calmed some of them down and no one had called the police.

Waving jauntily to one last staring woman in a thick spa bathrobe, Nicholas stepped back inside the house. They all needed some rest, some time to recharge.

Nicholas knew in his heart Grossman was long gone. He recognized a fellow operative when he saw one. Grossman had been formally trained in counter-surveillance, like Nicholas. He'd slipped in, taken what he needed, and gotten out again in under five minutes. He'd only maimed, not killed; he clearly understood the level to which he could go without creating a serious problem for himself. Breaking into an FBI agent's home was one thing. If he'd killed Nigel, or Mike, that would be a whole different story.

If Nicholas weren't so pissed off, he'd admire the man.

Where did the Pearces fit into all of this? Adam Pearce, especially, the young hacker with clear abilities to gain access to very private information. The kid was another ghost. Where **was** he? How did a nineteen-year-old evade a city-wide dragnet?

By getting out of the city, obviously, right under their noses.

He walked into the house to see Mike sitting on a small loveseat inside the front door, lightly rubbing her jaw. She was still spitting mad; he was pretty sure her anger was the only thing keeping her upright.

"How are you feeling?"

"The EMTs said I had a purple bruise which would fade to a lovely lavender, my pride is pretty well trampled, but other than that, I'm fine. Do you know Nigel wanted to make me a cup of tea? I told him to make himself some tea and go to bed."

"Perhaps you should have let him. I hate to tell you this, but you look like you need a bit of a lie-down."

She squeezed her eyes shut and got to her feet, held her hands up in front of her. They didn't waver. She opened her eyes. "See? Solid as a rock."

He was dubious, but said, "Okay, then, if you're up for it, Gray's sent what he had of Pearce's files to my server. Let's go back to the library. I can access everything Grossman stole from us and maybe we'll see exactly what's going on here. I don't suppose you recall what I told you when you entered the library at gunpoint?"

"No, the hit to my jaw knocked it right out."

"Pearce and Adam were looking for a

German U-boat, **Victoria.** It was lost at sea—on eternal patrol—in September of 1917. Adam's been breaking into the satellite imagery from various defense contractors' very secret LEO-synchronous satellites for the past six months, ever since the technology was developed to allow the satellites to look **through** land to the water beneath. It's similar technology to Thales's Sentinel-Two satellite—very high-resolution imaging. The files show he'd narrowed the search to the North Sea, on the northern coast of Scotland."

"So why is this submarine so important? I mean, 1917, that's World War One. A lot of U-boats went down, right? What did **Victoria** have on board that was so special, even after nearly one hundred years?"

"You may be onto something there. According to Pearce's files, the sub was stolen from the Germans, and went down with some sort of key on board, and, of all things, some of the kaiser's gold, though I wouldn't count on that being accurate. No, what's vital to everyone is this key.

That's as far as I'd gotten in the files when you showed up with our friend Mr. Grossman, and he liberated my laptop. And my Tardis, I'll bet I never see it again. I loved that thumb drive. At least Grossman doesn't actually have anything, either."

"You really managed to wipe everything before he got his hands on any of Pearce's data?"

He nodded. They reached the library, and Mike didn't fight him when he pointed at the couch. She knew she was okay, but Nicholas seemed to like nursing her, and she couldn't say having him hover over her was the worst thing that had ever happened in her life.

Nicholas took the beat-up leather chair opposite her. She noticed he fit into it like it had been built around him. He pulled out another laptop.

"How many computers do you have?"

"Oh, a few. You never know when an operative is going to break in and steal one."

"An operative? You think Grossman is a spy?"

"I do. And a very good one, too. No doubt in my mind he's had covert training. To best Nigel, who's trained in hand-to-hand combat, and to best you, as well? To sneak in here like a thief in the night and confront us? And to put together the operation in only a few hours? He had no idea who we were until he came to Ariston's this morning. Yes, to plan and execute this so quickly, get past my security and my butler? And you? He's a pro."

"Maybe you need a dog."

He laughed. "Not a bad idea. Nigel would walk him and he'd hate that. Yes, that's good."

"Do you have any idea what Grossman's real connection was to Jonathan Pearce, and to Sophie?"

"Not yet, but I'd wager there was something in that book Sophie passed him this morning. She was so adamant he receive the package. You could tell he wanted it badly."

Mike said, "When Grossman had me around the neck, he said something I've heard you say—**There's a good girl.** And he sounded British before he realized it and reverted back to perfect American."

Nicholas perked up. "Interesting. No one ever checked him out, did they?"

"We had a lot of balls in the air today. I do remember he said he owned a pub. It won't be hard to see if he was telling the truth. We'll have to ask Ben, he can do a background on him. If Grossman's even his real name, of course. So Sophie's in on it since she did hand off the book to Grossman, plus she wasn't at all anxious to help us. And Adam, of course."

"Yes, the whole bloody family. A family enterprise."

Mike said, "All right, so tell me this, who does Grossman work for?"

"Haven't a clue. Not yet, anyway. This Havelock character, perhaps, or another bad guy who wants to benefit from Pearce's sudden knowledge of the submarine's location. Speaking of the sub, Adam's finding its exact location seems to be the trigger."

Mike sat forward, excited. "And once Adam told his father he'd located the sub, his father wrote to the list of fifteen men on his computer, the ones whose correspondence was sprinkled with code. You're exactly right—finding the sub was the precipitating event. Bad guys converged on New York. And here we are."

Both of them were thoughtful, silent. Mike said, "So we know the sub's resting place was narrowed down to the northern coast of Scotland."

"Correct. Actually, I know exactly where it is," and he waved a piece of paper.

She jumped up from the couch, grabbed his arm. "Nicholas, that's it. What Pearce said to Mr. Olympic when he was dying— **The key is in the lock**? That's exactly right, only it's not a lock on a door. It's a loch, L-O-C-H, like a Scottish lake."

He smiled. "You're amazing, you know that? Even though your jaw is a deep purple."

"Don't you start." But she grinned, so tickled she did a little dance, finished it off with a bump and grind and high-fived him. "Okay, James Bond, looks like I've done the heavy lifting—your turn now."

43

Nice moves." He settled more comfortably into the chair, clicked the track pad of his laptop and read. After reading for a while, he looked up. "Okay, here goes. You're perfectly right, Mike—the coordinates Adam texted to his father match a loch in northern Scotland, a Loch Eriboll. It's isolated, desolate, but it's also one of the few deepwater lochs in Scotland. The Royal Navy has used it for years. Submarines go in and out, frigates, everything. It was a perfect staging area, more so in World War Two than in World War One. Brit ships would sail into the loch, anchor for the night, for the week. Whatever was needed. There's even a spot where the sailors would disembark and use the white granite stones to spell out their boat's name on the hillside above the western edge of the loch."

"If it's so active, how in the world did they miss this?" Mike said. "There's been a German U-boat in the loch since 1917, and no one knew it? How can that be? I mean, I've never seen one in person, but it's a loch. They aren't **that** big, are they?"

"This loch is very deep, but you're right, it isn't very big. **Victoria** has been concealed all this time under a shelf of granite, deep under the water, but near the shoreline, and no one's ever seen it. Pearce and his son have been searching for it for years, but it wasn't until the satellite technology caught up that they could see through the mass to the submarine beneath. It's been cozied up in there for nearly a century."

"Holding a key and the kaiser's gold." Nicholas tossed her a bottle of water and she drank deep. "Thanks. Now, what is the key to? Is there an explanation in their files?"

"Didn't see it, but I'll look deep now that Gray's downloaded his file copies."

"Obviously it has something to do with the polonium and Havelock."

"Yes, which is rather unsettling. An unstable man looking to get his hands on some sort of a secret weapon? But it was 1917, what could it possibly be?"

Nicholas's house phone rang. "I see Nigel didn't toddle off to bed. Maybe he's ill, maybe—" He answered, and relief flooded his face. He listened for a few moments, then said, "Fine, fine. I will. Yes, I swear. Go to bed, Nigel. Now."

He clicked off, set the phone on the table beside him. "Nigel sends his best wishes for a good night's rest, and made me promise to get some sleep myself."

Mike nodded. "He's a good man. A good friend, too."

"That he is. Stubborn as a mule, though."

"He worries for you."

"I'm worried for **him,** damn it all. Bloody sod's being a bloody hero about the whole thing."

I wonder where he learned those moves. Mike laughed. "Relax. He's fine. I'm fine. Why don't you tell me the big surprise? Come, what did you just read?" She stretched and yawned. "And then we can get some sleep. This couch is very comfortable."

"I'll get you set up in one of the guest rooms."

"Aren't you going to sleep?"

He shrugged. "I will in a bit. I want to work some more first."

Mike curled into herself on the sofa. "Then I'll stay here. I like the sound your typing makes. It's very soothing."

She reached up and pulled the ponytail holder from her hair, slipped it onto her left wrist. She scratched her head and turned her head a bit, not too much, and her hair settled around her shoulders. She pulled a dark blue throw over her legs. "Tell me, Nicholas."

He'd been watching her. Now he tapped his fingers on the arm of the chair. "I found something. This is where it gets very interesting. It's a German sub, no doubt about it. According to Pearce's files, it belonged to Kaiser Wilhelm the Second, which makes sense, I guess, since his gold is supposedly on board. Some say Wilhelm was crazy, whatever, he got Germany into the war, as the leader, he cocked things up royally and they lost. He ended up abdicating the throne."

"Come on, Nicholas, what is it? You're

grinning like a madman."

"I'll tell you, but then you have to promise to go to sleep. It's late, and we have an early morning."

"That's so not fair."

"You need rest to heal. I want you to close your eyes and sleep for a bit."

"No, I don't need to—" And she yawned and yawned again, wider this time, covering her mouth with her hand. "Okay, so I'm a little tired, no big deal."

Even as he said, "Please, Mike, rest," she yawned again. He smiled at her. "I'll keep an eye on you."

She curled up against the couch pillows, settled in and closed her eyes. "Nicholas? Thank you, you saved me twice today."

Thank goodness he'd been able to. "Go to sleep, Mike. I'll be right here, watching over you."

"Okay." She opened her eyes and gave him a heartbreaking sweet smile. "But first tell me the big secret. Was **Victoria** important only because she belonged to the kaiser?"

Nicholas said, "No. Until Adam Pearce

found her, she didn't exist."

But her eyes were closed again, and she was under.

He got up and pulled the throw up over her shoulders, then sat back in his chair and watched her. She looked very young asleep, open, vulnerable, that sharp brain shut down.

He was very glad she was okay.

He read some more, then set the laptop on the floor and swung his legs over the side of the chair. He glanced at his watch—1:00 in the morning. Talk about a long day. He took a last look at Mike's still face, saw the small smile on her mouth and wondered what she was dreaming, certainly not about today. He saw Nigel's face again, confused, disoriented after the assault, but all right, and then, finally, he saw the faces of the two men who'd died at his hands today.

"Five minutes," he said to himself, and shut his eyes.

44

Lower Slaughter, Cotswolds
September 1917

William Pearce, 7th Viscount Chambers, was late, very late. A damnable tire of his brand-new Lagonda had given out near Burford and it had taken him nearly an hour to change it. He would have much rather traveled with his man Coombe, allowed him to handle the tire, but this was a top-secret mission, and Coombe wasn't cleared for this level of service.

Pearce was dirty by the time he finished, but no matter. He prayed the wheels would get him to the cottage, at least.

Fifteen minutes later, he pulled into the lane, and drove up the track to the small cottage. According to protocol, he parked in the trees and walked to the cottage. And was greeted with a horrific scene.

He drew his Webley. The cottage was pockmarked with bullet holes, chips of sharp stone littering the ground. The windows were gone, shards of glass daggered from the corners. The door was wide open, hanging loose on its hinges.

His heart pounded fast and hard, and he pointed his Webley in front of him as he slowly pushed the door farther back and stepped into the cottage. He knew the smell of death from the battlefield, and it was rich and hot in his nostrils, as was the smell of rot, human rot.

He sent up a silent prayer that his enemies were dead, not his friends, but his prayers were not answered.

He counted quickly. Five men. All shot, all gone. But where was the sixth? He counted again. It was not his imagination. There were only five bodies. Josef Rothschild was not among the dead. Where was Josef?

He moved through the cottage, stepping over broken glass and the ruined bodies of his comrades. These brave men. Fighting for the freedom of their country, their families, themselves. Sorrow overwhelmed him, but there was a single spark of hope.

A terrible thought came to him. Clearly

they'd been double-crossed, despite their many precautions. But by who? Not Josef, that was an impossibility. Josef Rothschild was the catalyst, the one who'd taken on the hardest role. Josef wouldn't ever betray them, not the man who'd saved him from the battlefield at Verdun. He saw him clearly, the German soldier approaching him with his bayonet fixed. Instead of running him through, he'd taken one look at the crown and star on Pearce's shoulders, knew he was facing a man of rank, and thrown down his weapon.

Without speaking, the German pulled him from the field and behind a screen of trees. Pearce couldn't fight; he was wounded too grievously. He assumed the Kraut wanted to take his time, do the job properly and thoroughly, but instead of slitting his throat, the big German had motioned for Pearce to stay quiet while he'd expertly stanched the flow of blood from the wound in Pearce's leg. He'd put a cigarette between his chapped lips and lit it for him, seemingly unconcerned that his hands and uniform were thickly covered with English blood. He sat back, lit his own cigarette, drew hard, blew out the smoke, and said in accented English, "We must stop this war, Colonel. Will you help me?"

It was an offer he could not refuse. And Rothschild was a man he'd trusted with his life, now many times over.

Pearce heard a noise toward the rear of the cottage, and rushed into the back bedroom. There was a small closet off the bedroom, and a trail of blood leading to the wooden door, not from.

There was a wounded man in the closet. Was it Josef? Pearce was a soldier. He knew what death looked like, in all its forms.

Still, Pearce was careful. He raised his Webley, stood to the side, and slowly opened the closet door. A shot came from the darkness. Thank all that was holy, he'd moved to the side.

Then he heard the cries of a child, soft, broken sobs.

He called quietly, "Who's there? Don't shoot. I mean you no harm."

The crying abruptly stopped.

Pearce edged forward, speaking softly, gently, telling the child he would not hurt him. He finally risked a look inside, and the scene broke his heart.

Josef Rothschild's broken body was inside the closet, in the arms of a very young boy. Josef's gun lay on the floor by the boy's hand.

Pearce did the only thing he could. He buried the men in the field behind the cottage, and took the boy home with him.

He knew the child's name was Leopold. Josef had told him that night on the hill at Verdun, while they smoked and plotted the downfall of the kaiser.

It was good Josef had told him the boy's name, for the child was deep in shock, the only witness to the murder of his father and five others, did not speak. He didn't identify the assailants. He only stared mutely for several weeks after the incident.

News of **Victoria** never came. The gold, Marie's key, and her book, were lost.

The war ended. Pearce and his wife, Cornelia, took Leo in as one of their own.

He legally adopted the boy before the year was out. In a house populated by women, it was a comfort for Pearce to have a boy at last.

Leo was a quiet, studious child. He did well with his tutors, and though he still didn't speak, he learned to read and understand English quickly, so that Pearce thought perhaps his mother, the kaiser's private interpreter, had already started him on the language.

Pearce caught the boy watching Cornelia at times, when she was reading to the girls. His heart ached because the boy watched her with sad longing, but he never complained. A boy needed a father, yes, but he needed a mother even more.

Every so often, Pearce would sit down with Leo to speak to him of the night his father died. To find out who had come to the small cottage in the Cotswolds, who had dealt the deadly blow to the Order.

Leo began to speak, but never about that night.

A small time of peace was upon them. The gold, the key, and the notebook were lost, yes, but the threat had been silenced, and the Order began to rebuild.

Leo Pearce went from a shy boy to a handsome lad to a smart, educated, but very quiet man. In 1936, he met a young woman named Grace, who didn't mind his silence. Within months, they were engaged to be married. In 1938, their first child came along, a boy they named Robert.

And in 1939, war came to them again. A war that clearly would outstrip the last one.

Soon after, Leopold Rothschild Pearce took tea with his adopted father. He carried a newspaper with him into the Carlton Club, sat down with his adopted father, pointed at a picture of a small dark-haired man, and said, "This is the man who killed my father."

Astounded, Pearce took the newspaper, and saw a photograph of a man standing on a dock, the forty-point headline screaming—**U-Boat Sinks America Freighter Ship.** The caption named the U-boat commander as Ludwig Reimand.

Leo's voice was soft and deep, his accent crisply British. "He was there. He was one of the three men."

Pearce was dumbstruck, and what he said was "I'm very glad you've told me, Leo."

Leo nodded. "I have been silent on this for too long. And you have been very kind to me."

"You are my son. I love you. And you are my heir."

This was said simply, and Leo swallowed back the emotion rising in him. Pearce smiled, and placed a comforting hand on Leo's arm. "Tell me about this man. Who was with him?"

Leo handed Pearce a sheaf of papers. "These men."

There were two more names—Dietmar Lusion and Wilfried Gobb.

"Lusion was the leader. He was the one who tortured my—Josef."

Pearce leaned forward, took Leo's hand. "No, no, Josef Rothschild was your father, and a very fine man as I've told you many times over the years, a brave man, a man who was willing to do anything to achieve an end to the war. He never gave them the information, did he?"

"No. He stayed strong throughout, but I heard his screams. I had an eye to the door, I could see the shadows of the boots passing the door as they paced, firing questions at him, trying to make him tell them where the kaiser's gold and the key were hidden.

"I believe the pain was too much and he suffered a heart attack, because one minute they were screaming at him, and the next, nothing. I heard them leave. I waited until I heard the car pull away, then I—"

Pearce touched his son's arm again. "And then I found you."

"Yes. There is more, sir."

Leo handed Pearce a letter. He read it quickly and looked up, face puzzled. "Your mother?"

"Yes. My mother was the one who stole the key from the kaiser. She was on the **Victoria.** She went down with them. They are somewhere north of Scotland.

Jos—my father, he told me about the weapon, about the mission, the gold, about my mother's final act of bravery." He played with the handle of his cup. "I did not think we would see the kind of war we experienced ever again. These men know about the key. They will be searching for it. We must find these men, and kill them."

Pearce studied Leo's beloved face. **You would be so proud of him, Josef, so very proud.** "Are you ready to join us, then, Leo? Join the Order? You of all people know it will be dangerous, very dangerous. You have a family to think about."

Leo Rothschild Pearce actually smiled. "You never hesitated, sir. My mother and father never hesitated. Even knowing they could die at any moment if they were discovered. So yes, it would be my pleasure, sir."

Pearce stood up, and Leo did as well. "We need to bring you to the Order. Come with me."

Leo said, "My mother's name was

Ansonia."

"I am very sorry." And he took Leo in his arms and held him close.

With the help of all of the Order's resources, it took three years for Leo and William Pearce to find and kill the three men who'd killed Josef Rothschild and the other members of the Order on that long-ago night in 1917.

William Pearce, 7th Viscount Chambers, passed away in 1962. After years of distinguished service, Leo Pearce, 8th Viscount Chambers, was named head of the Highest Order in June of 1963.

In 1964, Leopold and Grace's son Robert married Lula Harstock, only daughter of Lord and Lady Wentworth of Kent, and she soon after bore him a son. Sadly, days after his son's birth, Robert Pearce succumbed to a fever, and died. Within a week, his wife Lula had died as well.

And so Leo and Grace named the boy Jonathan, and raised their grandson. Leo told him the stories of their family—about the kaiser's gold, a lost key, and Madame

Curie's notebook, and her weapon, but most of his stories were about a brave and tragic young couple named Josef and Ansonia. Some of his grandfather's stories frightened Jonathan, but he loved to hear about his great-grandmother and Leo loved to talk about her.

Jonathan was a studious boy, like his grandfather, fascinated by books, and once he'd read a rare first-edition **Robinson Crusoe**, his path was set.

DAY TWO

45

London
6:00 a.m.

He hadn't slept.

The knowledge that they were so close, and that all he'd been working toward for so many years was about to come to fruition, kept him awake. Kept him from Elise's side as well. He couldn't focus on pleasure, or pain, in this state.

Havelock was good at waiting, he'd had to be. Learning patience was his first challenge in life. He knew how patience worked. Patience had gotten him through the hours at the hands of his mother. Patience had forced him to study, to get his degrees early, since the only way he could escape his mother's cruelty was to leave the house and never return.

Yes, he had always been good at waiting. And that wouldn't change now. He'd bide his time until everything was perfect, until he held the weapon in his hands, and then he'd strike like a cobra, fast and hard, and no one would be spared, unless he wished it. The world would be on their knees, and he would hold their fate.

He'd called for his plane at 3:00 and they left Brandenburg at 4:00 in the morning. London appeared on the horizon an hour later.

Havelock placed the call as they started in for landing. A screen emerged from the wall, transparent until Weston's face filled it. He looked alert, already dressed for their big day.

Havelock wasted no time. "Where do we stand?"

"Good morning to you, too, Manfred. If I'm not mistaken, you're calling from your plane. Am I to assume you'll be arriving shortly?

"Don't try my patience, Edward."

Weston's lips moved into what might be called a smile. "Fine. Grossman went wheels up at eleven-twenty p.m. New York time. He called from the plane; Ms. Pearce is safe and unharmed. He'll be on the ground in an hour, with Ms. Pearce in hand. Incidentally, he also managed to capture the data Nicholas Drummond copied from Pearce's computer this morning. We have everything we need. I cannot give you specifics since there was no wireless on Alex's plane.

"Now all that's left to acquire is Adam Pearce. He is the only one with the coordinates. Without him, we're where we were nearly a hundred years ago. Then there's getting into the submarine. I trust you have a plan?"

The look on Havelock's face was transcendent and eerie, frightening. Weston felt his blood run cold. Not for the first time, he wondered if he would make it out of this treachery alive. Aligning with Havelock was his only choice, he knew that, but the man wasn't entirely sane, and it was never more clear than when he wanted his own way.

"I do. My ship is in northern Scotland and is in position to move at a moment's notice. Get me Adam Pearce, Edward, and I'll have the key in my hand by evening."

"What about the FBI?"

"The Americans? By the time they figure

out what's happening, along with all the other law enforcement entities across the globe, it will not matter. We will have the upper hand."

"We need to watch our backs. This Nicholas Drummond character, he's smart, and I don't like having him in the mix. And you know who his father is."

"Then eliminate him, my dear Weston. I would set März to the task, but he has more important things to handle today."

"Killing an American FBI agent might not be the wisest course of action."

Havelock screamed into the screen, "He is of no consequence to me! Kill him!"

Havelock was breathing hard, too hard, he was out of control, and that wouldn't do. He smiled, outwardly calm again. "The only person who matters now is Pearce's son. I took the liberty of having him messaged—the poor boy believes he's smarter than I am, and broke into my business systems overnight. He did not succeed, though he believes he did. I sent him a message he won't soon forget. Now, find him, Weston. And take the girl to your estate in Oxford. She'll be secure there."

"Why take her there? Shouldn't we keep her close?"

"Edward, do as I say. I want her guarded. It's called leverage, Edward. Do you understand?"

He nodded curtly.

"Excellent. Adam Pearce will be in London soon, mark my words. And when he arrives to help the Order retrieve the key, we will be there to alter his path. I have all the insurance we need, ready to go at a moment's notice. If the authorities try to intervene, I will deploy the MNW."

Weston tried not to show any fear, any concern. But this? The miniature nuclear weapons were the last resort. "Have we come to that, then?"

"Perhaps not yet, but we must be prepared. I will not be stopped, Edward. Today is the day the Order goes down and a new one arises in its place."

46

Over the Atlantic

The sun hit Sophie's face. But that couldn't be right. Then she heard an odd, low background purr and was suddenly jostled a bit.

A plane. She was on a plane. She had an ache in her neck, and felt the slightest bit hungover. Grossman had stuck a needle in her.

She whipped around to see Alex Grossman sleeping on the seats opposite her, a small table in between them.

All she wanted to do was kill him, but he must have cat senses, because as she threw off her seat belt to attack him, his eyes flew open and he caught her arms midair.

He couldn't push her back into her seat because the table was in the way. He held her locked motionless for a moment, looking at her, just looking. "Don't be afraid, Sophie, I'm not going to hurt you. I'm trying to protect you."

"Yeah, right. Protect me? By kidnapping me?" She jerked her arms free and punched him in the face, but he caught her wrists this time, wouldn't let her move. They were still leaning toward each other, close, the table between them.

"Good shot."

"Give me a gun and I'll show you a good shot."

"Sit down now and we'll talk. I'll tell you everything, okay?"

What choice did she have? She nodded and he lightly shoved her back into her chair. The plane hit another pocket of turbulence. "Put on your seat belt."

She did, then watched him fasten his. "Where are you taking me? Where is this plane going?"

He glanced at the flight path on the screen in the table. "To London. We're about an hour from the London City Airport. After we land, we're headed north, to a safe house, where you'll be protected by the Order until we get our hands on the key and the book."

"Don't forget the millions of dollars in

gold bars. And after Adam tells you the exact location of the sub, I'll be free to go?"

"Of course."

"Where is Adam?" **You bastard** was unspoken but clear.

Grossman frowned a bit, stroked his chin. "I was hoping you knew. He called you last night, gave you instructions to run. Where were you heading, when I met you in the garage?"

"France."

"Well, no matter, now you're in England. Your disguise was top-notch, your passport as well. I was impressed. Adam does good work. He was going to meet you in France?"

"That's none of your business. Who are you, really?"

"I work for the Order, it's the truth."

"That book I wrapped for you this morning, there was something inside, wasn't there?"

"The SD card with the exact location of the sub, among other things. Your father was supposed to have it waiting for me."

"What do you mean? It wasn't in the book? Then where is it?"

"That big son of a bitch British FBI agent took it from your father's apartment before he had a chance to put it in the book. I took the liberty of getting the files back. They do belong to us, after all." He pulled Dr. Who's Tardis thumb drive out of his pocket and waved it, nodded toward the laptop on the chair beside him.

"Where did that ridiculous Tardis come from?"

"Drummond had already uploaded all the information from the SD card onto this nifty thumb drive, easier to deal with."

"Did Agent Drummond see your face?"

"Yes. There was the FBI woman as well, a good dirty fighter, but not good enough."

Sophie lowered her head in her hands. "Great. The FBI had me under surveillance, and you stole the info from them. You know they're going to come after us. How did you get me out of the garage without their seeing us?"

"In a diplomatic car, you were tucked nice and snug in the trunk. As for the FBI, we're in England now. They won't come here. You'll be safe. Sophie, please, I'm telling you the truth."

"Your American accent slipped. You're British, aren't you?"

"Yes. I'm from Cambridge originally, but my folks moved to London when I was a boy."

"All right, keep talking."

He sat forward, his hands clasped together on the small table. "Your father was the Messenger for the Order for years, as you well know. He was responsible for moving delicate information around to the members. However, as of yesterday, everything's changed. Three members of the Order are suddenly dead, and our channels were compromised beyond repair. Here's the bottom line. It's up to us now. You and me, and Adam. You know what's in the missing sub, don't you?"

"Gold, a key, Marie Curie's books, instructions, I heard Dad say."

"The key is to a very powerful weapon, a weapon we can't allow out into the world. No government can be trusted with it." He thought of Manfred Havelock. "Nor any single individual. We must find the key and the book and destroy them."

How could a weapon created by Marie Curie a hundred years ago be of any use today? Radium, yes, she and her husband had discovered both radium and something else—polonium. But what good would either do today? But she didn't ask. She saw Grossman was still looking at her, studying her face. Did she believe him?

"You've known me for a couple of years, Sophie. You know your father trusted me. And now that he's dead, my only purpose is to keep you and Adam safe and to protect the Order and what we stand for."

When she remained silent, he pushed a can of orange juice her way. She cracked it and took a big sip.

"The drug I gave you, it makes you thirsty, so drink up."

She finished the can. She pushed her hair back, realized he'd taken her wig. "You said three people in the Order died? Who besides my father?"

"Wolfgang Havelock—he had a stroke last month. On the surface, it looked like natural causes; he'd had an aneurysm clipped the year before, but after what's happened today, I've changed my mind. This morning, about the same time your father was killed on Wall Street, Alfie Stanford, the leader of the Order, was murdered as well, here in London, and the contents of his safe, with all our fail-safes and the other SD card, were taken."

Alfie Stanford dead? She hadn't heard. It didn't seem possible. Both Stanford and her father. They'd been close friends since before she'd been born. "That's crazy, it sounds like a B movie."

Alex leaned back in the chair, his eyes on her face. "B or C, doesn't matter. The fact is, the Order is under attack. It's Edward Weston who is now the acting leader. Do I trust him? He has been a member for over thirty years, so yes, I suppose I do. But our files have been compromised, both by Mr. Stanford's murderer and by the FBI. Sophie, I'm afraid, for the Order, for the future of mankind."

Did she believe him? "Who **are** you?"

He crossed his arms on his chest. "Alexander Shepherd, at your service."

"So you're like a super-secret double agent or something?"

He smiled, and his face changed utterly. He no longer looked terrifyingly brutal, not with that white-toothed smile. He was wearing a gray jacket over a white button-down and jeans. She'd never noticed him dress like that before. She'd always seen him in casual gear, chef's gear, perfect for running his restaurant.

He looked younger than she'd thought, younger and more vital than the quiet, watchful book lover who'd stopped by the store on the weekends when she worked.

"Or something," he said. "I'm not a full member of the Order. I'm sure your father has explained how it works, it is your legacy, after all. I'm rather like you, aware of the Order's existence, its mission, and its goals. Then I was assigned to be your father's backup, for lack of a better term. I was in place to keep an eye on him, to make sure he was never compromised."

"So you don't really own a pub?"

"I do, but it's a cover. I love the place, it's become a passion of mine. One day, I might even own one for myself, more a restaurant than a bar and grill, I think. I like to cook, I'm good at it." He paused, his hand tightened into a fist. "No time soon, though, I doubt."

"Are you really a book enthusiast, or were you just pretending?"

"I love books. I loved Ariston's. I hope, when all of this is over, you'll be able to keep the store open. It would be such a shame to see it go away. I know your father wouldn't want to lose it."

She swallowed, hard, fighting back tears. "I don't know what I'll do. My dad was the one with the grand passion."

Alex leaned across the table. "There's more, Sophie. I was also tasked with protecting you, should something happen to him. That's what I'm doing. If anything, be glad I removed you from the FBI's scrutiny."

She looked at her hands clasped together in her lap. "I still don't understand why you had to drug me and kidnap me. Would it have been so difficult to simply tell me the truth?"

"Please forgive the attack, the needle. I felt it best to eliminate your options last night. I needed you safe on the plane before I went to the Brit's house to get the SD card before the whole world found out about the Order."

She stared at him, slowly nodded. "I'll forgive you if you tell me one thing."

"What's that?"

"This weapon that could destroy the world in the wrong hands. What is it, exactly?"

"It's better, safer, I think, that you don't know. If—when—this all works out, then I'll tell you. Then you can decide if you wish to continue with your father's work or continue in your current career as a translator. Okay? Will you accept that?"

When she didn't answer, he reached out his hand to her. "Trust me."

"No," she said, ignored his hand, and looked out the small window to see London below. "You said you're afraid they're trying to get their hands on Adam. Who is 'they'?"

"It's a he. The man's name is Manfred Havelock, the son of the Order member who died last month."

"Or was murdered, you think. By his own son?"

"I don't know, but given who Havelock is, I wouldn't doubt it. Tell me how you were supposed to contact Adam."

She reached into her pocket for her phone. It wasn't there.

"He was going to call me. I suppose you left my phone behind in New York?"

"Yes, but I spoofed it first before I kicked it under a car in the UN garage. I was hoping he was going to call." He handed her a new phone, similar to hers. "This one's clean, a burner. When he does call, it will scramble the signal, moving from your number through multiple servers to this one. It's the most secure way I could come up with on short notice."

"And the FBI won't be able to track it?"

"They might, but we're far enough ahead of them it won't matter. We're about to land."

47

Nicholas's brownstone
5:00 a.m.

He had strange dreams of being locked away in a tiny cage, being dive-bombed by killer bumblebees. How ironic—death by bumblebee. He flicked a hand to make them go away, but they flew closer, and they were loud, right in his face now—the bumblebees morphed into his phone, vibrating on the table next to him.

He fumbled for his mobile, saw the time—5:05 a.m.—and who was calling. Zachery. That brought him instantly awake. This wasn't good news. Mike hadn't stirred, still asleep on her back on the couch, an arm thrown over her eyes.

He shook his head to clear out the last two bumblebees as he answered. "Sir?"

"Drummond, I need you here immediately. You and Agent Caine. You're being reinstated right now."

He jerked to attention. "Reinstated?"

"Yes. Now, get your butt in here, double

time. We have a big problem."

"Sir, what's happened?"

Zachery sighed into the phone. "Sophie Pearce has been kidnapped, right out of the private garage at the UN last night."

Nicholas was on his feet. "But she was under our surveillance, wasn't she?"

"Digitally, yes. There was nothing amiss with her phone. We found it in the UN garage. Get in here, and I'll brief you. I don't suppose Agent Caine is with you?"

Yes, but it's not what you think. "She's asleep on the couch. After our visitor last night, I thought it best she stay here where I could keep an eye on her. I'll wake her."

"Hurry, Nicholas, they're hours ahead of us."

He hung up, and Nicholas slipped his mobile in his pocket.

"Mike, wake up." She rolled and stretched, then opened her eyes. The look on his face brought her upright fast. "What's wrong?"

"Sophie's been taken."

"How? We were watching her, weren't we?"

"Clearly not closely enough. How's your jaw?"

"I'm good," she said and stood, looking for her Glock.

He said, "It's on the table. You looked uncomfortable, so I took it off you."

She smiled at him. "Thanks. Tell me you didn't keep working all night?"

"No, no, I slept a few hours."

She clipped the Glock to her waistband. "What color am I this morning?"

"Your bruise has faded to a nice lavender, probably quite fetching with the right accessories."

"Yeah, yeah, make me laugh. What are we supposed to do about this?"

"It appears I've been reinstated. Zachery wants us downtown, fast."

Mike's blood stirred, she felt energized, as did Nicholas, she thought, as they hurried down the stairs, past the landing where the NYPD had decided Grossman had entered the house. Through the windows, Nicholas could see it was still dark out, the sky an inky black edged in silver, the darkest hour before the dawn.

"Hold on a moment. I need to check on Nigel."

His worry was unfounded. He found Nigel sitting in an armchair in his living room, reading a book.

Nicholas said, "Needed a wee bit of edification this morning, did you?"

Nigel closed the book and started to his feet. Nicholas gestured for him to stay put. He looked fine, just tired.

"Everything okay?"

"Yes. I couldn't sleep. Shall I make your breakfast?"

"We've been called in. You, stay put and rest. Orders. Understand?"

Nigel saluted smartly, smiled after Nicholas as he ran down the stairs to the foyer, where Mike was waiting, listening to a message on her cell phone. They went out the front door and onto the street.

He said, "I'll drive, where are the keys?"

Soon he was headed south, through the darkened streets of Manhattan, as Mike listened to her voice mail. She said, "Ben left me a message. He found Adam Pearce on the crime scene video from Wall Street yesterday morning, and again from videocams, at the shoot-out at his girlfriend's apartment." She shook her head. "To know both his father and his girlfriend were murdered and not be able to do anything about it—that had to be very hard."

Nicholas drove around a slow-moving cab trolling for an early-morning fare. "It feels like someone—Havelock, maybe—is systematically driving this kid toward a specific goal, and that's gotta be this key, which, in turn, leads to some sort of fantastic weapon. He has some seriously bad people sending him hard messages."

"And now they've got his sister, for leverage. I hope we find Sophie with him, and they're both safe. That's wishful thinking, isn't it?"

He nodded.

She said, "It strikes me we missed something at Allie's apartment. Neither of the Germans had the files on them. So who took it?"

"Adam. Clearly."

"Maybe that's why he was on the video.

He was at Allie McGee's apartment to get the files, but he was obviously followed. They probably also followed him to Ariston's yesterday morning too, wanting to get their hands on the SD card."

"Sounds good to me." He pulled around a garbage truck, got the finger from a driver.

"We need to get eyes on this Havelock character. Let's be sure to call Menard after we're briefed on Sophie." She punched his arm. "Hey, no SIRT for you."

"Unless there's some rule I don't know about," he said as he turned into the garage under Federal Plaza.

When the doors opened on the twenty-third floor, Mike slapped her access card against the reader and the door unlocked. They went straight into the senior staff hallway.

The offices were already a hive of activity, people hustling about, hurrying down the halls. It was not an atypical scene. The New York Field Office routinely did 5:00 a.m. "knocks," serving warrants to criminals. These knocks were witnessed by the team in a control room, with multiple wide screens on the walls. Almost as good as being there themselves.

But there wasn't a knock this morning, and the people who were here had only one thing on their minds: finding and saving Sophie Pearce.

When they came into Zachery's office, he rose to stand behind his desk. "Come, come." Zachery looked utterly whacked, Nicholas thought, his eyes bloodshot, his fine suit on the bitter edge. At least he'd been able to put on a fresh white shirt and shave.

Zachery said, "You made good time. Follow me."

He led them to the control room one floor down, where Ben, Gray Wharton, and Louisa Barry were already assembled.

The wall of screens was up and running as well. Mike took one look and said, "That's the front of the United Nations. They took her from the UN? It's one of the most protected spots in New York."

"Watch the tape," Zachery said.

Gray Wharton looked even worse than

Zachery, clothes wrinkled, his salt-and-pepper hair sticking straight up, bags under his eyes. "Here we go," he said and queued up the scene for them. He hit play and the feeds began to roll.

Zachery said, "So the United Nations security people knew Sophie's father had been killed. She came in yesterday afternoon—after you interrogated her—and stayed until after eight-thirty p.m. They saw her leave. Gray?"

Gray moved the tape forward a few minutes, and Sophie Pearce walked down the grand glass stairs in the UN's front lobby.

"So far, so good," Zachery said. "But when the security team recycled the feed for the day, one of them spotted Sophie again. She hadn't left after all; she'd just ducked into a doorway. One that leads down to a private garage below the building."

The view on the wall changed.

They were now inside a well-lit parking garage. The view was of the door to the space. A woman with black bobbed hair and dark sunglasses stepped out of the door.

Mike leaned closed. "Freeze that, and blow it up. Are you sure it's Sophie? It doesn't look anything like her."

Gray said, "Watch." He hit a few buttons and another screen popped up with a picture of Sophie Pearce on one side, and the half-silhouette from the garage on the other. "I ran facial recognition on the feeds as soon as we got them. It's her, all right." He hit the button, and the parameters started to align. Mike watched the red triangles layer over both faces until they flashed green. He was right, this was Sophie Pearce.

"And who's our friend there?" Nicholas asked, pointing toward the main screen where a man wearing a baseball cap was leaning against a car, slightly out of view of the camera.

Gray said, "He stays out of the frames, but I caught a jawline profile, and it was enough to make a match in the system. The guy in the garage is the same one who visited Ariston's yesterday."

Gray pressed another button, and a different series of pictures flashed up onto the screen. Mike was shocked when the photos aligned.

The man they showed wasn't wearing a hat. He had a closely shaved head, and stared out at them, ready, focused, eyes on Sophie Pearce.

She said, "Alex Grossman. He's the son of a bitch who broke into Nicholas's place last night and clocked me on the jaw."

Nicholas said, "He took Sophie first, then came to my house. Show us the rest, Gray."

They watched the short fight, the needle in the neck, Grossman laying her in the trunk of a diplomatic car.

Nicholas said, "Very fast, very smooth. What's his involvement here? Is Grossman his real name?"

Gray shook his head, a small frown playing on his lips. "Not according to Interpol. It took some back-end work, but I identified him. Grossman is an alias. His real name is Alexander Shepherd. And he works for MI Five. British intelligence," he added. "He's been on special assignment for the past three years, reporting directly to the Exchequer, Alfie Stanford."

Nicholas started laughing, shaking his head and laughing. He said, "You mean to tell me the bastard's on our side?"

48

26 Federal Plaza

"Yep, that's exactly it," Gray said.

"Bloody MI Five doesn't even bother to inform us they have an operative on our soil, in our operation? I'm calling them immediately. There's no excuse." But it was Alfie Stanford giving the orders, he thought, and now that he was dead, who was directing Grossman?

Zachery held up his hand. "Here's the bottom line. You and Mike are going to London. New Scotland Yard, MI Five, and FedPol all want a crack at this submarine. And to reward you, I suspect, since you are the ones who found the coordinates to the sub, you're to be allowed to be on the ground in Scotland when they bring her up, if that is even possible."

Nicholas said, "So we're actually going to be involved in recovering the sub? In getting the key?"

"Yes," Zachery said. "They will provide you diving gear. I know Mike doesn't dive, but I assume you do, Nicholas?"

"Yes, sir."

Well, of course he did. She wanted to punch him. No, she should learn, and she would.

"Good. All of you listen up now. A naturalized American citizen was killed for his knowledge of this submarine, and now his daughter has been kidnapped. We're a part of the international investigation now. And you're in luck, the director has sent his G-Five for you to use. We need totally secure communications while you're in the air, and he clearly feels you're the right agents for the job, or he wouldn't have given his blessing to this little junket. The Gulfstream is waiting for you at Teterboro."

Mike said, "Submarine rescue aside, why do you think Sophie's been taken to London, sir?"

"Gray? Would you like to explain?" Zachery said.

Gray put another image onto the screen. "I ran facial recognition on every airport, bus terminal, and train station in New

York. This popped up."

There was a grainy image of a man carrying a woman across a tarmac. Mike recognized the pair as Alex Shepherd and Sophie Pearce. He'd pulled off her wig and her dark hair was tangled over his arm.

Nicholas asked, "Where is this?"

"Teterboro, late last night."

"Did you get the tail number of the plane?"

"I did. It landed at London Airport about an hour ago, the private airport. They're already off the grid again."

Mike said, "London makes sense, since the majority of the men Pearce were in contact with were in the UK."

Zachery said, "Gray has prepared a laptop for you uploaded with all the additional files. I understand he already replaced all the SD card files Grossman tried to steal. It's good you managed to erase everything before he got his hands on it. In the meantime, Nicholas, I expect you to show me some of that razzle-dazzle magic computer work you're famed for.

Find out why a group of international leaders want this lost submarine so badly, and what the hell the key in Loch Eriboll opens."

"With pleasure, sir."

Zachery turned to Mike. "Mike, once Nicholas decodes the files, you will share with Interpol and Scotland Yard what the link is between the fifteen men Mr. Pearce was conversing with, and start rounding them up for questioning. And find out everything you can about Shepherd and this connection of his to MI Five."

"Yes, sir."

Zachery flicked off the screen. "People, we're an inch from figuring out what this weapon is, and why Havelock's been buying up polonium. The Brits claim not to know; let's see if they're being truthful with us. If they're involved, they very likely have a line on Adam Pearce. Find him, find Sophie Pearce. The two are clearly tied together."

Gray handed Nicholas the laptop. "Everything I hadn't already sent you has been loaded, plus a few extras you might need along the way. I'll be linked to you in real time."

"Brilliant. Thank you."

"One more thing," Zachery said. "There's a full-scale international alert for Manfred Havelock. He's gone to ground. He was in Berlin as of last night, but his jet took off very early in the morning, and they didn't file a flight plan. Gray is going to keep looking for him; he did such a great job finding the Fox when she snuck off to France, I'm sure he'll find this guy."

He leaned on the table, suddenly serious. "You two listen to me. You be careful. We have multiple agencies involved. You're going to be on foreign soil, and this time, Nicholas, you work for the FBI, you represent the United States, so there will be no rogue Bond crap. I regret taking all the fun out of your life, but no bombing, no shooting, no kidnapping of thieves. You hear me?"

The corner of Nicholas's mouth kicked up. "Roger that, sir. Who is our contact on the ground in London?"

"Who else? Your old boss, Hamish

Penderley. Now, go find Sophie Pearce. Find her alive, and her brother, and recover this weapon, whatever it may be, and don't kill any more people, unless it's absolutely necessary, or so help me God, don't bother coming back."

49

6:00 a.m.

Per standard operating procedure, Nicholas and Mike had small go bags stashed in their desks—a change of clothes, a spare weapon, ammunition, two disposable cell phones, and a tablet computer. Nicholas had also included a bevy of computer cords and other tools of the trade he felt might be necessary.

Mike looked at the clean jeans, the clean blouse, the clean underwear, and couldn't wait to wash and change in the plane lavatory. No one had said a word about her wearing Nicholas's white shirt. Things were so tense, so focused, maybe no one had noticed.

They grabbed their bags and their Glocks and Gray met them in the hallway. He handed them some papers.

"Here are your official papers allowing you to operate on foreign soil, so there'll be no running afoul of the British government."

Mike clapped him on the shoulder. "You always think of everything. Thanks, Gray. Listen, why don't you go take a twenty-minute catnap? We'll be in touch as soon as we're up and running on the plane."

He smiled. "I look that bedraggled, eh? Smell a little ripe?"

"No, nothing like that. You're going to make Nicholas think FBI agents don't ever sleep."

"What did you say? We're allowed to sleep?" And Gray laughed. "I wish you'd told me sooner. You two be careful." He tapped his temple. "I'll be ready for you when you're in the air. Twenty minutes will do me fine."

Ben was waiting for them in the garage by the Crown Vic. "I'm going to drive you to the airport. There's more, and Zachery needed to get you guys on the plane as soon as possible."

When Ben eased into traffic, he said, "Now, about the brain implant. I've been doing some research. Havelock's company is the only one I could find that's close to having patents in this area. He's really advanced. I mean, this stuff is space-age. There's nothing like it on the market. The composite material alone beingbiologicalinnatureisgroundbreaking stuff. If Havelock **is** behind this, he could have eyes on the ground everywhere."

Nicholas said. "Do you think our MI Five friend, Alex Shepherd, has one?"

"It's possible, depending on who he's working for now, what with Mr. Stanford murdered. Like you said, Nicholas, he's supposed to be on our side, but he certainly hasn't acted like it. Is he now one of Havelock's soldiers? Was he all along? I mean, taking Sophie, what's that all about? I'm hoping when you talk to MI Five, Mike, they can tell you what's going on now. At the very least, they might know enough to help you guys guard your backs. In any case, we need all the information we can get on those implants."

"Let me guess," Nicholas said. "You want me to break into the computers of Havelock's company."

"You're quick, Sir Nick. I didn't want to mention it in Zachery's office, but that's it exactly. If this brain implant is what we think it is, a live feed which can be sent anywhere in the world undetected, maybe there's a program on his computers to control it. And at the very least, we can find out who he has in the field, and what they're looking at, specifically."

"I'll do my best, Ben, and don't call me sir. No luck on the German in a coma?"

Ben met his eyes in the rearview mirror. "He had the gall to die an hour ago."

"I see." Another man dead at his hands. But he felt not a lick of remorse. Both of those men would have happily dispatched him and Mike, after they'd murdered Allie McGee to get to Adam Pearce.

Mike said. "Yeah, and here I was hoping we'd have a chance to interrogate him. Since neither of the Germans had implants, they were only hired muscle sent over to do a job, probably didn't know squat. I wonder why Havelock sent some operatives into the field with the brain implants, and some without."

"That's a question we need to address," Ben said. "Were the second set of thugs under Havelock's orders or someone else's? We haven't considered there might be more players in the game."

Nicholas said, "It's a good point, Ben, especially if there's been a leak about what's in the submarine. Very high stakes, evidently. What we do know is that Adam Pearce is the staked goat in the middle. Everyone would want him."

Mike said, "Ben, did you see something that made you think there are multiple people with the implants?"

"No, but I have a gut feeling about this."

"Good enough for me," Mike said. "We'll be on our guard, then." She looked back over the seat at Nicholas. "With any luck, Mr. Computer Whiz here will be able to get into Havelock's files and we'll know."

Ben nodded. "You two be careful."

And he pulled through the gates at Teterboro.

Ten minutes later, they were wheels up.

Their pilot, who'd flown three different FBI directors, came over the intercom. "Dan Breaker, at your service. We'll be on the ground in London in five hours. Agent

Caine. I've turned on the secure communications system. Feel free to plug in. Hit the green button if you need anything. There's food and drink in the galley, help yourselves. I'm going to be hauling ass across the Atlantic. This lovely beast will do four hundred eighty knots, and it's windy up here, we have a great tailwind of almost eighty knots. My copilot, Tom Strauss, and I, we're going to see if we can break a record getting across the pond."

Mike pressed the green button. "Does the director know you two are speed demons?"

A ghostly laugh from the overhead. "Yep. Who do you think bought us this beautiful baby?"

They didn't waste any time. Mike headed for the lavatory to clean up and change, and Nicholas opened the loaded laptop Gray had given him and inserted an earwig into his right ear. "Gray, are you awake?"

"I'm here, Nicholas."

"Good. I'm going to break through Havelock's firewalls and put a worm into his security system on his website, then see what information I can pull down. It will flow directly to our computer. It's going to take a while to see any results, but it's a start."

"Sounds great. I'll work the back end for you." Nicholas watched the computer screen in front of him segment, saw Gray in the upper right corner. Gray started to type, and Nicholas turned to Mike. "Hey, you're looking good, all clean and polished, and the lovely lavender of a few hours ago has faded to a light pink, with a touch of green to add interest. We're wired in. Are you all set?"

"Absolutely." She waved the case file at him. "I have plenty to look at myself, and I'll make some calls, see what I can turn up."

"If you see me with my eyes glazed and my tongue hanging out, I promise I'm okay; it's just me off in the code zone."

Mike wasn't kidding about the work ahead. Gray had given her a thick case file with everything their researchers had managed to find on both Adam Pearce and Havelock. After a while, she looked up at Nicholas. He was focused on the screen in front of him. It felt oddly reminiscent of their first case together, flying to Europe on the tail of the Fox.

"You're staring," he said, without raising his head or slowing his typing. "What's wrong?"

She said, "It's hard for you, isn't it?"

The typing stopped, but the head stayed down. "What do you mean?"

"Being constrained by our rules."

He looked up then. "Oh, Hamish Penderley of New Scotland Yard constrained me plenty. And Zachery was kind enough to request my razzle-dazzle. Penderley never did that. I fully intend to do my best."

He would, too. She grew quiet.

"What is it, Mike? What's really wrong?"

"I'm scared. We're not chasing a diamond this time. We've stumbled into a big conspiracy, fully operational well before we got involved. We're up against a multinational group, and all we know is they're after something that could destroy the world as we know it. Supposedly."

"Worry not, Agent Caine. By the end of this flight, we'll know exactly who we're up against. And once we do, we'll do what we're good at—we'll catch the bad guys and keep the world safe." With a pirate's smile, he dove back into the files.

She thought, **I guess it's up to me to keep you safe, and yes, then the world,** and returned her attention to her files.

50

Highest Order Headquarters
London
Noon

Edward Weston knew it was time to cajole, to persuade, to manipulate, even to bribe, time to do whatever was necessary. He looked down the long mahogany table at the members of the Order assembled in the elegantly appointed room. He knew some were worried, others scared. There was excitement, too, in those on his and Havelock's side. Nearly a century of work begun before any of them were even born, and yet they would be the ones to succeed. And with his leadership, with Havelock's, the Order would forge ahead on a new path, one he—and a few of the others— felt long overdue.

The fifteen men around the table represented Great Britain, the United States, Germany, Russia, China, India, Brunei, and Israel. They were some of the wealthiest, most influential people in the world. Power brokers. It was Weston's belief that power should be used overtly, not the discreet traditional behind-the-scenes machinations meant to stabilize the world. It was time to throw off secrecy, time to show themselves as the true world leaders.

It was up to Weston to make it happen. And Havelock, he thought, always Havelock.

He cleared his throat, and all the faces focused on him.

"Come to order, if you will."

Cups were set down, notepads straightened, pencils arranged. Then they all settled and waited expectantly.

It would not do to show anything but profound regret and sadness, and so Weston's voice was calm, respectful, the man to comfort, the man to lead. "It is with a heavy heart I've called this meeting. As you know, we have lost two more members of our brethren. Gentlemen, it was unclear until yesterday, but now I know we are under attack. I do not know who has taken action against us, but I do know our only choice is to band together, as we always have through the years, and find a way to stop these unseen enemies before the Order is destroyed and many of us murdered as well."

Alastair Burrow, one of the remaining six Brits in the Order, said, "Do we truly not know who ordered Alfie and Jonathan murdered on the same day?"

"No, Alastair, I'm sorry to say we do not. Unfortunately, we are currently limited in how much we can do, since the results of the inquest on Alfie must be kept secret. If it were to get out he'd been murdered, the British government would be under fire. We must keep this silent. The public must honor Alfie as a soldier and a leader, not as a murder victim. Better to let him fade away, the victim of an untimely heart attack, than risk the world finding out who we are, and what purpose our organization serves."

Dmitri Zachar, a former leader of Chechnyan rebels who now headed a Russian oil conglomerate and was almost single-handedly responsible for bringing his country back to life, said from the end of the table, "Two of us murdered. Who of us is next? And why?"

Weston said, his voice firm, confident, "No more of us will die and that is because we will find the submarine and the instructions on how to find Madame Curie's weapon. Then we will be safe."

Mason Armstrong, technological wizard and the sole American in the Order, said, "And how are we going to do that, Weston?"

Now came the tough part. "I know this is not standard protocol, that new members should be carefully considered, but gentlemen, we find ourselves in desperate times. First we must inaugurate new members since our numbers must be at fifteen in order to proceed. Then we must secure the weapon before it is used against us. And I have a way to do it."

There was open disagreement as members argued among themselves. Oliver Leyland, head of the Bank of England, brilliant, steady, ruthless, raised a hand to quiet the group. Jonathan

Pearce and Alfie Stanford had been close friends, and he was feeling both grief-stricken and wildly angry, and he didn't like Weston, didn't trust him. "Weston, you know we try to keep these positions in a hereditary line. However, Jonathan's son, Adam, isn't in a position to become a member of the Order, and from what I've heard, we don't even know where he is in any case. Alfie's son is dead, his three grandsons ignorant of the Order. I know Alfie left instructions for his successor, but those papers were stolen along with the Order's protocols by his murderer. With that in mind, then, may I ask who you are putting forth?"

The moment was at hand, Weston thought, and said firmly, "Manfred Havelock. His father would have named him his successor, had he been given the time."

Leyland's thick brows shot up. "Wolfgang Havelock had six years as a member of this group to name his son as heir to his position, Weston, and he didn't. Don't you think if he had wanted Manfred to have his seat, he'd have said so?"

Weston said, "Wolfgang's death was unexpected, and he hadn't been questioned by this group on his wishes. Leyland, I know you aren't a fan of the younger Havelock, but—"

"Too right I'm not. The man's an egomaniac, and barking mad. What he could do to the Order doesn't bear thinking. Which is exactly why his father hadn't named him heir."

"On the contrary," Weston said, "Manfred Havelock is a brilliant scientist who can bring untold abilities to our group."

Leyland half stood, his hands splayed on the table in front of him. "Abilities? Dear God, the man travels around the world with that bizarre woman at his side, who, I might add, is said to lay the whip on for pleasure. And look at the people he employs—that März character in particular—I've heard he's a sadistic animal.

"Manfred Havelock is not the type of man to belong to the Order, the type of man to look at the world objectively, and sanely, without self-interest, and come to agreement with other members. How could he possibly be a benefit to our community?"

"He has money," Claude Benoit, France's finance minister, said frankly, "and money is something we always need. Also he has the ear of the entire scientific world. He has the means and the intelligence to raise the submarine."

"We have to find the damned thing first," Leyland said.

Weston nodded. "As you know, Adam Pearce has finally located the sub. When we have the exact coordinates, we will share this information with Havelock. He not only has the technology to retrieve the key from the sub, he can do it without alerting the military to our presence. For this ability alone, he would prove his true worth to the Order. I believe he is also in a position to locate Adam Pearce. We've never had someone with Havelock's leverage before."

Had he said too much, or still not enough? He waited.

The Sultan of Brunei, Omar Hakim, a tough old hawk who was known to disappear his enemies, said, "Leverage? Whatever do you mean, Weston?"

Careful, man, don't make Havelock sound like the promised land. Back off a bit, let them find their way to the answer. "Perhaps **leverage** is too strong a word, Omar. Let me rephrase. Havelock has a foot in a world we don't. The closest we come to the scientific community is Mason, and he admits he's very limited in his technical scope."

Omar said, "I do not see what the rush is to vote in new members. We should take our time, do things properly, according to the bylaws of the Order. We can certainly act, even though our numbers are not at our mandated fifteen. It is an emergency, after all."

Huang Chén, a wealthy Chinese industrialist from Beijing, all of seventy, with a brain fast as a striking cobra, said in fluent English, "The bylaws allow for emergencies, Omar, and as you said this appears to be a big one—someone is trying to destroy our world, this same someone who had Jonathan and Alfie murdered, and now I believe it imperative that we get back to strength immediately. I for one have no intention of allowing Marie Curie's weapon to be used against us or anyone else. If we don't find it, and control it now, the world could be in very big trouble."

51

Oliver Leyland looked at the men around the table. He was shaking his head. "Jonathan and Alfie aren't even cold yet. Surely this can wait until we have buried them properly."

"I fear not, dear Leyland." It was Stuart Niles who spoke, the eldest member of the Order, and a leading British member of Parliament, a hard-line old autocrat, verbally skilled, intelligent, looked up to by the other members. Weston once would have voted to euthanize him, but not now. Niles was on their side. Even though he spoke in an obnoxious stentorian voice, the other members usually followed his lead. "Weston is right to move quickly in this matter. I have heard rumors the American FBI have been investigating, and are aware of the submarine's general location." He turned his attention to Weston. "The simple fact the American FBI have the location, and we do not, is a disgrace. Should they retrieve the sub and the key before we do, the weapon would be in their hands. You said we still do not have Adam Pearce, Weston?"

"He is adept at hiding in plain sight." Weston smiled, allowing a bit of nostalgia into his tone. "His father taught him well."

"I ask myself," Leyland said to the group, "why wouldn't Adam Pearce come to us immediately? Why is he hiding? From us? And the answer is, of course, that Alfie was murdered, his safe cleaned out, his own father was murdered, and Adam Pearce isn't a fool. He fears there's something going on within our Order, and that's why he hasn't run to us. And now you wish to add Havelock? I tell you, it's insanity."

"Leyland, I must correct you," Weston said. "Adam Pearce ran because the FBI is after him. He has no fear of us."

"Leyland, the bottom line is that Havelock has the resources right here to find Adam Pearce and go after the sub," Stuart Niles said. "The rest of it, we will deal with in due time. My friends, the last thing we want is to be outed to the world." He paused a moment, then his orator's voice rang out. "I move we have a vote. Today. Right now."

Weston wondered what Havelock had given Niles to bring him over. He wasted no time. "So moved. Do we have a second?"

Alastair Burrow raised a meaty paw. His voice was better suited to television, deep and throbbing with sincerity. "I second the motion."

Weston said, "All in favor of extending membership in the Order to the son of Order member Wolfgang Havelock—Manfred Havelock, who has a hereditary right to the position—say aye."

A super majority ruled. It was rare they found themselves divided, in any case, but today was different. Today the vote was the narrowest in Order history.

There were twelve men in the room. Six hands raised immediately. After a few moments, Dmitri Zachar assented, giving them seven. Who would be the eighth? Weston looked around. Not Leyland, he was against this, sitting upright in his chair, clearly angry. Weston watched Omar

Hakim bite his lip, then slowly, he put his hand in the air.

Weston wanted to yell his victory, but he said nothing, merely raised his own hand in the air. He made the ninth.

"The ayes have it. Manfred Havelock will be inducted into the Order straightaway. I will let him know immediately," Weston continued. "You know Alex Shepherd. He's proved his loyalty time and again through his covert operations on our behalf, most recently his three-year stint in New York with Jonathan Pearce. Some of you believe Shepherd should go back into MI Five and work his way up. One day he could run the British intelligence services, and if he did, he'd be a true asset to their group. Therefore, I also would like to move that Alex Shepherd be made a full member of the Order and take over as Messenger for Jonathan Pearce. He will continue his nominal position with MI Five because it is to our advantage that he does and he has expressed an interest in taking over for Pearce."

Alastair Burrow said, "So moved."

"Seconded," Niles said.

"All in favor?" This time, to Weston's relief, all the hands raised.

"Excellent," Weston said. "Alex will be well pleased by this news. I will tell you, he is currently with Sophie Pearce, who is cooperating fully with helping us locate her brother. As you know, Adam Pearce has the exact coordinates of the sub, and, as I said, he wisely ran from the FBI. We will have him with us again, very soon, and we will keep him safe from the FBI.

"Alex tells me Sophie Pearce is passing him a message to come in, and we will guarantee him safe passage from the FBI and any further persecution on the Americans' behalf. As soon as I have news, I will send our new Messenger to you."

There were murmurs among the group. It was time for the last play. Weston drew in his breath. He knew this was going to be tricky.

He cleared his throat to bring all their attention to him. "Gentlemen, before we adjourn for the day, we need to nominate and vote in one last member. This will bring us back to full strength and we can then move forward, helping Havelock retrieve the key. Alfie Stanford relayed to me his desire to see Heinz Gernot take his place. You're all familiar with the man; Gernot is the head of Germany's—"

Oliver Leyland banged his fist on the table. "Wait a minute, Edward. Gernot would change the balance of the Order. We always have eight Brits. This would give the Germans two seats."

Weston smiled. "As I said, Alfie told me Gernot would be ideal, with his obvious influence in the EU. Indeed, he was quite insistent we begin to branch out, to lessen the British grip a bit. And Gernot is a friend of this country. Why, last month he—"

Leyland jumped to his feet, fury pouring off him. "No. I will not go along with this. We will not be forced into yet another new member, not until Alfie's papers are located and we can actually read his wishes and reasons."

Weston met his eyes and asked in a very quiet voice, "Are you calling me a liar,

Leyland?"

"I don't see Alfie nominating Gernot," Leyland said. Of course Weston was lying. But why? Leyland looked around the room at the faces that seemed content and those that were clearly disturbed. He took a mental count. Something was very wrong here.

He turned back to Weston. He had to stay calm. "You already seem to have a majority vote, Edward. Another few days without a fifteenth member won't matter and you all know it. We should wait until we actually have the key and the weapon is secured before reworking nearly three centuries of practice.

"Gentlemen, allowing Havelock to join is a mistake, one we will come to regret. Adding Gernot is insanity."

Leyland was eloquent, damn him. The other members began talking among themselves. Weston threw up his hands. He knew better than to push Leyland further. "Fine, fine. We will wait. But there is one more bit of business. We need a pro tem leader until all fifteen members can meet and vote for a new one." He cleared his throat. "I am willing to proceed in the role until such time as we can have a clear vote."

Leyland met Weston's eye, and barked a short, humorless laugh. "It seems you've already taken over, Weston. We'll see how long that lasts."

He stalked out of the room, leaving the remaining Order members to look after him.

Weston watched him go, and calculated. Could Havelock safely eliminate Leyland?

He turned back to the group. They looked uncertain. **Get them back on board, man, or you might have trouble.** While Havelock had been voted in, he still wasn't a full member and wasn't supposed to be given the secrets of the Order until that ceremony was complete. But Havelock already knew as much as any of them. Weston had seen to that. He thought briefly of the ten million pounds safe in four different Swiss bank accounts. He thought of the power Havelock promised him once they had Madame Curie's weapon, once he and Havelock together would decide what to do with it.

He held up his hands. "All will be well, my friends. Leyland is right, these are difficult times for us all. We can table the newest member for the time being, until this crisis has passed," and he nodded to each of them in turn, now the man in charge, their leader. He fully intended to remain in charge.

On the street below, Oliver Leyland stepped into his waiting Jaguar XJ, slammed the door, and waved for his driver to proceed. He immediately rang one of his oldest friends. Thankfully, Harry Drummond answered on the first ring.

"Harry? It's Leyland. We have a very serious problem."

52

Over the Atlantic
8:00 a.m. ET

Nicholas's fingers hadn't stopped flying over the keyboard since they'd left Teterboro. Mike had heard him talking to Gray, much of their language too technical for her to get more than the gist.

She'd eaten her fill, then set a steaming cup of coffee and a few muffins at his right hand. He'd eaten and sipped from the coffee absently, never stopping. She'd never seen him coding before; he wasn't kidding about being in another world.

She was on her second cup of coffee and debating a third when she spotted a report from deep in the FBI files about an organization they'd identified as the Highest Order. What a highfalutin moniker that was.

Then she read on and her heart began a wild hoedown. This was it, she was sure of it. She finished reading the dossier. It was maddeningly brief, but gave her at least some background on who they might be dealing with.

"Nicholas. Take a break. I've found something."

He didn't miss a beat. "Is it important? I've only a few minutes left here until Gray and I are done."

"Stop, now. You need to hear this."

He stood, stretched, and actually focused on her now. "Ah, that's better. I'm very close here. What's your news?"

"It's a dossier, prepared about seven years ago about a group called the Highest Order. I think this is who we're looking for. These are the fifteen men from Pearce's files."

"The Highest Order?"

She nodded. "The information was lifted off the computer of a diplomat who visited the U.S. with a British delegation a decade ago. It's incomplete, but at least we can get an idea of what we might be up against."

He stood over her, hands braced against the ceiling of the fuselage. "Rather rude to invade the computers of a foreign delegate.

Is that common practice? And how'd you do it?"

"The easy way. The Brit logged in to an unsecured wireless network in his hotel, and welcomed us right in. But no, this isn't common practice. He must have been under surveillance and tracking software was put on his computer."

"Who was the diplomat?"

"Well, he's dead now. Callum Chatterton was his name. They were here to speak at the UN. He worked as a researcher in the office of Stuart Niles."

Nicholas whistled. "Stuart Niles is now a leading member of Parliament, and would have your heads if he knew his people had been spied upon."

"But he didn't know. This is from the dossier: **'The Highest Order was formed in 1714 before the death of Queen Anne by a small group of powerful Englishmen and Germans who did not want to see the son of the deposed James the Second make a grab for the crown when the crown should rightfully go to the Hanoverians because of** the standing law forbidding Catholics to rule England, thus taking away the risk that England would again be plunged into bloody religious persecution. Through their efforts, the Jacobites were defeated in the rebellion of 1715 and the Hanoverian George the First was crowned king of England.

'The Highest Order's goal immediately shifted to stand as protectors of England's supremacy. They were successful in maintaining England's stability during all the revolutionary unrest throughout Europe in the mid–nineteenth century, an extraordinary accomplishment. They were succeeding admirably until the onset of World War One, which they fought to prevent but failed due to the extreme fanaticism of Kaiser Wilhelm the Second.

'After the Great War, the group expanded to include members from America, and in the seventies and eighties, they added Israel, representatives from the Middle East, India, Russia, and China.

'The members themselves are in positions of power in their respective countries, and are incredibly wealthy. They quietly effect change in their individual countries by open communication with other Order members, and exacting influence and pressure in the appropriate quarters.

'Today, the Highest Order remains a small but powerful multinational group of fifteen high-powered men whose primary goal is to maintain the safety and security of the world by helping countries avoid wars and other destabilizing events.

'In the beginning of the twenty-first century, however, it became obvious that a new element began to make inroads into the Order. Questionable actions were taken, deals were struck with questionable allies. They should be watched to ensure they don't use their power to subvert the peaceful objectives of the Order.'"

She looked up. "They sound like something like the Trilateral Commission."

He nodded. "And different as well, since the Trilateral Commission is a more public group and their actions are both well documented and incredibly controversial."

Mike was nodding. "But like this Highest Order, the commission is also a consortium of influential leaders who work together to help the world stay safe.

"Nicholas, the Trilateral Commission doesn't date back three hundred years, they're newbies. Why do I have the feeling we haven't even scratched the surface of what the Highest Order is up to?"

He said, "Because they're supposed to be working for good, and they have someone like Manfred Havelock involved with them?"

"Exactly. You don't seem terribly surprised by this."

"I don't? I am, I assure you."

"Come on, Nicholas. I can see data running across that brain of yours like a stock ticker on crack. What's going on?"

He focused on her. "Very well, it was something my father said when I called to talk to him about Alfie Stanford's death.

He said if Alfie's death **was** murder, and had been committed from inside Downing Street, as we suspect it must have, it was a bigger situation than anyone could imagine. Then he steered me away, told me the Brits had it well in hand, and to stop thinking about it." He turned to stare out the window, then he pushed the green button. The pilot's disembodied voice came through the air.

"Yes?"

"I need to make a call. A private call. Will our security measures do an appropriate job scrambling the signal?"

"Absolutely. Use the phone in the arm. Hit nine. That will fully encrypt the call. Thanks for letting me know, it makes my instruments squirrelly while you're connecting. By the way, we are now under two hours from landing." He snapped off the speaker.

Mike looked at her watch. It was only 8:00 a.m. "He is breaking airspeed records. It's one p.m. London time. We'll be there by three o'clock, and we should have plenty of daylight to get north to the loch. Assuming they haven't left without us. Assuming Adam has given them the exact coordinates."

He reached into the arm and pulled out the secure phone. "I'll bet anything he hasn't."

"Who are you calling?"

"The one person who might have some insight into what's really going on here." The phone clicked a few times, then he heard the familiar tinny double ring. He nodded to Mike. "I'm calling my dad."

53

North of London
12:30 p.m.

Could she trust Alex? Even though he'd assured her the Order had only her best interest at heart, Sophie simply didn't know. Her father was dead. What was the Order doing about that? And the murder of Alfie Stanford? If they did want her safe, why hadn't they simply told her, rather than sending Alex Grossman—no, Shepherd—to kidnap her?

Alex was driving a Vauxhall that waited for them in the airport's short-term car park. Driving in downtown London was craziness, but he expertly maneuvered in and out of traffic until they hit the M40 and it became less populated, the city streets giving way to green fields.

Near High Wycombe, he pulled to the side of the road and put the car in park. He looked at her.

"Why are we stopping?"

"I'm going to give you a choice."

"About what?"

He dug in his pocket and pulled out a syringe.

"Oh, no, don't you even think about it, Alex whatever your name is. You try to stick me with another needle, it will be the last move you make."

He reached into the bag he had in the backseat and pulled out a length of black fabric. "This is your choice, the needle or a hood."

"A hood? Like terrorists use on people they're going to behead? Are you nuts?" She yanked at the car handle, only to find it locked. By him. To keep her a prisoner. She didn't look at him, she was too angry.

"Either I can knock you out again or you can put the hood over your head. One or the other. No other choices."

She didn't know much about guns, but she wished she had one right now. She held out her hand for the black hood. "And you expect me to trust you? Why should I believe you won't kill me when you find Adam?"

He crossed his hands over his heart. "I

swear to you, Sophie, I would never hurt you. You may not believe me, but I promise I'll keep you safe, or die trying. Now, would you please put the hood over your head so we can get this over with?"

"Where are we going?"

"Someplace safe."

She searched his eyes, but he said nothing more. "How long?"

"Fifteen minutes, tops. And please lie down in the backseat. Wouldn't do to have people staring as I drive past with a hooded woman in my front seat."

He grinned and she wanted to punch him. No choice. She climbed into the back and lay down. She pulled the hood over her head. Utter and complete black. She hated it. "Fine. Go."

"Don't even consider peeking. If you fiddle with the hood, I'll have to stick you with the needle."

He pulled back onto the road.

Sophie hated this, hated the darkness, the suffocating feeling of the thick black material. She couldn't breathe properly, started to raise the bottom edge so she could get a bit of air.

"Sophie, don't."

Of course he was watching. "I can't breathe."

"Not long now."

Sophie had a general idea where they were. Now she had to concentrate on which direction the car moved, the turns, anything.

She counted in her head, left, left again, then a tight turn right, straight. She guessed they'd entered some sort of drive. Nearly there. Her heart was thudding. She was afraid, very afraid.

"Can I take the hood off?"

"You'll have to keep it on until you're in your room. You must be starved. I'll make sure you're given food and drink. Please, Sophie, don't worry, we only want to keep you safe. I'll be nearby."

The car stopped and Alex helped her out. She could make out no light, nothing. She began to feel claustrophobic. He heard her breathing quicken. "Relax. Not long now. Here's the steps."

She stumbled once, but he steadied

her. She listened, but heard nothing to give her a clue where they were.

Up three flights of stairs, he walked her down a long hallway, then stopped. "This is your room. One second more."

She heard him open the door. Once they were inside, he pulled the hood off. He actually ran his fingers through her hair before she jerked away.

He stood by the door and watched her look about the room. Dark walnut canopied bed, yellow-and-white striped wallpaper. It was beautifully appointed. She turned back to him. "What happens now?"

"I'll be back soon."

She grabbed his arm. "Don't you dare leave me here, you bastard."

He pulled away her hand, squeezed it. "Sophie, you'll be fine. Try to relax. I'm going to send someone up with food and tea."

When the door closed behind him, she heard the sound of a key turning.

She wasn't meant to be kept safe. She was a prisoner, pure and simple. He'd locked her in. He'd lied. She shouldn't have pulled the hood over her head, she should have forced him to try to stick that needle in her, and she'd have fought him, maybe hurt him badly. But no, she'd trusted him, taken the easy way.

She felt numb as she walked to the window. She had to keep it together, she had to stay calm and think.

She was on an estate, and clearly the house was big. She looked out over a large expanse of gardens. She saw a fence running away from her, and a very long tree-lined graveled driveway. All she knew was she was north of London, in the country, locked in some rich person's house.

No phone, no computer, and no way to get out. The windows were locked. Even if she broke a window and shouted, who would hear her? She saw no one outside, not a single gardener to maintain those beautiful gardens.

She was studying the ledge outside the window when someone knocked on the door. She heard the key turn, and the door opened. She ran into a young girl bringing in a tray. The tray went flying, scones and jam hit the carpet and the hot tea splattered both of them and the girl yelled, then ran.

A chance. Sophie burst into the hallway. Not six feet away stood a large man. He wasted no time and was on her in an instant. "Get back in there, stupid bitch." He grabbed her arm and pushed her back into the room. She stumbled against a wall as he slammed the door, locked it.

He was armed, she'd seen the large gun at his belt. An armed guard, in the middle of nowhere.

If Alex Shepherd had walked into the room at that moment, she would have tried to tear his throat out with her teeth.

She was a prisoner, but Alex wasn't. Even as she prayed, she knew this was not going to end well.

Over the Atlantic

Harry Drummond answered the phone on the first ring. "Nicholas. Calling me twice in two days. If you keep this up I might think you're doubting your decision to move to America."

"I'm glad you can still joke, Dad." But he'd heard the tension in his father's voice. Something was happening and his father knew what it was.

Harry paused. "Is everything all right?"

"No, I'm sorry to say it isn't. I'm on a secure satphone on a plane on my way to London. I need you to be honest with me. I need you to tell me what's going on over there."

"Nicholas, I told you we have Alfie's murder well in hand. Why are you coming to London? You're FBI now. You have no business here."

"On the contrary, I do. Which is why I'm calling, to tell you what's bringing me to London with an official invitation from

New Scotland Yard, as a matter of fact. A principal in my case was kidnapped and we know she's been taken to England." And he told his father all of it, including the break-in. "As if this weren't enough, Dad, have you ever heard of a group in England called the Highest Order? Or simply the Order?"

Absolute silence. "Dad? Are you still there?"

"Where, exactly, did you hear the name Highest Order?"

"So it does exist?"

"The Order is a very secret organization, Nicholas. It's not something bandied about in polite conversation. Where'd you see the name, Jonathan Pearce's files?"

"An old FBI dossier, actually."

Harry Drummond cursed.

His father never cursed. "Dad, isn't it time to tell me what's going on over there? I'm coming. I'm going to be in the middle of it. Don't make me come in blind. I'm on a line as secure as is humanly possible, and it's scrambling from your end as well. We couldn't be more private if we were sitting in the center of the labyrinth out back. So out with it. Please. Sir."

Harry said, "I must caution you, Nicholas, what I'm going to tell you, you must keep it between us. Do you agree?" He paused. "Of course I don't want you blind, Nicholas."

"Yes, sir, of course I agree."

"Very well. The Order has been around hundreds of years. They've gone global now, and honestly, all I truly know for certain is it's an organization of powerful men dedicated to keeping the world as safe as possible, which isn't saying much, is it, given the violence in every part of the globe?"

"Above the governments, above the people? How does that work?"

"The Order has always worked for the common good. At first, admittedly, its purpose was to keep the English throne Protestant to avoid bloody war. It changed, of course, but still, the common good continued to benefit England only. That's really all I can say, Nicholas. You have to trust me here, this isn't the kind of conversation we want to be having on the phone, regardless of how secure it is."

"Dad, have you heard of a man named Manfred Havelock?"

Dead-cold silence, then, his voice heavy, his father said, "I knew his father, Wolfgang. He passed away recently."

"I know that. I saw it when I was looking into Havelock the younger last night."

Now Nicholas heard urgency in his father's voice. "May I ask why you were looking into Manfred Havelock?"

"We believe he's directly tied to the murder of Jonathan Pearce. We've also learned he's been quietly gathering polonium from the black markets. The assassin he sent to kill Pearce had a brain implant which worked as a type of recording device. The man's mad, it seems, a genius who's toppled over the edge. We're looking for him, beating all the bushes. His last known location was Berlin, but we believe he may be heading to Scotland. He's looking for a submarine called **Victoria,** which went down in 1917."

"Nicholas."

Nicholas heard the alarm, the urgency in his father's voice. "What is it?"

"How far out are you?"

"We should be on the ground in two hours. Dad, what's going on?"

"When you arrive, you need to see Oliver Leyland. Go directly to his home in Mayfair. Do not stop anywhere else. Do you understand?"

"The head of the Bank of England? That Oliver Leyland?"

"Yes. I will tell him you're coming."

"Dad, what is going on?"

Harry said, "Wolfgang Havelock was a member of the Order, too. High-ranking."

"Too?"

"Alfie Stanford, Nicholas. He was the head of the Highest Order, their leader for many years. And now Manfred Havelock's been inducted. This is bad, very bad. Get to Leyland, Nicholas. He'll tell you what's happened. I do know the Order is under attack. Nicholas? Be careful, be very, very careful."

Harry hung up, and Nicholas stared at the phone. He didn't like this, didn't like it at all. Oliver Leyland, then. Very well.

Mike was leaning toward him. "What in the world was all that?"

Nicholas placed the phone back in the armrest. "All I'm sure of at the moment is that the first person we're to see in London is the head of the Bank of England, Oliver Leyland," and he told her what his father said.

When he finished, she said slowly, "Alfie Stanford, Wolfgang Havelock, and Jonathan Pearce, all members of the Order, all murdered. I'd say they're under attack."

"Yes, remember the diplomat's dossier warned that the Order was changing, and not for the better. My father agrees. I think Alex Shepherd is now working for Havelock against the Order. That's why he's kidnapped Sophie, as leverage against Adam to get the final coordinates of the sub. I think it's time we call Hamish Penderley, see if they've sussed out anything important."

But Mike wasn't listening anymore. She was sifting through the files, tossing pages to find what she needed.

"What are you doing?" Nicholas asked.

"I saw something a few minutes before you called your dad. Give me a second, I'll find it. Here it is. Now, it was reported that Wolfgang Havelock supposedly died of a stroke, following an aneurysm repair, right?"

"That's what Savich said. Why?"

"His autopsy report is in here. Gray found it. I can't believe I didn't put it together sooner."

"Mike, take a breath and tell me what you're thinking."

She shoved the paper at him. "Wolfgang Havelock didn't have a repaired aneurysm. He had a brain implant. He had one of his son's brain implants in his head."

55

London
1:00 p.m.

Once all the members of the Order had departed, Weston hurried to the flat he'd secured for Havelock in the building.

He didn't knock, simply opened the door, walked in, and stopped cold. Havelock was standing spread-eagle in the window, his shirt off. His woman, Elise, held a cat-o'-nine-tails in her left hand. When Weston entered the room, Elise turned and saw him, bent her head in a silent nod of greeting, then hauled off and whacked Havelock square in the back. Havelock jumped with the force of the blow and strained against the ropes that held his wrists bound to the window frame, but he didn't make a sound.

Weston stared, disbelieving, horrified. "Stop this now! Havelock, what are you doing?"

Havelock grunted a command in guttural German, and Elise reached up and released first the left wrist, then the right. She handed Havelock his shirt. He said, as calm as a judge, "Thank you, Elise. You may go now. I will see you soon." He kissed her cheek. She gathered her things gracefully and left the room.

Havelock buttoned his shirt, tucked it into his pants. He didn't look embarrassed or in pain. He looked as if Weston had walked in on a tea party. "Hello, Weston."

Weston was without words.

"Ah, I see you're upset. Please don't concern yourself. I felt the need for release. Elise is always very accommodating, and excellent at her chosen métier." He walked to the small wet bar in the corner of the room and poured himself a scotch. "Tell me, how did the meeting go?"

Weston swallowed bile, forced the look of awful disgust from his face. "You've been voted in. You're a full-fledged member of the Order."

"Were there any dissenters?"

"Yes. Oliver Leyland was the most upset, at least verbally. My mention of Gernot sent him stomping out of the room. I backed off since I saw other members were listening to him. Alex Shepherd was voted in as well."

"And Adam Pearce?"

"Has not been located."

"This is unacceptable, Weston."

"There may be another way. The FBI agents, Nicholas Drummond and Michaela Caine, are on a plane to London as we speak. It's possible they can flush out Adam Pearce once they're on the ground."

Weston watched Havelock sit down, lean back and stretch. How could he do that after the beating she'd given him? But Havelock didn't seem to feel a thing. He seemed cool and collected, ready for anything.

"I do believe the FBI has outlived their usefulness," Havelock said. "It is time to eliminate both them and Leyland. I will see to it."

Weston shook his head, appalled. "Surely that isn't necessary."

"Oh, yes. It is."

"Leyland knows something's up. He won't be an easy target."

"März will take care of Leyland personally. And I will deal with the FBI. Now, Sophie Pearce resides in your home?"

"If she's not at West Park now, she will be shortly."

"I will go there. She and I need to have a small talk."

Weston knew exactly what sort of talk Havelock had in mind. He wondered to himself if he'd done the right thing. All that lovely money, the promise of more power than he'd ever dreamed. The time for questioning was long over.

Havelock had a point. With Leyland gone, they would be able to force a vote for two more Order members, which would give them the majority vote. And they'd recover the weapon and have the power in the palms of their hands.

"How will you eliminate the FBI?"

Havelock smiled wickedly. "I'm sure you'll hear it on the news very soon."

56

Over the Atlantic

Nicholas read Wolfgang Havelock's autopsy report, then read it again more slowly. Mike was right. He looked up at her, sitting forward, so excited she was nearly bouncing on the seat.

She said, "They found the implant, but evidently it must have been a prototype, not as obvious or as well defined as the one Dr. Janovich found. Maybe its capabilities weren't as advanced as the one in Mr. Olympic's head since British ME believed it to be some sort of advanced German technology for the aneurysm, an 'aneurysm chip,' is what they wrote. They also wrote they'd never seen anything like it."

"So he implanted his father at the beginning. To see what the Order was up to, that makes the most sense."

She nodded. "Either his father agreed to it or he didn't know about it, and that raises the question, How did Havelock do it without his being any the wiser?"

"A question we'll have to ask Manfred when we get cuffs on him, but it makes the most sense he was implanted with the chip during his aneurysm surgery." He added, "If the father wasn't the good guy we all think he was, then he was in on all this maneuvering with his son." He shook his head. "That doesn't make sense. If the father was in on it with his son, then all he had to do was tell him everything. I don't think Havelock senior had any idea he'd been given an implant."

Mike nodded. "And then Havelock starts buying up polonium, and through his father's implant he gets a direct feed into Adam Pearce, the sub, the key, and suddenly, he doesn't need dear old Dad anymore. With Dad gone, Havelock has a sure line into the Order."

Nicholas said, "I buy Havelock using Daddy to spy on the Order. Maybe he was pushing his father to convince the Order members to go a certain way, and his father refused. Dad's implant is triggered, and he's gone, clearing the way for

Manfred to step into his place and take the weapon they've been searching for for nearly a hundred years into his own hands.

He stared down at his clasped hands on his knees. "Then this key to this weapon that's in the sub, it has to be something Havelock needs to make the mini-nukes work properly or make them more powerful."

She bounced in her seat again. "Yes, that's it. Nicholas, I've got it, I know what the implants are for."

"What?"

"You said it yourself. It's a trigger." She pointed at the autopsy sheet. "It all makes perfect sense now. The micro-nukes. They need a trigger. The implants are the trigger."

"I have to say," he said slowly, "this is so much worse than anything I imagined. I hope you're wrong."

"But you know I'm not. We have to get that key out of the sub and find that weapon, Nicholas."

"Yes, we absolutely do. Soon we'll have access to everything Havelock has in his databases. And then I'll call Penderley."

He tapped on his laptop for no longer than a minute, then closed it. "Done. We'll have all Havelock's files momentarily. But before I call Penderley, we need to look again at Pearce's files. I want to see if he'd caught on to Havelock. The coded messages from the past few days might have answers." He clicked a few buttons, and Pearce's e-mail came on the screen. He clicked on the in-box, started to type, then stopped.

"Wait, what's this?"

Nicholas watched the screen of his computer light up, then go completely black. Then a small face floated into the center of the screen, rotating and spinning. Nicholas looked closely at the image, squinted at the small face. He recognized it instantly.

"That cheeky bugger."

"Nicholas? What are you talking about?"

He turned his laptop to face her. "Adam Pearce has hacked into my computer."

"How did he manage that?"

"I don't know. But I'm going to find out."

And he clicked on the face.

A link popped onto the black screen. He recognized part of a word embedded in the string. **Ariston**.

Normally, Nicholas wouldn't get anywhere near something like this, knowing full well it was a hack, and that whoever was on the other side could bring mayhem on his world. But if Adam Pearce was reaching out, he had to know.

He clicked on the link.

It took him to Jonathan Pearce's secure e-mail.

He combed the messages. Clearly he was meant to see something here, but nothing jumped out at him. "Maybe I'm supposed to go back in time. Look at yesterday's e-mail."

Mike stepped behind him and pointed to a message. "No, wait. It's right there."

He looked at the message she was pointing to. "That's spam, only an advertisement for a sale on British Airways."

"Yep. One that so happens to invite Pearce to come to Scotland for a holiday.

Click on it. Right there, on the northern coast of Scotland, where the small star is. That's what we're looking for."

"What are you seeing that I'm not?"

"Adam Pearce is trying to give you the exact location of the sub."

He clicked the message.

Instead of a normal e-mail coming up, a text message box filled the screen. Mike gave Nicholas a big smile. "Tell Adam I said hello."

Nicholas wrote in the message box—
It's Drummond. We're here.

"Hopefully he's paying attention. Want to tell me how you knew this was the one?"

Mike said, "There are some private websites with hidden embedded links inside their home pages. It's one of the ways child porn works. Believe me, I've seen too much of that."

"What made you think this particular e-mail was the one?"

She flipped out her phone, opened her e-mail. "Because I get e-mails from British Airways all the time, and the one that came today was advertising a trip to Machu Picchu in Peru. Not to Scotland."

He stared at her. "You're very clever, Agent Caine."

Before he could go on, the cursor started to blink on Nicholas's screen. The words spilled into the small chat space.

"It's Adam," he said.

They have my sister. You have to help me. I'll do whatever you want.

Nicholas wrote back.

We know they do, we are trying to help. Alex Shepherd—Alex Grossman—kidnapped her last night. Do you know where they've taken her?

Shepherd works for the Order, and now for Havelock. No idea where Sophie is. You have to help me find her.

We're coming.

"Mike, are you seeing this?"

"I am. Ask him where he is."

Where are you? We need to speak in person.

Meet you at Leyland's.

You're already in London? We'll send the Metropolitan Police to pick you up. My people. They'll keep you safe.

No. Havelock has people everywhere. When you get to Leyland's I'll tell you everything. We must stop Havelock. Promise me you'll save Sophie.

That's the plan. You must come in.

Will you expunge my record? I got an offer from the wrong side to do that in exchange for info on where to retrieve the key.

What's more important to you? Your sister or saving your own hide?

Both. I want to be on the right side of this. My father would want me to. We can't allow Havelock to win. Have to go. This channel has been open too long. Leyland's ASAP.

And the chat box disappeared.

57

Notting Hill
1:00 p.m.

Leyland had left Adam a key. He'd come in and eaten his way through the fridge and found some of the weird fizzy lemonade they passed off as soda. Then he'd gone outside with his laptop and reached Drummond. And now here he sat on a bench behind Leyland's house, looking out at the beautiful, peaceful gardens, everything opposite of how he felt right now.

Where was Leyland? The house was too quiet, too empty. Adam was getting spooked.

Oliver Leyland, his godfather, had been a good friend to him and it wasn't the first time he had stayed in his house, in what was considered his own room, hiding out from one government or another after him at the time. Adam was a white hat hacker, breaking into secure systems to show them their security flaws. He never profited from his hacking, though he certainly did make a great deal of money designing the code on the front end. And when he discovered the weaknesses, he didn't sell that information to the highest bidder like most of the other hackers he knew. He wasn't interested in taking down governments or anarchy, he wanted adventure, the chase, the excitement of changing the world, one keystroke at a time.

As tense and uncertain as this situation was becoming, Adam had to admit he liked the FBI agents on this case. Especially the Drummond guy, the big Brit. He was smart, and a computer geek, like Adam. Maybe when all this was over, he could sit down with him and they could talk.

It hit him like a punch to his stomach— the deadening pain made him gasp aloud. He hadn't allowed himself to grieve, not for Allie, not for his dad. But now he shook with pain. Smart, sweet Allie, his friend for two years, his girlfriend for less than six months. Now she was gone and it was all his fault.

He saw his dad, bleeding out on the street twenty feet away, and he knew he'd never get that image out of his head. He hadn't told Sophie, couldn't, the pain of it was too deep, too raw.

He felt tears sting his eyes, swiped them away. He wouldn't break down, not with that crazy bastard Havelock after the key. He realized with sudden clarity that he was willing to die if necessary to make sure it didn't happen.

He said aloud, "You're nineteen and you're ready to throw yourself under the bus? You're an idiot."

"No, not an idiot unless you want to throw yourself under the wrong bus."

Oliver Leyland stood in the doorway, a big man, a strong man, with a lion's mane of thick white hair, now smiling at him, welcoming him, his arms held wide. Adam burrowed against him, and let the grief pour out of him. His godfather held him, saying nothing, simply letting him grieve, giving him what comfort he could. The boy was only nineteen and his world was tilting. As for his world, it didn't look much better. He said, "I am so sorry, Adam. So very sorry."

Adam nodded, finally drew away, and once again swiped his hand over his eyes. "What are we going to do?"

"Honestly?" Leyland streaked a big hand through his hair. "At this point we're going to have to pull in some of our contacts in the Security Service. Havelock's too far ahead of us on this. He's been voted into the Order, Weston saw to that, and there are others. Havelock had Stanford and your father killed to precipitate this crisis so he could be voted into the Order. He probably killed his own father, too. Three seats open, he gets one, arranges for his own people to take the other two, and he and his people swing the vote. It's as simple, and as complicated, as that.

"First, I need a cup of tea. As for you, I assume you'd like a real meal?"

"Well, I did eat all the jelly and bread. I guess I could eat something more."

"Ah, to be young," Leyland said, hugged him again, then set off for the kitchen.

"Havelock wants Curie's weapon, doesn't he?"

Leyland nodded. "Oh, yes, and the key to the weapon and the book of instructions. And don't forget all the kaiser's gold bars, probably at least a billion dollars' worth, maybe more, I don't know.

"Havelock's power-hungry, and he's quite mad. You add in that he's a scientific genius and we have the makings of a disaster of epic proportion."

"Then we have to stop him, sir. But how?"

"The same way we've always stopped people who wanted too much—we find a way to eliminate him, and quickly. Dismantle his technologies, discredit his work. When we're finished with him, it will be as if he was never born. We owe your father that level of revenge, at least." Leyland opened the fridge, poked around. "How about some bubble and squeak?"

At Adam's blank look, he smiled. "Fried leftover potatoes and veggies, some onions in there, too."

He dumped ingredients into a pan,

started the heat.

Adam said, "Well, the bastard doesn't have the final coordinates of the sub. Only I know them and he's not going to get me. So I'm the key to the key." No reason to tell his godfather Drummond had the coordinates.

"No, Adam, two of us will have the coordinates. You're going to tell me exactly where the **Victoria** is, since I already have our people standing by." He stirred the mash, turned off the heat. "Nice and hot."

Adam thought for a moment. "Are you sure, sir?"

"I am, yes. Get the forks out of that drawer over there. I think I'll join you."

The house alarm double beeped. A door had been opened.

Leyland grabbed Adam's arm. "I wasn't expecting anyone. I sent everyone away for the afternoon so I could meet with you alone."

They heard people moving through the bottom level of the house, heavy steps, heard a man's voice giving directions.

Leyland calmly pulled a Walther PPK

from his pocket. "Adam, I want you to go upstairs to your room and lock yourself in. Don't open that door for anyone. Wait for me to come for you. Don't worry about me, go, now," and his godfather was gone.

Adam ran up the back stairs to the third floor, stopped, and listened. He heard Leyland shout, he heard fighting, no mistaking the sickening sound of bones cracking, the grunts of pain. Then a popping sound—a silenced gun. He couldn't lose his godfather, he simply couldn't. He ran to the front stairs and started down, hugging the wall, one stair at a time until he reached the entrance hall landing.

He saw three men standing over his godfather. Oliver wasn't moving. His prized Walther was on the floor near his hand.

Was Oliver dead? No, no, it couldn't be. Rage roared through him. Adam couldn't stop himself. He ran down those steps, yelling, "Leave him alone!"

Three men turned to stare at the skinny boy racing toward them, his fists raised.

"Well, now, boys, what have we here?"

Adam heard that thick German accent, recognized the scar that sliced through the man's cheek. The man smiled at him, making the scar pucker and redden. It was Havelock's vicious right hand, the man known only as März.

"I do believe we have Adam Pearce."

Adam had read about this man in Havelock's files, but he hadn't realized—his godfather moaned. März turned and casually shot him with a suppressed Beretta, the sound no louder than a polite cough.

He turned back to Adam, his smile still in place, and gestured with his gun for him to come down the stairs.

Adam snapped. He charged the man, kicking, punching, screaming. He wasn't a fighter, but his fury was profound, fueled by his grief. He caught the men off guard, but still, it only took a couple of seconds for them to grab him and hold him. One of the men raised his knife, but März shouted, "No! We need him." The man cursed but drew back. Still, they'd gotten in a couple of licks. Adam's face hurt, and he knew his lip was split and bleeding.

März said, "You're a brave little cock, aren't you? I wonder if you will be marked, like me."

Adam licked the blood from his lip. "You've killed my godfather! You've killed him," and Adam tried to break away, but this time it was no use.

"Enough!"

"Did you send the man to kill my father? Or was it your boss, Havelock? Oh, yes, I know who you are."

Again, that awful smile that widened his mouth and made the scar push up and pleat. "What would you do if I had?"

"I'll kill you, you bastard."

März laughed. "Come along, little boy. We have things to do, a short trip to take, then we'll have a nice long chat." He nodded to Leyland's body.

Adam watched the two men carry his godfather up to the second landing, turn and simply toss him over the railing. März laughed. "There, that should ensure the old man is dead."

Adam couldn't bear it, he yelled and

charged März again.

Adam felt a sharp sting in his neck. His heart speeded up, his breathing came fast, too fast. Then he couldn't breathe, he was drowning. As everything went black, he heard März say, "You shouldn't have done that, little boy."

He fell to his knees, dizzy, knowing he was going to die. The last thing he saw was the blood on the floor from his godfather's body seeping toward him. Everything went dark.

58

Over the Atlantic

Penderley answered Nicholas's call immediately. "Drummond. Finally. Are you on the ground?"

"No, sir, we're still about an hour out. First, let me thank you for the official invite. Now let me fill you in on what we've learned. I may need some of the lads to help us out." He told Penderley everything they'd discovered on the flight over.

Penderley listened without interruption. When Nicholas was finished, he said, "You can have all the people you need. I will station a team at Oliver Leyland's house straightaway, see if we can't snatch young Adam before Havelock's men get to him. Also, the inquest on Stanford confirms he was murdered—injected with a large dose of ketamine, enough to stop his heart very quickly. We're trying to keep it quiet until we have this well in hand. So tell your pilot to hurry."

"I will. Thank you, and sir, we—"

The plane jerked hard to the left, throwing Mike out of her seat, sending Nicholas's laptop crashing to the floor. Pages flew through the air, their coffee cups, half full of liquid, sprayed across the windows. The plane pulled back left, banked hard, and they heard yells from the cockpit.

Nicholas tried to get to his feet, tried to reach Mike, but the plane was jerking and twisting in the air like it had hit a patch of ice. It spun right, then started to nose down.

Mike yelled, "What's happening?"

Nicholas stumbled up the short aisle to the cockpit, threw open the door. Dan Breaker was half out of his chair, unconscious. Copilot Tom Strauss had a hand over his eyes, moaning. Nicholas righted him and saw a slash of red across the man's eyes. A burn.

He shook Strauss. "What in bloody hell happened?"

Strauss managed a strangled whisper, "Green. Flash," and passed out.

Nicholas pulled him out of the seat, took the copilot chair. He had to get the plane under control.

He saw Mike was holding the edges of the cockpit doorway for dear life. "The pilots are injured, they're both unconscious. I'm going to have to land the plane."

Nicholas was trying to get the plane stable on the horizon, but the navigation display was off. There were four large flat-panel displays across the front of the cockpit, and the HUD—the heads-up display—was blank.

Something had destroyed the electronics in the plane.

Nicholas hit the elevator too hard and the plane whipped to the right, throwing Mike into the cockpit and against the instrument panel.

"Engage the autopilot," she yelled.

"I have. It seems to be damaged. I'll have to fly it myself."

He saw her face was perfectly white, but she was there, with him, ready to act. She said, "Tell me you know how to fly a plane."

"I know enough. Best get your parachute

on, just in case."

"Parachute?" She tried to sound calm, but her mind was screaming, **Oh, please, no. I don't want to jump out of this plane into the ocean.**

She felt the captain's pulse. Thready, but he was alive. The skin across his face was horribly burned, red and blistered. She unbuckled his seat belt and began pulling him from the seat.

"What happened? How did he get this burn?"

Nicholas was adjusting instruments, turning knobs, one hand on the yoke. The plane seemed to soften. The mad shimmying and spinning lessened, and finally, finally, after a lifetime, the plane began to even out. Nicholas said, "The copilot said 'green flash' before he passed out. The only thing I can imagine is he was hit with a green laser. There's nothing commercial grade that can cause this kind of burn. It has to be military. Or private sector."

"Are you saying another plane hit us with a laser, or were we hit from the ground?"

"I don't know." He took a deep breath. "I think we're okay now. I need to get in touch with the tower at London City Airport, let them know they have a guest flying the plane. And then—"

There was a second loud boom, and the plane began to shake and shimmy, harder this time, like it was breaking apart. The instrument panel turned red. "Son of a bitch."

Mike watched the engine light begin to flash on the control panel.

Nicholas shut the engine down and grabbed the radio. "Mayday. Mayday. This is FBI Gulfstream Five. We've been attacked, repeat, we've been hit. Our pilots are down and we've sustained damage to engine one. We need to land immediately."

Mike fought panic. All she could see ahead and to the left and right was blue. A wide expanse of blue. They were over water. There was no land in sight.

"Parachutes, Mike. Now. If we have to jump, we can't go out the door, we'll be sucked into the engines or hit the wings, even at a low speed. We'll have to go out the baggage hatch. So keep that in mind. When the time comes, don't open the cabin door."

She stumbled to the back of the plane, above the galley, where she knew the chutes were stashed. She pulled out four. After fighting her way back to the cockpit, she managed to get both pilots into chutes.

She'd done an emergency egress once before, during the Academy, out of a plain old Cessna with a jump instructor strapped to her. Not something she ever wanted to do again. She prayed harder than she ever had in her life—**Get the plane on the ground, Nicholas, in one piece, you can do it.**

The plane was shuddering, flinging itself about, as if it was fighting the air itself.

"What's happening?"

"We've been hit again. The laser is coming from the air, not the ground. There's a plane up here shooting at us, but I haven't a clue with what. It whipped past a few moments ago. It looks like a retrofitted private jet of some sort—it's definitely not a military jet. Whatever it hit us with damaged the fuselage."

She handed him a parachute, saw her hands were shaking. "You need one, too."

He looked up at her, gave her a smile and nodded toward the yoke. "Hold it steady. It's going to take a bit of strength, since we have no instrument help."

She took the empty pilot's seat, clutched the yoke in a death grip while Nicholas threw his arms through the pack, tightened it down.

"Trade." They switched seats. He did a quick check of the instruments. "All right. We're hanging in, but the stress on the other engine is beginning to show. There's a backup for the engines, so keep the faith, Mike. While you were getting the parachutes, I spoke to the nice gentlemen at the RAF base in Cardiff, Wales. That's where we're going to land, only about a hundred miles to go. Listen, if something goes wrong, and I say jump, we jump. They're with us, they know we're in distress. We'll be rescued before the sharks nibble our legs."

"Happy thought. Nicholas, honestly, can we land? Can you get us to Cardiff?"

"We'll soon have an RAF escort, and they'll see us into the air base. With any luck, they'll identify the plane that's shooting the lasers at us. I can fly us in a straight line, but I can't run us through a dogfight."

She realized he hadn't answered her question.

59

Nicholas wasn't at all sure he could land the plane, but he wasn't about to tell Mike that. He'd done flight simulators before, flown with instructors, but he'd never done a solo landing.

The radio squawked in his ear, and the tinny voice of a British NATS air traffic controller spoke calmly. "We're going to begin your talk down now, Mr. Drummond. Come round to heading two-four-zero."

"Coming about to two-four-zero." As the plane turned, Nicholas squinted out the glass. Land ahead.

Mike saw it, too. "Land ho, Nicholas," and she gave him a shaky smile.

"Very good, Mr. Drummond. Keep to this heading and slow your airspeed to three hundred knots."

He was throttling down when a flash of white burst into his field of vision. "It's that bloody plane again."

It whipped past them, and he saw a bright green light begin to flash.

"Mike, shut your eyes and duck!"

They both ducked, hitting their heads together over the throttle with a sickening crunch. The plane began to shudder again, the fuselage beginning to give way under the pressure of the laser beam.

"What are they doing?"

"Trying to blind us and cut through the metal to create an even bigger problem. Stay down." He keyed the mike to the radio. "We are under attack, repeat, we are under attack. The plane has a laser, that's what incapacitated our pilots to begin with. Burned their skin, blinded them. The laser seems to be able to penetrate the fuselage of the plane."

The NATS controller said, "Hang tight, Gulfstream Five. Keep on this heading. Help is on the way."

Nicholas risked a look. The sky in front of him was clear. He sat up, and Mike followed. The plane came back into their sights, whipping around in the sky in front of them, trying to disrupt the second engine by making them fly through its jet wash. Nicholas saw the plane bank hard, coming around until it was aimed straight for them.

The NATS controller said, "Stay the course, don't move your flight path. Keep your speed. You're going to see a Tornado on your port side. They will eliminate the threat. When they signal, you'll need to bank hard. Make your heading four-four-seven, and hold on tight."

Sure enough, a moment later they saw the gray metal Tornado fly up beside them. The pilot gave them a salute. They watched an ASRAAM missile drop from the underside of the wing, a white tail streaming out behind it. Nicholas heard the Tornado pilot's transmission, "Fox three away."

There was a large explosion that rocked the air around them. Nicholas twisted the knob to move the plane out of the blast radius and away from the falling debris.

"Nicholas, look! They shot him down. Did you see that? They shot him down!"

There were few things more deadly than a short-range air-to-air missile off a Tornado. Nicholas said, "Good. That plane was attacking federal agents in British airspace."

"But who? Who in the world would attack our plane? They tried to kill us."

He said grimly, "When they fish the pieces of the plane out of the Bristol Channel, we'll find out. But I think we know who might want us dead and gone."

"Havelock."

"Oh, yes."

"You do know what you're doing, right?"

He gave her a cocky grin. "We'll see, won't we?"

Nicholas kept his hands steady on the yoke, and the radio spoke to him again. "You're clear, Gulfstream V. Follow the Tornadoes home, sir. Come to heading two-two-zero, drop your speed to one hundred fifty knots. I'm handing you off to Cardiff Tower, they're going to talk you down. Good luck."

Mike had headphones on now, heard the exchange. "Where are we going, exactly?"

"I would expect we're heading to Ministry of Defense—MoD—Saint Athan. It's a Royal Air Force base in southern Wales.

It's where the Tornadoes scrambled from."

"I wonder if Prince William will be there to greet us."

Nicholas laughed. "I'm glad you can still joke at a time like this."

She started to say it was better than hysterics, but she didn't. She stared straight ahead and prayed for all she was worth.

The tower at MoD St. Athan hailed them. "Hello, Special Agent Drummond. I'm Daniel Healy, the National Air Traffic Services general manager here at Cardiff Tower. We work both landing strips because of the proximity of the base to our airport. I understand you're hand-flying the plane; you have no autopilot and your ILS has been knocked out?"

The man's voice was wonderfully calm and Mike felt some tension ease.

"Correct. Our electronics are damaged. And engine one is out as well."

"That **is** vexing. Have flying experience, do you?"

"Some. In a Tornado simulator. A few years ago."

Healy laughed a bit. "Roger that. You'll be fine. Now, the airport should be at your ten o'clock. Do you see us?"

"I do."

"Set your flaps to twenty, and make your speed one hundred twenty-five knots. Be prepared, we have some low-level wind shear, you'll want to flare as you're landing, then do an idle reverse to slow yourself down."

"Easy for you to say."

They lined up, and the landing strip at MoD St. Athan appeared on their horizon a few moments later, a long snake running straightaway from them. The runway was lined with emergency vehicles, their lights flashing.

"Looks like they're throwing us quite the party, Nicholas. Champagne and caviar, I hope."

"I'll take most anything you put in my hand at the moment. Okay, focus. This is the fun part."

Mike did what Nicholas told her, twisted the knobs to new headings, dropped the landing gear. Healy talked them down, making adjustments here and there. The ground rose up. The plane skidded as Nicholas reversed their single engine and applied the brakes, setting it into a sickening sideways spin, but finally it groaned to a stop half on and half off the runway.

They were alive, on the ground safely. Mike jumped up from her seat and hugged Nicholas tight. She said against his cheek, "You did it! And we're even in one piece. The plane is still in one piece, too." She gave him a whopping big kiss on the mouth. "What's best? No sharks. You're not going to be a lamebrain for at least a month." And she gave him another kiss.

He said against her ear, "Twice? That's good. I'll take what I can get."

60

MoD St. Athan
Wales
3:00 p.m.

The emergency personnel attended the pilots, both still unconscious, their burns deep and purpled. They'd both been staring at the laser when it had struck. Mike and Nicholas watched them carried away on stretchers to the waiting ambulances, and heard some cheers from the men below.

It was a pity about the beautiful Gulfstream, Nicholas thought. The laser had bit directly through the metal, leaving deep gouges in its sides, and blackening the glossy white paint around the left engine. A few more hits and they'd have broken up midair.

Mike came up to stand beside him. "The director's not going to be too happy about what we did to his baby." But she was grinning like mad. It felt great to be alive.

He hugged her, this time kissed her. "We

made it."

They were escorted into the RAF Headquarters, and given hot tea while they were debriefed. Once everyone was satisfied, the base commander told them the plane that attacked them, the one the Tornado shot down, was being recovered. They'd know soon enough who it belonged to, though Nicholas had no doubts as to who was behind the attempts on their lives. And he thought, **So you're really that scared of me, are you, Havelock? You've a good reason to be. I'm going to bury you, you sodding bastard.**

The commander told them the pilots were being treated for burns and flash blindness by the base medics and were both expected to recover fully, though both would be scarred.

The commander also confirmed the laser wasn't commercial grade, it was even beyond military grade. It was a very powerful weapon, and no one had ever seen one used in the civilian or military theaters. They would start a full-scale investigation immediately.

The base commander's XO told them they were to be choppered to London on the double, on orders of one very irritated man named Hamish Penderley.

Nicholas pictured his former stiff-necked boss in his mind—this little kerfuffle was guaranteed to get the old buzzard's blood pumping.

Their gear was retrieved from the Gulfstream, and when they walked back out onto the tarmac, Nicholas saw Mike eying the green Chinook helicopter with something like dread.

"What's this? I thought you loved a good chopper ride."

"Right now, all I'm thinking about is how nice it is to be on terra firma, but no, back we go bounding back up into the air." But she hopped into the seat, put on her headset, and pulled her seat belt very tight.

The British Royal Air Force was true to their word, and thirty-five minutes later, they were buzzing the Thames, ready to set down at RAF Northolt.

As they watched the copter lift off back

to its base in Wales, Nicholas said to Mike, "Remind me to send a thank-you note to our friends at the National Air Traffic Services."

"Let's send flowers, too. And chocolates. Maybe my firstborn—and yours, too."

A black eyebrow went up.

She gave him a manic grin. "I didn't mean it to come out quite like that, sorry."

"Whatever, interesting idea."

There was a modified black 5 Series BMW waiting for them on the tarmac. Against it leaned Hamish Penderley, detective chief superintendent of the Metropolitan Police's Operational Command Unit. Since there'd been distance and time between them, looking at him now Nicholas would swear Penderley could billboard the benign grandfather. Penderley even smiled at them, a warm smile, something Nicholas couldn't remember ever seeing, but then boom—"The prodigal returns. Did you have to do it with such a splash, Drummond?"

"Not a splash, sir, we managed to make

it to land."

Penderley shook his head. "What a cock-up."

"No, sir, it wasn't my fault."

Penderley gave a bark of laughter, shook Nicholas's hand.

"Of course you remember Special Agent Michaela Caine."

"Yes, of course." Penderley shook her hand. "I still remember that hat you wore the day of Elaine's funeral. Welcome back, Agent Caine. I see you're still walking and talking, quite a feat in this chap's company."

Mike said, "Good thing I come from hardy stock. But you know, sir, around Nicholas, you're certainly never bored."

A grizzled eyebrow flew up. "I'm still recovering. I still can't get my head around the fact that he's now an American FBI agent. And he thought I was strict."

She'd liked Penderley when she'd met him at Elaine York's funeral back in January. "We're lucky to have him, sir. His mind would be a terrible thing to waste."

Penderley laughed heartily. "Right. You're welcome to it, all it ever did was cause me trouble. Come along."

Once the BMW moved into traffic, Penderley got down to business. "We've blanketed Leyland's house in Notting Hill. It appears no one's there, and we've had eyes on the house for the past two hours. No one's heard from Leyland, either. His people said he had a meeting at noon today and hasn't been seen since.

"I'm beginning to worry. Special Branch is making all sorts of noise, wanting in on this. We won't be able to put them off much longer, especially now that they know about this phantom submarine and Loch Eriboll, is it? Near the North Sea?"

"That's right. Loch Eriboll. I have the exact coordinates for the sub."

"Bringing up a sub isn't something just anyone can do. The planning has begun, but they won't be able to be in place to raise it until tomorrow at the earliest."

"A problem with that plan, sir. Havelock is surely making his own preparations to raise this sub, if he hasn't managed it already. He needs Adam Pearce for the final coordinates, so we need to find this kid before Havelock gets his hands on him.

"It's scary stuff. With Havelock's assembling polonium, going off the grid, and this unknown weapon, there's no time to waste. Adam Pearce told us to meet him at Leyland's. Hopefully he's there now staying out of sight. Then we'll head to Loch Eriboll, locate the sub and find this mythical key everyone's searching for."

"What's the key to?"

"Possibly to something created by Madame Curie way back in the early part of the twentieth century. Something that can go with the polonium Havelock's been gathering. Putting together the two supposedly will make a very powerful weapon. We need Adam Pearce and Sophie. They're the only ones who know the whole story."

Well, also all the members of the Order knew, but his father's request, no, more a plea, sounded in his head. **Protect the Order, keep the police away from them.** Very well, he would remain quiet for the time being. But if everything went arse up, he himself would arrest every last member he could find, and be damned what happened to the Order.

Mike was watching him. He had the odd sensation that she knew what he was thinking.

Nicholas said, "Any sign of Havelock?"

"His plane landed in London, then departed again. We have no idea where he is."

His mobile rang. He glanced at the screen. "Who's this, 01856? That's the Oxford code, isn't it?"

Mike said, "Answer it. Maybe we'll get lucky, and it's Adam Pearce, calling to say he's saved the day."

"Perhaps." Nicholas put it on speaker and answered. "Hullo?"

A woman's voice, low, frantic. "Agent Drummond? It's Sophie Pearce. You have to help me."

61

West Park
Oxford
3:45 p.m.

She had to get out of this room, out of the house, back to London, to find Adam. She looked toward the fireplace, looked again, and knew what to do.

She picked up a poker, two and a half feet of solid, tempered iron, and hefted it in her hands. She went to the door, took a deep breath, and screamed.

"Help me! I'm sick, help me! Something's wrong with me. I'm going to vomit. Please, you have to let me use the bathroom."

The guard was still out there. Good. He yelled, "Shut up."

"Please. I'm so sick. Something's wrong. You don't want to get in trouble for—ooh!" She started making gagging noises.

She heard the guard curse, then the jangle of keys.

As he opened the door, she shoved hard against it, knocking him off balance, and struck him in the chest with the poker as hard as she could. She slammed the poker into the top of his head.

He was out cold. She hit him again for good measure, then ran down the long, wide hall, nearly dark because all the doors on either side were closed. She was almost to the stairs when she heard voices from below. Someone must have heard her yelling about being sick, or they'd heard the guard. No time. She ducked into the nearest room, pulled the door closed behind her, and threw the bolt.

She was in a private study, oak floor covered with antique carpets, bookshelves climbed the walls, dark as the paneling. A computer on a large mahogany desk, and a phone.

She grabbed up the phone and started to dial Adam's cell. No, better, the FBI agent, Nicholas Drummond. It didn't matter that she'd lied to him, and he'd known it, that he'd taken her father's SD card and now knew about the Order. But what if he hadn't come to England, what if—no, she knew he'd come. What was his number? She forced herself to calm, pictured the card he'd handed her with his cell number scrawled on the back. She let the image coalesce—as she did when learning a new language—and the letters and numbers took shape, rearranged themselves into patterns— and there it was. She dialed. **Please, please, know where I am, please be able to find me.**

"Hullo?"

"Agent Drummond? It's Sophie Pearce. You have to help me. Please tell me you're in England."

"Sophie? Yes, we're here. Are you okay? Where are you? We've been looking for you."

"I don't know. North of London, but Alex made me pull a hood over my head near Weymouth. I think it was about fifteen minutes later when we stopped. There was a long gravel drive and the house I'm in is big, and there are gardens and acres and acres of land. I'm on the third floor. Oh, no, I hear people coming."

"Don't panic. You must stay on the

phone, keep talking to me. We'll triangulate the call." He spoke to someone out of her hearing, then came back. "Do you know who ordered you kidnapped?"

"It had to be the Order, to protect me, Alex said, but I don't think it's true. Have you found Adam? Is he okay? Do you know about the sub?"

"We're looking for Adam right now and, yes, I know about the sub."

"They want to find out where the sub is, and Adam's the only one who knows. Unless you managed to decode the SD card?"

Drummond said, "Yes, I did and I know exactly where the sub is. Describe the gardens for me, tell me about the grounds of the estate. Maybe you'll see something helpful."

She left the phone and ran to the window. The view was slightly different here, she could see more of the house, more of the land. She was back on in an instant. "It seems like it's in the middle of nowhere. The long driveway, there are trees on either side in two perfect rows. I'm facing west, there seems to be some sort of big turret to my right, and the house is sand-colored stone."

"Well done. Where's Alex?"

"I don't know. His name isn't Grossman, it's Shepherd."

"We know. He's MI Five."

"No, that can't be right. He was working undercover to protect my father, that's what he told me, but now I don't know. MI Five?"

"He does both. However, he hasn't acted like a man with your best interests at heart, has he?"

"He spent the whole plane ride telling me the Order was going to protect me, but then he brought me here, locked me in a room and put a guard on the door. I managed to trick the guard into opening the door and I bashed him with a poker." She heard footsteps outside the study door. "They're here—please, find me soon!"

"Keep the line open."

She heard his words even as she looked around the study. No place to hide. She watched the deadbolt slide back.

The door opened, and a tall, lean, middle-aged man in a beautiful gray suit stepped in. He was handsome, objectively, but when he smiled at her, she felt fear slam into her.

"Hello, Sophie." His voice was smooth, his accent odd, some British, some German. "Ah, I see you've made a call. Hang up the phone now."

"No. I won't do it." She ran back to the desk and grabbed up the phone. "Please, help me!"

He crossed the room in three strides and slapped her, hard across the face, slammed the phone down into its cradle, and yanked the cord from the wall. Still smiling, he threw the phone across the room. It crashed against the marble fireplace.

He turned back, grabbed her hair, and hurled her toward the bookcase. She landed hard on the floor, her back hitting so hard two books fell off the shelves to land beside her.

He came down on his haunches in front of her, grabbed her hair again, forced her face up. "Don't ever disobey me again. Do you understand?"

His hand was so tight in her hair she could barely nod.

"Good. Now you will stand and walk over to that chair. You will sit down and then we will have a conversation."

He gave her his hand, a long narrow hand, long, thin fingers. She felt her heart pounding, fast and hard, felt her brain blur, and she wanted to run and scream and scream—hysteria. No, she had to get herself together. Her scalp hurt and her back was sore from striking the bookcase, but she could move. She took his hand and wanted to scream again. His flesh was dry and cold. "Who are you?"

"Dr. Manfred Havelock, of course. I'm looking forward to our getting to know each other."

He pulled her to the desk, shoved her down into the chair.

62

West Park
4:00 p.m.

Sophie was sitting backward in the chair. Havelock jerked her arms behind her, making her groan with the pain, and bound her wrists together. He tied a thin gag in her mouth. He straightened and stood for a moment, looking down at her. He picked up the letter opener, lightly glided the sharp edge along her cheek, and laughed softly. Then he was behind her slashing the letter opener down, ripping her shirt to her waist, and he spread the fabric apart. He sliced through her bra strap, and looked with pleasure at the flawless expanse of white skin. He touched a fingertip to the slight mark from her bra, rubbed it away.

"Tell me the coordinates of the submarine."

"I don't know. I swear to you I don't know!"

"Of course you do, dear heart."

"No, no, I don't. Adam wouldn't tell me. He said it was better I didn't know, it'd be safer." Now, that was a joke. She waited, so terrified she could scarcely breathe.

He said no more, merely looked down at her. Oh, her back would mark so beautifully. But he had to be careful and not get carried away. What was important now were the coordinates to the submarine. März was already on the **Gravitania** with Adam Pearce, and the damned boy was refusing to tell him anything. März wanted to beat it out of him, but Havelock knew März didn't have the talent to do it properly. He'd fall into a rage that turned his world red and he wouldn't be able to stop and the boy would be dead. So it was up to him. He knew exactly what to do.

He looked up to see Elise slip into the room. "Come here and look at her, my dear. Her eyes—can you see the fear in them? I have asked her the coordinates. I have been polite. She swears she doesn't know. So I will move on. Watch what your master can do."

Sophie pulled and jerked her wrists.

Havelock said, "Go ahead, Ms. Pearce, struggle to your heart's content." He ran his hand down the length of Sophie's spine, his eyes on Elise the whole time. Ah, now she was thrashing about, making frantic yipping sounds. Elise ran her tongue slowly over her bottom lip and he stilled, but only for a moment.

He hit a button on his cell phone. While it rang, he said, "Now, Ms. Pearce, we're going to play a little game." The call connected, and he spoke into the cell.

"März? Do you have the boy close?"

"Yes, he is here. He is listening."

"Then by all means let's allow them to speak to one another."

Havelock punched the speaker button and set the phone down on the desk, close to Sophie. He smiled as he reached inside her shirt and caressed one breast. Then he slapped her hard on the back. She rewarded him with a muffled groan through the gag. Havelock walked around to the side of the chair so she could look at him.

"Very good, very good. Now I want you

to cry for your brother."

Her dark hair tangled in her face and he pushed it out of her eyes. He saw fear, panic, but, alas, determination.

"Stubborn, are you? I think a little added incentive will make all the difference."

He took Elise's favorite cat-o'-nine-tails, the one with small lead weights on the ends of the soft suede, perfect for leaving marks on the flesh without opening a wound, moved into position, and struck.

Not terribly hard, he didn't want her to think this was the worst it could possibly be, not yet.

The whip whistled through the air and landed against her back. She jerked, her breath heaved out, and she grit her teeth.

He did it again.

"Your father told the Order he'd found the sub. I've been waiting for this to happen, you see. I'd been watching him, watching the communications between your father and your brother. I've been waiting for so long, so many years, so much planning."

He struck her, but she made no sound.

"Yes, I had to identify exactly who would help me, how I could get into the Order."

He struck again, harder, and then again. She was crying behind the gag, low, retching sobs.

"Your father wasn't supposed to die. It was incompetent bungling and I regret it. He had so much knowledge, and it was a true waste, losing him." He hit her twice more, once from each direction. "Ah, Elise, the stripes are rising, a lovely red, and there is bruising beginning over the ribs." He leaned forward and jerked the gag from her mouth and struck her again.

She yelled. It was delicious, too delicious. He had to keep himself focused, couldn't allow himself to enjoy this the way he'd prefer. **Pay attention, pay attention.** "Perhaps you're an exceptional liar, sweetheart, perhaps you don't know the coordinates after all?"

He grabbed her hair and pulled her head back. "Tell me, come on now, tell me."

"I don't know the damned coordinates!"

He paused. "Yes, I believe you. So now you must tell your brother to give März the coordinates, or we're going to move on to the real show. You believe I've already hurt you? You have no idea what I can do."

He held the phone to her lips. "Tell him."

She was breathing hard, pain choking her. Her back was on fire. She met his eyes and slowly she nodded. He put the cell phone to her mouth and Sophie yelled, "Don't tell him anything, Adam!"

Havelock shook his head at her like a mournful parent. "That **was** a mistake, my dear."

He set the phone next to her head, selected the smaller of the three whips he had with him, the leather one studded with small iron rivets. He knew from personal experience the pain was extraordinary, when applied correctly.

The first blow brought round welts out on her skin. The second drew blood. And she screamed and screamed for him. He paused, breathing hard, and picked up the cell phone.

"Do you hear that, Adam? She's bleeding now. I'll move on to other, more persuasive methods if you do not tell me the coordinates immediately."

He heard sounds of a struggle, März's curses, then Adam Pearce's furious voice spoke in his ear. "I'll tell you, you sadistic bastard. Don't touch her again, swear to me you'll let her go."

Havelock slowly slid the whip down Sophie's spine, smiled. "Of course I swear. Where is the sub? I want to hear the coordinates myself."

Adam choked out a series of numbers, latitude and longitude.

A moment later März got on the phone.

"We've confirmed the coordinates. Right where you believed it was, northern Scotland, in Loch Eriboll."

"Excellent," Havelock replied. "Send the coordinates to my cell phone, and move the **Gravitania** into position. I will be there shortly."

Havelock slipped his cell into his pocket as he looked dispassionately at Sophie Pearce's back, spun the chair around to see the tears streaming down her face. He'd done a nice job, he doubted Elise could do any better. He struck palm open across her face for good measure, then kissed her softly on the forehead and untied her wrists. "Come along. We have a quick trip to make."

He grabbed her hair and dragged her out of the study and into the hallway, Elise behind him, no expression on her face.

Alex Shepherd came running toward him, saw Sophie, and stopped cold. "You're not taking her anywhere. You and Weston promised she would be okay, that she would be safe here."

"Move out of my way, Shepherd."

But Alex didn't move. He drew a gun, but Havelock was quicker. He already had a gun in his hand and shot him in the chest. He dragged Sophie over his body, and half dragged her down the stairs.

At the bottom of the stairs stood the guard who'd allowed Sophie to escape. He was holding his head. He looked up, an excuse halfway out his mouth when Havelock shot him in the forehead.

Edward Weston came through the front door at that moment, looked at the dead guard, at Sophie Pearce. He asked calmly,

"Do we have what we need?"

Havelock shoved Sophie at him. "Get her in the plane. Let's go."

"Where's Shepherd?"

"Dead."

Weston threw out his hands. "What? Why? We need him."

"No, what we need is the key, and now I know exactly where it is. Now, let's go." He signaled to Elise, who looked through Weston and followed Havelock out the front door.

"No, he's not dead," Weston said.

Havelock turned to see Alex Shepherd coming slowly down the stairs, his gun locked on Havelock. He raised a brow. "My, my. Still alive, are we? Wearing that armor I had made for you? I suppose I should have shot you in the head. No matter, you can bring her." He pointed the gun at Sophie's temple. "Let's go."

63

Notting Hill
4:00 p.m.

Penderley said, "The tech lads are saying the phone has some sort of scrambled signal, bouncing off relays throughout the country. The call may not have originated in Oxford after all, but we'll be optimistic. We'll find her." Nicholas only hoped they'd find her in time.

They parked a block away from Leyland's house so they wouldn't alert Adam Pearce or Oliver Leyland, if he was there. The windows of Leyland's white stucco town house were dark, the four-story mansion silent in the cool spring air.

Dark low-hanging clouds were piling in. The wind had kicked up, swirling through the town houses on Lansdowne Crescent and the green communal gardens of Notting Hill. Rain was coming soon. Mike shoved her hair out of her face. "It looks like we're about to have nasty weather."

"Yes, it does, doesn't it?" he said. "It's

good to be home." He saw himself at Old Farrow Hall, running through the labyrinth hedges toward the center even as the rain battered down. What was he, twelve years old?

Penderley said, "My team are set up outside the perimeter."

Nicholas said, "And you promised to keep them there, sir. It's only the three of us. Gareth? You ready? I don't want to make Adam think I lied to him."

Gareth Scott walked up, patted his chest, bulky with body armor. "Ready as I'll ever be, let's get it done, mate."

They moved silently toward the house, Nicholas and Mike, weapons at their sides, following Gareth. They skirted the black-fenced front steps and forest green front door and moved to the side of the house to another entrance.

The side door was slightly ajar. There were clear rake marks on the lock. It had been forced.

Gareth gave Penderley a running commentary through their radios as they entered the house from the side entrance.

They were on the lowest floor. There were a dozen windows, and despite the dark clouds overhead, light spilled into the hallways and rooms, making it easy to see. They split three ways, clearing the ground floor quickly. No signs of a struggle, no signs of Adam or Oliver Leyland. No signs of anything.

Nicholas didn't like this, didn't like it at all.

They met in the grand foyer under a centuries-old crystal chandelier and began up the massive wooden staircase.

They found Leyland's body on the first-floor landing, his head leaning against the panels. His legs were bent backward, his arms dislocated, making him seem a crumpled marionette, his strings cut and dropped straight down from the landing above.

Mike swallowed. "Is this Leyland?"

"Yes, it is."

"Somebody pushed him over."

Gareth fell to his knees beside Leyland. He looked up. "Sir, do you read me? Leyland is down. Repeat, Leyland is down.

He was hurt badly, sir, before he died. We're moving to the second floor. Do not send anyone else in here until we've cleared the place."

Gareth skirted Leyland's body, signaling to Nicholas he was going to move to their left. Nicholas nodded, taking the low side right. Mike was in front of him going straight.

The gunshot came out of nowhere, suppressed, like a pop, but they knew what it was.

64

Nicholas only had time to see Gareth fall before he was tackled from behind. He went down hard on his knees. Mike whirled around, right into the waiting arms of a big bruiser nearly twice her size, hard with muscle, strong as Rocky.

Nicholas shouted to her, but she couldn't move. Rocky's arms were tightening more and more, he was going to crush her ribs if she didn't break loose. Gareth was down, Nicholas was under attack—she had only herself.

Rocky let up a bit, banged her hand against her leg, and she let the Glock go. She pulled an old trick—let herself go limp. It surprised him enough to give her time to force her shoulder under his forearm and twist hard to the right, and despite his weight advantage, she sent him over her shoulder to sprawl on his back on a thick Berber runner. The carpet cushioned his landing and he was back on his feet, a surprising shock for such a big man, and he was coming at her again, fists up, protecting his face.

He kicked her leg out from under her and she went down on her knees. His hands went around her throat, his fingers bent inward to gouge her eyes. She jerked and heaved so he couldn't get to her eyes, twisted onto her back and kicked him hard in the gut. He windmilled backward, then started cursing her. She kicked him in the kneecap, but it wasn't enough, so she kicked him in the groin as hard as she could. She realized in one part of her brain that she was out of control. She wanted to kill him, she wanted to obliterate him.

He was strong, fast for his size, and despite the blow to his groin, he was up and dancing toward her again. **Bring it on, Rocky, bring it on.** No way was she going to let him beat her. She blocked the next punch to her face, saw her chance. She slid her thigh in between Rocky's legs, and crashed her left leg down hard, at the perfect angle. He went down with a howl, and she stomped on him again, in the exact same spot, and was rewarded with the fine crunch of bone. She'd blown out his knee.

Mike flipped him onto his stomach and cuffed him. He was yelling, cursing, so she hit him hard in the back of the head with her fist, knocking him out. At last he shut up.

She took a huge breath, felt all the bruises along her ribs, but she was okay, she'd won. She sent a prayer of thanks to her FBI hand-to-hand combat coach, press-checked her Glock, and yelled, "Nicholas!"

She found Gareth first. He'd taken a shot to the neck not an inch above the top of his body armor and was bleeding, but it wasn't too bad, not an artery, thankfully, a through and through. She ripped his sleeve off and pressed it to his neck. He groaned and his eyes opened.

Of all things, he smiled up at her. "Alive, am I?"

She laid her palm along his cheek. "You're going to be okay. Hold this." She pressed the shirt sleeve to his neck, guided his hand to it. "Help's on the way."

"No, it isn't. They cut our comms. I called

to Penderley, but no one's come in after us. Where's Nicholas?"

"I'm going to go find him now."

But first, she tested her comms unit. Gareth was right, no communication. Disruption technologies were one of the FBI's greatest fears, from knocking out comms to taking down planes and setting off EMPs, Havelock had clearly figured out how to make it happen.

She had to find Nicholas, but first she had to let the Brits outside know they were in trouble. She couldn't shout, she didn't know how many bad guys were in the house.

She fired her Glock through a big glass window that gave onto a garden, straight down into the dirt. It was loud, a blast in the quiet. The shot that had gotten Gareth in the neck was suppressed. Hers wasn't. That should bring them running. She tore off a sleeve of her shirt and attached it to the window as a signal.

"Go find Nicholas, Mike. I'm okay." Gareth pulled out a knife, thin, deadly sharp.

She listened hard as she ran quietly toward the stairs to the upper level. She heard nothing.

Her ribs were on fire, but she paid no attention. She had to find Nicholas.

She saw a trail of fresh blood drops on the stairs, teardrop shaped, the fat end of the blood drops closer to her. Since the velocity pattern was moving away from her, she knew whoever was bleeding had gone up the stairs instead of coming down.

65

Mike followed the trail of blood up the stairs. There, windows were fewer, making it darker. It was silent as a tomb.

Come on, Nicholas, where are you? And where are you, **Penderley? Come on!**

Mike cleared room by room. The last door at the end of the hall was slightly ajar. She paused, listened. She heard breathing. Whoever was in there was waiting for her.

She edged sideways and looked through the crack. She saw Nicholas lying on his back under a large square window. Rain was coming down hard, slamming against the windowpanes. He was deathly still.

She kicked open the door, but forced herself not to run in, to keep to the side.

Five shots blasted out. She closed her eyes a moment, again blessed her training.

She aimed into the breach between the frame and the door and fired, praying the bullet wouldn't ricochet and hit Nicholas.

There was a yell, then silence.

She'd hit him, whoever him was.

Adrenaline shot through her. Time to take a chance. She went in low and fast, rolled across the floor, coming up in a perfect crouch, arms extended, facing the now open door. The shooter wasn't anywhere to be seen. Another door—she yanked it open and ran through a bathroom and back out into the hall and saw splatters of blood. The hall was empty.

She heard Nicholas moan. She shut and locked both doors, and dropped to her knees beside him and pulled him into her arms. She saw a syringe sticking out of his neck. The plunger wasn't depressed, and a thick, viscous gold liquid was still in the tube. Still, he must have gotten a bit of a dose. She jerked the needle from his neck. The wound began to bleed, and she blotted it with her remaining sleeve. His eyelids began to flutter; he was coming around.

"Nicholas. Wake up." She shook his shoulder. His eyes opened. He shoved himself away from her with such force she landed on her butt.

She scrambled back to him, grabbed

his arm. "Nicholas, there's another shooter in the house. They cut our comms, I fired a shot outside, so I hope Penderley realizes we're in trouble."

Nicholas was on his knees, facing her, weaving a bit. Slowly, he raised his hand to his neck. She saw his pupils were dilated, saw he still wasn't with it.

She shook him as hard as she could. "Come on, Nicholas. Pull it together."

"Trying." His voice sounded nearly normal.

"Okay, okay, stay still." She rose and looked through the thick pounding rain down into the garden, but they were on the wrong side of the house. No Penderley.

Nicholas grabbed a chair and pulled himself up. "Whatever that ruddy bastard shot me with is strong. My head's still spinning."

"He got out through the bathroom, over there. When I got back to the hall, I didn't see him, but I saw a blood trail, so I gave him a shot for you." She helped him to his feet, her shoulder under his arm. She got him up and into a chair.

He tried to smile at her. "My lips are numb, and my hands, but I'm okay."

"Good, because we need to get out of here in case that bastard comes back with reinforcements."

"Where's Gareth?" Nicholas got slowly to his feet. He finally managed to straighten.

"He was shot in the neck, but he'll be all right."

"Good. Good. You look like you had quite a dustup. You won, I hope?"

"I did. Rocky's on his belly, nicely handcuffed. I blew out his kneecap."

"Remind me not to get on your bad side. You're all right?"

She nodded. "Don't worry about me. We need to catch whoever's running around this house with a gun and a stack of syringes. How did he get you?"

He looked surprised. "I have no idea. One minute the three of us were going up the stairs, the next I woke up in your arms." He gave her a look. "Rather enjoyed that part of it." And then he lightly cupped her face, then shook his head, and dropped his hand.

"Yeah, yeah, can you walk without help?" Actually, she'd have enjoyed it as well if she hadn't been so scared.

He took three steps to test and nodded, then realized, "That bloody prat took my Glock."

"Give me your spare magazine, I'm down three bullets."

He handed it over and she switched them out. "Okay, let's go. Slowly. You're still not too steady on your pins."

There was a clear blood trail down the hallway, then suddenly it stopped. He must have bound the wound. They went down another flight, paused on the small, dark landing.

They both smelled the blood. They heard him wheezing, each breath an effort. She'd lung-shot him, but he was still on his feet, still ready to fight, waiting for them by the main staircase. He probably realized Penderley's men were right outside and he was stuck in here. And he was fully prepared to kill them.

Mike dropped and rolled to the top of the stairs, came up on her elbows, and as the man raised his gun, she pumped four bullets center mass. He stared at her in surprise, dropped his gun, then quietly fell backward onto the beautifully appointed foyer just as Penderley's tactical team burst through the front door.

66

Nicholas watched the paramedics wheel Gareth to the curb. His face was white, he was clearly in pain. He touched Gareth's arm as he passed. "I'm glad you're okay, mate."

Gareth managed a crooked smile. "You're going to owe me for years."

"I'll stand you a pint at the Feathers when you're up on your feet."

"You'll stand me a pint for the next ten years," he called out as the doors closed and the ambulance pulled away.

Oliver Leyland's body stayed in the house, along with the two shooters, one dead, one unconscious and cuffed, while Mike told Penderley and his team what had happened inside, her voice calm, emotionless, but she wanted to yell, **I won, I won, I took down both of them.**

When there was no more to say, Penderley patted her on the shoulder. "Well done, lass. Damn well done."

Mike said, "I don't know how they cut our comms. Both Gareth and I tried to call you."

"We heard a gunshot, that was good enough. We were with you less than three minutes later."

Mike couldn't believe it. Only three minutes? No, at least an eon had passed. "Hopefully, Rocky will talk." And then she had to explain.

Penderley patted her shoulder again, making her smile, then he turned to Nicholas. "Only Leyland was inside? No sign of Adam Pearce?"

"No sign. Can we pull CCTV feed on the street, see who entered Leyland's house and when?"

"We're working on it now. Also working on IDs for the two men who tried to kill you and Mike."

"I'm going to bet you'll find they're German nationals. Havelock has a history of sending his own men to do his dirty work, not using local talent."

"Understood. Also, while you were inside, the call came in from the boys at MoD Saint Athan. That missile did its job thoroughly, only small pieces of the tail of the plane that attacked you were located. It was a Gulfstream, though. A private jet."

"Ten to one it was Havelock's. Who else would have tried to stop us coming over?"

Penderley said, "First the chancellor of the Exchequer is killed, and now the head of the Bank of England? FBI planes are being attacked with lasers, there are two Americans on British soil being held against their will, and we haven't the foggiest idea where to start looking for them. Not to mention the world press has already reported on Alfie Stanford's death. When they find out about the murder of Oliver Leyland, they're going to be asking questions. You know they'll put it together soon enough, then all hell will break loose. This is a disaster." Penderley looked ready to stick his head in the noose.

"Sir," Mike said, her hand on his forearm. "Once we have the weapon and Havelock, once we show the world what he is, what he has done, including the murder of these two fine men, the world media will crucify him."

Penderley gave her an odd look. "Do we tell them we have saved the world from disaster, Agent Caine?"

She grinned. "That will be up to the leaders of our two countries, I would imagine. Let's go do our jobs now, sir, let's get this done."

"Drummond, you agree?"

"Yes, sir, I do." Nicholas touched his fingers to his neck. The injection site throbbed and pulsed. He wished he could remember exactly what had happened, perhaps it would all come back. Would he be dead if Mike hadn't gotten there in time? Yes, it would have been all over for him. But he was here and breathing, his brain finally working again. Mike was right, time to get it done. He said, "We know Adam Pearce was in the house at some point since your team found a laptop and gym bag stuffed in the back of a bedroom closet. We also know he was taken. The team's still up there, with Adam Pearce's things?"

Penderley nodded.

"Good," Mike said, "let's see if there's

anything of use on the computer."

They were careful not to step in the blood that pooled on the landings. There were crime scene techs everywhere.

He saw Mike didn't look at the man she'd shot. Her back was ramrod straight, her ponytail was a little off-center, her shirt ripped, but she was excited, he could feel it pouring off her.

"Mike?"

She stopped. "Nicholas? Is something wrong?"

He gave her a long look, shook his head. "Let's see what's on Adam Pearce's computer."

67

After making certain Adam's laptop wasn't bugged or trip-wired or attached to a microscopic explosive, Nicholas powered it up. A few moments later, he began to smile.

"Yes, this is definitely Adam's computer. It's a hacker's dream. He's got a sophisticated and completely custom operating system that I've never seen before. And it's encrypted to the hilt." He hit a few keys, testing the security. "This is one of the strongest encryptions I've ever seen. All this from a nineteen -year-old."

Mike said, "Impressed, are you?"

"Very. This is beautiful work."

"Can you beat it?"

Nicholas cocked an eyebrow. "Oh, I can beat it. He may be fresh and new, but I've been around the block a few times. Let's see how his new work stands up to my old-school hacking skills."

He uploaded his decryption program and set it to run.

While Nicholas worked on breaking into Adam's computer, Mike looked through his bag. "Underwear, toothbrush, and look here, about five thousand in cash. Where'd he pick that up?" She dug deeper. There was a burgundy-colored passport in the bottom of the bag, issued from the United Kingdom, in the name of Thomas Wren. "This is how he got here. A false passport. It's a good one, too." She gave it to Nicholas, who looked it over, then made a quick call. Five minutes later his mobile rang. Customs at Heathrow showed Thomas Wren had entered the UK in the wee hours of the morning, off British Airways flight 176.

Nicholas said, "Adam flew first class, mind you, on a commercial flight out of New York. He's got a good disguise, no wonder the NGI database didn't pick up on it."

She thought of how he'd looked at Ariston's yesterday morning and shook her head. So much had happened. Yesterday felt like ten years ago. She watched the rain lashing down, obscuring even the cars parked in the neighboring drive. The media must really be committed over here to run around in this weather. She didn't know if she could get used to this all the time.

Nicholas's mobile rang. He listened, agreed, and punched off. "Penderley's preparing a statement about Leyland. He told me to hurry with the computer, see what we have. He says the media has picked up on our presence here. Look here, Mike."

She stared down at the screen. File after file opened, stacking window upon window of encrypted code, each being run through Nicholas's powerful program and coming out the other side in plain text. It was in computerspeak, techy code she couldn't read, but Nicholas clearly could. Not only read it, but understand what it meant.

Nicholas paged through the files for a few moments, then he said, "Yes!" His face changed. He shook his head, his look disbelieving.

"What is it?"

She saw alarm in his eyes. "What? What is it?"

It was as if he had to force out the words. "I know what the weapon is, Mike. We must stop Havelock. We must stop him now."

68

Nicholas stood, slapped the laptop closed. "We must get to Loch Eriboll immediately. You know Havelock used Sophie as leverage to get Adam to tell him the coordinates. He has them or he's close to getting them. We have to get the key before Havelock."

Mike grabbed his arm. "What is the weapon, Nicholas?"

He grabbed Adam's computer. "Let's find Penderley, he needs to know this, too."

She ran after him down the stairs to the kitchen, where Penderley was hovering over a crime scene tech.

"What is this? What have you found out?"

Nicholas motioned both Penderley and Mike into the elegant dining room. "Both Adam Pearce and I cross-hacked the files of Manheim Technologies, we both have his research. I didn't have the time to look deeply at it, but Adam did. He left me a pretty clear trail of bread crumbs.

"Sir, I told you about the implant we

found in one of his men's heads. Havelock's been making micro-nukes—it's all here. The nukes are so small, they could be taken and remotely detonated.

"We know he's been gathering polonium-two-ten. It's because he wants to use it as the base for a much bigger weapon. He's well past the theoretical stage. All Havelock wants now is a bigger payload."

Penderley frowned at him. "What payload? Be clear, man."

"Havelock is after a very old radioactive isotope at least one hundred times stronger and more lethal than polonium -two-ten."

Mike said, "What do mean **more** lethal? A single drop of polonium-two-ten will kill you."

"Yes, but we're not talking simple polonium here. If Havelock can get his hands on this ultra-robust polonium, and combine the two, we're talking about micro-nukes, hidden in plain sight, that could kill millions. This is our worst nightmare."

Penderley shook his sleeve. "Explain this ultra-robust polonium? Who came up with that?"

"Marie Curie."

Mike and Penderley stared at him. She said slowly, "Marie Curie worked over a hundred years ago. There's no way she could have discovered something this advanced, there wasn't the equipment, the technology, this—wait, she died of radiation poisoning, didn't she, from working on radium and—"

"Yes, and polonium. Evidently, she realized polonium was unstable, and had a very short half-life. She believed polonium was much less useful than radium and so that's where she focused her energies. Or so we thought."

Mike said, "What do you mean, or so we thought?"

"Historical records show that Curie spent her time developing radium, and left polonium alone. But she didn't. She found a way to increase its half-life, evidently to make it indestructible, potent and viable in five years, in a hundred years. Adam had a document in his files explaining it all. Sir, we need to move, fast."

"All right, Drummond, but first, you have to tell me where is this ultra-robust polonium of hers? Is it in the sub and that's why Havelock wants it so desperately? How could it possibly be potent and viable after being underwater for one hundred years?"

"It isn't the ultra-robust polonium itself that's in the sub, it's her key that leads to where she kept it. That's why Havelock has been trying to find it. Curie's book would indicate where she locked it away, and how to use her polonium's enhanced properties, and the key would unlock whatever it is, a door, a deposit box, a safe, whatever.

"Sir, we have to get to Loch Eriboll right now. Havelock is no doubt going for the sub tonight. He must already have the coordinates. And he's poised to get there ahead of us."

"How do you know?"

He shook the laptop. "It's in Havelock's files. Adam Pearce hacked into Manheim Technologies, pulled down all of Havelock's personal files. He owns a ship called the

Gravitania. It's a high-end salvage vehicle. He rents it out to treasure hunters, people who dive shipwrecks and the like. Yesterday, he ordered it to move into position in the North Sea. He's going after the sub, right now. We must beat him."

"Or you believe thousands of people will die. But, Drummond, I told you already it would take at least a day to get our gear in place."

Nicholas took a deep breath, put his hand on Penderley's shoulder. "If you've never trusted me before, sir, I ask that you do now. The safety of our people, all of our people, our very country, lies in the balance. We can't wait. We can't let him get to the sub first. I don't care who we have to call, what favors we need to pull, it has to happen, and it has to happen right now."

Penderley looked at him thoughtfully for a moment, then pulled out his mobile phone, dialed and put the phone to his ear. There was a brief pause, and he said, "Sir? It's Penderley. We have an emergency."

69

The rain was coming down in sheets when they got themselves into Penderley's BMW, Nicholas behind the wheel.

Penderley rang off his mobile, and turned to Mike, who was hanging on to the grab handle, "We're headed to Northolt. You'll be in Scotland in less than two hours. We're borrowing a Hawker from the prime minister; the only way to get you there faster is strap you and Nicholas into Tornadoes. They're clearing the airspace for you, shouldn't be much more than an hour up there. You'll land north of Inverness, at RAF Tain, and they'll chopper you to Loch Eriboll. You're going to the back end of Scotland. That far north you'll have a little more daylight to work with."

Mike thought about their near death in the director's Gulfstream and gulped. She'd rather drive, or take a train, even a bicycle.

Nicholas saw her face in the rearview, turned to flash her a grin. "By car it's only about eleven hours, with hundreds of roundabouts."

"Stop reading my mind, particularly when I'm mentally whining."

Penderley ignored the both of them. "They've diverted a Type twenty-three anti-submarine frigate, the HMS **Dover,** to intercept the **Gravitania.**"

"Anti-submarine?" Mike asked. "I thought the **Gravitania** was a ship."

"It **is** a ship. One that's being used to search for sunken treasure and bottomed-out shipwrecks. Its registry is Bahamian, and shows an MIR-two submersible on board, a three-person mini-sub, perfect for deep-sea exploration. Havelock's prepared. So that means you'll have to dive to the sub. The **Dover** will have the right equipment to make that possible.

"Children, our countries are on the line now. Keep me informed. We have a few more minutes to Northolt. Talk, Drummond, tell me all of it. Start with Manfred Havelock. And don't bang up my car," he added, when Nicholas swerved around a big black truck at the last minute.

When there was a break in traffic, Nicholas said, "Manfred Havelock is a German scientist who has revolutionized the nano-biotech field with his brain implants for amputees, among several other huge discoveries. Our medical examiner found an implant in the brain of the man Havelock sent to kill Jonathan Pearce in New York. Unlike his official work, this one was being used for real-time intelligence gathering, video and audio, on American soil.

"The worst part is Havelock also seems to have developed multiple mini–nuclear weapons which he's tied to these intelligence-gathering implants. The implants are the triggers. We don't know how far they're deployed, but they could be anywhere."

"So the people who carry the implants are walking triggers?"

"Exactly. And if Curie's creation of this ultra-robust polonium is added to the mix, catastrophe."

Nicholas turned onto the A40. Northolt wasn't far.

"I'll notify Homeland and Downing Street. What do Oliver Leyland and Alfie Stanford have to do with Havelock?"

Nicholas thought of his father's urgent plea to keep quiet about the Order. He said, "Still unknown at this point, sir. Once we stop Havelock's attack, we can sift through the rest."

"Who does this sunken sub belong to?"

"It belonged to Kaiser Wilhelm, went down in 1917."

"I know there's more, but we're here." Nicholas stopped at the Northolt guard gate. Penderley pulled out his ID and handed it to the guard. His mobile rang. "I hope they've found Sophie Pearce." A few moments later, he shut off the phone and looked at Nicholas strangely, then said, "Your plane, it's right over there. You can drive to it."

"Did they find her, sir?"

He shook his head. "They've found where the call originated from. Let's get you on the plane and I'll tell you the rest."

70

**London
5:00 p.m.**

Once inside the plane, Penderley waved away the pilot. He stared at them, through them really, and he looked stunned.

"Sir? What's wrong? Was Sophie at the location? Is she dead?"

"Our people found the location, just outside Oxford, like we thought. They're on their way there now. Hold on to your pants, Drummond. The call originated from an estate called West Park, a country estate owned by Edward Weston."

Nicholas stopped cold. He began shaking his head, back and forth. "No, sir, that can't be right, not Weston."

"I'm sorry, Nicholas. The call absolutely came from inside Weston's house." He reached out, laid his hand on Nicholas's shoulder. They stood together silent for a moment.

What was going on here?

Finally, Mike said, "All right, who is

Edward Weston and why are you surprised, and why does Nicholas look like he's been smacked in the head?"

Nicholas didn't want to tell her, and she knew it, but it didn't matter. She laid her hand on his arm. "Tell me."

Nicholas nodded. "Remember hearing about a small **issue** I had in Afghanistan?"

"You've never told me what that **issue** was, but yes, I remember some sort of problem."

"A problem?" Penderley shook his head. "A problem doesn't come close. Tell her, Nicholas. but be quick about it. You've got to go."

Nicholas said matter-of-factly, "First you need to know that Edward Weston is currently the second-in-command of MI Five."

"You've got to be kidding me." Mike couldn't believe this. **MI5?** "Tell me what happened."

"Weston was a special attaché to the embassy in Kabul. He saw himself as the king on the chessboard, and we young ones as pawns to move around at his whim. He sat back in the embassy, happily getting relays on what was happening outside the walls, while I was crawling around in the muck, drinking barrels of chai and passing out cigarettes to the Afghan soldiers, pulling in as much intelligence as I could."

He shook his head, remembering the anger and frustration. "The very people our military were training would turn on us. They were actually working for the Taliban. They used the training and information we provided to attack convoys, set off suicide bombs and car bombs. Anything to hurt us."

Mike said, "It happened to the Americans, too."

"Yes. I was tasked with finding where the Taliban were getting their information. I heard a solid rumor one of these insurgents was a high-ranking official, one that Weston himself had recruited and ran as an asset. His name was Bahrambin Dastgir.

"On the surface, Dastgir looked clean. He was bringing us scads of information, helping us run operations on the ground. No one believed he could possibly be a threat, not with all the solid intel he'd given us. Dastgir would sit down to tea with Weston and spout the party line about wanting the Taliban and their informants out of Kabul, out of Afghanistan.

"But he didn't feel right to me. I came to believe he was a plant. I found his mistress, and in exchange for a wad of cash, she gave him up. I went to Weston, told him what I knew, told him I wanted to bring Dastgir in and interrogate him, but Weston wouldn't hear of it. He insisted the man was a friend."

Mike said, "But you were right?"

"Yes. Two days after I warned Weston about Dastgir, an IED exploded very near our command post. Everyone rushed to the scene, including Dastgir, in the makeshift mobile command unit. He was well-known, they let him in."

Nicholas fell silent, seeing it all again. "He got right into the thick of it, and flipped his switch. He was strapped into a vest filled with ball bearings and nails. The bomb not only took out our mobile command, it killed my entire team and ten civilians. I realized he knew his mistress had sold him out and he knew his time was short, and he wanted to ensure his martyrdom and kill as many of us as he could. He succeeded. The two bombs killed upwards of fifty people that day."

"And Weston?"

"He doctored data, making it appear that I'd been the one to bring Dastgir into our midst, that I'd been too blind to see what he was doing, and what he really was, and that I'd refused to consider Weston's spoken concerns about him. He was, of course, a fanatical Taliban member who wanted all of us to die. It was his word against mine and he held the higher rank. He had more juice than I did. And he knew I wouldn't go to my father to get things changed. And I should have, but I didn't.

"Truth is, I screwed up. I should have gone over Weston's head right away when he refused to act.

"My fieldwork days ended rather quickly

after that since Weston made it a point to blow my cover before he left to become the high commissioner in Rawalpindi.

"I ended up riding a desk, as you Americans put it, instead of being boots on the ground, where I belonged. I left the Foreign Office not long after, because Weston made sure I had no future there. And now you know the whole story."

Penderley tapped his watch. "Nicholas, given Weston chose his own survival over the truth, why is he working with a madman like Manfred Havelock?"

"Unfortunately, it plays perfectly. Weston's a lot like Havelock, unstable and unpredictable, and maybe not as mad as Havelock, at least overtly, but inside, he's close. When I knew him he was a liar and he didn't care who got killed, and now? He sees Havelock as a genius who can rule the world with Weston at his side."

"Then our people will get inside West Park, see if there's any evidence there to tell us what's happened to Sophie Pearce. I'll get them looking for Weston, too."

Penderley shook his head. "And this man is in MI Five."

He clasped both their hands. "Whatever else he is, Weston's no fool, so watch your backs. Get to Scotland and stop these maniacs. I'll tell the PM exactly what's on the line and that Weston is up to his neck in it."

He left the plane, and the pilot secured the door. Moments later, they lifted into the air, banked right, and began the quick run to Inverness.

71

GRAVITANIA
Loch Eriboll, Scotland
6:00 p.m.

Adam awoke to the sound of helicopter rotors. **Helicopter rotors?** Where was he? He realized he was lying on a narrow cot, his wrists tied in front of him. He seemed to be rocking. He was on a boat. But how could that be? He felt as if he had fog in his brain. He lay perfectly still, thinking. Something was very wrong, but he couldn't put his finger on it, everything was a blur. He only knew he shouldn't be here on a boat with helicopter rotors whooshing. He was supposed to be in London with his godfather. **His godfather.** He saw his body, the men standing over him. It all came back to him.

Adam quickly got the knots apart, shook his hands to get feeling back, and looked around the small stark cabin. There was a bucket to his right, and to his left, another cot, and there was a person, with long, dark tangled hair.

It was Sophie, on her side, facing him. Her eyes were closed, and she wasn't moving.

He rolled off the metal cot and stumbled over to her, afraid she was dead. Like their father, like Oliver. He looked down at her, afraid to touch her. He leaned close. "Sophie, wake up."

She moaned and rolled away from him. Her shirt was ripped open and he saw her back, the raw welts still oozing blood. "That bastard beat you," but of course he already knew that, he'd heard her screams over the phone while März stood over him, smiling the whole time. And he'd yelled out the sub's coordinates to make that madman stop beating her. He remembered the needle coming into his neck, März still smiling as he plunged it in.

He leaned over her and slapped her cheeks. "Come on, you can do it. Wake up, Sophie."

Her eyes opened. As gently as he could, Adam turned her back over onto her side to face him. She lifted her hand to touch his face. "Adam? Is that you? Really? Thank God, I thought they'd killed you." She started to move, gritted her teeth and held perfectly still.

"Sophie, I know your back hurts. I'm sorry but there's nothing I can do about it. No, no, you've got to stay with me. We've got to get out of here."

Sophie wanted to scream, but she wasn't about to, not with her brother looking so afraid. She had to keep it together. "Where are we?"

"One of Havelock's ships. We're also very probably in or near Loch Eriboll."

"You gave him the coordinates."

"I had no choice, Soph, you were screaming and I had to make it stop."

The door opened. Adam jumped to his feet, ready to fight.

He knew the man slipping in the cabin, had known him for three years. Alex Grossman, their friend, their father's friend. "Alex, what are you doing here? Are we being rescued?"

Sophie grabbed Adam's wrist. "No, he's not here to help us, Adam, he's with

Havelock, he's the enemy. His name isn't Grossman. It's Shepherd."

Alex quietly closed the door behind him. "I'm not your enemy. Don't attack me, Adam. You must be quiet, both of you." He looked down at her back. "I didn't know, I swear I didn't know. Weston is my boss, in the Order and at MI Five. I trusted him for three years. But now—" He shook his head. "I was dead wrong. I had no idea Havelock had come to West Park, no idea what he was going to do. I'm so very sorry. They wouldn't let me take care of you."

Adam said, "What do you mean Edward Weston is your boss? And at MI Five? Are you some sort of spy?"

"Weston is the frigging deputy director general, which is why I trusted him, but he's working with Havelock now, maybe he was all along, I don't know. There's a lot to explain, but we don't have time.

"Half the British military will be here soon. I left a note for them at Weston's house. I heard Havelock talking about your call, Sophie, before he caught you. They'll have triangulated it. Now I've got to get you two off this boat and to safety. There's a small rescue raft lashed to the port deck. That's our lift. Havelock's gone down to the sub to find the key."

He looked down at Sophie's back. "I nicked a first-aid kit. Hold still and I'll do the best I can to make you feel better." He sat beside her and set to work. Since there was no water to clean her back, he uncapped a large tube of medicinal cream and lightly rubbed it into the welts. The blood made the cream turn red. He knew he was hurting her, just as Adam did. Adam took her hand.

"Done," Alex said finally and rose. "I know that hurt." **Hurt** wasn't the word she'd have chosen, but at least she hadn't made a sound. Alex wrapped the entire roll of gauze around her while Adam held her up. He pulled off his shirt and helped her into it.

"You're wearing a bulletproof vest under your T-shirt," Adam said.

"Yes, and a good thing because Havelock shot me back at West Park." He tapped a round hole in the armor. "Now, Sophie, do you think you can walk if I help you?"

She wanted to hold herself perfectly still so the pain would lessen. She said, "Of course I can walk."

Adam watched Alex Grossman—no, Shepherd—help Sophie out the narrow cabin door. What to do? Who to believe? He hated being helpless. He saw a wrench sticking out of some oily rags in the corner and picked it up.

Adam's brain was near full power again. He remembered this particular ship was one of three in Havelock's personal fleet, two hundred fifty-one feet from stem to stern, and she had all the latest technology. When they reached the deck, he saw Havelock's helicopter tethered to its platform, but the MIR-2 submersible was gone. No one was around.

Adam caught up to Shepherd. "There should be forty hands on this ship. Where are they all? Who's running this thing?"

Shepherd said quietly, "Havelock put the crew off on another of his boats before we sailed into the loch. He doesn't trust anyone. Everything's on autopilot. Only

März and Weston are on board. They're up on the bridge. I'm supposed to be bringing you water. That was my excuse."

Adam's hands fisted. "That man, März, he drugged me and brought me up here, after he murdered my godfather."

Shepherd stopped cold. "What did you say? Leyland's dead?"

Sophie was shaking her head back and forth. "No, this can't be happening. Not Oliver."

When Adam told them what had happened, Shepherd closed his eyes against the enormity of it. "I am the biggest idiot alive."

Sophie said, "You didn't know, you couldn't know."

Alex said, "I met Oliver Leyland when Weston assigned me to protect your father three years ago. It was Leyland who told Weston I should be in the Order. I admired him, believed he could move mountains. He was honest, an excellent man. He was my mentor and now he's dead. Because of Havelock."

Adam laughed. "But you want to know

the big joke? Weston's supposed to keep Britain safe." He broke off, swallowed.

"Sophie, Adam, we have to get off this ship."

"I don't think so, Mr. Shepherd."

It was März and he was pointing the same gun at them he'd used to kill Oliver Leyland. "I knew you couldn't be trusted when I saw the look on your face. You're betraying us because of this useless bitch. You think you can outsmart Havelock? You can outsmart me? You can't. Now you will lose everything. We will all go back to the cabin and I will lock the three of you in. Mr. Havelock can decide what to do with you."

Adam saw the slight nod. He grabbed Sophie, jerked her back against him as Alex Shepherd turned. His right leg came up and kicked out so fast it was a blur. The gun flew from März's hand and skidded across the deck.

März cursed, grabbed his wrist, then came at Alex. Adam couldn't get to the gun because the two men were fighting in front of him, the kicks brutal, both men heaving and grunting. Alex kicked März in the kidney, whirled about and sent his foot into his neck, but März was strong and fast and when he kicked Alex in the groin, he went down. He bounced up, but then there was a shot.

It was Weston and he'd shot Alex in the shoulder. März grabbed Shepherd around the neck and slammed his head against the rail. Alex went limp.

März cast a dispassionate eye at Shepherd, who was oozing blood onto the deck.

He looked at Adam and Sophie. "A taste for you of what happens if you don't do as I say," and he lifted Alex's body off the deck and dumped him into the cold waters of the loch.

"No!" It was Sophie. März was nearly on her when Adam went for his throat.

Another shot. Weston called out, "Enough, Mr. Pearce, it's over."

März was smiling. "You two. Come with me."

Weston called out, "März, when you are finished, come to the bridge."

72

Nearing Inverness
6:00 p.m.

They ate crusty French bread and soft cheese and grapes, and washed it down with tart lemon-flavored Pellegrino.

Mike wiped up a last bit of cheese with a fingertip. "Isn't it nice the PM keeps his plane so well stocked?"

Nicholas grabbed the last grape. "Maybe next time, more cheddar." He cleared the tray off the table, then opened Adam Pearce's laptop. "Now, Mike, if it's okay with you, I'm going to read aloud about Marie Curie and her polonium according to Adam's files from the Order. It's easier that way."

"Read away. I can't believe you ate the last grape."

"I'm a right pig." He tapped the screen. "Adam left an encrypted note inside two other files with my name on it. When I decoded it, it sent a message to my server. What Adam wrote isn't complete, but it's enough.

If you're reading this, Drummond, this is my take on what has happened. This I know for sure. Everything has gone wrong. Havelock is trying to get his hands on Marie Curie's weapon.

Madame Curie was a member of the Highest Order. The Order funded a great deal of her research. When it became clear Britain was struggling in the war Curie set out to develop a weapon that would prove so chilling in its consequences that it would prevent countries from ever going to war, or in this case, stop World War I in its tracks. (I see Curie evaluating this weapon like the scientists on the Manhattan Project doubtless did—they were both committed to creating something incredibly deadly in order to bring about peace—to me this reasoning is flawed. In Curie's situation, though, I think she really believed she could put a stop to the war with an über-weapon without ever using it, and create a world peace keeper. She obviously had too high an opinion of her FELLOW HUMANS.

She herself was committed to peace and so she worked on it day and night. She discovered another variant of the radiological element polonium-210. (Of course, all of this is far too technical for me to understand completely.)

Curie somehow managed to enhance the short half-life of polonium-210, to retain its efficacy. She believed it would grow stronger over time, and she was pleased because if she could determine how to deliver it, the threat of it would stop the war. Then she discovered her new super-enhanced polonium meant death to all who even chanced to touch it and she quickly realized there would be no controlling it and she'd made a big mistake. She didn't want to open Pandora's box. She knew now that she couldn't allow anything this powerful to be in England's hands, in any country's hands, for that matter, and so she went to the head of the Order at the time, William Pearce, 7th Viscount Chambers, and told him the weapon she'd developed didn't work, and she couldn't figure out how to make it work.

Though Pearce suspected she was lying, she didn't change her story.

No doubt in my mind that Curie both hated and was in awe of what she'd created, otherwise how to account for the fact that she didn't destroy the weapon, destroy all her notes, destroy her secret lab? But she didn't. She couldn't bring herself to do it. Why? Perhaps because the monster she'd created was so magnificent she simply couldn't bear to destroy it. I think she was obsessed with what she'd found, amazed, really, and couldn't let it go. Perhaps she was already ill from radiation poisoning, and wasn't thinking clearly, but whatever the reason, she didn't destroy her discovery.

Curie did the next best thing—she locked everything up, including the weapon itself and her notes on how to manufacture it. Perhaps she believed that if her lab was ever found in the distant future, her weapon could be used for good. (Not very logical reasoning, given mankind's endless violent history. We will all suffer for her decision if Havelock finds it.)

Curie walked away from the Order and continued her research into radium. The war went on.

But Curie was betrayed. (I can only imagine what she must have felt—questioning her own decisions, so much remorse, dread, because she'd be the cause of Armageddon.) A young colleague of hers was a German sympathizer. He stole her notebook and the key to her secret lab and made his way to Germany. He gave the key to Kaiser Wilhelm and told him for the right price, he'd tell him the location of Curie's secret lab, and the kaiser would be able to have the weapon.

Pearce found out through his spies in Berlin and immediately notified Curie. She realized she'd been betrayed. She couldn't allow the kaiser to get his hands on the weapon, (probably she decided better the devil you know), and so she told Pearce the truth about the what she'd created and why she'd lied to him. She told him the weapon wouldn't kill a few people, it had the capacity to kill them all.

Even though Curie no longer had the key to her secret lab, she could have figured out how to destroy it, but evidently before she could act, Pearce told her he'd arranged for a spy to steal the key and the notebook from the kaiser. All he ever told her was that the sub with her key and notebook on board sunk, and they didn't know its location. She must have been very relieved to learn this, and thus, why destroy her lab? No point.

Nicholas looked up, his voice quiet. "That's it. That's all he had time to write."

Mike said, "Mini-nukes with a new radioactive element. Here we've been worried about suitcase nukes. But,

Nicholas, if Havelock gets his hands on the über-polonium Madame Curie developed, and makes a nano-nuke with the bigger load, creating a massive fallout, we don't know what the results will be."

Nicholas nodded. "And unlike dirty bombs that can be detected, these nano-nukes could go anywhere, no one the wiser. And since we don't know the makeup of Curie's extreme polonium, we don't know how big a payload it can deliver." He paused. "Über-polonium, extreme polonium, enhanced polonium—hard to know what to call it. Like Adam, I don't understand how it would work, either, only that it does."

"**Deadly** will do the job since all we really understand is the consequences would be bad."

The pilot of the Hawker came over the intercom. "We will be on the ground in five minutes. The chopper is waiting to take you to Loch Eriboll. The **Dover** is looking for the **Gravitania** now."

Mike fastened her seat belt. "Clearly something went wrong along the way if the Order lost the key and Madame Curie's notes. And now Havelock is close to having it."

"We'll get there first, Mike. We must."

Mike looked out the window, to the barren hills below. "I wonder where Curie's secret lab is located."

"We have to find Adam Pearce alive to get the rest of the story."

73

Ten minutes later they were buckled into the seats of a Merlin chopper on their way to the frigate HMS **Dover**. The pilots were curious; it wasn't often they were diverted to a closed air base to pick up two civilians for a ride up to the North Sea.

The pilot said, "Be prepared, it's choppy as hell out there right now, so buckle up. We'll have you over the loch in thirty minutes and land you on the **Dover.** She's waiting for us. The minute we're on board, the boat will head into the loch. This ship you're searching for, the **Gravitania,** they've already moved into position, they're in the loch as we speak."

Nicholas said, "If that's the case, can you put us down on the **Gravitania**?"

"Unadvisable, sir. It's an enemy ship, we don't know who or what's down there. Our captain would have us for breakfast if we pulled a stunt like that."

"Gentlemen, I am not lying to you. This is a matter of national security. All of our lives are going to depend on you getting us on that ship."

"No can do, sir."

Nicholas looked at Mike, raised his eyebrows, then said, "Alert me when we are nearing the ship."

"Roger. I have a call to patch through, from a Superintendent Penderley. You want it?"

"I want it."

There was static for a second, then Penderley's voice came clearly through their headsets.

"Drummond, there's blood all over Weston's Oxford house, but no sign of Sophie Pearce. There was one dead man in the house, shot through the head, no idea who he was. There had also been an MI Five agent on the grounds, Alex Shepherd. He left us a note saying they'd gone to Scotland, to the **Gravitania**.

"Looks like Havelock and Weston are together, with Sophie Pearce. The note has a time on it. They left less than an hour before we got here."

Nicholas said, "Then they're all on the **Gravitania** now. Sir, I need another favor.

You have to get us on board that boat. I can't waste time landing on the **Dover**, then sailing into the loch. It's all going down on the **Gravitania.** If I get there first, I may be able to stop this whole mess before it goes up in smoke."

When Penderley remained quiet, Nicholas said, "I promise I can stop them, sir. Can you get me on that boat?"

Penderley heaved a huge sigh. "Do try not to get yourself killed, Drummond."

The call abruptly ended. Mike shouted into her headset's microphone, "Say they pull it off and get us on Havelock's boat. Do you have a plan?"

"Oh, yes. You and I are going to put down on the **Gravitania,** shoot the bad guys, and hand the ship over to Her Majesty's Navy. Then we're going to stop Havelock before he gets to the sub and steals the key."

"Well, okay, sounds like a good plan to me. Let's do it, sounds like fun."

He grinned at her, and she thought to herself, **I'm becoming as mad as you are. In any case, it didn't matter, they**

had to pull it off, there was too much at stake to believe otherwise.

Should she call Zachery, tell him what was happening? She looked at her cell, then shoved it back in her pocket. She caught his eye, and read his unspoken words clearly—**Good call**.

The chopper was skimming the land below, its flight path on a northerly heading. The moors of northern Scotland spread before them in a glorious multicolored pattern, greens and browns and oranges muted into rusty grasses and yellow fields, colors Mike had never seen before.

It was bleak, desolate beauty. Sheep dotted the fields like tufts of white cotton, and the fields ran up the hills into thick, green forests. Fog was threatening; her map showed the Firth of Moray to the east, but the late-evening sun was keeping the fog at bay.

The hills swelled into sudden mountains, gray and forbidding and sharp-edged. The chopper flew over misty peaks, swooped down the lee edge of the mountain, letting the wind take them, and the moor spread again before them. The loch appeared suddenly, a long, blue finger of water, and she could swear she could smell the peat fires burning below.

She said to Nicholas, "That has to be the most beautiful fifteen minutes I've ever spent."

"Lovely, isn't it? Cold as the dickens, though."

The pilot broke in. "You must know some pretty impressive people, sir. We've been instructed to put you down on the **Gravitania.** The ship's too small for us to land, you'll have to fast-rope onto their deck."

Nicholas punched his fist in the air. "Great news. Now, do you have a few weapons we could borrow? I don't feel like going up against a whole ship of bad guys without some serious firepower."

The pilot laughed. "Check the cabinet to your left. There's some C-Eights in there. Plus ammunition. You're going to need backup. I'm going to send Lieutenant Halpern here to watch your back when you drop on."

"Perfect." Nicholas reached over and unstrapped the cabinet, pulled out two C8s, paused for a moment, then took an emergency first-aid kit.

He handed one weapon to Mike, and a pair of thin, sticky gloves. "This is like the M-Four assault rifle, but the barrel is up instead of down. It takes a thirty-round clip." He pulled out two and handed her one. "So here's a spare. It's a little heavier than the M-Four, so it's gonna kick. Set it to burst."

He'd gone operational on her, his perfect, crisp, posh British accent was changing into adrenaline-driven military-speak.

"You've fast-roped before?"

"Yes, in training. It's been a while."

"It's our only decent ingress. It's going to be windy, so plan to go fast. Slap that strap over your shoulder, the rifle will lay nice and snug against your back. The minute we hit the deck, you spin it around and cover me."

"Roger that."

He looked at her then, really saw her. Her face was pale, composed and set, but her eyes, he could tell she was excited, blood pumping, locked and loaded. She was holding the C8 in a death grip.

He said, "When we've wrapped this all up, I'll buy you a proper meal."

"No haggis," she said.

"You're in luck, it's not haggis season. A nice cottage pie, that will warm you from the inside."

He broke open the first-aid kit. He was in luck, God bless Her Majesty's Navy.

He shook out the pills. "Here, Mike, take two—potassium iodide. It will protect us from radiation."

She swallowed the pills. "I'll bring the first-aid kit along. We don't know what we're going to encounter down there."

The chopper was swinging low over the loch now. A herd of red deer sprang away from the cliff's edge, running away from the noise.

Mike tucked the kit inside her jacket. The adrenaline was starting to pump hard through her body. She took a few deep breaths to tamp it down, pulled on the gloves, grateful she wasn't going to have to try this bare-handed.

She ran through the weapon, checking it, as she'd been trained to do. When she was comfortable with it, she set it square in her lap and tried to empty her mind of everything but each action she was going to undertake. She was glad she'd put on a heavy sweater under her leather jacket. She had a sinking suspicion it was going to be freezing cold once they slid out the doors of the chopper.

The pilot came over the air again.

"Two minutes to jump."

"Roger," Nicholas said, then opened the chopper door. The cold breeze whistled in.

"One minute to jump."

She took a deep breath, moved into position. There was a thick black coil attached to the floor of the chopper, the ropes they were going to slide down. The copilot joined them, his own weapon at the ready. He shouted, "I'm Lieutenant Ryan Halpern. I'm going to cover your insertion. Careful to keep your feet free of the rope, ma'am, since I'll be right behind you."

Mike gave him a thumbs-up. She saw the **Gravitania**'s lights below, bobbing in the waves.

The pilot said, "We've circled twice, I don't see any activity of any kind from the ship. We're going to insert you low, so if there are bad guys down there hiding, they'll come out like lice so you'll have to be ready to rock 'n' roll. You'll have a thirty-foot slide, okay?"

Nicholas smiled at her. "Mike, you ready?"

Her heart jumped into her throat, blood thundered in her head. She gave him a mad grin, took the thick braided rope in her hand, fed it around her arms and left her legs free.

The pilot said in her ear, "Fast-rope on my mark—three, two, one, jump, jump, jump."

And they went out the door, snaking down the lines onto the deck of Havelock's ship.

74

GRAVITANIA
Loch Eriboll
7:00 p.m.

The moment they hit the **Gravitania**'s deck, the helicopter peeled off, the whump of the rotors fading slowly until they were surrounded by nothing but a pervasive silence. Mike got the C8 into her hands immediately, Nicholas did as well. Where was everybody? They had to be hiding somewhere. They kept quiet and used hand signals: Nicholas to lead, Mike behind him, Lieutenant Halpern bringing up the rear to cover.

The ship rocked a bit in the still waters, listing gently from side to side. The mountains on either side of the loch rose like silent sentinels.

Nicholas saw a small T-shaped spit of land about one hundred yards away, a bleached wooden hut on the spit, and what looked like caves fronting a small beach. Like the **Gravitania,** the land and hut seemed deserted.

They moved out, stepping lightly, and worked their way through the ship. There was no one aboard. The **Gravitania** was empty.

"Where is everybody?"

"Havelock must have off-loaded them," Nicholas said. "Why? I don't know."

Lieutenant Halpern moved closer. "If so, he probably has another ship nearby. I'll call it in."

Nicholas again looked from side to side. "Lieutenant, after you make that call, take another circuit. Mike, let's go to the bridge, see if we can figure out what happened here."

With a quick nod, Halpern melted away. They heard him speaking quietly. Mike followed Nicholas up the steps at the rear of the boat. The spit of land was on their port side. A small Bell helicopter blocked most of their view of the stern. Mike looked over at the small hut. Still no sign of anyone.

The ship was anchored, the engines were off, but the electrical system was still running. On the bridge they saw a sophisticated multiscan sonar system, perfect for skimming the waters beneath them, and a side-scan sonar buoy in the water off the port side. There was a small blip flashing steadily on the screen in front of them, two hundred degrees astern.

Havelock had been trolling for the exact location of the sub, and he'd found it.

Nicholas stepped closer to the sonar display. He tapped the screen, then pointed left.

"There," he said.

Mike said, **"Underground?"**

He nodded. "That's why no one has ever picked up on it. To regular sonar, the blip would appear to be the land itself, but it's not. It's under a rock ledge."

Mike looked at him. "How deep is that water?"

"The channel is sixty-eight meters. Along the edges, it's probably twenty, twenty-five. Deep enough for a German U-boat to nestle itself in. If it's first generation, it will be about forty meters long, less than four meters high. Not small, but small enough."

"And they've been hiding for a century, tucked up under this spit of land. Amazing."

"A secluded spot, even with the seagoing vessels coming in and out. This is the only sea loch on the northern coast of Scotland. It's far from civilization, the perfect spot for a sub to hide."

"Who's idea was it, do you think? To hide the sub here?"

Nicholas shrugged. "The captain of the sub, if they'd been damaged and he didn't want anyone to find them."

Mike looked again toward the wooden hut. "We don't have time to wait for the **Dover** and a submersible. Nicholas. As you know, I can't dive."

Halpern came onto the bridge. "I dive, sir. What's more, I saw all the dive equipment we'll need. But before we go down, there's something you need to see. I found one of the crew."

Halpern led them down the stairs, to the stern of the boat. There was a man, half off the back of the boat, caught in netting that had most likely held a small rescue raft. He was pale, waxy, nearly the same color as the graying sky. And wet. He was wearing a T-shirt and a bulletproof vest. His hand stretched onto the deck of the boat, and there was blood smeared along his arm.

Suddenly, he moved. "He's not dead!" Mike shouted and ran to him.

"Mike, no, get back!"

She was on her knees beside him. "Nicholas, it's Alex Shepherd. He's been shot."

He was alive, barely.

"I'd as soon leave him for the crows," Nicholas said.

Alex grabbed her hand, and looked up into her face. "Help. Me." There was a pause, he dropped her hand. She barely heard him whisper, "Please." He was out cold.

Nicholas said, "We do need to know what happened on this boat, and I suppose that means helping the bastard."

"He did leave us a note at Weston's house to tell us where to come. We need to call the **Dover** right now, get them to send the chopper back and airlift him out of here."

"You do it, Mike. Use channel sixteen."

Nicholas and Halpern pulled Shepherd free of the netting, two hundred pounds of deadweight. They hauled him to a small cabin off the stern.

Mike ripped open his T-shirt, unstrapped the body armor Velcro. Once they pulled it off him they saw the huge bruise on his chest. "Somebody shot him dead center. From the color of the bruise, it wasn't all that recent."

The second shot had happened very recently. It had missed the vest—a small hole high on Shepherd's shoulder, blood still oozing, a through and through. He groaned, tried to jerk up, but Mike pressed him back down. "It's okay, lie still. I'll try to fix you up. Help is on the way."

Halpern went back to guard the door. Nicholas stood over Shepherd. "Time to tell us everything, Shepherd. First, is Havelock already in the submersible?"

Shepherd's eyes were closed, his teeth gritted against the pain. "Yes, but I don't know how long he's been down."

"Where are Sophie and Adam?"

"Probably with März, Havelock's familiar. He's dangerous. They aren't safe."

"Is Havelock alone?"

"I don't know. I was in the water, hanging on to the anchor, when I saw März and Weston help him get the submersible in the water, then I think Weston took Elise to the other boat."

"Who is Elise?"

"Havelock's mistress. He likes pain. She's a dominatrix."

"Why did they shoot you?"

Shepherd opened his eyes, blue as a summer day and filled with pain. "Havelock whipped Sophie because he wanted to break Adam. I was trying to get her and Adam off the boat when März stopped us. Weston shot me. März kicked me overboard. I played dead, then I climbed up the nets and managed to hang on until you found me."

Nicholas said, "What is your role in all this?"

"My loyalty is to the Order. I worked for

Stanford. He assigned me to guard Jonathan Pearce three years ago after his former guard retired."

Nicholas said, "We know MI Five didn't have a problem with this assignment since Weston is deputy director general."

Alex moaned. Mike put a cup of water to his mouth, let him drink.

He fell back, panting. Mike said, "I'm sorry, I know it hurts. A little longer and I'll have you all bandaged up."

He closed his eyes against the pain, whispered, "You've got to listen to me. Weston betrayed the Order. He works for Havelock. I failed Sophie and Adam. I failed Jonathan. One of Havelock's assassins killed him."

His voice was thready; Mike didn't know how much longer he could hang on. He wasn't shaking with cold too much, and that was good, but the pain and the exhaustion were pulling him under and there was simply nothing else she could do for him. Where were the medics from the **Dover**?

Alex couldn't let go yet, he had to tell

them, had to. "Weston told me Jonathan Pearce's death was a mistake. Havelock only wanted Adam Pearce. Massive screwup. Havelock's man was only supposed to take Adam when he showed up on Wall Street. Havelock didn't want Jonathan dead. Jonathan was the secret keeper as well as the Messenger, the only one in the Order who knew the entire story."

"What story, exactly?"

He was fading fast. Mike and Nicholas leaned close.

"What story, exactly?" Nicholas asked again.

He whispered, "Josef and Ansonia."

Mike lightly squeezed his hand. Ansonia, he recognized her name from Jonathan's files. "Who are they, Alex?"

"The key. They stole the key."

Nicholas hunkered close. So they were from long ago. Shepherd was nearly out. Nicholas said quickly, "You said Weston went with Elise to the other boat. Where is the other boat?"

Barely a whisper. "North," he said, and

he was gone.

Mike said, "He's lost a lot of blood, Nicholas. I've done the best I can. I hear a helicopter."

Halpern said from the cabin doorway, "The medics are here for Shepherd."

Nicholas said, "Good. Time's up. Ryan, you and I have to dive down to the sub, now."

75

Nicholas climbed into his thick neoprene dry suit, ran through the equipment, tested his regulator and tank.

He caught Mike watching him, and smiled. "Havelock came prepared. He prepped his boat with all the cold-water equipment we need. The dry suit's a must since it's going to be bloody cold down there. Don't worry, all right?"

"Is that your way of telling me you've got this under control?"

He nodded. "It is. I do. Don't fret." And he was ready. He said more to himself than to her, "Now I wonder where will I find a key so small it will fit in my palm."

"You'll find it. Be careful, both of you."

Both men nodded. They needed to hurry, the sky was changing color, going a soft, warm yellow-gray. The sun was nearly behind the westerly mountains.

Mike shook his arm. "How are you going to get in the sub?"

"I'll bet you Havelock's already done it for us." He took her shoulders. "Have faith,

Mike."

She had to believe if the key was on the sub, he'd find it.

She let him go, watched him turn to Halpern. "Ready, Lieutenant?"

"As I'll ever be."

They made their way to the stern. The sun was descending rapidly now. It would be dark when they came back up.

Halpern checked Nicholas's equipment, and Nicholas returned the favor. "It's going to be sketchy down there, sir."

Nicholas only nodded. He'd dived several times onto shipwrecks, but never into a sub. He knew there'd be choking silt and zero visibility. It had scared the crap out of him since he was a bit claustrophobic, and now he was doing it again.

"All right, then. Bottoms up."

They donned their masks and dropped off the end of the boat. Nicholas waited a moment, allowing the cold air to lap against his face. The water was very cold, but the dry suit kept him comfortable. After a minute, he cleared his mask and

signaled to Halpern. With a quick wave to
Mike, and a prayer, he started down.

Nicholas flipped on the camera feed
attached to his mask so Mike could see
what he was seeing. They fired up their
propulsion devices and started to dive,
the lights cutting a path through the murky
water.

Beneath the surface it was an odd
blurred gray. Large fish swam away from
them, salmon, Nicholas thought.

They didn't see Havelock's submersible.
They followed the radio signal on the side
sonar buoy. Within five minutes, they were
at the spit of land. They dropped deeper.

And there she was.

Victoria lay on her side, wedged under
the wall of granite. She was in surprisingly
good shape. They'd been hit and the
captain had managed to limp his sub into
the loch. Whether the captain had been
able to wedge her under the shelf on
purpose, or it was the serendipity of the
tides and chance, they'd never know.

They swam closer, saw beds of mussels
attached to her stern. They swam along

the outside length of the sub to the bow and there it was, not a small torpedo hole, but a wide jagged opening, only minutes before blown apart so Havelock could fit through.

Nicholas set his DPD against the side of the sub, then signaled to Halpern to remain at the opening and carefully eased through the jagged tear. His torch was powerful, and it needed to be, he knew, because of all the silt Havelock had stirred up. He followed the ghostly light into the black interior. Fish swam past his face.

He found himself in a long narrow tube, divided into individual compartments. He concentrated on not becoming disoriented. He saw that the first hatch was open, and could make out ancient equipment through the veil of silt, strings of algae flowing off the edges of the sub's walls and ceiling, waving like ghostly arms.

He swam slowly into the second compartment, through the fog of silt. He saw bits of human bodies, several long bones swaying in the dark water, three skulls loose, the empty eye sockets staring up at him through the torchlight. There was no way to know how many men had died on the sub because the thick beds of refuse and the blinding sediment hid so much. There had to be more than three, he knew, and he paused a moment to pray for these men entombed here for so long. And for the families these men had loved, who'd grieved and prayed.

Every man on the sub had known he was going to die, so they'd locked themselves in this chamber, all of them together in their final moments.

Nicholas slowly swung his torch around the space, and saw something glittering on the far wall. He swam closer, rubbed his gloved hand along the shiny spot. It was a single gold bar. He wiped away more silt. He saw not only one gold bar, he saw a wall of them, stacked from floor to ceiling, maybe six bars deep, shining faintly in the torch beam. He hung in the water, perfectly still, waiting for the water to clear, staring at the unbelievable sight. There was a king's ransom of gold on this sub. Of course Havelock had known about the kaiser's gold, but he'd been so focused on finding the key he hadn't even noticed.

Nicholas swam toward the bow through several more compartments—a small mess hall, rusted pans, ceramic bowls and plates, still whole, and through sleeping quarters with only the wire and steel frames left, open rusted metal lockers.

He saw that the hatch to the bow compartment was smaller than the rest, with some sort of thick corroded rubber gasket around the edges. This hatch was closed.

He spun the wheel, and slowly pulled the hatch open.

Nicholas flashed his torch around the small room, no more than eight by ten feet. He saw a bunk in the corner, blankets floating off in the water, lanterns hanging over it, and a small table, all still intact.

He felt a punch of shock. On the bed was a body, floating inches above the disintegrating mattress, in much better shape than the skeletons scattered in the black waters behind him.

76

He realized this small compartment must have been completely sealed and airtight, dry for a hundred years, until Havelock had forced the hatch open. The body was mummified, almost perfectly preserved, wearing the uniform of a German naval **Kapitänleutnant**, the uniform cloth still a deep pure black.

But there was no mistaking the long, flowing hair. A woman. No woman should be aboard a sub, impossible, so what did this mean?

Her mummified body would soon be reduced to bones like the rest of the small crew. She hadn't drowned, he realized, she'd starved to death, trapped in the ship's womb, unable to get help for herself or her shipmates.

The names Alex Shepherd had said— **Josef and Ansonia.**

Had he found the Ansonia from Pearce's files?

And suddenly, the bits and pieces from the Highest Order's files started to make sense.

He floated in the water, staring at her, her body slowly rising, nearly to his outstretched hand now. He saw that her left hand was missing. Nicholas realized that as she lay dying, she'd held the key and Curie's book in that hand and Havelock had snapped it right off.

He heard a tapping noise. It was Halpern. He looked down at his dive computer. Halpern was warning him. He'd started with sixty minutes of air and planned to spend only fifteen minutes in the sub, but that hadn't happened. He'd spent too much time inside.

He swam slowly and carefully so as not to stir up more of the blinding silt, past the skulls, as he emerged out the enlarged torpedo hole. He felt suddenly like he'd been released from hell itself, and breathed deeply. He looked up, searching for fins and bubbles, but he didn't see Halpern. Instead, he saw a white flash of metal, bearing down on him, four lights shining in his eyes, the water churning around it.

It was Havelock's submersible. It looked

straight out of a science fiction movie, like a giant metal bug, with three large portholes like eyes along the bottom.

Nicholas grabbed up his propulsion device to get away, but it was no match for Havelock's submersible.

He saw the submersible had stopped. Had Havelock decided it wasn't worth the time to try to run him down?

He prayed Halpern had escaped and he was already on his way to the surface to warn Mike. Nicholas knew he couldn't get to Havelock down here, he had to get back up top. Suddenly the submersible shot past him, clipping his foot as it passed, knocking him around in a lazy circle.

Havelock had changed his mind. The submersible was turning to come at him again. He had to get to the surface now, but he couldn't move. The submersible had shot off a net, trapping his legs.

He pulled his dive knife out of the sheath on his thigh and began sawing at the ropes. He sensed movement out of the corner of his mask, looked up to see a diver bearing down on him, a knife in his hand.

As the man swam closer, Nicholas saw through the face mask a scar bisecting the man's eye and cheek, and a rictus of a smile around the regulator in his mouth. It wasn't Havelock.

This must be the man März.

Had he come off the submersible? Yes, that was why Havelock had backed off for a moment. Nicholas swam backward and up, still sawing on the ropes.

Nicholas realized März didn't want to get into a knife fight, he wanted to cut Nicholas's air hose.

The submersible was backing away, its lights growing dimmer. Nicholas hoped März hadn't killed Halpern.

Nicholas used his DPD as a shield as März came at him and kept cutting away the net on his legs. Finally, he kicked free of the netting as März swam over him, knife ready to slice through the tubing on Nicholas's back. Nicholas corkscrewed in the water and thrust his own knife at März's thigh as he swam past.

He missed.

März grabbed Nicholas's tank and got his arm around his neck. He cut through the air hose to Nicholas's regulator, sending a cloud of bubbles bursting upward. Nicholas twisted, felt März's knife slash through his dry suit and into his arm, then his knee struck Nicholas's hand and he dropped his knife. Nicholas managed to jerk free and swing his DPD around, hitting März in the face, shoving him backward.

There was a sudden whooshing sound and Nicholas could swear he saw a torpedo shoot through the water not six feet away.

He couldn't begin to understand what was happening. He was running out of breath. He grabbed for the secondary regulator on his shoulder, but he didn't have time to suck in a breath. März turned a tight somersault and reversed fast, right in Nicholas's face, his knife up and ready. Nicholas punched his fist into his mask, knocking it half off his face, then he ripped the mask all the way off, and caught März's face between his hands. He shoved his thumbs into his eyes and pushed, hard.

There was a loud boom. The concussion tumbled both men backward, grappling for a hold on each other.

Nicholas heard the screech of metal, but he knew Havelock hadn't sent a torpedo into the sub, otherwise the concussion of the blast would have killed them.

So who had fired at what?

Nicholas's arm was bleeding, he was getting light-headed but knew if he passed out, he'd be dead. He grabbed März's foot, and jerked him backward, until he was able to flip him around. März struggled even as the stirred-up silt blinded him. He got his thumbs into März's eyes again and squeezed. A moment later, he felt something give way.

März jerked and danced in his hands, ribbons of blood curling around their heads. Nicholas ripped the regulator from März's mouth, and sucked in air. Then he held März's body between his legs and twisted his neck until he heard the crack of bone. He shoved his secondary air in his mouth, took a huge breath, and let go of März. He was facing Nicholas as he fell away, his eyes black holes, his head now dangling sideways. Nicholas watched his body hang limp in the water before slowly, slowly gliding downward.

Nicholas checked his air tank. His air was low, too low, but he hoped there was enough to make a decompression stop on the way up.

He started a slow ascent, carefully breathing in and out. Mike suddenly appeared in his brain, arms crossed over her chest, tapping her foot. Was she calling him a lamebrain? A set of fins came into view. It was Halpern, he was alive and waiting for him. He'd never been happier to see someone in his life.

Nicholas saw the air gauge on his dive computer was flashing red. He made a cut across his throat. Halpern quickly gave him his own regulator, and pointed to his dive watch, signaled three minutes.

Nicholas pointed to his arm where blood

snaked into the water, and Halpern grabbed on to him. They hung quietly, off-gassing for a full three minutes, sharing the regulator back and forth.

Together they rose in an octopus ascent, skimming gently higher and higher, minute by minute, careful and smart, hanging still for another agonizing three minutes, then finally broke the surface. Nicholas saw the **Dover** not fifty feet away, and the men on deck shouting to them. Nicholas followed their pointing fingers and saw that Havelock's ship, the **Gravitania,** was on fire, raging flames amidships, her nose now pointing to the sky. He watched as she slipped silently into the sea.

77

9:00 p.m.

Mike paced the deck of the HMS **Dover**, watching for Nicholas and Halpern. She'd had a firsthand view of everything Nicholas saw until März attacked. The initial impact had knocked the camera free. She'd never been so afraid in her life. She prayed, promising every good deed she could think of if only the right men would surface. She wouldn't believe März had won.

The sun was gone, the air brisk and cool. They were using the ship's big lights to scan the water. A young sailor joined her. "Ma'am? The captain's asked for you. We have a hit on our sonar. We believe it's the submersible you're looking for."

The **Dover** had steamed into the loch at the same moment Nicholas and März faced off. They'd gotten both Mike and Shepherd off the **Gravitania,** and onto the deck of the **Dover**. Shepherd was being treated in their sick bay, and Mike had briefed the ship's captain. He'd immediately set to work looking for Havelock's submersible. And now they'd found it.

Captain Kinsley showed her the spot on the screen. "It came from that narrow strip of land over there about five minutes ago. We can take it out with a single shot, it's not moving fast enough to outrun us."

"You're sure it isn't Drummond and Halpern?"

"It's too big to be men, it's displacing too much water, and moving at about four knots. I'm sure it's not divers."

But they could be close, she thought, too close, and she closed her eyes against the possibility. She gave it only a moment's thought. The key didn't matter, killing Havelock eliminated the threat of the micro-nukes.

"Light it up, Captain. The man on that submersible is an enemy of both our countries."

He smiled, signaled to his man, who said, "Firing, firing, firing," and the torpedo was free. It hissed away, and there was an impact. Mike felt the concussion.

"Direct hit, sir. The submersible is down."

Havelock was dead. It was over.

A second explosion, this one from above the water, made them all rush to the rails. The **Gravitania** was on fire, flames spreading through the ship as if following a trail of gasoline.

Mike shouted, "Did you hit it, did the torpedo hit the ship and not the submersible?"

The captain shook his head. "The torpedo was on a completely different path. That explosion was internal to the ship, not external. And there's no one aboard, so it was probably on a timer of some sort. You didn't see a bomb on board?"

Mike shook her head, realized her hands were shaking. They'd been plucked off the **Gravitania** and brought on board the **Dover** only twenty-two minutes before.

Everyone but Mike watched the ship sink. She was staring down at the water. She knew how much air they had, and it was gone. She had to face it, Nicholas and Halpern hadn't made it.

The surface of the water began to bubble. When she saw Nicholas's head break the water, she didn't say a word, so grateful, she stood mute, heart pounding, thinking over and over, **You did it, James Bond, you did it.**

Nicholas and Halpern were chilled to the bone. The medics from the **Dover** wrapped both men in special heat-trapping blankets, stitched Nicholas's arm, dropped a pain pill down his gullet. When they finally let Mike in to see him, she went straight to his bed and hugged him hard, and kissed him. His lips were cold, his teeth chattering, but he grinned at her.

Mike said, "Didn't we have a talk about you pulling death-defying stunts? You scared me to death."

Nicholas ran a hand over her hair, rested it on the back of her neck. "At one point down there I saw you clear as day—did you call me a lamebrain?"

"Not this time, I was too scared. You're all right, Nicholas, you're all right."

"I've got to admit I didn't think I was

going to make it up, and I wouldn't have if not for Ryan." He called out across the sick bay, "I owe you one, Ryan, you saved me. What was the explosion? Tell me what happened above water."

"They hit the submersible with a torpedo. If Havelock was still in it, he's dead."

"So I didn't dream it, then? I thought I saw a torpedo whiz by. Havelock dead? Somehow I can't quite come to grips with that. I have a lot to tell you." He realized he was still holding her close and pulled his hand away. She didn't move for another moment, then slowly straightened, and he told her about the billions of dollars in gold bars in the sub, about the woman he'd found in her own private tomb. He mentioned briefly März's attack once he came out of the sub. After they thrashed it all out, she pushed him again about März. Nicholas said only, "He knifed my arm, but in the end, I killed him. As for the key and Curie's book, Havelock took them."

"Do you think this was the woman Shepherd spoke of? Ansonia?"

"I do. Is Shepherd awake? I'd like to hear

more."

"Shepherd was in and out of consciousness the whole time you were down. He's messed up pretty bad. They had no choice but to operate, possible because they've got a small operating room on board." She looked at her watch. "They took him in for surgery maybe twenty minutes ago. It's going to be a while before he's coherent enough to talk."

"Has there been word on Adam and Sophie?"

Mike shook her head. "I would assume they're probably off on this phantom boat Shepherd talked about, with Weston and Havelock's whipstress. But there's been no sign of it."

"His what?"

"I made it up. Sounds fitting, doesn't it?"

He burst out laughing, startling the medics, who rushed over to make sure he was okay. "I'm fine, I'm fine. Agent Caine's a comic, that's all."

The captain strode into the sick bay. "We're receiving some sort of distress signal from that long piece of land and someone's waving a white flag at us. We're sending a boat over, and the chopper for support, in case. We'll have whoever it is on board shortly."

They heard the chopper's rotors whining, heard it lift off, and they waited.

78

HMS DOVER
9:30 p.m.

After a reluctant nod from his captain, the medic unhooked Nicholas from his IV and discharged him from sick bay. He and Mike went up onto the deck of the **Dover** to watch the rescue.

The lights of the chopper swung crazily along the coast of Loch Eriboll, the granite cliffs shining white in the beams of light. A small rescue craft scooted over the water, sending out ripples across the surface. The chopper hovered, spinning up debris and rocks, then set down next to the hut.

Five minutes later, the boat was headed back, no shots fired, no trouble at all. When the boat drew close enough, Mike let out a shout. "It's Sophie Pearce!"

She was a mess, bedraggled, bruised, exhausted, still wearing Alex Shepherd's shirt, the gauze bandage still wrapped tightly across her back, but she managed to climb the ladder to the deck of the

Dover. Both Nicholas and Mike wanted to speak to her, but a medic said, "Nope, first we take care of her."

Sophie smiled at the medic towering over her. "A moment, please." Before he could answer, she grabbed Mike's arm. "You have to go after Havelock. He took Adam with him."

Mike said, "Please tell me you don't mean Havelock took Adam down in the submersible."

"No, no, he forced Adam to go with him on his helicopter."

Mike's blood pressure dropped back to normal. She'd been scared Nicholas would be too close to the submersible when she'd given the order to fire the torpedo. She hadn't even thought of Adam.

"Okay, then, that means Havelock set the submersible on automatic and sent it back into the loch. And then the **Dover** blew it up—it was all a diversionary tactic."

"Sophie, where did Havelock take Adam?" Nicholas asked her. "Where did they go?"

"To get Madame Curie's weapon. Havelock has the key and the book, he can open the lock now. We have to stop him, please, you have to save Adam."

"Sophie, what lock? A lock to a door? Where did they go?"

Sophie stopped cold. "You mean you don't know where Curie's weapon is?"

"No, do you?"

Sophie shook her head. "All I know is it's probably somewhere in Paris."

79

Quai d'Anjou
Paris
Midnight

Havelock arrived at his house on the Quai d'Anjou just before midnight. He hurried inside with his package, still unopened, his hands shaking in excitement. He couldn't believe he finally had both the key and the book.

Elise forced Adam to a second-floor room, a Beretta against his spine, and locked him in. She joined Havelock in his study, and together they spread the mummified fingers. Havelock carefully, gently, pried the package from the palm.

He had no idea how a woman came to be on the sub, nor why she was sealed in the waterproof compartment, nor did he care. All he knew was she'd held in death the gift of a lifetime.

The package was wrapped in thick oilskin, protected as best they could manage. He eased the edges apart, but the old wrapping paper inside crumbled at his touch. And there was the key, long, heavy, brown with rust. It had an ornate bow with a series of interlocking four-cornered fleurs-de-lis, a thick, twisted shank, and a dual bit with a complicated series of bit wards etched into the metal. It wasn't an everyday key for Curie's time, it was a key meant to protect as well as deter.

Havelock caressed the key with long trembling fingers, felt its weight in his palm, then finally, he set it gently on the desk. He turned to the book, encased in a separate waterproof pouch. The cover was black, the book slender, the edges rounded. He slipped on soft white gloves. If there was anything he'd learned from Pearce, it was how to deal with very old pages.

He slid his finger beneath the cover and lifted gently. The pages inside were yellow and the words were in French. Curie's handwriting was faded but legible.

His heart pounded. With the book and the microgram of intensely amplified polonium, polonium that she'd managed to make grow stronger over time, he was ready. It was waiting for him in her lab to formulate a new kind of atom to be added to his bombs. And then he would own the world, nothing and no one could stop him.

He wondered, what should he name his new compound? Curie had named polonium after her beloved Poland. He felt no such love of homeland.

Havelockium?

He giggled. No, better to wait until he witnessed the new element in action, then he'd give it a proper name.

He turned carefully to the last page of the book. He saw a series of numbers and letters.

19 . G . 13 . R

There it was, the directions to Curie's lab. He read the letters and numbers again. What was this? It made no sense, there was no address like this in Paris. Then he realized what the letters and numbers meant, and smiled. What a clever woman.

She was about to make him the most famous man on the planet.

He turned to Elise with a manic smile, pulled her into his arms, and danced her around the room, spinning her as they swirled and dipped. When he ferried her back across the room to the desk, he released her reluctantly. "Who would have imagined her hidden address would be so ingenious? And yet it makes sense— nineteen, G, thirteen, R. How very brilliant she was."

Elise cocked her head to the side. "Nineteen, G, thirteen, R? What do the numbers and letters mean?"

"It always made sense to me her secret lab had to be here since this was her home. But you see, Elise, her lab wasn't **in** Paris, it was **under** Paris. Her lab is in the tunnels. And now, my dear, I must go. You stay here and guard the boy. If he does anything you don't like, feel free to kill him. I will be back before dawn."

Elise saw his eyes were glittering, his pupils dilated, his excitement was that huge. She leaned up and kissed him on the neck, bit him deep, then licked the blood. "Be careful," she said.

He stared at her mouth, at his own blood slicked over her lips. No, no, it wouldn't do to celebrate too early. But later, later.

He made a brief phone call. The man answered on the first ring.

"Allo?"

Havelock spoke in rapid French. **"I have the key and the directions. Bring the lamps and tools. I'll meet you at the Sorbonne, then we're going to the sixth arrondissement."**

"Oui, d'accord. Five minutes."

Havelock hung up, stashed the cell in his pocket. He popped a handful of potassium iodide pills, gently eased the book and the key inside a small backpack, along with a Maglite and a bottle of water. Elise walked him to the door, kissed him again, and he set off into the dark Parisian night.

80

Over the Channel
Paris
11:00 p.m.

Captain Kinsley arranged to chopper the three of them down to RAF Tain, north of Inverness, where the PM's Hawker was waiting to fly them not to London, but directly to Paris.

They left Shepherd behind, but took Sophie with them. She still had a lot to tell them. Nicholas wasn't taking any chances with her safety, not now.

During the chopper ride to Inverness, Mike called Zachery and explained what was happening and where they were headed. She didn't mention how close Nicholas had come to being killed.

Zachery gave them his consent, and thirty minutes later, they were off to Paris.

Once they were settled in with food and drink, Nicholas leaned forward, studied Sophie's face. "How do you feel?"

"I'm fine, really. I only want to find Adam."

She was probably telling the truth—both of them were feeling little discomfort, he thought, thanks to the pain meds swimming in their bloodstreams. His arm was sore, but the pain was tamped down.

He said, "Tell us what happened when you landed on the **Gravitania.** With Shepherd."

She accepted a cup of hot tea from Mike, took a sip, then another. She sighed. "I was wrong about Alex. He was trying to protect me the whole time. He was working for the Order, reporting to Alfie Stanford. Then Stanford was murdered and Weston took over. But he also trusted Weston not only because he was a member of the Order, but because he was high-ranking in MI Five. Alex didn't know Weston had joined forces with Havelock until we were leaving Weston's estate near Oxford. Alex told Weston Adam had found the sub. He set the wheels in motion without meaning to.

"When we were on board the **Gravitania,** he came to our cabin to help us escape." She told them of the fight, how Weston had shot Alex and März had thrown him off the boat, and taken her and Adam to the hut on the mainland. She paused. "Thank you for saving Alex."

Mike said, "He didn't give up. He'll be okay," and she hoped she was right.

Sophie drank more tea. "There are limestone caves right below that skinny slice of land, close to the hut. Havelock brought the submersible right into the edge of the caves—there's a deep bay there, and a small dock. You can't see it unless you're right on top of it.

"Adam and I watched Weston help Havelock climb out of the sub, and he looked like some sort of mad scientist. He had something in his hands and I knew he'd found the key and Curie's book. He told Weston and Elise that März had gotten himself killed. All he did was shrug and say, 'It's a pity. März served me well.' And then he sent the submersible back into the loch. I think it had some sort of remote control. We heard an explosion. And Havelock laughed and called them fools. We didn't hear him say anything about the gold."

"Do you know," Nicholas said, "I don't think Havelock even saw the gold, he was so focused on getting the key and the book."

"Was it an amazing sight, all that gold?"

"Yes, scores of bars. I don't know how many."

"So what happened after that?" Mike asked her.

"Havelock was in a hurry. He knew you'd be right behind him. Havelock took Weston, Elise, and Adam. They left me tied up. I remember thinking I was going to die in that hut, but then I saw a glass bottle lying in the corner and managed to break it. I used a shard to get my ropes cut off and signaled to you. And that's the whole story."

She fell silent. Nicholas watched her.

"Has Havelock gone to Paris because that's where the weapon is?" Mike said.

Sophie nodded. "He took Adam with him because he's not finished with hacking into all my father's files. Alex told me killing Adam wasn't part of the plan, at least until he had everything he can get from him." She paused, then looked at Nicholas. "If Adam refuses to cooperate, Havelock will kill him, won't he?"

"Not on my watch," Nicholas said.

"Is there more, Sophie?" Mike asked.

"Oh, yes. I suppose I need to tell you everything now, don't I?"

"Yes, start with the Highest Order in World War One," Nicholas said.

Sophie drank more tea, then drew a deep breath. "It all started at the Battle of Verdun, with two men—William Pearce, Seventh Viscount Chambers and a German soldier named Josef Charles Rothschild, and his wife, Ansonia."

81

Sophie said, "Please remember this account comes down from Josef's son Leo to his son Robert to my father and then to Adam and me. Some is historical fact, but a lot is what Leo imagined must have happened.

"Ansonia was my great-grandmother. She was born in Königsberg in 1890. When her family realized she was a language prodigy, they sent her to her wealthy grandmother in Berlin in 1900, and she saw to Ansonia's formal schooling.

"Ansonia spoke seven languages and was brought to the attention of the kaiser in 1909. He hired her as his translator, and she became part of his household.

"She met my great-grandfather, a handsome young **Kapitän** named Josef Rothschild, and married him in April of that year. Their son Leo was born in 1910, and war broke out four years later.

"Ansonia began to see the kaiser for what he was, a misogynist, not very bright, a man who wanted no one to disagree with him or there'd be hell to pay, and so she began to work against him when the war started. Leo remembered hearing his father and mother talking about her efforts on the inside—rewritten letters, forged instructions, certain correspondence not translated quite correctly—and how they were helping screw up the Germans' plans.

"What happened next came down to us from William Pearce. For most of the time Josef was on the front lines. He saw the horror of nerve gas, the starvation and sickness, the brutality. In the weeks leading up to the Battle of Verdun, he knew his wife was right—it had to stop.

"At Verdun, Josef saved William Pearce's life and Pearce realized what a friend England had in my great-grandfather. Pearce was the leader of the Highest Order, working with a brilliant young scientist who was developing a very powerful weapon unlike anything seen before. But the scientist was betrayed, and the formulas and key to her secret lab went missing. This was Marie Curie, of course.

"Evidently, Ansonia overheard the conversation between Curie's lab assistant and saw German marks and a small packet change hands. She didn't realize the impact of this until the leading German scientists of the day came to the house. She heard them speak of a weapon with unimagined power.

"Josef knew exactly what was in the packet because Pearce had told him about the theft. He and Ansonia devised a plan to smuggle the packet out of the palace. Josef would take it himself to England, get it safe into William Pearce's hands. Pearce had promised to protect the key and notebook with his life.

"A week before their mission, Ansonia learned the kaiser was sending handpicked men to Paris to bring the weapon back to his scientists in Berlin. She realized there was no way Josef could make it to Berlin in time to steal the packet.

"Ansonia had to steal it herself. She notified Josef to meet her and Leo in Bremerhaven. Then Josef would travel to

England, and give the packet to Pearce. She arranged for Leo to travel with his old nurse to Esbjerg, Denmark, then take a boat to Edinburgh, where Josef would meet them.

"Leo believed his mother learned that the kaiser was moving his private treasury of gold bars to a new location because the Allies' spies had gotten too close. The gold had been put on board a U-boat named **Victoria,** after the kaiser's grandmother, Queen Victoria. Leo heard Josef tell Ansonia they'd found the U-boat near Bremerhaven tucked away on a private, well-guarded wharf. Josef and his men managed to steal the U-boat. Can you begin to imagine his jubilation? England would have the key and instruction book to Curie's secret lab and the kaiser's gold. It would be a killing blow.

"But things fell apart. Leo overheard his mother telling her old nurse that the kaiser's men were nearly there. They were in danger, and the nurse had to take Leo to Esbjerg right away without her. She'd kissed him and told him they would soon be together again and he was going to have a grand adventure. That was the last time he saw her.

"A week later, Josef found Leo in Edinburgh in a poor inn, sleeping on the floor next to the old nurse, who lay dead, probably from the influenza. On their wild journey back to the Cotswolds, Josef had to tell his son that his mother was dead."

Sophie fell silent, tears in her eyes. "You know the rest. No one knows if **Victoria** was torpedoed by the English or the Germans in the North Sea off Scotland. All we really know is they didn't make it."

82

Nearing Paris
1:00 a.m.

Sophie stretched, careful not to hurt her back. She smiled sadly. "Until the day he died, Leo remembered the massacre at the cottage, how they'd tortured his father, and William Pearce had found Leo holding him in his arms. Leo watched William bury the men, including his father. He remembered Pearce's tears, he remembered seeing his terrible rage as he dug six separate graves for men he'd admired and loved.

"My father told me that Leo didn't speak for nearly a year after William Pearce found him, and once he did speak again, he was quiet, reserved.

"As for the key, the book, and all those gold bars, they were lost until Adam was able to use the satellite imagery to locate the sub."

"Sophie, did Josef know the sub ended up in Loch Eriboll?"

Sophie shook her head. "I don't think so."

Nicholas asked quietly, "Did Leo or William Pearce ever discover who betrayed the men in the Cotswolds?"

"No one ever was identified, but the Order wasn't attacked again. It was commonly believed the betrayer was killed either in the war or in the influenza outbreak. He clearly was someone close to the kaiser. But William and Leo Rothschild Pearce did find the three men who killed the Order members in the Cotswolds, and eliminated them."

Nicholas sat forward, his hands clasped between his knees. "We have got to get that key."

Sophie said, "The key is important, yes, but it's the book that's critical. It contains Curie's notes on how to make the weapon, and the directions to her secret lab."

Mike said, "Adam sent us a note about Curie's secret lab."

"So you know the whole story," Nicholas said.

"Quite a bit of it, yes. I know that after

the war, the Order decided they had to find the sunken sub and destroy the key and Curie's notebook. They didn't want to take the chance that Curie's special polonium would ever find its way into the hands of a hostile government.

"So now you understand why Adam and I are so important to the Order. We're more than institutional knowledge. We're also the last physical link to the Order's past, to Josef and Ansonia Rothschild."

"So Paris seems by far the best bet since this is where Curie lived and worked," Nicholas said. "But the question is, where in Paris?"

"I honestly don't know. But her book is the only way to find out the location of her secret lab." Sophie sighed. "And now Havelock has it."

83

**Quai d'Anjou
12:30 a.m.**

They'd blindfolded Adam on the plane, but he knew they were flying to Paris, where Curie's secret lab had to be located.

He wasn't a linguist like Sophie, so he didn't understand what Havelock was saying to Elise. His specialty was all binary code and obscure numbers. Havelock's rapid-fire German sounded incomprehensible to him.

Adam heard Havelock mention Weston several times and wondered what had happened to him. Weston couldn't return to his life at MI5 since he and Havelock had both overplayed their hand, and were both wanted by the police. Havelock had probably killed Weston because he was of no more use to him. Havelock must also have realized the Order would never let him through the doors now.

They landed, got into a car, and drove for at least twenty minutes. When the car stopped, Adam heard the sound of water lapping against a wall. He managed to angle his head to he could see the street name. quai d'anjou. He was on the Seine.

They removed his blindfold and shoved him into an elaborate entryway. He saw high ceilings, antiques, an expanse of tile floor before Elise stuck a gun in his back and forced him up two flights of stairs, then put him into a dark room. A key grated in the lock. He was alone and, unfortunately, still handcuffed. Adam stumbled around in the dark before he managed to run his fingers along the wall by the door. He finally found a light switch, nudged it up with his shoulder, and the room lit up with a soft glow.

First things first. He had to get the handcuffs to the front so he could use his hands. He relaxed his shoulders and stepped back with one leg, working his foot between his hands and his butt. His hands were now scissored between his legs, and he stepped back with the other leg, and his hands were in front of him.

He saw a lighted keypad next to the

door—the room was alarmed and that meant he had no chance of breaking out, not without alerting Havelock and the woman. He'd have to find another way.

He turned then and looked around at a maritime museum, the walls wainscoted in rich, warm walnut, painted white above the paneling, and covered with magnificent paintings of old ships, set beneath individual soft lights.

The room was full of naval memorabilia. As he walked through the long room, he realized the old maritime equipment was not only authentic, it all had been lovingly restored, set in vitrine cases with museum-style lights. He saw letters and old ships' logs, sextants and astrolabes, even a full-size weathered wooden wheel with a gold roundel at its center.

This room would have been Christmas for his father. But Havelock? He couldn't imagine him assembling, much less displaying and caring for this incredible collection.

He walked slowly around the room again, this time looking for anything he could use to communicate to the outside world. He went back to the alarm system, checked it thoroughly. There was a small button with a lowercase script letter l. It looked similar to the intercom system they had at home.

He pressed the button and heard Havelock's voice, and he was speaking English. He was crowing, he was so pleased with himself. He was talking to Elise. Havelock said, "Who would have imagined Curie's hidden address would be so simple? Nineteen G thirteen R. How very brilliant she was."

Elise: "Nineteen G thirteen R—what do the numbers and letters mean?"

Havelock: "It always made sense to me her secret lab had to be here since this was her home. But you see, Elise, her lab isn't **in** Paris, it's **under** Paris. Her lab is in the tunnels. And now, my dear, I must go. You stay here and guard the boy. If he does anything you don't like, feel free to kill him. I will be back before dawn."

Then silence. Then he heard Havelock speaking French to someone. On his cell phone?

Adam felt adrenaline shoot through him. Those numbers and letters Havelock had discussed with Elise, they had to be directions to Curie's lab in the tunnels beneath Paris.

He saw two lights on the pad light up. Then there was a small beep, and the two lights went off. Havelock had left the house through the front door. Adam hurried to the window, and saw Havelock walking quickly down the street. He was going to get Curie's weapon.

He had to work fast. He needed a computer or a phone. Anything.

He made another circuit of the room, looking under the cases, against the wall, for wires.

Then he saw it, in a case across the room—an old Morse code transmitter. It was in pristine condition, but that didn't matter. Without something to transmit to, he'd never be able to use it.

But it gave him an idea. What other communication or navigation equipment was in this room?

It only took him a few minutes of searching to find an old hand-crank ham shortwave radio.

He needed to get both items out of their cases, then he had to crank the hell out of the ham radio, and start sending messages. Someone would be listening. They always were.

He had to break through the glass of the display cases and his fists wouldn't do it.

He lifted the wooden wheel off its stand, muttered an apology, and smashed the spokes through the top of the vitrine case.

84

Near Paris

The pilot came over the intercom. "We will be landing in ten minutes. There is a call for you, Agents. From an FBI special agent in charge Zachery."

"Thank you," Nicholas said. "Please put him through."

"I hope they've found Havelock," Mike said. "It would make our jobs a lot easier."

Nicholas's armrest vibrated once, gently. He answered the phone. "Sir, we were about to call you, we've—"

Zachery interrupted him. "Quiet, Drummond. We've received a shortwave radio transmission on a private, secure frequency normally only known of, and used by, the American government agencies. Someone has managed to hack into the radio transmissions of Air Force One, the DEA's evening broadcast, and the CIA's feeds to Mumbai. Secret Service is understandably livid, the CIA is breaking down the director's door. The

DEA aren't too happy with us, either, since they were in the middle of an op, which has since gone south."

Nicholas couldn't help himself, he grinned like a fool. Adam had managed to upset three major government agencies in a very short amount of time.

"I hope the message will make sense to you since the sender has been using your name liberally in his transmissions. Know Morse code, by any chance?"

"I do, sir. Play me the message."

"Hang on. Gray will upload it for you."

Nicholas said to Mike, "We've got him. Sophie, your brother is amazing."

For a moment, there was nothing, no sound, only static. Then he heard the clicking. He listened carefully. It started with a series of repetitive clicks, over and over and over again. Then a series of coordinates, the words **Paris, Curie, Lab**, and a series of seemingly meaningless letters and numbers—**19 G 13 R**—followed by a brief explanation of their meaning, and the name **Havelock**, three times.

Nicholas asked Gray to play it for him

again, then a third time. He finally looked up to see Mike's excited face.

"Is this what I think it is?"

Nicholas nodded. He tapped Sophie on the hand with his pen. "Your brother is alive, and in the process of pissing off the government. I'll say it again, Sophie, your brother is amazing."

"You know where he is?"

Nicholas nodded. "Adam's managed to give us both his location and the location of Madame Curie's secret lab."

85

Paris
1:15 a.m.

Nicholas called Pierre Menard of FedPol to help clear the way through the French bureaucracy.

The call was answered on the first ring.

"**Allo,** Nicholas. When you call in the middle of the night, I assume bad things are happening."

"Good things, for once, my friend. But I do need your help."

He explained some of what was happening. "Our plane is due to land in ten minutes. We have an address for Manfred Havelock, but I don't think he's there at the moment. We believe he's gone into the Paris underground after something quite priceless. We need to find him, Pierre, now."

"The weapon you discussed with me last evening?"

"The very same. We have to move fast, as if there is an imminent terrorist attack on Paris, but we need a needle to handle this, not a sledgehammer. Can you help?"

"Of course. Tell me exactly what it is you need, and I will make it so."

"Send the police to the address on Quai d'Anjou and rescue Adam Pearce. Then we'll need a guide, Pierre, which is why I thought of you. Isn't there a group of revolutionaries who meet down in the catacombs and cause a ruckus?"

"I don't know if we could call them revolutionaries. The French police call them cataphiles."

"That's it, cataphiles. I recall reading about a group of cataphiles who have mapped the tunnels between the limestone quarries that run under the city. Not the quarries the city turned into ossuaries, I'm not speaking of the Empire of the Dead. This would be the uncharted areas, north into the sixth arrondissement. I believe they call themselves the Extreme Underground?"

"**Oui,** I have heard of these people."

"Since it is illegal to be in the tunnels, and I know the Paris police are quite serious about rousting the cataphiles, do you think there may be a name in their files, someone who may be a leader of this organization?"

"**Oui**, you do indeed need an experienced guide, Nicholas, but not one of the cataphiles. They would not cooperate even if you offered to reward them handsomely.

"I believe you would be better served by using the skills of an elite police unit responsible for the catacombs. I will contact the commander of this unit. Do you have any idea where to start?"

"Near the Sorbonne."

"I will have someone meet you there."

"Hurry, Pierre. Havelock has quite a head start."

"I will. Oh, yes, we have no records of Manfred Havelock owning a home on the Quai d'Anjou. We will have to look further."

"Check the name **Elise**—I don't know her last name. Perhaps she is listed as the owner. Call me when you recover Adam Pearce, please."

"Very good. Once we get you through

security, you will proceed to the Sorbonne, and wait at the corner of rue des École and rue Saint-Jacques. You will be met. I will handle the rest."

"Thank you, Pierre. I owe you one."

"Good luck. Be very careful in the catacombs. It is a very dangerous place."

An hour later, they were standing in front of the limestone buildings of the Sorbonne when a handsome dark-haired woman approached them, six officers in tow. She introduced herself in lovely accented English. "I am Commander Beatrix Dendritte. I will be taking you into the tunnels."

They shook hands. "I'm Special Agent Nicholas Drummond and this is Special Agent Mike Caine. And this is Sophie Pearce." Nicholas looked at her and came to a decision. "She is our—civilian consultant. She'll be coming with us."

"Pierre said you know where we are to go?"

"We have an address of sorts, but we don't know how to get there."

"An address?" She laughed. "**Mon**

Dieu. You are already far ahead of the normal. There are street names in the underground, carved into the walls, some dating back to the beginning of the **Révolution** in 1789. Some street names are written even now by the cataphiles to map new tunnels. What is this address you have?"

Nicholas gave her the numbers. "Wherever we are headed, this will be on the wall. It's how we'll know we are close. Nineteen, G; thirteen, R."

She wrote it down. "And you think the Sorbonne is the closest starting point?"

"The person who hid the items we're looking for worked here in 1915. The space this person created would have needed to be within walking distance of the Sorbonne. We're looking for some sort of room, guarded by a wooden door with a lock, which has been there for over a century."

"A wooden door? I don't think I have ever seen such a thing in the tunnels, but it does not mean it is not there. The cataphiles, they dig, they create entrances, new exits. They also put up walls of stone to rearrange the connecting tunnels. It not only confuses things but it hurts the structural integrity of the ceilings, so we must have a care." She shrugged. **"Alors.** Perhaps we will find this door. And perhaps we will not**."**

Mike said, "Commander Dendritte, this is a matter of life and death."

The commander gave her a long look, then another shrug that said everything and nothing at all. **"D'accord.** This life and death, that seems always to be the case. Okay. We look."

She spread a large piece of paper on the hood of her Citroën. "Do you have anything other than these numbers to go on?"

"I do not."

She wrote the numbers and letters on a sticky note and affixed it to the map. She pointed at them with her finger.

"The thirteen R, that is easy. It is the thirteenth year after the end of our **Révolution**. It was written on the walls in about 1812. Nineteen G—I believe it is

Guillermo's signature. He was the leader of a group of Rats who lived in the tunnels after the **Révolution**. Nineteen—I do not know."

Sophie said, "Are there rats?"

The commander looked at this young woman who was too pale, who was possibly in pain. Special consultant? Why was she here if she was injured? "Do not worry, the rodents, they only come two or three a year. **Non,** I speak of Rats, a gang of revolutionaries. Even today, the gangs of Paris meet in the tunnels. But this"— she pointed at the map—"I believe we need to go down at rue Saint Jacques. This numbering is familiar, and I think I know where to start looking." She folded the map.

Nicholas asked, "Is there an official entrance into the tunnels?"

Commander Dendritte pointed down to the street. "There are ladders down from the manholes in certain places. It will be best to start there."

86

Paris Underground
Off rue Saint-Jacques
2:00 a.m.

Their flashlights barely made a dent in the dark. The air smelled ancient, musty, and dead flat, like a tomb. Mike wondered how Marie Curie could stand to come down here day after day. She looked at Sophie, saw her face was white and set.

As they walked, their feet crunched on trash and broken glass. She saw rivulets of water running down some of the walls and wondered where the water came from. And wondered why it didn't simply burst through the tunnel ceiling. She stepped over and through puddles of stagnant stinking water, eyes ahead, trying not to dwell on how alien and terrifying this world was.

They'd climbed at least forty feet down a series of wooden ladders, then struck out in the direction Dendritte pointed. The ceiling over their heads was lower in some places, making Nicholas bend down.

There were only the four of them. The rest of Dendritte's cops were stationed around the aboveground area, with photos of Manfred Havelock, guarding known exits out of the underground in case they were too late. They were the fail-safe—if the four of them didn't return in an hour, her other men were to come in after them.

Dendritte was right, there were street names, of a sort. Some were very old, carved into the stone, some much newer, spray-painted on the walls. They went deeper and deeper, sometimes angling up, then down, mostly downward, lower and lower beneath the real world above. Dendritte seemed like she knew exactly what she was doing, where she was going.

They saw walls covered in red and black graffiti, insults written by the cataphiles to the police. She'd heard Dendritte say the cataphiles used the tunnels to host parties, drink with their friends, or escape from the police after committing crimes.

Mike wondered if they would cancel their parties if they knew what was down here behind a locked door in a hundred-year-old lab.

She heard Sophie breathing heavily behind her. Despite the pain meds, Mike knew her back had to be hurting badly, but she hadn't said a word. Sophie had guts.

Sophie stumbled and Nicholas caught her, righting her before she slammed headfirst into Mike.

"You okay?"

"I am. This place—it's like it's dead, yet I can almost feel it breathing around me. Isn't that strange?"

Nicholas agreed. He wondered about Commander Dendritte. Why had she chosen this assignment? He couldn't imagine trying to track a criminal down here, with only a flashlight and a map that was always changing. And that meant Havelock had to be somewhat familiar with the catacombs, or had a guide like they did. Even so, he was taking a huge risk.

Dendritte stopped, shined her light on the walls.

"**Regardez-vous.** Look at this."

They gathered around her. She ran her

hands along a carving in the stone wall. "See? rue jacques. In the **Révolution**, the street names with **Saint** in them were dropped. The Rats have made certain that guideposts down here match what is above. And see the other numbers? We are twenty-five meters below the street. That is over eighty feet," she added to Mike.

Mike glanced at Nicholas. "As deep as the sub under the loch. Incredible."

Sophie asked, "Are we close?"

Dendritte dropped her light from the walls. "**Oui,** yes, very close. Follow me." She walked for another one hundred feet, then stopped and shone the light on the walls again.

"Ah, **ici.** Here, you look."

Mike shined her flashlight on the wall as well. "Nineteen G thirteen R. This is it. We have found the spot. I do not see a door, only the wall—"

The wall began to crumble. The cinder base slid open with a loud grind and two men burst out. There was an odd whistling sound, and the commander suddenly fell to the ground, her flashlight spinning to hit against the tunnel wall. Nicholas grabbed Mike and Sophie and dragged them down to the floor behind her. In that instant Nicholas realized exactly how Havelock had known where to come. He'd hired Rats, and they'd not only showed him the way, he'd set them to guard the tunnel entrance. They were dressed in heavy overcoats, big boots, their faces unshaven and brutal.

Mike grabbed the unconscious commander to protect her from the two men, but one of them was coming her way. Before she could draw her Glock, he hit her hard in the back with his fists, then wrapped his big hands around her neck. She heard Nicholas and the other Rat scuffling next to her. She tried to kick back at him, tried to twist away, but he was squeezing harder and harder. She was getting light-headed and dizzy.

A second later, the beam of a single flashlight began bouncing around. Sophie, she'd found Dendritte's flashlight. The sudden light distracted the Rat and she was able to jerk free and whirl around to face him. She looked into the man's face as she kicked him hard in the hip, then launched herself two steps up the wall, twisted hard in a somersault, landing behind him, and slammed her Glock on the back of his head. He fell hard, landing on her ankle, twisting it under him. She had no choice but to fall as well; it was that or let the ankle snap.

As she went down, she saw Nicholas and one more man, this one even bigger, punching each other, twisting, kicking. But this Rat wasn't März. Nicholas kneed him in the face, then knocked him onto his back. Then he was on him, his neck between his hands, and Nicholas was choking him. It didn't take long. When Nicholas let his head drop, he came slowly to his feet.

"Mike?"

"Here. I'm okay, but this idiot is unconscious and he's pinned my leg. Where are Sophie and Commander Dendritte?" She yelled their names, and their names came back to her as a hollow echo.

She yelled again. There was no answer. The two women were gone.

87

Nicholas heaved the man off Mike's leg and pulled her to her feet. She cursed under her breath, but Nicholas heard her and tightened his hold around her. "My ankle's sprained and isn't that just wonderful?"

He said, "At least your thick boots kept the ankle from breaking. Can you walk?"

She gritted her teeth and took a couple of steps. It hurt, but she could do it. Mike said, "Those two men—the Rats—they ambushed us to take the commander and Sophie?"

He played the light in the tunnel behind them, then up ahead. "Maybe. Havelock knew we would come down here after him. How, I have no idea."

They found Dendritte in an adjoining tunnel. She was moaning softly. Nicholas knelt beside her, felt the pulse in her throat. It was steady. "Are you all right, Commander?"

"Bad knock on the head," she whispered. "The Rat must have flung a rock at me.

Go, go, find Sophie. I'll be all right."

Nicholas said, "Where do we go from here, Commander?"

But Dendritte's eyes were closed.

"Nicholas, look!" Mike shone her light on the wall, to the spot where the two Rats had burst out. She realized it was cracked open, meant as the escape for the Rats after they'd killed her and Nicholas. "Through here, look, there's another tunnel. See, the floor slopes down, going even deeper than where we are now. This is it, Nicholas."

He felt Dendritte's pulse again. Still steady.

There was nothing they could do for her. He stood. "Let's go."

Nicholas shoved against the walled door. It was old, maybe built by Rats in the nineteenth century. Once through, he shined his flashlight on the ground. "Yes, this is it." Nicholas leaned down to look at the scuff marks in the dirt floor, long drags. "There was at least one more Rat. He took Sophie and dragged her through here. Can you walk, Mike?"

Oh, yes, she could run now, if she had to.

They went deeper, slapping away cobwebs. The smell of rot and slime was nearly overwhelming. Something skittered away from Nicholas's foot. This narrow tunnel seemed untouched by man for a very long time—maybe since Madame Curie had walked through here a hundred years ago.

The corridor narrowed. Nicholas's shoulders touched the wet walls. He closed his eyes a moment, breathed through his nose. This was worse than diving to the sub.

Mike called out, "It widens out again down here, Nicholas. And I see it, a chamber."

He swallowed and followed her. She was right. The tunnel was getting wider, the ceiling higher. His breath came easier now.

Mike was shining her flashlight along one long tunnel wall. They stood shoulder to shoulder, staring at four side-by-side wooden doors, each with warped brown wood panels and rusted black hinges. They looked half a foot thick. On each door was a big lock. "They look like dungeon doors," Mike said, only to hear her own voice echo back to her. "Why four doors? Are there labs behind all of them?"

"Look above the doors, at the carvings," Nicholas said. "Gargoyles of sorts, mythical figures—griffins and dragons and chimeras."

Mike whispered, "They're meant as warnings, to scare away anyone who stumbled across this place. But why four doors? Are there chambers behind each one? Did she use them all?" She looked back over her shoulder and gave him a smile. "Four doors—you pick the one you think is Curie's main lab."

He whispered in her ear, "Step back. I'll shut off my torch. Radium can be luminescent; perhaps Curie's new polonium is as well. Let's see if it can help us choose the right one."

They shut off their lights, and the world turned black. And they saw that the third door glowed in the darkness, a bluish light that seemed to seep out of the wood itself. They realized the door wasn't completely closed.

"I have a theory," Nicholas whispered.

"And what would that be?"

He looked dead serious. "If you do bad things, bad people will come visit you." He pulled his Glock and started to push the door open.

He sensed the slash of a knife through the darkness.

Another Rat, this one bigger than the other two. He seemed to come out of nowhere, with no warning. Nicholas caught his arm as the blade came down, and the knife disappeared between them.

The man was growling, panting, cursing him in French. They grappled in the dark. Slowly, inch by inch, Nicholas was turning the Ka-Bar knife until he had the Rat pressed back against the tunnel wall. He jerked the man's hand up, twisted the knife inward and shoved it into the big man's throat.

88

Madame Curie's Lost Laboratory
Paris Underground
3:00 a.m.

Havelock was sadly disappointed when he'd unlocked the third door. The lab was old, but then what could he expect? He couldn't imagine having to work day in and day out in this dank hollowed-out room with its dead air, a hundred feet below the street. There weren't any precautions then against radioactive materials. He thought of Curie's long, slow death.

Beakers were lined up on the counters with liquid still in them; the chamber was practically airtight. There were two microscopes, state-of-the-art for the time, that is. Was one for the assistant who'd betrayed her?

Havelock found the small microgram of super-polonium in a cabinet, unsecured, in a glass bottle with a stopper. It glowed an eerie kind of bluish yellow in the tube.

It was lovely, a color not on the spectrum. He supposed he'd have to name that as well. **Elise**. He'd name it for her.

It wasn't safe to transport as is, but that was no matter. Using specially made gloves, he picked up the tube, and brought it over to Sophie Pearce.

Havelock's heart speeded up as he looked at her. He wanted to see the marks of his whip on her back. He knew she was frightened, her face utterly white in the soft lights in Curie's old lab. He wondered if the Rat who'd taken her from the tunnels and was now guarding the door had been more frightened than she was when he'd looked around Madame Curie's lab. He'd hired him and his two cohorts because they knew the tunnels well and they knew how to kill.

He said in a voice eerie and strangely hollow in the closed confines of the ancient lab, "You do realize, Ms. Pearce, that you are in the presence of genius and a hundred-year-old weapon of such magnitude, only I can make it what it was meant to be? I thought it only fitting that

Rothschild's blood was here in the chamber with me. When I finish the assembly, I will take you back to the house and kill both you and your wretched brother." And he and Elise would celebrate.

He wanted to sing. He'd won, he'd won. Soon his Rats would be back from finally ridding him of those FBI agents.

"You're scared, aren't you? But you're trying to act brave. It's charming."

Sophie stared through him, saying nothing.

If only he had a whip with him. He wanted to kiss that pale pinched mouth, but he'd have to remove the crude gag. And then she would scream, and he didn't want that, it would break the exalted moment.

"Isn't it pretty, my dear? Something worth dying for, don't you think?" He mimed pouring the small bottle on her, and he thought she'd faint, but she made no sound.

He laughed, moved back to the table. The microscopes still worked, though they were in poor condition. It was a crude workplace, but serviceable. He prepared his station. A scalpel to break open the seal on the tube, then to work the stopper free. The polonium, warmed by the movement, glowed merrily, as if happy to see him.

Using a specially made pipette, he gently extracted a tiny amount from the tube, and carefully, carefully, placed it into the trigger mechanism from the small box sitting on the table.

The reaction was immediate. The bluish yellow turned a deep violet, the color of a dying sunset, or a freshly made bruise. The atoms bonded together, and the new element was formed. He'd done it!

He reverently closed the lid. He'd made the world's first micro–nuclear weapon, ready to be deployed, with a payload that could kill thousands of people with a single small explosion. His own personalized MNW.

His other miniaturized bombs were paltry in comparison. This was his masterpiece. The explosion itself would take down a block at least, and the radioactive cloud would disperse into the air and people would breathe it in. Death on the wind. And he controlled it all.

He stashed the MNW into the metal briefcase he'd made for it, secured the polonium in its own separate metal casing, then put both back into his backpack. They were ready to go.

He reached for Sophie's arm. "Shall we, my dear?"

A man's voice said from behind him, "Yes, we shall."

Havelock turned slowly. The two accursed FBI agents stood in the door to the lab. His Rats had failed.

Havelock jerked Sophie to his side, and pressed the tip of the scalpel into her neck. "No, the two of you will stay right there. Agent Drummond, you killed März. I must admit that astonished me. No one's ever beaten him before. However, enough is enough. I have had it with you people. You need to learn how to die."

Drummond said, "No, I don't believe so. Put down the backpack, Havelock, and let Sophie go."

Havelock laughed. "You haven't a clue,

do you? There is nothing you can do to stop me."

Mike said, "We can shoot you."

He laughed again. "And risk poor Sophie's life?" He pressed the scalpel in, and a drop of blood appeared. Sophie stared out at them, white-faced, silent.

"And you. I know all about you, Michaela Caine. You are not like your partner here, Nicholas Drummond. He would have no qualms about shooting me dead where I stand. He's done it before, he'll do it again. But—" He pressed the scalpel deeper into Sophie's neck, her blood now a steady drizzle. "I suggest you put down your weapons, or I will dig around until I slice her carotid artery.

"You see my backpack? If you try to shoot me, Drummond, I'll drop my precious little bundle, and it will go boom and we will go boom with it. How much of the world up there will it bring down? You want to test it out?"

Nicholas said, "Nothing will happen." He looked around. "You can't make your weapon in this lab, it's a wreck. I've seen your files, I know what you need, and it wasn't here. Put the knife down, now."

"Snooping into my company? You and young Adam. You don't seem to understand what I have in my hands, Drummond. No great need for modern equipment, Madame Curie left me the final ingredient I needed. Now both of you will immediately place your guns on the floor and kick them to me, or I will slit this sweet girl's throat. Can you imagine how much blood will spray out of her?"

Nicholas and Mike slowly bent over and set the guns on the wooden floor.

"Kick them to me!"

They did. Now they were unarmed, and he had the control, the power. Havelock breathed in deep and smelled the strawberry scent of Sophie's hair mixing with the sulfur breath of the room, the perfect combination of heaven and hell.

"Tell me why, Havelock," Nicholas said. "Tell me why you murdered your own father, betrayed your friends and all you've ever known to get this weapon."

"Betrayal, murder? Who truly decides

these things, my dear Drummond? Even Madame Curie had to make a choice all those years ago. She could have given the polonium to the Order, as they'd planned. Instead, she decided to keep it all to herself, and hide it down here. And it's taken someone like me to find it. I know exactly how to use her weapon to its best advantage. Listen to me, both of you, and listen carefully. I will stop wars. I will end centuries of violence. I am giving the world a gift.

"With my technology, with my tiny little implants, you'll be able to see things happen even as they're being communicated. I have single-handedly changed the gathering of intelligence. I will be able to target the real villains, our true enemies, and I will destroy them before they do any more harm."

Nicholas said, "You actually believe that another weapon of mass destruction will save the world?"

"Of course. With my power, and your knowledge and acceptance of my power, every country in the world will do exactly as I say. No longer will one country have dominance over another. No longer will one country be rich at the expense of another. All the power will reside in the palm of my hand, in a four-inch-square box. I will give the world peace and hope, and the will to lead a better life."

"With you making all the decisions? How people will act, what their futures hold? Will you have everyone bow before you? Will you have huge statues of yourself erected everywhere so that people may bow down and worship you?"

Havelock appeared to consider this. He smiled. "Perhaps inside buildings there will be walls with my image on them, always watching. So no one will forget."

Mike said, "Every law enforcement agency on the planet is after you. There is no way you will make people bow down in front of you. You're certifiable."

89

Havelock merely nodded at his backpack. "Ah, Agent Caine, how little imagination you have. Think, dear girl, I will be the one giving all those precious law enforcement agencies the orders."

The longer he talked, Nicholas knew, the more likely it was that the commander's people would come looking. Keep him talking, it was their best chance.

Sophie's hands were tied in front of her, Havelock's scalpel digging into her neck. She couldn't move, except for her eyes. She was staring at Nicholas, and she began to blink rapidly, her eyes never leaving his face. Then she turned her head a bit to the right. He looked, but didn't see anything. What was she trying to tell him?

And then he saw it, a small glass beaker with a yellowish substance inside, and it was within her reach, if only she could pull free of Havelock.

Havelock was still talking about how he wouldn't dismantle the law enforcement agencies because, after all, there were still criminals in the world. Nicholas began coughing, bending over, grabbing his stomach.

Havelock yelled, "What is wrong with you?" In that instant of distraction, Sophie jerked away from him and grabbed the glass beaker. Before he could stab her, she whirled around and smashed the beaker into Havelock's face. The glass shattered, and he started to scream.

Nicholas sprang forward, stopped in his tracks. Havelock's face was melting, the skin pouring off the bone. Whatever the acid in the beaker was, it had sat brewing one hundred years.

Nicholas grabbed the backpack from Havelock's arms as he fell to the ground, screaming, screaming, clutching at his face, and screaming.

Mike picked up her Glock, put the muzzle against Havelock's head, and pulled the trigger.

Havelock's body twitched, then went still. Eyeballs stared blankly from the bones of his face at the ceiling of Curie's lab.

"You okay?" Nicholas said and she looked at him and smiled faintly. "I am."

Sophie pulled the gag out of her mouth. She stood over him. "He was a monster and he was mad." Sophie suddenly sucked in her breath and looked down at her hand. A tiny bit of the acid had gotten on her skin and had left an angry red burn. Who cared? She looked up. "Thank you both for saving my life."

Mike untied her wrists, cupped Sophie's hand. "We need to get you aboveground, quickly. We have no idea what that acid is."

"It's **esprite de sel.** Spirits of salt, also known as muriatic acid," Sophie said. "It was on the label, and I knew what it would do." She laughed through a sob. "I wonder why Madame Curie abandoned this lab but left the muriatic acid behind. Was she using it in her experiments?"

"We'll never know," Mike said. "There's no one left to tell us."

Nicholas took Sophie's arms between his hands. "We didn't save you, Sophie, you saved us. Well done."

"We need to go get Adam," Sophie said, but Nicholas held up a hand. They could hear Dendritte and her people shouting from higher in the tunnel.

Nicholas picked up the backpack that held Havelock's MNW. "No one can ever say a word about what is in this box. We can't let anyone, any government, any technology company, get their hands on this weapon. Agreed?"

Mike and Sophie nodded. Mike watched him shoulder the backpack. The shouting grew closer. Commander Dendritte burst into the room with several cops on her heels.

She took in the scene, eyes wide when they landed on Havelock, and then she reholstered her weapon, and said, **"C'est fini, non?"**

Nicholas nodded. **"Oui. C'est fini."**

90

Paris
6:00 a.m.

The Paris dawn was bright and fresh, a new day beginning. The people of the city were waking up and preparing for their day completely unaware of the battle that had raged beneath their streets overnight.

Sophie was tended to, Adam had been rescued and brought to them, Elise arrested. They did a quick debrief with Commander Dendritte. When Mike's stomach growled loudly, the commander grinned and suggested they eat something while she started on the mountain of paperwork.

Over freshly baked croissants and hot **café au lait,** they talked. When Nicholas told Adam that not only Havelock was dead, but also März, Adam whooped and gave Nicholas a high five.

Then Sophie and Adam talked about Ansonia and Josef and their son Leo. Sophie said, "I even owe my affinity for languages to Ansonia."

Mike raised her cup. "Here's to the direct descendants of the Rothschilds."

Sophie raised hers as well. "Now Adam and I will do our share so there will be more descendants for the next hundred years. May Ansonia and Josef never be forgotten."

They clicked cups. Mike looked back and forth between brother and sister. "Amazing. All of it is absolutely amazing."

Adam said, "You're pretty amazing, sis. Look at you, you destroyed Havelock. You saved the Order. Not to mention the world." He paused for a moment. "I wish I could have seen him."

"I'm glad you didn't, Adam. He looked like a monster out of a horror movie."

Adam looked over his shoulder, then leaned close across the table and whispered, "Did you get the weapon?"

Sophie didn't say a word.

Nicholas fiddled with his spoon a moment, reached over and wiped a spot of foam from Mike's chin. "You needn't ever worry about the weapon again,

Adam. It's been taken care of. Something that powerful, that deadly, no person, no government should ever have control of it. I've destroyed Curie's notebook and Havelock's files."

Mike said, "For now, Havelock's company's been closed down. All the technology he's discovered—it needs someone who isn't mad as a hatter to guide it properly, to see it's used for good."

Sophie said, "We can only pray there's not another mad genius like Havelock to resurrect it all again."

Mike thanked the good Lord above Dendritte hadn't known what Havelock had been after in Curie's lab. If she'd known about the MNW, there'd have been hell to pay. She could hear the howls from French government loud in her head.

Nicholas said, "I identified the man from Havelock's files, code name Mr. Z. He was Mr. Stanford's secretary, Trevor Wetherby, and he was the one who killed him. He was working for Weston, of course. Word leaked late last night that the inquest found Stanford's death was murder. As you can imagine, the media is having a field day with this. Who knows where it will head?"

Sophie asked, "What happens to Adam?"

Nicholas sat back in his chair, his hands steepled in front of him. "I suppose it depends on Adam."

Nineteen, and the kid was already surpassing Nicholas's own skills. It felt strange, he had to admit.

"I'm willing to do whatever you want, sir."

"Are you? You're willing to go to jail? Because that's where you belong."

Adam's face fell. Mike kicked Nicholas in the ankle under the table. "Quit torturing him, it's not nice."

Nicholas said, "All right, so we'll make a deal. But Adam, there will be some jail time, no way around that. You've hacked too many sensitive agencies, stepped on a lot of very big toes, thumbed your nose at too many important people. But if you're willing to work with me, to tell me everything you've done, and how you did it—we may be able to get your jail time reduced."

Adam looked appalled. "Are you saying I'd have to work for the Man?"

"Forever, probably," Nicholas said, and felt ancient. "Don't look like you're going to throw up. Get used to it. We need minds like yours. So if you're willing to cooperate, we could plead you out as a misdemeanor, and you'll be out in well under a year.

"Ah, I see Commander Dendritte waving to us. I believe she wants to speak more with you and Sophie, probably more grilling for Mike and me as well. Then it's back to New York."

"And then? I know, I know, after the slammer, it's the Man. Okay, I can do that." He flashed a big smile. "Within reason, of course." Nicholas paid for breakfast and they went to see Commander Dendritte. They made a date to come speak to the higher-ups in the Parisian Sûreté. Mike and Nicholas watched brother and sister follow the commander, Adam's arm slung around Sophie's shoulders. He turned and mouthed **Thank you** to Nicholas and gave him a thumbs-up.

Nicholas smiled down at Mike. "They'll both be okay now."

"Now that I've had sustenance, I need sleep, at least until we have to report in for more talk, talk, talk."

"I do as well."

Mike said, "And then we debrief for Zachery, and, and, and—"

Nicholas took her hand. "All of that, but sleep first. Where shall we go?"

"I was thinking of a little pension, maybe a bit on the seedy side, with no hot water—"

He laughed. "Do you think instead you could put up with a shabby two-bedroom suite at the Ritz?"

She slowly nodded. "Well, if you insist. I remember I liked that place okay—especially the soft bed."

91

Early the next morning they were eating breakfast and watching the continuing media frenzy about Alfie Stanford's and Oliver Leyland's murders on the BBC when Mike's cell rang.

"It's Zachery."

Nicholas groaned. "I knew he'd have more questions, but now? It's midnight in New York. Doesn't the man sleep?"

"He probably wants us to get ourselves back to New York today. Hello, sir. It's a lovely midnight in New York, right?"

"No, it's raining. Listen, you two," Zachery said. "As you know, the world press is going nuts with all that's happened. But since that isn't your problem you will simply say to anyone who asks that you have absolutely no comment."

Mike met Nicholas's eye. "Yes, sir, we know nothing at all."

"Good. Now, I have to tell you there is still no sign of Edward Weston. He appears to have disappeared off the face of the earth. Our agencies are beginning to believe Havelock killed him and buried him deep. No one knows."

Nicholas wished it were true, but he didn't believe it. "No, sir, I know to my boots he's out there somewhere. And he's got money, from where, I don't know, but he's waiting, that's all."

"Well, perhaps you're right. You'll be pleased to know you have three governments who are very happy with you right now. And one who is rather peeved."

"The Germans?" Nicholas asked.

"How'd you guess? They're claiming the gold belonged to Kaiser Wilhelm and want it back. I hear they're cheering in Scotland, claiming all that gold belongs to them, right of salvage."

Nicholas said, "Well, it's going to cost big bucks to clean up the pollution caused by Havelock's blowing up the **Gravitania.**"

"I haven't heard Scotland use that argument yet, they've all still got golden bars before their eyes. In any case, it's not your problem."

Nicholas said, "Oh, yes, have you seen to Adam Pearce?"

"Yes. He's agreed to our terms, so all is good in nerd land. Well done, you two. Both of you have done a wonderful job. You and Mike get back here pronto. The director wants to know what exactly happened to his plane."

Nicholas said, "Does that mean no SIRT review?"

Zachery laughed. "No, there will still be an inquiry, for you both, but I'm sure we'll find a way to make it as painless as possible." Zachery laughed again. "When you save the world, those things happen."

"We'll catch a plane this afternoon. Any chance of a ride home?"

"After what you two managed to do to the director's plane? It's Air France for you. Enjoy the flight."

When Nicholas hung up, Mike said, "It was a good try."

"Perhaps I'll give Penderley a call. We didn't bung up the prime minister's plane."

"What, you're too good to fly commercial now?"

He grinned back at her. "I really don't care what we fly, I only want to go home."

And she thought, **New York is home.** She rose and stretched. "Time to pack my pathetic go bag." She leaned down, laid her palm against his cheek, something Nicholas was getting used to, and quite liked. "No stitches to pull this time. That's good."

His go bag was sitting beside the door of the suite. He heard her bedroom door shut. He had one more call to make.

His father answered on the first ring, asked immediately, "Are you all right?"

"I am."

There was a slight pause, then, "What's wrong, Nicholas?"

How did a parent always know? "Dad, what is your role in the Highest Order?"

"You know this isn't a conversation to be had over the phone."

"I need to know. Please, don't put me off. Tell me."

"All right. Alfie named me to replace him. It was in his will, a private one, meant for me and the other members of the Order.

And I've accepted. We've lost so many people, and several more are corrupt. I will see to it they are rousted, and the Order's ranks are filled with men and women who want the best for their countries, who won't pervert the power given them by wealth and privilege and society."

"In that case, Dad, I have something for you, something I know the Order didn't ever want found because no person or government should ever have this sort of power."

Harry sucked in a breath. "I will send someone for it immediately. As far as the world is concerned, no one will ever know it even existed. Now that you've destroyed Havelock, the Order can refocus. Do what's right for the world. When it's time, Nicholas, I trust I'll be able to count on you to do the same."

"Me?"

"It is a hereditary organization, when possible. Alfie's eldest grandson will be stepping in when he's finished his tour of duty. When it is my turn to leave the group, you will take my place."

Him, part of the Highest Order? "But I have no influence."

Harry Drummond laughed. "You have more than you know, Nicholas. More than you know."

Epilogue

Two weeks later
New York

Alex Shepherd's shoulder still pulled and ached. It would be another two weeks, the surgeon told him, before he could consider lifting even a three-pound weight. But he was here, at last, in New York, resigned from MI5, and now exactly where he wanted to be, in Sophie Pearce's living room. Today was the reading of her father's will and she wanted him there.

She appeared in the doorway, standing straight once more, her back mostly healed now. She looked absolutely beautiful, her dark hair loose around her face, and she wore not a black dress, but a soft yellow, her father's favorite color. Alex walked to her, lightly took her arms in his hands, and told her the news. "The Order has asked me to replace your father as the Messenger. I accepted the offer and resigned from MI Five. My cover remains the same. A full-time barkeep and restaurant owner. What do you think?"

She cocked her head to one side and considered. "I think you need a new chef. I really didn't like my spaghetti the last time I ate there." And she leaned up and kissed him, whispered in his ear, "Yes, oh, yes, it's perfect. Dad would have been so pleased."

They stood awkwardly facing each other, since he was afraid to put his arms around her still-tender back and she was afraid to hug him because of his shoulder. He kissed her again, and sighed. "Actually, it was Agent Drummond's father, Harry, now the head of the Order, who asked me to continue in your father's place. Isn't it a small world?"

"If his father hasn't already told him, you can tell Nicholas today at the reading. I asked both him and Mike Caine to be there. It seemed only right since they—"

"Yes, since they went through everything with us."

As they walked out of Sophie's building into an incredible June day, Sophie saw the forty-two-point headline of the **New**

York Post: Treasure in the Tunnels— the True Story.

"Another true story," Alex said, and they simply shook their heads. Both knew the media would continue having a field day for months to come. The layer of tunnels beneath the tunnels of the catacombs had been world news, and tomb raiders and scientists and archaeologists and sociologists alike were flocking to the Paris underground to uncover the secrets of **Les Quatre Chambres**—the Four Chambers. The truth was that the other three doors hadn't been locked and they'd all been empty, except for the very small antique ruby ring found under a clot of dirt in a corner, eighteenth-century, given the style of the ring. No one knew who it might belong to.

Once in a taxi, Sophie said, "How I wish Adam could be with us. They're doing a video feed from the prison."

Alex took her hand, rubbed his fingers over her knuckles. "Last time I spoke to Drummond, he said the prosecutor was recommending only six months." He grinned at her.

Sophie laughed. "And then when he comes out of the slammer, he works for the Man. He'll still be only nineteen when he gets out."

The taxi pulled up five minutes late to the Elcott Building on Seventy-first Street. The building was old, but the plumbing and wiring had been updated and it was an excellent address. The sixteenth floor was a modern oasis with beautiful high ceilings and molding painted in soft cream. They were shown into a large conference room, a long glass table running along the center, a dozen black leather chairs cozied close. On the mahogany sideboard were carafes of coffee and tea.

Sophie accepted a cup of coffee, went to the windows, stared out over Central Park, a stunning sight, green and gold and blue skies. It was a perfect early-June day. Alex joined her. She said, "Dad wanted his ashes spread over Loch Eriboll. Adam will go with me once he's free. I couldn't bear to do it alone."

Alex said, "All three of us will go."

They turned from the window when Nicholas Drummond and Mike Caine arrived, both looking vital, in charge of their world, a handsome couple. No, not couple, Sophie thought, they were partners, FBI agents. Still—Sophie hadn't seen them since they'd returned to the States, on the prime minister of England's jet, Alex had told her, and how had they managed that?

Mike joined Sophie at the window. "I won't hug you, not yet. How are you, Sophie?"

"I'm good," she said, then sighed. "It's a difficult day. But Alex is here and you're here and we'll soon see Adam on video."

Mike touched her on the shoulder. "I know I've said this probably half a dozen times before, Sophie, but what you went through, it was tough, but you did it, saved all of us from Havelock."

"The nightmares," Sophie said, never looking away from the view, "the nightmares hurt more than my back ever did." She raised her hand. There was a small scar where the drop of muriatic acid had touched her skin. "I didn't really believe what I'd read about muriatic acid, but it was true. His face melted off his bones. I see his face in my dreams, hear his screams."

Mike was silent a moment. "As you know, Nicholas and I spent only the one night in Paris. I woke up to hear his yells from the other room. He was dreaming about that fight with März in Loch Eriboll. He never told me exactly what happened, but I know it was bad, and it was close." Mike smiled. "The nightmares will go away, Sophie. What's important is you're the one who saved us all. You're the heroine. That's what I told Nicholas as well—you won, he won, we all won."

Sophie drew a deep breath. Mike was right. It was over, they'd won. But she didn't mention that her other nightmare was when she believed Alex Shepherd was dead. Nor did she mention the raw ache in her chest whenever she thought of her father.

An assistant came in to set up the video feed with Adam, followed by Jonathan

Pearce's longtime friend and lawyer, Franklin Jones.

"He looks happy," Sophie said, when Adam came on.

He was going to serve six months in a minimum-security prison, fixing the prison's computer system, and, he'd told her, the warden wasn't a bad guy at all. And when he came out he was going to be a part-time consultant for the FBI while he finished college, and then what? Who knew?

Franklin Jones cleared his throat, nodded to Adam. "Jonathan's will is straightforward. All his property is split evenly between his two children, you and Adam. Sophie, you are the executrix. You are responsible for his far-reaching financial holdings, he always wanted you to keep Ariston's alive." He paused a moment, looked over at her. "Do you plan to do this, keep Ariston's thriving?"

"Yes," she said. "I will hire a manager, but both Alex and I will keep it flourishing."

Franklin Jones nodded. "Excellent. Your father would be very pleased. Now, I have a letter to you and Adam from your father." He handed her a thick envelope. "Jonathan wrote this last year, and had it attached to his will. There is also another folded paper that is much older. I do not know who wrote it or its contents. Would you be so kind as to read both aloud? As per your father's instructions, I will excuse myself for a moment."

Jones left the conference room and Sophie opened the letter from her father first.

Dear Sophie and Adam,
If you are reading this letter, it means I am gone, and I'll never again be able to tell you again how much I have loved you both from the moment I felt you in your mother's womb.

Sophie paused a moment, choked down the tears, and cleared her throat.

Adam, I had once believed you would replace me as the

Order's Messenger, but I've realized for several years now your path will be a very different one. Whatever you choose to do, do it well and always act for good. I imagine that eventually it is Alex who will follow me as the Messenger, he has the skills, the determination, plus he's a book lover.

Sophie, membership in the Highest Order is hereditary, as you know. I wish you to take my place. I can see you saying, but Dad, there's never been a woman in the Order. You're wrong, there have. Madame Curie, for one. Ansonia Rothschild, for another. You are the first woman in the new millennium, true, but not the last. It seems to me the women of the Order are the true heroes. We men have sat back and blathered for a century.

She smiled, looked at her brother, all spiffy in his jumpsuit, sitting in a chair behind a small table, the walls behind him blank, painted a bilious green, and he was grinning.

"Are you okay with this?"

"Of course. Dad always understood both of us very well."

Sophie said, "Nicholas, are you a part of the Order as well?"

"Eventually, it seems. Alfie Stanford named my father to lead the Order. You'll meet him when you fly to London for an Order meeting next week. You'll like him. And you'll be able to trust him completely."

She nodded, then read the rest of her father's letter.

If there is such a thing as reincarnation, I will ask to come back as a first-edition Mark Twain. Sophie, take care of me if you chance upon me. Good-bye, my children.

"He'll make a great first edition," Sophie

said, and swallowed down the curious mix of laughter and tears. She picked up the other letter, yellowed with age. She opened it carefully, and saw the date, written in a curly, old-fashioned script, and the words, in German, which she could translate easily.

She looked up and a huge smile bloomed. "Adam, Dad never showed me our great-grandmother's final letter to Josef, and now he's passed it down to us."

She read:

26 August 1917

My darling Josef:
  I have little time. The kaiser's men are nearly here. We leave as I put this letter in Leo's pocket and send him on his way to Denmark then to Edinburgh with his old nurse, since now it is far too dangerous for him to travel with me. You know where they will be. There is no choice now,

I must be the one to get Madame Curie's key and instruction book to England, to William Pearce, and the wondrous gift of the kaiser's gold bars.

I will sail immediately on the VICTORIA and will meet you in Scotland. When you see me I will be wearing your spare uniform and you and Leo will laugh and we will be together again. We will beat the kaiser, I know it in my heart, and what we do will end this unspeakable war.

Josef, I love you more than my life. Soon now we will be together again and safe—

Ansonia

The only sound in the room was the crackle of the old paper as Sophie slowly refolded Ansonia's letter.

Adam said, "I knew she was a hero, but

I never realized—it's because of her that we're all still walking this earth."

Sophie said, "It's so sad, to have it all end for her, dying entombed on that submarine."

Alex said, "No wonder your dad was so passionate about finding the sub. He was a brave and good man. He always did want to right the world's wrongs." He took Sophie's hand. "It's in the blood, Sophie, it's in the blood."

Nicholas said, "It wouldn't surprise me if there's a first-edition Mark Twain making its way to Ariston's as we speak."

As they rode the elevator down, Mike said, "This has to be the most incredible story I've ever heard."

Nicholas smiled at her. "The most incredible story you've heard—so far."

"Maybe you have some lovely mysterious skeletons in the Drummond closet?"

"Oh, Agent Caine. You have no idea."

As they walked out of the building, Nicholas's mobile screamed out the Rolling Stones' "Sympathy for the Devil."

He glanced at the screen, arched an

eyebrow at Mike, and answered quickly. "Savich? Is everything okay?"

Savich's deep voice came through the speakers. "No, Nicholas, it's not. I've cleared it with Zachery. I need you and Mike to fly to D.C. right away. We have a big case for you two."

"Both of us?" Mike asked.

"Oh, yes," Savich said. "Both of you."

Author's Note

I have frequently been asked how I could reconcile family life with the scientific career. Well, it has not been easy.

MARIE CURIE

Marie Curie was an intensely private and brilliant woman, winner of two Nobel Prizes, in 1902 and 1911 (in Physics and Chemistry), who discovered both radium and polonium and developed the theory of radioactivity. Her husband and collaborator, Pierre, an extraordinary physicist himself, helped to make sure she got the credit she deserved for her discoveries. She gave birth to a future Nobel Prize winner as well.

Marie Curie was born in Warsaw, Poland, in 1867, studied in Paris, barely surviving on very little money, met a professor at the Sorbonne who was a confirmed bachelor, and together they dazzled the world. She died of aplastic anemia, brought on by her exposure to radiation in 1934.

Curie also worked on the front lines in World War I to help bring the benefit of X-rays to the wounded. She was one of the first modern "open-source" scientists, who didn't trademark her discoveries because she believed knowledge should be shared. And to top it off: she was the first woman professor at the Sorbonne.

A derivative of one of Curie's discoveries, polonium-210, is famously used for political assassinations. It is a sure and painful death. And this is where truth and fiction diverge. Curie never created any sort of weaponized polonium, but for the sake of the story, she does. When she realizes the enormity of its destructive power, she stops work immediately and hides it away where no one will ever find it. Nor was she a member of the Highest Order, since, alas, the Order did not exist.

The actual Marie Curie was far more impressive. She was an incredible scientist, an incredible human being.

Marie Curie is, of all celebrated beings, the only one whom fame has not corrupted.

ALBERT EINSTEIN